HOLLY'S TRILOGY

BOOKS 1-3: HOTEL SERIES

EBONY OLSON

EBANDMUSE
PUBLICATIONS

Published 2020

Published by

EbandMuse Publications

Sydney, Australia

http://ebonyolson.com/

CONTENTS

HENDERSON
Hotel Series
EBONY OLSON

To Kate, who froze her bum off in an ice skating rink week after week, just to see what I would write next.

For my poor fingers, that survived me writing this all by hand in the freezing temperatures.

CONTENTS

CHAPTER ONE

My name is Holly Claire. I'm twenty-eight, and the night manager for Hotel Henderson. I started working here at age twenty-two, a fresh graduate from hospitality school and looking for a job that would pay the bills. I worked as a receptionist initially, moving my way up until the opportunity to progress into management became an option.

I entered the management traineeship the same time I became the day concierge. Three years ago, I finished the traineeship and took the role of night manager. Wednesday to Monday, I made sure the guests of the original Hotel Henderson had a comfortable and enjoyable stay. This, of course, meant I saw a lot of things I probably could have done without, but I was pretty sure I'd seen it all now.

"Holly, you about?" The night concierge's voice came through my ear piece.

"Just about to go on my break, Ellen, what's up?"

Ellen Patterson was terrified of confrontation, which was

hilarious considering she stood six feet tall and had the shoulders of a line backer.

"We are getting complaints about a disturbance in room ten sixty. Nearly every room around it has called now. I've tried calling, but I'm getting no response. The honeymooners in sixteen ten have ordered room service, so I'll take the newlyweds if you take the brawl?"

I dropped my head. "Okay, I'll head up," I announced, dumping my gym bag back into my locker. I usually swam laps in the hotel's subterranean lap pool for my one-hour break. I guess it would have to wait.

Pinning my brown hair back into place, I put my blazer, embroidered with the Henderson Hotel insignia, back on over the tunic dress uniform, and made my way to level ten. As soon as I exited the elevator and started down the hall, I could hear it. A woman screaming before a thundering crash carried down the corridor.

"Jarrett?"

"Here, Holly," Jarrett, our night security guard responded.

"I'm going to need you up here, and the police, please."

"Domestic?"

"And a lot of property damage," I explained.

"On my way." Jarrett had been working here since before I started. He was an imposing man at nearly seven feet tall, but the sweetest person you'd ever meet. Well, until you got him angry.

I knocked on the door of ten sixty. "Hotel management, could you open the door please?"

A woman screamed for help. "Shut up, bitch!" A man's furious voice followed.

I put my ear to the door. There was thumping, like someone kicking the wall and choking sounds. "Shit!" I inserted my master key into the lock, threw the door open and charged inside.

The brute was holding a petite woman against the wall, choking her with one of his hands, the woman kicking her feet against the wall to try and free herself.

"Sir, please put the woman down," I asked cordially. First rule of the Hotel, always be polite.

"Fuck off, bitch, or do you want to take her place?" He snarled. He turned his body toward me so I could see him stroking himself as he suffocated the woman.

I'd been trying to ignore their nudity until then. I assessed the state of the room, the bloody cuts and bruises all over the woman, including her face, and made the deduction she had not consented to being beaten and choked to death for this man's sexual pleasure.

"Sir, I will ask you one last time, put the woman down."

The man let her go and made a quick grab for me. I stepped out of reach and dodged his grab. He snarled and threw himself at me. He wasn't tiny; there was no way of avoiding his flying mass in the confines of this hotel room.

I fell back under the weight of the man and had the wind knocked out of me. He knelt back and punched me in the face. Lights danced in front of my eyes, pain searing along my cheek and jaw.

"Okay, bitch, let's see you turn blue." He wrapped his giant hand around my throat and squeezed.

I felt my eyes bulge as he cut off my oxygen. Blood rushed to my ears, muffling all other sounds. A moment later, his hand was gone, distorted sounds of grappling, grunts, scrapping furniture filtering in. Glass shattering filled the room and broke me free from the static. I sucked in precious oxygen, rolling to my side to assist my body in expanding my lungs.

I climbed unsteadily to my feet, leaning on my own legs to support of my body, and observed Jarrett pinning and hand cuffing the brute. I moved to the unconscious woman and checked her pulse. She was breathing and alive. I sighed with relief.

"Holly, are you okay?" Jarrett came over to me.

"Yeah, I'll be fine. Let's call an ambulance for this poor woman," I winced when I licked my lip.

Jarrett turned me to face him and frowned. "He's busted your lip, and you're going to have a shiner tomorrow," Jarrett assessed.

"I'll put ice on it. Go bring the police up."

Jarrett nodded and left. Walking to the bathroom, I grabbed a robe for the naked woman, tucking it around her, so she wouldn't be exposed to the police when they arrived. Then I started searching through the broken furnishings for her purse.

"She's just a whore," the brute spat at me as I walked past him.

I looked down to where he was lying on his flabby gut and aimed a kick right between his spread legs. The man howled as my foot connected with his still swollen sack.

"She's a woman, and half your size at that, though, I understand why you'd need to pay for it."

I grabbed a bag from the corner and moved back to the woman as the door opened. Jarrett escorted the police and paramedics in. I didn't need to explain, Jarrett had already done that. The police took photos of the room with their phones and then escorted the man out, after wrapping a towel around him.

The woman was rushed to hospital with suspected internal injuries and a second ambulance was called to check me over, despite my protests. After half an hour with an ice pack and paracetamol in my office, I made my way back upstairs to do a stock-take of the damage.

With a thorough list of damage, I headed back downstairs to write up the report. The elevator stopped on level nine and Lance Petts, one of the bell hops, stepped into the lift.

"Holly, you look like shit," he assessed me worried. "Did I miss something?"

I stepped forward, handing him my ice pack to hold, and straightened his tie. "Got in the middle of a domestic. You know the rules about sex with customers during work hours," I tsked. "Was she worth risking your job for?"

Lance gave me his naughty smile and patted his groin. "You can taste her if you like? She was delicious."

I laughed shaking my head. "I'll take your word for it and suggest you use condoms."

"I'll take your advice on board."

"Just know, if Betsy or Colin catch you, you're out the door.

Mr. Henderson is very strict about this," I warned. Betsy was the day manager and Colin the day concierge.

"I'm doing the hotel a service," Lance argued teasingly.

"Mr. Henderson sees it as stealing from him. He's not paying you to get your rocks off," I reminded Lance. "You want to get paid for sex, go see Oliver about a job." Oliver was a male escort who frequented the hotel. You get to know who's here for work, play, or both pretty quickly.

The elevator doors opened, and I stepped out, wishing Lance a good night, and made my way to the manager's office. I typed up the report, estimating costs, then printed it out. My alarm went off, telling me it was morning reporting time. I left my office for the staff room where the staff coming onto shift were being fed breakfast and coffee while being debriefed; one of the initiatives I'd convinced Benjamin Henderson would assist with staff job satisfaction.

I loved Monday mornings; they were the end of the work week for me. I debriefed the front desk staff, services manager, catering manager, the day manager, Betsy, and the day concierge, Colin.

"Are you okay?" Betsy asked over her coffee.

"Just a bit tender. I'll be fine."

"Does Henderson know yet?" Colin asked between mouthfuls of scrambled eggs. He was really the only staff member here I couldn't stand. The man was arrogant, juvenile, and above all else, a horrible concierge. His idea of customer service was up his arse.

"Not yet, I'll report to him next." I bid everyone goodnight and made my way back to the manager's office.

Mr Henderson was sitting at my desk when I walked in. He lifted his sea green eyes from the report I'd left on my keyboard and looked me over. He was eleven years older than me but didn't look a day over thirty-five. "Jarrett told me you got hurt saving that woman."

"Will she be okay?" I asked deflecting.

"A few broken bones, but she'll live." Benjamin put the report down and folded his strong arms across his chest. He donned his usual suit and tie, his light brown hair in a shaggy styled mess which made you think he didn't try to look good. "How bad is it?" Benjamin asked.

I took a deep breath and handed him my financial impact report. "Furniture damage, repairs to the room itself, complimentary breakfasts to those in the surrounding room, plus, the room being out of commission while repairs are carried out."

Benjamin took the report and looked it over unhappily. He was from a family of successful business men, his father a media mogul giant. For his twenty-first birthday, Benjamin was given a cheque with more zeros than I would ever see and told to make his mark in the world.

Hotel Henderson was his starting point. There were now fifty hotels in the Henderson Hotels conglomerate worldwide, but Hotel Henderson was his baby. He loved this place so much, he lived here, in one of the three top floor penthouses.

Benjamin sighed and put the report aside as he stood. "You handled the fallout well and did a good job."

"Thank you."

"Two things happened last night which I'm unhappy with how

you handled them," Benjamin stated, putting his hands in his pants pockets.

My mouth gaped open. Not once in the years I'd been giving morning report to Benjamin had he ever given me negative feedback.

He held up a finger to count. "The first is that you put yourself in danger. Jarrett told me he had to pull the man off you."

"He would have killed that woman," I defended.

"You should have waited for Jarrett," Benjamin lectured angrily. "Don't ever put yourself in that situation again, understood?"

I nodded, swallowing my rebuttal.

"Good."

"The second thing?"

Benjamin's eyes became dangerously vibrant. "I stopped by the security office on my way back from the pool this morning."

Benjamin spent an hour swimming laps in the pool every morning, before it opened to guests. That was after a forty-minute run and thirty-minute weights session. He got up at five every morning just to work out, something seriously reflected in his physique, which no female on staff had complained about.

"Jarrett left me a message about the incident, so I was in the office and witnessed your elevator ride with the bell hop on the security camera."

I lowered my eyes and pressed my lips together to prevent from swearing.

"Did you fire him?" He knew I hadn't.

"No."

"Are you going too?"

"No."

"That's what I suspected you would say, so I took care of it myself while you ran the breakfast debrief."

"Damn it!" I muttered under my breath.

Benjamin raised a brow. "The boy hit on you after fucking a customer, and you think that is acceptable?"

"If anyone else had done it, no. Lance needs this job, and we do have female regulars who come back to see him. Women who happily spend money on suites and room service while they stay here," I defended.

Benjamin laughed. "You let him get away with it because it's financially good for business?" I shrugged. Benjamin stepped forward. "I'm not running a brothel, Holly."

"Close enough," I muttered under my breath.

Benjamin shook his head and touched his thumb to my cut lip. I pulled back a little. "I would have fired him just for hitting on you, Holly. I don't share well with others." He moved me closer to him and kissed me gently. His tongue darted across my bottom lip as he pulled my dress up, hands grabbing my arse and rubbing me against him so I could feel his growing interest.

Did I mention I was screwing my boss? For two years now, every morning after I finished my shift, and Wednesday evenings before I started work.

When I first became the night manager, I'd only met Benjamin once, at the interview for the position. I was the manager for just over six months when I walked into the security office to discuss an issue with Jarrett and found Benjamin there. He had a couple of spare football tickets and asked if I wanted them. I said yes and informed him I'd give them away to a member of staff who had performed well over the past month.

The positive feedback reached Benjamin, and he turned up in my office a few weeks later giving away show tickets and eager to hear what other ideas I had for a happier and motivating workplace. The debrief breakfast started a month later, the sex, another two months after that.

By the time Benjamin made a move on me, I was pretty smitten. The first time he kissed me breathless, pushed up my dress, pulled my knickers aside and slowly fucked me against the office wall, I'd been powerless against his charm to say no. After that, I just didn't want to. Even now, as he laid me back on my desk, moved his way between my thighs and slid into me, I was absolutely and utterly under his control.

Every morning in my office, I bit my lip and lost myself to the power this man had over me. I was his mistress, even though we were both unattached. I wasn't stupid enough to consider myself his girlfriend.

I couldn't define what it was between us. It was more than sex, less than a relationship. Neither of us had been involved with anyone else since our affair began, which indicated an undiscussed commitment. It just wasn't what society labeled as a romantic relationship.

We talk Wednesday nights. We ate dinner together and

discussed our lives. Even now, as we finished and righted our clothing, we spoke.

"Are you going out with Trisha tonight?" Benjamin asked.

Trisha Godfrey was my flatmate and best friend. She was an air hostess. "No, she's on a long-haul flight today and won't be back till Wednesday." I took a breath and started packing up. I picked up a pile of papers and looked at them confused. "Are you holding the interviews today?"

Benjamin observed me carefully as he took the papers from my hand. "Yes, we are interviewing for the day manager's role today. Betty finishes up in two weeks, and I'd like to have someone on board by then."

I frowned. "I didn't get an interview? Did you not get my application?"

Benjamin's face closed down. "I got it; there were just other candidates more experienced for the role."

I studied Benjamin and instantly saw it for what it was. I think it was the first time he'd ever lied to me. "Bullshit! I know this hotel and staff. I'm a good manager and you know damn well I'd be a good day manager."

"I want you in nights, Holly."

"You want me on your dick every morning, and that can't happen if I'm busy getting the day staff on track," I argued back.

Benjamin looked like he'd swallowed a sour lolly. I knew I'd understood correctly why I wasn't getting an interview.

"I have never given you preferential treatment, Holly. I'm not about to start now. You are the best manager I've ever had. I want to keep you on nights. The other candidates are more experienced. That's all I'm going to say on the matter."

The door opened, and Betsy stepped in as Benjamin said that last sentence. "Sorry," Betsy apologised and covered her pregnant belly as if to protect it before she closed the door again.

I grabbed up the keys to my locker and logged out of the computer. "I saw Colin's name on that list, Benjamin. He's a shitty concierge, and he'll be a lousy manager, so don't feed me that bullshit."

"Holly," Benjamin growled in warning, "it's my business, my call."

I opened the office door to leave. "Your call sucks." I walked out leaving the door open for Betsy, who was holding an impromptu meeting with one of the bellhops in the corridor, in other words, she was eavesdropping.

If the staff knew about our affair, they never commented or eluded to it in my presence. Betsy had walked in plenty of times when Benjamin first started coming down to talk to me. We would always be sitting talking about the hotel and ways to make improvements. I think that created an acceptance of friendship. Since no one has walked in on us fucking, thus far, the assumption of friendship only was still there.

Right now, knowing I was being passed over for promotion because I was sleeping with the boss, pissed me off. I grabbed my bag from the locker and walked out to catch my bus home.

CHAPTER TWO

"You really need to relax, Holly," Mitchell, my yoga instructor scolded, massaging my shoulders. "You will get no benefit out of today if you can't turn your mind off."

"I know," I moaned.

Mitchell assessed me. "Come into mountain, Holly."

I stood straight and took a deep breath.

"Now close your eyes and breathe."

I obeyed.

"Now open your eyes and see me," Mitchell cajoled.

I opened my eyes and met Mitchell's hazel eyes. "Focus on me, Holly, my eyes, my voice." Mitchell smiled at me, his thumb brushing under my split lip tenderly.

Mitchell asked about it as soon as I walked into class yesterday. Not only did I have a black eye and split lip, but my neck bore the purple imprint of the brute's hand from Sunday night. Mitchell flipped.

"You've been unfocused since this happened," Mitchell removed his thumb. "If you are feeling insecure, I can give you some defense lessons?" Mitchell taught martial arts most nights and did house-wife yoga during the day. He lived next door to me and dragged me along to his morning lesson on my days off.

"No, it's not this," I touched my lip.

Mitchell stepped back looking at the class. "Okay, slowly step back into downward dog," he instructed.

I flowed into a forward bend, then stepped back, blocking out everything except the sound of Mitchell's voice. The rest of the class went a lot better for me.

"Holly," Mitchell called to me as I gathered my things to leave after the lesson. I stopped and waited for him to catch up. "Let's get a drink tonight," Mitchell suggested. "You can tell me what has made you so unhappy, though, I could take a guess and say work."

"Good guess," I muttered, "you're at least half right."

"Not a hard guess. You live and breathe your job. I'll pick you up at six. We can get dinner, then go out dancing."

I smiled. "Sounds good. See you at six."

Mitchell kissed my temple and left for his private lessons. He'd been the first person Trish and I met after moving here, four years ago. He helped us move in, and until I became a night manager, there had been a lot of dinner parties with his flatmate and us.

By seven that evening, I was sitting in Mitchell's favourite Thai food restaurant in the city, dressed in my favourite 'dance all night' dress and heels.

"So, spill," Mitchell demanded as he spooned a helping of saffron rice onto his plate.

"I didn't even get an interview for the day manager position," I sighed.

"What? Why not?" Mitchell asked disbelieving.

"Mr Henderson said the other candidates were more qualified."

"What a load of horse shit," Mitchell looked outraged. "You've worked your arse off. You at least deserve an interview."

"It is bullshit because he interviewed Colin Fine for the role and that guy couldn't organise a root in a brothel," I growled.

"Did Henderson explain why?"

"Yes. He told me I'm the best night manager he's ever had and he wants me to stay on nights." I spooned Panang chicken onto my plate angrily. "The day manager organises the roster and makes the hard calls on a lot of decisions. I've effectively been passed over for promotion, but I'll have to play clean-up on any bad decisions the new day manager makes."

Mitchell frowned. "So, he hires some dick as the new manager, it makes your job unbearable."

"Exactly."

"So, go somewhere else."

I sighed. I'd already thought of that, but what would that mean for Benjamin and me? "I like working at Hotel

Henderson. I just want," I took a deep breath. "I want a life. I want to be able to go to my friend's parties, have dinners with my friends, go out dancing on the weekends, hell, I want to go on dates." I exhaled. "I haven't been on a date in three years."

Mitchell winced. "That's hard to hear, Holly. A beautiful girl like you should be out there playing the field." He reached over taking my hand. "You know, there is a really good-looking guy sitting a few tables away who hasn't taken his eyes off you since he walked in ten minutes ago."

I blushed. "I already have my hot date tonight."

Mitchell laughed. "Tonight, yes, but you could get his number." Mitchell shook his head. "You so don't know how to do this dating thing, do you?"

I put my hands up. "Guilty as charged."

Mitchell smiled. "We'll learn quickly. Mr Hot-steamy-date is coming this way." Mitchell sat back as a navy tailored suit entered my peripheral vision.

I looked up and swallowed, my laughter dying immediately. "Mr Henderson."

"Holly," Benjamin greeted. He looked down at me, a smile on his face belying the anger in his green eyes. "Are you going to introduce me to your friend?"

"This is Mitchell, my yoga instructor," I introduced. "Mitch, this is my boss, Benjamin Henderson."

Mitchell stood up shaking Benjamin's hand. "We were just talking about you," Mitchell smiled.

"Really?" Benjamin's eyes flicked back to me unhappily.

"Yes. Holly was just telling me how disappointed she was not to be given an interview for the day manager's role," Mitchell stirred. "I've suggested that if you are unable to see what a great asset Holly is to your company, she should take her skills elsewhere."

Benjamin pressed his lips together unhappily. "I am well aware of Holly's abilities and what an asset she is. As I explained to Holly, there were just better candidates to consider."

"Did you offer the job to one of those other candidates?" Mitchell asked.

"Yes, and he's accepted the job offer." Benjamin shoved his hands in his pockets watching me for a reaction. I picked up my glass of wine, taking a long mouthful. Okay, maybe several mouthfuls. "I'm sorry you don't agree with my business decision, Holly," Benjamin sighed.

I looked up, meeting those seductive eyes. "As you said, Mr Henderson. It's your business, your call." I gave him a sarcastic smile. "You should get back to your dinner guest." I encouraged. I looked over to see Colin Fine sitting at the table, not too far away. Colin waved, a Cheshire smile across his face. I returned my gaze to Benjamin. "You gave Colin the job?"

"Holly," Benjamin used his warning voice.

"Did you take Betsy out to dinner to celebrate her accepting the role?" I asked. Benjamin just glared at me. "So, this business decision is actually you giving preferential treatment to a friend."

Benjamin put his hand out to Mitchell. "It was a pleasure meeting you. I was going to ask you to join us for a drink, but I think I've disturbed your date long enough."

Mitchell shook Benjamin's hand. "Not to worry, Holly is used to staying up all night. We are really only just getting started." I felt my jaw drop when Mitchell winked to further his insinuation.

Benjamin's shoulder's tensed visibly. "I see, well, enjoy your evening." Benjamin strode away, returning to his table with Colin.

Mitchell sat down and I glared at him. "I can't believe you just did that."

"What?" Mitchell tried for innocence but failed.

"You implied we would be having sex all night to my boss."

"Well, I am hoping to be up having sex all night. The fact I'll be waking Tony up to get it, and you'll be crawling into bed alone, is beside the point." Tony was Mitchell's male flatmate. They just happened to share a room and bed. They were the most masculine homosexuals I'd ever met.

"Jesus, Mitch." I hid my face in my hands.

Mitchell chuckled. "You skank. How long have you been performing extra duties for your hot-as-hell boss?"

I looked through my fingers at him and groaned. "Two years."

Mitchell sat forward removing my hands from my face. He met my eyes, intent and serious. "Does Trish know?" I shook my head. "Did you not get this promotion because it would change the arrangement between you two?"

I exhaled. "I thought so, but now I think it's because Colin is his friend."

Mitchell lifted a brow. "What does that make you?" I rarely

ever saw this stoic side in Mitchell. Tony was the serious one.

"A dog's breakfast," I murmured. "At least, that's how I feel."

Mitchell nodded. "End it."

"How?" I asked honestly. "I love being with him."

"Do you love him, Holly?" I closed my eyes unsure how to answer that. "Better question. Do you think Benjamin Henderson loves you?"

I opened my eyes and met Mitchell's wise ones. "No, Mitch, Benjamin does not love me."

Mitchell nodded. "It's been two years, Holly. Put him in your spent bank and move on to greener pastures. You deserve more than being his fuck buddy."

I held back a sob. "I thought I was."

Mitchell gave me that look. The one Trish always gave me for being naive or gullible. "Your innocence is endearing, but the sooner you realise all men are pigs, the better off you'll be."

"You're not a pig," I debated.

"Do I have balls and a giant cock, Holly?"

I laughed. "I don't know about the giant part."

"I do," Mitchell laughed. "It's huge. The bigger a guy's cock, the fatter the pig he is."

I smiled. "I don't believe that, Mitch."

"I'm forty-three, Holly. Older guys hide it better." Mitchell gave me a sincere look, his eyes flicking to Benjamin before pointedly staring at me. He'd noticed the age difference. "Now, let's eat and get that hot arse of yours on the dance floor."

CHAPTER THREE

"Ms Claire?" A male voice queried through my Bluetooth earpiece as I entered the hotel lobby on Wednesday evening. Normally I would be upstairs eating dinner, or, being eaten by Benjamin by now. However, after a night of drinking and dancing with Mitchell at his favourite gay bar, I'd slept in.

"Speaking."

"My name is Roger Holmes, from Holmes Resort Corporation," He introduced himself. My eyebrows lifted in surprise. "Lance Petts gave me your name and number as a reference. Would you be free to talk for a few minutes?"

I waved to the staff on reception as I made my way back towards my office. "I'm just about to start my shift, Mr Holmes, so if you could be quick?"

"Of course, Lance mentioned you were the night manager for Hotel Henderson." Mr Holmes cleared his throat. "Would you recommend I hire Mr Petts?"

"I would," I confirmed. "Lance was a good worker, very customer focused, friendly, and efficient," I summarised as I stuck my bag in my locker.

"Can you expand on why Mr Petts left Hotel Henderson?"

I exhaled slowly. "If I'm to be honest, Mr Henderson let Lance go due to a difference of opinion."

"I see," Mr Holmes inhaled. "Could you clarify further?"

"I would prefer to make it clear that I would not have fired Lance. I didn't have an issue with his behaviour."

"You didn't agree with Mr Henderson's decision?"

"No, but that seems to be quite common of late." I shrugged, trying not to let my annoyance turn audible. "Mr Henderson makes the decisions. The staff can only try their best to work with them."

"Well, thank you for your candidness and your time, Miss Claire." Mr Holmes responded happily.

"You're welcome, Mr Holmes. I do hope you hire Lance. He really is a hard-working employee and shows considerable concierge potential."

"I will take that into consideration. Good evening."

I wished him farewell and hung up. I stepped into the office to find Betsy standing bent over the desk, breathing heavy, and a puddle of clear fluid on the floor beneath her. "Shit, Betsy, please tell me you just wet yourself?" I pleaded. I wasn't ready to work with Colin yet.

"I'm sorry, Holly," Betsy panted. "Can you call an ambulance?"

I picked up the phone and requested an ambulance, then took a rather breathy report from Betsy while we waited. An hour later, I walked into the staff room for debriefing. The managers had just finished giving their report when Benjamin stepped into the room, brows low, eyes scowling at me.

"Thank you, everyone. Before you all leave, there is one more thing. As you may be aware, when I arrived for work today, Betsy went into labour, so, it looks like she will be starting her maternity leave earlier than expected." I smiled while the staff made cooing sounds. Colin looked like a cat who caught the mouse. "Luckily, interviews for a replacement have already concluded. Mr Henderson has come down to speak to you about it," I deferred to Benjamin, trying not to laugh at the surprise on his face as the attention turned to him. If he thought I was informing the staff their new boss was Colin, he was wrong. Everyone looked to Benjamin with expectant smiles, and a few even winked at me.

Benjamin cleared his throat. "Evening everyone. I won't keep you. As of tomorrow, Colin Fine will be the new day manager of Hotel Henderson." The smiles disappeared off nearly everyone's faces, except Colin and Benjamin's. Silence descended over the staff room for a moment. Many of the staff's eyes turned to me as if asking if this was a joke. Benjamin's face fell at the response. "Please join me in congratulating Mr Fine on his promotion." The staff clapped haphazardly and unenthusiastically while I collected my iPad and notes. I wasn't clapping for Colin. Something Benjamin's eyes noted.

"Okay, everyone," I took over, "Thank you for your hard work today. I hope everyone has a good night."

Everyone stood to leave, not one person offering Colin

personal congratulations. Instead, I was headed off by Katie Dale, the housekeeping services manager. "What the hell happened? We thought for sure the position was yours?" Katie asked, two other staff, nodding in agreement as the crowded around me. "Did you not apply?" Katie whispered confused.

"I did," I assured. "Mr Henderson didn't even offer me an interview. Apparently, those he did interview were better qualified."

"Bullshit!" Katie cursed loudly, then quickly covered her mouth.

"It is," Sally Gayle, one of the front of house staff grumbled. "Colin is Mr Henderson's half-brother from his father's fourth marriage to Marion Fine. They have lunch all the time and are really close," Sally gossiped.

A light went on in my head. Blood was thicker than water. "Well, if that's how Mr Henderson wants to run his business, it's his choice," I responded quietly.

"Ladies," Benjamin interjected, walking up behind Katie as she opened her mouth to speak. "Is there a problem?"

"No, Mr Henderson," I smiled sweetly. "I was just relaying that Betsy promised to visit with the baby before she goes home with it."

"I can't wait to meet the little thing," Sally cooed.

"As soon as I know if it's a boy or a girl, I'll organise a gift hamper to be sent from all of us," I decided.

"Just let us know how much to put in." Katie touched my shoulder. "No paying for it out of your own pocket."

"I'll pay for it," Benjamin announced, handing me his credit card. "I'll get that back off you when we meet for reports tomorrow morning."

"Sure," I agreed taking the card. "I should get my staff organised. Excuse me." I stepped away and made my way out to start my work day… night shift.

Just before my break, I knocked on the door to the security office. Jarrett opened the door with a smile. "Holly, heard you had an exciting start to the day."

"Disappointing more like. I thought I had two more weeks of competence up my sleeve."

Jarrett chuckled. "He may surprise us."

I lifted my brow in disbelief. "While I hope, for all our sakes, that is the case, I doubt it."

Jarrett nodded but said nothing more. "Benjamin was looking for you earlier. He wasn't happy."

"What time was that?" I asked looking at my watch.

"Two hours ago," Jarrett smiled. "He waited in here with me for an hour, watching you do your rounds. By eleven, he needed sleep."

"Well, at least he knows I actually do the job I'm hired to do, not sitting on my arse all night," I dismissed. "I'm going on my break if anyone needs me."

"Okay, Holly, enjoy the swim," Jarrett smiled shutting the door.

I made my way to the pool and dived in, ready to do forty minutes of laps. When I finished, I pulled myself from the water and enjoyed five minutes of peace, lying beside the pool with just my legs hanging in the water. My alarm went off on my phone to the side of the pool. I sighed, standing up. I silenced the alarm, picking my phone up and taking it to the shower with me. As I approached the shower, Benjamin was standing there in just his tracksuit bottoms and a shirt. "Benjamin, shouldn't you be sleeping?"

"I couldn't sleep," Benjamin answered watching me approach, his eyes raking over my body. "You came to work late tonight?"

I frowned stepping past him and into the ladies' bathroom. "I was here an hour before my shift started."

"Which was an hour late for our meeting and dinner," Benjamin stated, following me into the change room.

"I had a late night out dancing with my friend and slept in," I explained dismissively. I unzipped my swimsuit and peeled it down my body. I stepped into the shower recess as I let my hair down out of its usual French roll, while I waited for the hot water to come through.

"Do you know, last night was the first time I'd ever seen your hair out," Benjamin commented.

I looked over my shoulder at him. "Makes sense. You've only ever fucked me in uniform." I stepped under the water and turned around to face him. "This is actually the first time you've ever seen me naked."

Benjamin's eyes were following my hands as I soaped myself up. "I am aware of that. I suddenly feel like I've been shortchanged the past two years."

I smirked. "Well, unless you are about to start going without sleep to catch me on my break, this will probably be the last time too." I hung my head back and washed the soap from my body.

"Best I make the most of it then," Benjamin growled. I opened my eyes in time to see him step into the shower with me naked. He pulled me to him and kissed me deeply as he slammed my back against the cold tiled wall. My breath rushed out of me in the form of his name. I couldn't describe how wonderful it felt to be utterly naked with him. Not that he hadn't been naked before. Most Wednesday nights he would strip entirely while he took me bent over his dining room table or his couch. Never once had we had sex in a bed. That thought occurred to me as he lifted my thighs to his waist, found my entrance and shoved into me. A sob caught in my throat as I realised how right Mitchell was. I was delusional thinking this was more than sex, that Benjamin felt something more for me.

"I know, Holly," Benjamin murmured in my ear. "We should have done this years ago." I held my tongue as my alarm started ringing again. "What's that?" Benjamin asked, thrusting harder, faster, to meet the urgency of the alarm.

"Breaks over," I gasped, holding on. Benjamin took the hint and pounded into me as he found his release. There was another first; I didn't orgasm with him. The brilliance of the hot quickie sex had diminished by the realisation that was all I was ever going to be to Benjamin Henderson. He held me for a moment before he gently released me and stepped into the running water to wash himself. When he stepped out to grab one of the complimentary towels from the shelf, I cleaned myself and turned the shower off. Benjamin silenced my alarm and handed me a towel. He watched me dress in silence, sitting down after he'd dressed.

Once I was fully-clothed, I turned to leave, trying hard to hold my hurt in till I was back in my office alone. Benjamin stood up grabbing my arm. "I forgive you, Holly."

I frowned. "Forgive me?"

"For last night," Benjamin clarified. "I know you are angry about not getting the chance to interview. Going on that date last night was your way to pay me back for feeling slighted. I don't want to know what happened with that guy last night. Let's just forget it, okay?"

I wasn't sure what pissed me off more. The presumption he had a right to chide me for going on a date, or that he expected me to feel guilty. "Let's get something straight," I began. "First, I wasn't on a date last night. Mitchell is one of my best friends. I've known him longer than you, and have been going out to dinner with him and his long-term partner for years. Something Trisha can attest to." I stepped closer to Benjamin, letting him see how angry I was with him.

"Second, I don't care how pissed off I am with you; I would never go and fuck some random guy just to get even with you. In fact, with how you've treated me, the exact opposite would be the likely scenario." I grabbed up my bag and stormed out to the pool area.

"How I've treated you?" Benjamin asked astonished. "What, because I passed you over for promotion?"

"Two years, Benjamin. Not once before tonight have you ever made time for me in your life as anything more than a sordid quickie," I blasted him. "Tonight was the first time you've seen me naked because you have never taken me on a date, come back to my place, undressed me and enjoyed me properly. I'm just a five-minute fuck over a desk. I could be anyone as far as you're concerned."

"That's not true," Benjamin refuted, eyebrows in his hair. "We've never been on a date because you work nights."

"Don't give me that shit, Benjamin. I have two nights off a week." I turned to leave. "You just had the opportunity to put me on day shift and make this thing between us something more. You instantly made sure that couldn't happen." I opened the pool room door.

"Holly, that wasn't even a consideration."

"I noticed." I turned to look at him. "I never have been."

CHAPTER FOUR

"Good morning," Colin greeted, hanging his overcoat up as he came through the door. "Winter is finally here."

"Morning," I answered, finishing up my written report for the revenue manager.

"How was your night?" Colin asked.

"Uneventful. Only a couple of complaints about pillows being too hard or soft. One couple complained about a couple in the adjacent room fornicating loudly, and a protest that the complimentary shampoo and conditioner were not a chemical free organic brand." I handed Colin a list. "I've researched and have a list of possible organic brands we could start using."

Colin took one look at the list, scrunched it up and threw it in the bin. "We'll stick with what we have."

"They aren't the first to complain, Colin."

"I'm the manager here, Holly, it's my decision," Colin bit back.

"That it is," I replied mildly, pressing send on my report. "Let's go do the breakfast debrief," I sighed standing up and logging out of the computer.

"Don't be in such a rush, Holly, or are you begging for it this morning?" Colin gave me a feral smile, which did nothing to endear him to me.

"I'm sorry?" I asked, giving him a chance to backtrack.

"You know because if you are that keen, I can help you out." He winked.

The son of a bitch winked at me! "Did you just proposition me?" I asked incredulously.

"Oh, I'm sorry, I thought older men who were your boss was your thing?" Colin stepped closer, his murky eyes taking in my surprise. "Yeah, I know about you and my brother, Holly. He told me about banging you in this very office after it first happened. I didn't work here then, and I wasn't sure if it was you or Betsy until I saw how pissed he was when he saw you with that other guy on Tuesday." Colin moved closer, taking my hips in his hands and pulling my lower body against his. "I'm not going to tell anyone, Holly, as long as you give me a reason to keep my mouth shut."

I grabbed his tie, pulling his face close to mine. "Tell anyone you like. I'm not going to fuck you. Touch me again. I'll file a harassment complaint." I pushed him away from me, grabbing up my stuff and storming to the meeting.

"Holly? Everything okay?" Katie called catching up with me.

I looked behind me, making sure Colin was nowhere near. "That jerk just threatened me."

"How?" Katie asked wide-eyed.

"He told me if I didn't sleep with him, he'd tell everyone I was sleeping with Mr Henderson."

"Oh please!" Katie rolled her eyes. "He started that rumour six months ago. Though, back then he would only say one of the managers."

I balked. "Why did no one tell me?"

Katie put her hand on my shoulder. "Honey, you are the only one who has closed door meetings with Mr Henderson, it was kind of obvious who Colin was implicating."

"I can't believe this."

"Look, Betsy walked into that office all the time without knocking and never witnessed anything other than professional behaviour. The majority of us were already suspicious. By the time Colin was blabbing about it, we'd already gotten over it. If you are sleeping with Mr Henderson it's been made fairly obvious that's all you are getting out of it. So, who cares?" Katie gave me a friendly smile. "Come on, let's get the debrief done so you can get out of here. You look exhausted."

The breakfast meeting went quickly. I was yawning by the time I walked back into my office and found Benjamin waiting. I left the door open and went to my desk. "Shut the door so we can talk, Holly," Benjamin directed.

I raised a brow. "No, it can stay open."

"Holly," Benjamin warned. "You don't want anyone overhearing what I'm about to say."

"Then don't say it," I returned evenly, logging into my computer. "Your brother is telling everyone we are sleeping together. I refused his offer to keep his mouth shut in return for letting him have the same privilege this morning."

"What?" Ben stood outraged.

"So, since we aren't sleeping together any longer, I think, for the sake of my reputation, the office door can stay open whenever I'm in here with either of you."

"Jesus, Holly!" Benjamin stalked to the door and shut it firmly. "What the fuck happened? In the space of four days, you've completely changed. Did not getting an interview piss you off that much?"

I stood up to face him. "I can't believe you are making this about me. You're the one who told your asshole brother about us."

"That was two years ago. He didn't work here," Benjamin yelled frustrated.

"He told me, right before he tried to bend me over the desk," I yelled back.

"My god, Holly. I always took you, to be honest and sensible. I never thought for a second you'd be so bitter about not getting a promotion that you would make this sort of shit up," Benjamin scowled. I stood speechless. Benjamin shook his head. "I'm disappointed in you, Holly, but you were right about one thing."

"What's that?" I asked on the verge of tears.

"We aren't sleeping together anymore. We are done." Benjamin yanked open the office door open with such violence that I thought it would come off the hinges. "Email me the usual reports."

I took a deep breath. "Actually," I straightened my back, "it is the day manager's responsibility to do these reports. Get your more than qualified brother to do them."

"Holly, you've been doing these reports for two and a half years. Colin was never taught this. Be fair," Benjamin requested, barely restraining his temper.

I logged out of my computer, picked up the reports I'd printed, and handed them to Benjamin as I stepped out the office door. "Here, give him these as a starting point. I've already emailed them to Elliot anyway." Elliot was our revenue manager.

"Holly, you're being unreasonable," Benjamin called after me.

"Good night, Mr Henderson," I waved over my shoulder. I grabbed my bag out of my locker and caught the bus home. I opened the door of my apartment to the smell of fresh coffee.

"Hey, you, what's been happening?" Trisha, my South American flatmate, asked from the kitchen. Her smile faded when she saw me. "Shit, who died?"

I sobbed. "Trisha, I've fucked up big time."

"Okay. Do you need me to help you move a body or something?" Trisha asked, which made me smile. She was deathly serious in her offer.

"I fucked my boss," I admitted, closing the door and taking the coffee she offered me.

Trisha looked surprised. "Only just today? I thought that shit had been happening for a year or more now?"

I stared at her. "Fuck!" I whispered. "Everyone knows." I walked to the couch and sat down.

"Well, I know yes. I am your best friend." Trisha sat next to me and placed her hand on my knee. "Who else knows?"

"Colin."

"Wait, the concierge who should never have been hired knows? How?"

"Not the concierge anymore." I filled Trisha in on everything she missed.

"Okay, so how did the dipshit find out?" Trisha asked, still gobsmacked by my news.

"Turns out, Colin is Benjamin's half-brother. Benjamin told him back when it first started," I explained.

Trisha's brow creased. "Then why is it a big deal now?"

"Because Colin started as the day manager this morning and his first order of business was to demand I drop my panties for him or he'd tell everyone about Benjamin and me," I mourned.

"That asshole!" Trisha exclaimed passionately. "Please tell me you told Benjamin?" I nodded, tears filling my eyes. "He didn't rip his brother a new one?" Trisha asked astonished.

I sucked in a shaken breath. "He accused me of making it up because I was angry about being passed over for promotion." I couldn't hold it in any longer. Hot tears spilled forward, cascading over my heated cheeks.

"That's bullshit! You don't have a vengeful bone in your body. It wouldn't even have occurred to you to do such a thing. Me? Yes. You, hell no!" She wrapped her arm around me. "I can't believe this has happened. What are you going to do?"

"The only thing I can do," I sobbed. "I need to find a new job before he fires me."

"You think he will?" Trisha asked soothingly.

"Yes." I was sure of it. The way he looked at me before he stormed out of the office played over and over in my head. "If I don't arrive tomorrow to find my notice has been given, I will be very surprised."

"Okay, then." Trisha stood up collecting her laptop from the kitchen bench. "Drink your coffee, Holly, and let's find you a new job."

Trisha sat back beside me and opened a job search site. I smiled at her. "You're the best friend I could have. You know that, right?"

"Sure do," Trisha smiled. "Now, let's see what kick arse job you can do next."

———

THURSDAY EVENING, I arrived at work early and used the office to meet with Ellen and do some forward planning. I hadn't taken any leave in nearly five years. I decided now was the time to cash some of that in. Ellen was more than happy to carry a little more responsibility for a few weeks. I suggested it as a trial so she could see what being a manager entailed. Once I'd organised dates with Ellen, I emailed Terry Patrickson, the General Manager for all the Henderson Hotels internationally. My phone rang twenty minutes later.

"Holly, is everything alright?" Terry asked in his usual kind voice. "I don't think I've ever seen a leave request from you."

"Where are you that you were awake to get that email?" I asked with a laugh.

"London. Now, what's going on?"

"I have five years of annual leave accrued and decided to cash in a month's worth," I explained. "I've already covered my shifts. Ellen Patterson will be fill-in assistant manager, Sally Gayle will trial as concierge."

Terry was quiet for a moment. "Okay, I'll sign off on this. So, two weeks and then you'll be on leave for a month?"

"That's right," I confirmed.

"Are you going to travel or do something interesting?" Terry enquired.

"Actually, I don't know yet, Terry. I only decided I needed a holiday yesterday."

"A-huh, the same day the new manager started," Terry laughed. "Is he that bad?"

"Much, much, worse, Terry," I smiled. "He's going to destroy this hotel's reputation, and I don't plan on being here for it," I informed him honestly.

Terry took a deep breath. "That your way of giving me advance notice, Holly?"

I sighed. "I don't know yet. I just know that for the first time since I started working here six years ago, the idea of walking in the doors of this place fills me with dread. That's a sure sign that it's time to move on, don't you think?"

Terry cleared his throat. "I'll be back there in a week. I can have a look and see if there is a position coming up at another of our hotels. I know there is a night concierge role opening up in Saint Kilda."

"Backwards step and moving interstate? No thanks, Terry." I smiled at his generosity. "I think getting away from Henderson Hotels is the only way forward for me. Thanks anyway. I'll see you next week."

"See you in a week, Holly," Terry answered sadly and hung up. There was a knock at the door. I called for them to come in.

Katie Dale walked in, her face red with anger. "You ready for this?" She asked holding a piece of paper.

"I don't know. Am I?" Katie handed me the piece of paper. I read the printed order of room cleaning and frowned. "What on earth?"

"Our new manager has decided that our current program is inefficient. He feels that the suites should be cleaned at the same time as every room on that level," Katie explained.

"Suites can have up to two hours later check out time," I discredited Colin's theory. "So, cleaning won't start till ten in the morning, and your entire team will work one level at a time?"

Katie shrugged. "This is how he wants it done. One level at a time. Hanging around up to two hours for suites to be ready, we'll still be only halfway through cleaning when the check-in opens at two."

I frowned studying the paper. "Fine. Let's split your staff into teams," I suggested. "Designate one team per floor, that way they can move from room to room as they check out still, but it will appear to Colin that you are following his new work plan." I made a few marks on the paper. "Whoever is designated to the upper two levels will start by cleaning the gym and showers. By the time they finish down there in the morning, they can go to the function rooms and bars, before going back to do the second clean of the gym and then up to the rooms on their levels. Each team will ensure the elevators are clean. Split the other areas amongst the lower level teams."

Katie smiled. "Basically, sticking to the way it already works, but presenting it differently?"

"Basically," I smiled.

"Thanks, Holly."

"Oh, I'm going on annual leave in two weeks. Ellen will be filling in for me while I'm away."

Katie's brows rose. "Anywhere good?"

"I'm thinking a cruise. I haven't been on one since I started working here," I admitted.

Katie smiled. "Take a plane to Hawaii with no luggage. Shop yourself silly and then catch a boat back. You'll have a ball."

"Sounds good. I might see if any of my sisters want to go. We haven't spent time together in years," I mourned. I missed my two older sisters.

"What is Nichola doing now?" Katie asked about the one sister she'd met regularly through the years.

"She's a personal assistant for a bank CEO," I chuckled.

"That's long hours," Katie shook her head. "Being a workaholic must run in your genes."

I stood up. "Speaking of which, best we get to the reporting meeting."

CHAPTER FIVE

Colin managed to annoy nearly every manager over the course of the next week. I arrived at work most evenings to put out the fires he'd caused during the day, and I left work late most mornings as I spent a lot of my time running around correcting his incompetence. Most recently, Colin decided that lilies were a boring flower and the florist should now supply gardenias for the lobby vases. I had a headache by the time I'd walked across the foyer to see what the staff were complaining about. They didn't need to verbalise the problem. I could smell it. A call to the florist and an hour later, and all the gardenias were replaced with orchards. I did, however, keep a bunch of gardenia's aside, which I put in my office and closed the door before I left. Just for Colin.

I hadn't seen Benjamin except in passing. He didn't even acknowledge me if we ended up in the same elevator. Thankfully, both times that happened, we'd had guests with us. I disembarked with the guests even if I was going to another level, just to prevent being alone with him. I received daily emails from the revenue manager asking me to confirm or correct Colin's reports. Most of the time I was making major corrections, which I made sure the general manager also received a copy of.

"Evening, Holly," Terry greeted as he approached when I arrived at work on Friday.

"Evening, Terry. Did you have a good flight?"

"I did. I arrived home Wednesday night and spent yesterday with the family. Do you have some time to talk before your shift starts?"

I looked at my watch. "All depends on how long my fix list is tonight, honestly."

"Yes, I've heard it's been quite the week. The newly proposed decor in the guest rooms is quite different."

Different? Ellen and I were wondering which brothel Colin got his inspiration from. I didn't say that to Terry though. "Yes, quite the departure from the subtle, clean lines that Betsy decorated the rooms in two years ago," I answered casually as I moved to my locker.

"How is Betsy?" Terry enquired.

"Good, it was a little girl. They are over the moon. She's bringing the baby in next Thursday morning for the morning debrief."

"I look forward to meeting the little bundle of joy." Terry followed me into the office and closed the door. "Complaints have nearly doubled in the last week, both from customers and staff."

"I'm aware. I check the reports daily."

"Check them? Don't you write them?"

"No," I sat down at my desk and opened my emails, "that is the manager's job, the one I wasn't qualified to even interview for," I replied evenly.

"I see," Terry grunted. "A lot seems to have changed since I was here a few months ago."

"You have no idea," I muttered under my breath. "Colin should be by soon to share whatever new change he's decided on shortly."

"He's been making a lot of changes?"

"He has a head full of new ideas, Terry, and is now in a position to inflict them on the rest of us," I responded dryly.

"Inflict, does he?" Terry studied me carefully.

I looked up and exhaled. "God, you're giving me the same look Mr Henderson did."

Terry's brow lifted. "What look is that, Holly?"

I sighed collecting my stuff together for the evening debrief. "The disbelieving one that says you think I'm being negative towards Colin purely because he got the job over me."

"It is very unlike you, Holly, and unless there is something else that has changed in your life recently, the common denominator to your sudden unhappiness does seem to be your new boss," Terry acknowledged reasonably. "Has anything else happened that I should know about?" I looked at my shoes, biting my lip. He was asking about Benjamin. Did everyone know? Terry blew out a breath. "Let's go to the debrief. I'm here for the week. If you change your mind and want to talk to me, just email me, and I'll find you." I nodded without meeting his eyes.

Everyone was in the staff room who needed to be, except, of course, Colin. "I think we need to start this meeting if everyone is going to finish on time," Terry announced taking the chair. "Firstly, Mr Henderson has provided me with two tickets to the symphony for Tuesday night for our monthly acknowledgement of a staff member. If you could all send me the name of the person you think is most deserving using our in-house communications app Holly created, I'll announce the winner at the end."

Everyone took out their smartphones and tapped out the name of who they thought worked the hardest this past month.

"Now, I'd like to say I understand a lot of you are unhappy with some of the changes made by the new manager. I personally would have liked the opportunity to sit on the interviews and see the other candidates so I could assure you we do have the best manager from the selection. Unfortunately, I was stuck in France at the time and was unable to even Skype in," Terry explained. "Having said that, everyone in this room was selected by Mr Henderson for their position, and we all know our team of managers has settled in and do a great job every day. I would ask that all of you trust Mr Henderson's judgement and give Mr Fine time to settle into his new position."

Katie raised her hand. "And if Mr Fine sexually harasses any other staff?"

Terry sat back jaw dropping for a second. "I wasn't aware there was a first incident" Katie's eyes flicked to me. Terry following before clearing his throat. "Was it reported?"

I stayed quiet. Katie sighed. "Holly would be able to answer that."

"It was reported directly to Mr Henderson," I informed Terry, keeping my voice even.

Terry swallowed. "What did Mr Henderson do?"

I met Terry's eyes. "He accused the victim of making it up." I sat forward as the other managers shook their heads unhappily. "Needless to say, the victim of the assault didn't bother taking the matter further."

"I see," Terry sighed. He wrote a note down. "Holly, I'd like you to follow up and get a formal statement from the staff member. Hand it to me directly. I will ensure it goes on file, so if there are any further incidents, a record of the behaviour exists."

"Of course, Mr Patrickson," I nodded writing down a note to kill Katie later. The door opened, and Colin walked in almost on cue. The grumbles around the table were almost synchronous.

"Mr Fine, so nice of you to join us," Terry grumbled.

"Sorry, everyone. I got caught up with a customer," Colin smiled walking to his seat. He unbuttoned his blazer to sit. The fact his fly was unzipped was evident to the room by the bright red underwear showing through the opening.

Terry cleared his throat and made a gesture subtly. Colin looked down, smirked, and zipped up. He looked across the table at me and winked. I rolled my eyes and tried not to vomit in my mouth. The rest of the meeting went as usual. Colin gave us the night's numbers, which I'd already pulled for myself, then proceeded to list off those with specific requests.

"Zoe Jephson's team are confirmed to check in tomorrow?" I asked already knowing the answer. Zoe was a big-name actress due to start filming her latest movie in town next week. She stayed with us previously and loved the service she received. For this shoot, she'd booked out one of the penthouses for the full three months of the shoot.

"If you say so," Colin dismissed. "Weekends are Mia's problem."

Terry raised his brows but said nothing to Colin. "Any special preparation needed?" Terry asked openly to the table.

I waited a few seconds to see if Colin had bothered reading the memo I'd sent out. Shaking my head, I looked to Jacob Atteberry, the manager of cuisine. "Zoe doesn't arrive till Tuesday, so nothing special till then, but it would be good to ensure your staff knows Zoe is a vegetarian."

"Will do, Holly," Jacob nodded making a note.

I looked at Colin. "Since Zoe will arrive while you are on shift, you will need to prepare a big bowl of M&M's for her room. Zoe is addicted, but only brown ones. She doesn't like the artificial colours, so she only eats the brown M&M's."

"Absolutely ridiculous," Colin huffed.

"Your opinion is irrelevant Colin," I lectured. "Zoe is a great catch for this hotel. Her only demand is a bowl of brown M&M's. It is your job to make that happen."

Colin sat forward, a nasty smile on his face. "I don't need you to tell me what my job is, Holly."

I closed my book. "Good, then try actually doing it." I stood up. "I have to get my staff on track. Good evening everyone."

"Night, Holly," The other managers farewelled.

"I haven't finished my report yet," Colin growled.

"Email me anything I miss," I replied with a false smile as I left. I finally looked forward to working the weekend. It meant four days Colin free.

THE NEXT MORNING, I dropped into my office chair after the breakfast debrief. I was exhausted after another night of cleaning up from Colin's ineptness. There was a gentle knock on the door. "Come in."

The door opened, and Terry walked in. His eyes went straight to the empty chair in the office and widened slightly as he stepped in. "I was looking for Benjamin. He's usually in here in the morning."

I shook my head. "Not for nearly two weeks now."

"Oh? Another change?" Terry inquired carefully. I nodded. "Would I be right in guessing this was the change that made work entirely unbearable?"

I met Terry's eyes. "Benjamin hasn't spoken a word to me since I told him about Colin and the sexual harassment."

Terry nodded and stepped forward placing two tickets on my desk. "The staff voted that you deserved these, Holly. I didn't catch you last night."

I picked up the symphony tickets. "I've never won the reward before."

Terry smiled. "I know. Apparently, your colleagues feel you deserve it though."

"Thank you."

"Well, I'll go find Benjamin. Any ideas?"

"Try Jarrett in security. He has the all-seeing eye," I reminded him. Terry laughed and left. I packed up my stuff and caught the bus home.

CHAPTER SIX

"Yay, you're home," Trisha smiled walking into our apartment an hour after me.

"I am. What are your plans Tuesday night?" I asked holding up the symphony tickets.

"Nothing so far. What are you taking me to see?"

"Symphony," I sighed.

"Argh, classical music, really?" Trisha looked ready to vomit. I chuckled.

"Think of it as a cultural experience. Plus, they are VIP tickets, so we get to sit in the company box," I coaxed.

Trisha gave me a sly smile. "Fine, but I expect you to put out if I sit through that."

I laughed. Trisha stood up. "Well, that means I need a respectable dress and so do you. Let's go shopping."

"Trisha, we both just finished a night shift," I groaned.

"Drink coffee, have a shower, and we'll be good for at least two hours," Trisha shrugged.

I smiled and dragged myself from the lounge. "I'll shower first; you make the coffee."

An hour later I had a mauve silk dress in the bag and waited while Trisha purchased her bright red sequined dress. "Holly?" A man touched my shoulder.

I turned to see Lance Petts smiling at me. "Lance, how are you?"

"Good. Great, actually. That reference you provided scored me a job at Holmes Resort as the concierge," Lance beamed. "Let me buy you a coffee to say thank you?"

"I'll take a rain check. I need my bed and sleep if I'm going to function tonight."

Lance frowned. "Wait, aren't you the manager now? Why are you working nights still?"

I released a long sigh. "Colin Fine got the manager's position. I've decided to leave Henderson's employment. Wednesday is my last shift."

Lance's brows jumped. "Wow! That's a shock. Who was lucky enough to score you?"

"No one yet, I'm still applying."

Lance pulled out his phone. "Roger, remember that excellent manager I told you about? Yeah, the one who gave me my reference? Well, she's job hunting." Lance winked at me.

"You'd be insane not to find a job for her if you want to make this hotel work," Lance assured. He grinned. "Just hold on, she's right here." Lance handed me the phone.

"Hello, Mr Holmes," I spoke shyly.

"Miss Claire. Would you be available to meet with me Monday morning?" Roger Holmes asked immediately.

"Yes, of course. What time?"

"Would zero eight hundred be too early?

I chuckled. "Mr Holmes, I've spent three years on night shift. Eight in the morning is an early night for me."

Roger laughed. "I'll meet you at the new undertaking for Holmes Resorts. Lance will give you the address."

"Thank you, Mr Holmes." I handed Lance the phone, and he checked it disconnected before giving me the address for Monday.

"I guess we are even?" Lance smiled.

"Thanks, Lance."

"Thank me if he gives you the job. I'll see you later, Holly," Lance waved and walked off.

Trisha walked up with a suspicious look. "Did you just score a date with that young hunk?"

"Better, I scored a job interview with Holmes resorts."

Trisha squealed and hugged me, startling everyone around us, including me.

———

I ARRIVED at the address Lance gave me with fifteen minutes to spare on Monday morning. I entered the old bank building which was still undergoing renovation and looked around. The hotel wasn't open to guests yet but wasn't far off. There was no reception staff, or bellhops to tell me where to go, which was kind of good, as it allowed me time to stand there and marvel at the beauty of the lobby.

Holmes resorts were usually just that. A beachfront resort. This was the first Holmes Resort to be city based. No water frontage, beach, or rain-forest in the city to connect to nature, which was the Holmes Resort trademark. However, I was seriously impressed when I walked into the city building and found myself standing on a glass floor above what looked to be a river bed. The sound of a waterfall drew my eyes to the right where a magnificent indoor waterfall fell from two levels up, from what looked to be an indoor forest.

"That's the Daintree restaurant," a male voice spoke to my left. I turned to take in the man standing next to me. He was early to mid-thirties and dressed in a tailored charcoal suit to match his hair. A slight touch of receding hairline barely noticeable with the short hairstyle. "I'm Roger Holmes, the owner. You must be, Miss Holly Claire."

"Lovely to meet you, Mr Holmes," I shook the hand he offered me. It was a good firm handshake.

"Call me Roger. Mr Holmes is my father," Roger instructed.

I smiled. "The lobby looks amazing," I complimented.

"It does, doesn't it?" Roger beamed. He gestured for me to walk with him. "My father challenged me to take an inner city building and turn it into a resort. I decided an indoor rain-forest to escape the concrete jungle was the most appropriate theme." We crossed a bridge over an open run of water that divided the entrance, cafe, and lounge areas from reception and access to the elevators. "May I ask, Miss Claire, why you are looking for a new job?"

I was ready for this question. "I've spent three years working night shift as the assistant manager at Hotel Henderson. I started there when I was twenty-two and worked my way up. When the position of manager opened recently, I applied. Mr Henderson didn't even give me an interview."

"Did he explain why?" Roger listened carefully.

"He wanted me to stay on night shift," I answered. "I've done three years straight. I've basically had no social life in that time. I've missed weddings, birthdays, wild holidays abroad, all under the belief that if I did my time, worked hard, and didn't complain, I would get my nights back as soon as the relevant position became available."

"That didn't happen, and now you feel hard done by?" Roger finished.

"There is more to it, but that is the base of the issue," I acknowledged.

Roger walked with his arms clasped behind his back, very military in his stance and appearance. He stopped as we reached the elevator and raised a brow. "Tell me the more?" He took out a card and swiped it as we stepped into an elevator before pressing the second-floor button.

"It is personal," I bit my lip.

"I will not share anything you tell me, Holly, but I do value honesty in my employees," Roger warned.

I cleared my throat. "The new manager is related to Mr Henderson. His first day on the job, he told me if I didn't have sex with him, he would ruin my reputation by telling everyone I was sleeping with a senior member of staff. I reported the incident. Mr Henderson accused me of making it up out of spite."

Roger hid any surprise or doubt well. "I suspect that has made your current workplace rather uncomfortable for you."

The elevator opened and we stepped into the Daintree Restaurant. It smelled like a rainforest. One full wall was a living wall of plants.

"Is that a snake?" I stopped walking, staring at a giant snake wrapped around the branch of the indoor tree.

"That is Mousetrap," Roger explained. "He's a diamond Python and has helped us rid the building of its rat and possum problem. I don't believe in using chemicals if I don't have to." Roger pointed to a large pond that separated the kitchen from the customers. "That pond is a natural filtration system. It cleans the water used in the waterfall and underfloor lobby river. The other bonus is that it attracts any insects that might get in here."

"They won't bug the customers," I nodded understanding.

"Literally," Roger smiled. He led the way to a table in the back. There were staff here doing training. "Do you want the good news or the bad news, Holly?" Roger asked as I took a seat at the table with him.

"I always believe in ending on a positive note, so let's go with the bad news," I requested.

Roger's face softened. "I've already filled the manager, assistant manager, and concierge roles."

"Oh," I forced a smile. "So, there isn't a role for me here?"

"That depends," Roger studied me, sitting forward to cross his arms on the table. "I've heard you are the ideas person at Henderson's. You came up with the breakfast staff meeting, a communications app, the staggered checkout times?"

I bowed my head. "That is correct, plus other things that only senior level staff are aware of because I never took the credit."

Roger grinned. "Then here is the good news, Holly. The job I'm about to offer you doesn't require night shift." I met Roger's eyes with curiosity. "I'd like you to be my staff manager. You will sit in on debriefs, take care of rostering for all areas, so you will need to work closely with the managers from all departments. You will compile reports on performance, sit in on any interviews, but most importantly, you will manage me," Roger finished.

"Manage you?"

"Yes," Roger laughed. "I need a lot of managing."

Roger said it without any suggestion, but I wanted to be sure. "Could you maybe give me a summary of what managing you consists of?"

Roger propped his elbow on the table, chin in his hand. "Huh, well, diary management, ensuring I get to where I should be and keeping me informed about what is happening in my hotel. I don't live here, so you will be my eyes and ears. What do you say?"

"May I be frank, Roger?"

"Please?"

"Are you married, or in a long-term relationship?" I asked hopeful.

Roger's brow furrowed. "I've been married for eight years, Holly. I love my wife and two children immensely. My wife has just found out she is expecting our third child actually."

I deflated in relief. "May I meet your wife? If she likes me and is happy for me to be working closely with you, I will accept the job."

Roger assessed me a moment. "Benjamin Henderson is single."

"Yes, he is." *Even more so now.*

Roger watched me for a moment then pulled out his phone and dialled a number. "Hi, honey..." An angry female voice came through the other end. Roger smirked rolling his eyes. "Yes, honey, I'm a prick for getting you pregnant, but if you recall correctly, you're the one who wouldn't let me pull out." More yelling followed. Roger tried very hard not to laugh. "Honey, you just made the woman I'm interviewing blush like a Beetroot. Well, she asked me to actually. Holly would like to meet you before she accepts the job." Roger lifted his eyes to mine. "I suspect because she is worried you might have an issue with us working closely together." Roger blushed at whatever his wife said next. "Yes, to both, Sammy, but she was relieved to find out I was married, so I don't believe that's the issue." Roger listened a moment longer then hung up. He watched me a moment. "Have you ever heard of Sam Ania?"

I frowned. "The hotel reviewer?"

Roger grinned. "Yes. When she isn't reviewing hotels, Sam Ania is Samantha Holmes, my wife."

I laughed. "I always thought it was a woman."

Roger smiled enjoying my humour. "You've picked a bad day. Sammy only just had the pregnancy confirmed. She's a bit cross with me about it."

I smirked. "I heard that. Did she not want a third?"

"We hadn't discussed it. Our second child is only twelve months old, and Sammy just returned to work." Roger took a deep breath. "It doesn't suit Sammy's plans to have three children under five." Roger stood up buttoning his suit jacket. "Sammy will meet us at a cafe up the road for breakfast." I stood and followed Roger back to the elevator. We walked two blocks up and entered a French patisserie. The smell of freshly baked pastries and coffee hit me the moment we entered. My stomach growled with sudden hunger. Roger looked at me and chuckled. "I'm guessing you haven't eaten yet this morning?"

"Uh, no. I don't like to mess with my routine for night shift on my days off. I usually don't eat before lunch." I explained.

"Have you just come off night shift?" Roger asked leading us to a table.

"Yes, I finished early to meet with you," I replied, the reminder causing me to stifle a yawn while I took the seat opposite him at the table.

"Mr Homes," a young waitress greeted handing us both menus. "Any drinks to start?"

Roger differed to me. "A large hot chocolate please."

"I'll have a long black please, Michelle, and another hot chocolate for Sammy."

"Yes, Mr Holmes." The waitress smiled and walked away.

An average height woman with a girl next door appearance approached our table. Roger smiled pulling out the chair next to him as he stood. "Sammy..."

"Na-uh," Sammy shook a finger at him, "I'm not talking to you." She took the seat furthest from the door and turned to me. "Samantha Holmes," she introduced herself, holding out her hand.

I shook it. "Holly Claire. It's a pleasure to meet you." I smiled. "I would congratulate you on your news, but I'm terrified you'd gouge my eyes out."

Sammy smirked. "You're safe; he's not." She put her hand on Roger's thigh and dug her nails in.

Roger grimaced and patted his wife's hand. "No foreplay in front of the potential employees, honey," Roger teased. Sammy's head whipped around to scowl at him. Roger assumed an innocent appearance. "What, it's not like I can get you pregnant again." He winked, and Sammy threw her hands in the air.

"Honestly," Sammy looked at me. "They say men in their late thirties are past their prime, but I have a hard time believing that. What do you think, Holly?"

I smirked. "My experience would also negate that theory."

Sammy smiled. "How old is your current boyfriend?"

"I don't have one," I answered honestly. "Part of the reason for me wanting a new job is to have the opportunity to date again."

Sammy looked confused. Roger patted her hand. "Holly is the assistant manager at Hotel Henderson. She's been on permanent night shift for three years now," he explained. "When the manager's position recently became available, Holly was passed over in favour of one of Benjamin's relatives. The new manager then used his position to try and force Holly to sleep with him."

I exhaled roughly as Roger revealed what he assured would be confidential.

Roger met my eyes. "I'm sorry, Holly. I should have clarified. Confidentiality meant everyone except my wife. I share everything with Sammy."

Sammy patted my hand as our drinks arrived. "Michelle, can we get three croissants, please."

"Any condiments, Mrs Holmes?"

"Jam please," Roger requested.

"Honey for me, thank you," I smiled.

Sammy rolled her eyes. "My French grandmother would smack you both." Sammy waved Michelle away and considered me. "I've reviewed Hotel Henderson regularly, both before and after you became the assistant manager. It's pretty well known you have been the driving force behind a lot of the improvements there. I'm surprised Benjamin took the risk of losing you." Sammy looked to Roger. "What did he tell us last year at the conference?"

"That his assistant manager was his ideas bank," Roger declared.

I frowned. "Not anymore, I'm not."

Sammy raised an eyebrow at my tone. "There is more to this than a sexual harassment claim."

I took a mouthful of my hot chocolate while the waitress placed the croissants and left. Then I explained to Sammy how Benjamin accused me of lying. "He wouldn't hear me, and it made me realise that continuing my employment was going to be impossible," I explained.

"So, you started looking for a new job?" Sammy asked. I nodded. "How much notice do you need to give?"

"A month," I answered casually. "I start four weeks of annual leave on Thursday. I intend to submit my resignation Thursday morning before I finish my shift and never return."

"Even if you don't have a job?" Roger asked surprised.

I swallowed. "I'm flying to Hawaii on Friday with my two sisters for four days, then cruising back home from there. That will leave me two weeks to find a new job after I return." I ran my finger around the lip of my mug. "I've not had a life for three years. My FU fund can sustain me a few months without work."

"FU fund?" Roger looked to Sammy confused.

"Her fuck you fund. In case you need to dump and run from a bad boyfriend, or work situation, as per her current work problem," Sammy explained. "A sensible woman starts saving the moment she gets a job, just in case. You don't want to find yourself stuck in a bad situation because your hands are tied financially."

"Do you have a FU Fund?" Roger enquired, surprised.

Sammy laughed. "You bet your arse I do." Sammy returned her attention to me. "Who will you be using as your reference?"

I took my resume out of my bag and handed it to Roger. "The general manager, Terry Patrickson has agreed to be my reference, so has Betsy Mills, the former manager. Ellen Patterson, the night concierge, will also be happy to talk to you about working with me."

Roger was looking through my resume when Sammy reached over, snatching it from him and stuffing it in her handbag. "What?" Roger asked startled. Sammy nodded her head to the door. "Oh," Roger cleared his throat and sat back. I peered over my shoulder and swallowed when I observed Benjamin ordering a coffee. His eyes scanned the restaurant, spotting me and then who I was sitting with. His green eyes hardened before he paid for his coffee.

"I like her, hire her, Roger," Sammy whispered.

"Holly, when would you like to start?" Roger asked quietly as Benjamin walked towards our table.

"Five weeks from today?" I asked.

"Perfect," Roger smiled. "The hotel will be a week from opening. I'll send you the paperwork tomorrow," Roger murmured and gave me a wink as Benjamin arrived.

"Roger, Sammy, Miss Claire," Benjamin greeted. "I didn't realise you knew each other?"

Sammy smiled. "The hospitality world isn't that big Benjamin. We are just having a celebratory breakfast."

Benjamin raised a brow. "And what are you celebrating?"

"I'm pregnant again," Sammy announced excitedly.

Benjamin's brows dropped in confusion, then lifted quickly in surprise. "Oh. Congratulations to the both of you." Benjamin shook Roger's hand.

"I was just discussing Holly's interest in becoming a mother with her," Sammy added with a Cheshire grin.

I nearly spat my hot chocolate across the table. Benjamin froze like Han Solo in carbonite. I recovered faster. "I was explaining that I would have to find a decent man worthy of being my husband before I could consider children, and that's not going to happen while I'm on night shift." I stood up. "Thank you for breakfast, Sammy. I should go if I'm going to make my morning Yoga class," I excused.

Sammy stood up and gave me a quick hug. "We'll see you when you get back from your trip," she smiled. I nodded.

"Trip?" Benjamin blinked surprised. Roger and Sammy looked between us.

I swallowed. "Yes. I start a month's leave at the end of the week," I divulged.

Benjamin's eyes bored into mine. "I wasn't told about this."

I shrugged. "It was approved through the usual channels several weeks ago. I'm going on a cruise with my sisters. I leave Friday." I stepped away. "Thanks again for breakfast," I smiled at Roger and Sammy, then made my way out of the cafe. I was two doors down when I heard my name being called behind me. I ignored Benjamin and kept walking to the bus stop.

"Holly," Benjamin growled, grabbing my elbow and pulling me to the side of the moving foot traffic. He cursed as his coffee escaped the sipper hole and splashed the cuff of his suit jacket.

"What do you want, Mr Henderson?" I glared at him. How dare he touch me?

"What the hell was that?" He snarled. "Was that a job interview?"

Technically, no, the interview happened before we came to the coffee shop. "Did it look like an interview?" Benjamin raised his brows at my tone. I shook my head and looked at my watch. "I'm off duty, Mr Henderson, my life is none of your business anymore." I tried to step back into the flow of pedestrians, but Benjamin pulled me back.

"Holly," he frowned and shook his head. "I miss you," Benjamin muttered moving his mouth closer to mine.

I put my hand on his chest pushing him back. "I don't miss what I never had, Benjamin," I responded, tears filling my eyes. My heart ached with the pain of his last words to me. Benjamin dropped his coffee cup, took my face in his hands and pressed his mouth to mine. I felt his teeth pressing around my heart. I shoved him away. "No. You made yourself abundantly clear, Benjamin. What was happening between us is over. I don't want to be your fuck buddy anymore. I am not a play toy for you and your brother-"

"My brother?" Benjamin startled.

"Find someone else, Benjamin. I'm not interested in wasting

my time on the likes of you." I swiped the tears from my eyes and took a deep breath as I stepped closer. "All those years I thought we were more than sex. I thought you cared for me, the way I felt for you."

"Holly," Benjamin's face softened.

"I was lying to myself," I admitted, shaking my head at my own stupidity. "I never lied to you, Benjamin. Can you say the same to me?" Benjamin just stood there watching me. I nodded, wiped away the tears and stepped away.

CHAPTER SEVEN

"You look amazing!" Trisha cooed as we stood sipping champagne while we waited to enter the concert hall on Tuesday evening. "Tell me you are taking that dress to Hawaii?"

I blushed and nodded. Trisha grinned. "Shall we go in?" I asked, setting aside my champagne glass.

Trisha drank the rest of hers down in one mouthful. "Let's." We giggled and made our way up the stairs to show our tickets. We climbed the stairs to the box we would be watching from and were shown our seats.

We stood at the balcony watching the symphony tune their instruments and other people making their way to their seats. Our seats were in the second row back from the front of the box. "How long since you've spent time with Nichola and Sadie?" Trisha asked as we moved to our seats. "It seems like years since I've seen them."

"Four years since I've seen them in person," I answered. I'd been surprised when I realised how long it had been. My four older siblings still lived three hours south, in Canberra where we grew up.

My older brother Justin had followed our father into politics and was now a liberal backbencher. Nichola, the eldest girl, married a politician twice her age and was the perfect trophy wife, until he was caught cheating. She returned to her personal assistant work after the divorce, and I'm pretty sure she was now involved with her CEO boss.

David, my second oldest brother, became a lawyer and has his own law firm. Sadie, my sister just older than me, is a former porn star turned domestic goddess. She quit the porn circuit at age twenty-five and married David's best friend and law firm partner. They now have three children at school, and the only videos Sadie stars in are her homemade cooking videos that she posts on YouTube. I was the youngest in our Irish Catholic family. Five years younger than Sadie, and over a decade younger than Justin. Despite Sadie's colourful youth, I was considered the rebel child. I left for university and never came back.

"Should be an interesting trip," Trisha grinned.

"I'm still surprised they agreed to come," I admitted. "Nichola and Sadie are even footing the hotel bill so we can stay at a five-star resort. They both booked suites on the cruise ship too, so I'm just going to crash in their room on the boat."

"What if you hook up?" Trisha winked at me.

I laughed. "Then I won't be crashing in their room."

"This way, Mr Henderson," A woman's voice sang. I tensed, both Trisha and I watching the curtain pull back as Benjamin entered with an attractive woman I recognised from television as one of the morning news anchors. She was closer to his forty years, and without the thick stage makeup, her age was very evident.

"Did you know he would be here?" Trisha whispered unhappily. I shook my head. "Did he know you would be here?"

I met Benjamin's eyes and saw the smile on his face. "Yes," I whisper growled back and turned my attention to the orchestra again.

"You know you're better off without the prick," Trisha announced conversationally. "He treated you like shit and never deserved you." I looked at Trisha, trying to work out what she was up to. She smiled. "Look, you'll go to Hawaii, probably meet some amazing American who knows your true value, he'll whisk you off to the altar, get you knocked up with his six kids, and you'll never think twice about the prick you left behind," Trisha beamed.

"Six kids?" I looked at her terrified.

"Of course," Trisha laughed. "Because girls marry their father, so he'll be strict Irish Catholic too, and you nutters breed like rabbits. I'm still trying to work out if you are just that fertile you fall pregnant every time you have sex, or your sex drives are ten times higher than the average human."

I burst out laughing at Trisha. "Probably a combination of both." As I turned my attention back to the symphony, I caught the fierce look on Benjamin's face and understood

Trisha's sudden rant. She was pissing him off on purpose. The orchestra started clapping, and the audience joined in as the conductor came out.

"I can't believe you brought me to a symphony, Benji," The woman in front of us groaned. "You better fuck like a demon for this."

Trisha took my hand and squeezed it gently in reassurance. I met her eyes in the dark and mouthed 'Benji' before miming sticking my finger down my throat. Admittedly, I was relieved to know Benjamin hadn't slept with this woman before. Concurrently, the heartbroken and angry sense of self, wanted to lean forward and tell the woman that fucking was all he was good for. However, I knew that was being spiteful. Just because sex was all he wanted from me, didn't mean he couldn't be more for someone else. There was that tightness in my chest again. I rubbed my sternum; breathing seemed harder than normal.

Benjamin looked over his shoulder at me. I moved my eyes to the stage and closed my eyes as the first violin began a solo. The music was haunting, crawling into your body through your ears and tearing open your soul, so you felt every agonising note. The first violin played solo, climbing to the apex, stealing the breath from my lungs with its sorrow, until it reached that climatic high note of genuine heartbreak. The rest of the orchestra joined in, the first tears broke free, my heart dissecting itself on the razor-sharp strings of the symphony. The music was soul shattering. By the time intermission arrived, my tissue was saturated. I quickly cleaned myself up and excused myself from Trisha before the house lights came up. I ducked out to the bathroom and fixed myself up. I looked like I'd been crying for months when I looked in the mirror.

When I returned to the bar area, Trisha was standing with two glasses of champagne, talking to Benjamin and his date. I took a deep breath and walked over to them. "Better?" Trisha asked quietly, handing me the champagne. I nodded and took a large drink.

"Are you enjoying the symphony, Holly?" Benjamin asked jovially. "Trisha and Liselle were just discussing how boring they find it."

"I quite enjoy the symphony," I answered politely. "I haven't been in years and had forgotten how powerful the music could be. It picks you up, steals you away into the composer's heart and soul, and lets you feel their emotions at the rawest level. It's how music should be," I explained its effect. "You should feel it, not just hear it." All three stood watching me surprised. I finished my champagne and put the glass down. "I'm going back in," I announced, forced a smile and walked away.

"Wow, she's rather passionate," Liselle commented.

"Holly, wait up," Trisha caught up to me, a smile playing across her lips.

"What?" I asked as we climbed the stairs.

"I get it now," Trisha whispered conspiratorially. "I mean, other than the looks, money, and big shlong. He does have a big one, doesn't he?"

"I'm trying not to remember," I sighed, remembering. Life could be cruel.

"Well, other than the superficial stuff, I get why you two were drawn to each other," Trisha squeezed my hand. "Just before you came out, Benjamin was trying to explain the reason people still go to the symphony. He basically said what you said, but without your utter conviction." Trisha turned to face me at the top of the stairs. "I thought he was going to kiss you the way he was looking at you while you spoke."

"That could have been embarrassing," I murmured. "I'd hate his date to think less of him if I punched him out."

Trisha rolled her eyes, and we moved to our seats. "My point is, you two, you make sense to me now. Of course, you were almost made for each other. The media giant's youngest son, the politician's youngest daughter."

"We can stop discussing something that never existed anytime now," I grumbled. "You're my friend; you're meant to hate him."

Trisha cooed. "Oh, I do. I just wouldn't be surprised, if, a few months from now, he seeks you out and begs forgiveness."

I snorted. "That will have nothing to do with your romantic notions and everything to do with his brother ruining his business."

"I'm just saying, Holly," Trisha warned, "he's still into you, and I don't think whatever this is, is even close to finished."

The curtain parted, Benjamin and his date walked in taking their seats. As the lights dimmed, Liselle sunk down in her seat, taking Benjamin's hand and placing it on her thigh. The music started and stole my attention. Ten minutes into the second movement, Liselle gasped and moaned. I looked at Trisha. Her jaw was set and her eyes shone fiercely. I observed the pair in front of us, it took me a moment to notice the small movement of Benjamin's arm and that Liselle's thigh was bare, her dress pushed up on the side closest to him. I felt my own jaw clench and moved my gaze purposefully back to the orchestra. Several minutes later, I felt something vibrating on my lap and cursed as I pulled my phone out. "Hello?" I whispered.

"Holly, its Zoe Jephson."

"Zoe, what's wrong?" I stood up, moving out past the curtain and into the stairwell.

"I hate to complain, Holly, you've always done a great job in the past. I just checked in and found the bowl of M&M's I requested," she explained.

"Good. I passed that you only eat the brown ones onto the day staff."

"Really? Because I've got every colour," Zoe grouched.

"What?" I asked shocked.

"I may as well have bought the pack myself, Holly. It's really upsetting. I'm not overly demanding," Zoe informed me. "It's the only thing I asked for."

I took a deep breath. "Zoe, I apologise profusely for the stuff up. I will ensure the oversight is corrected within the hour."

"Thanks, Holly. I knew I could count on you," Zoe hung up.

I dialled work and Mia's connection. Mia Downer was the part-time assistant manager. She worked days during the weekend, and nights on Monday and Tuesday. "Holly, aren't you at the symphony?" Mia answered surprised.

"Yes," I whispered. "Look, Mia, I just got a call from Zoe

Jepson. Apparently, the bowl of M&M's was not sorted so that she only received the brown M&M's."

"But, you left specific instructions," Mia replied surprised. "Colin assured me he would see to it personally at this mornings' debrief," Mia groaned.

"Did he just?" I huffed.

"What do you want me to do?" Mia asked.

"Head down to the kitchen and get a bowl ready. I'll stop by the seven eleven on my way to the hotel and get some more M&M's. Then I will help you sort them," I advised.

"Holly, you can't pay for this out of your own pocket," Mia argued.

"Oh, I won't be," I assured. "I'll see you shortly." I hung up and walked back into the box. Benjamin and Trisha both watching me walk back in. I hit Benjamin on the shoulder and bent to his ear. "I need the corporate credit card," I told him then stepped passed Trisha to collect my clutch and jacket.

"What's going on?" Trisha asked.

"Have to go in to work. Sorry for ditching you," I excused.

Trisha gathered her stuff. "I'll see you to the hotel then get a bus."

I nodded. Benjamin stood up pulling out his wallet. "What's happened?"

I snatched the card out of his hand. "I'm going into work on my night off because your new manager decided to fuck with me by pissing Zoe Jephson off," I snapped. "So now I have to go fix it, just like I've been doing every night since he started."

"Holly," Benjamin snapped my name in warning.

"Don't," I growled back. "I'm tired of fixing problems that shouldn't exist, and I'm done with you pretending that I'm the problem in your life. I'm done, Benjamin." I walked out, moving as fast as I could down the stairs.

CHAPTER EIGHT

TRISHA AND I STOPPED AT THE SEVEN ELEVEN, BUYING EVERY pack of chocolate M&M's they had, then went to the hotel. Trisha handed me the bag she was carrying, then headed home. I made my way down to the kitchen and spent thirty minutes sorting M&M's with Mia, till we had a bowl full of brown ones. "I'll take this up," I sighed as Mia started putting the remainder M&M's into glass jars for the staff. I went to the top floor and rang the bell for the penthouse. Zoe opened the door and smiled when I handed her the bowl. The smile faded when she saw my dress.

"Holly, were you on a date?" Zoe asked surprised.

"The symphony, with my flatmate," I smiled.

"Oh, God, Holly, why didn't you tell me you weren't working tonight?" Zoe looked ashamed. She was the most down to earth young adult celebrity I'd met.

I shrugged, "You called me directly." I cleared my throat. "Actually, do you have a minute?" Zoe nodded and opened the door for me to come in. I stepped inside and waited for her to shut the door. Zoe walked over to the lounge and plonked herself down, placing the M&M's on the coffee table. She took a handful then sat back and made eye contact to tell me she was ready to listen. I sat down and faced her. "I thought I should let you know that I'm going on leave on Thursday for a month-"

"Oh, wow. Are you going somewhere nice?" Zoe asked.

"Hawaii-"

"Where are you staying?" Zoe cut in enthusiastically.

"Cassidy Resort," I smiled.

"That place is awesome; you'll love it. The owner actually works as the manager. He's very hands-on in making sure his guests are happy," Zoe informed me.

"So I've heard," I smiled. "Zoe, I'm not returning to Hotel Henderson after my holiday. I've been offered a position with another company, and I've decided to accept it."

"Oh," Zoe stared at me. "If both you and Betsy are gone, I'm not sure I want to stay here. The new manager isn't very nice. Where are you going to?"

I smiled sincerely. "Zoe, I'd get in a lot of trouble if it was even suggested I poached you to my new employer. I just wanted you to know that tomorrow is my last night here. If you have any issues, Ellen who will be taking over from me, will be more than willing to help."

Zoe looked utterly depressed. She was quite young, emotionally. I was only two years older than her, but she seemed so much younger. Probably why she could play teenagers still. Suddenly Zoe perked up. "You know, I'm absolutely wired, still on L.A. time. Want to hang out and watch a movie with me? Please?" Zoe begged. "You can watch the new Skarsgard movie with me."

I frowned. "I didn't think that was out yet?"

"It's not. The studio sends us copies of movies since its nearly impossible for actors to go to the cinema and watch a movie peacefully. So, I have an advance copy," Zoe preened.

I chuckled, kicking off my shoes. "Okay, you've twisted my arm." I picked up the phone and dialled the kitchen.

"Good Evening, Miss Jephson, what can we get you?" Mia answered.

"Mia, can you send up a big bowl of popcorn with extra butter to the penthouse please?"

"Sure, Holly," Mia laughed.

Zoe pushed the DVD into the machine and smiled at me. "Popcorn? Excellent idea!

The Skarsgard movie turned out to be Stellan Skarsgard, not his son Alexander. Never the less, the movie was quite good. One movie turned into three and lots of on-set, behind-the-scenes stories from Zoe. Just before five in the morning, Zoe fell asleep. I grabbed up my handbag and headed out to the elevator. I heard a door behind me open and turned to see Benjamin stepping out for his morning run. He looked me up and down with a frown. "You're still here?"

"Yes," I answered shortly. "Your credit card is in the office. I will give it to Terry to give back to you," I informed him.

"Do I want to know?" Benjamin asked stepping into the elevator with me.

"Probably not," I stifled a yawn. "Mia will report it though. I've given her all the details."

Benjamin turned suddenly, pinning me against the back of the elevator. "Holly, you were never just sex. I need you to know that. I thought you were happy with our arrangement. You never asked for more, never indicated to me you weren't happy."

"Jesus, Benjamin. I watched you date for years before we hooked up. I saw how quickly the girls who asked for more lasted." I swallowed painfully. "When I told you I wanted more, that night in the pool shower, you kicked me to the curb only hours later. I knew, Benjamin. I just thought if I didn't push, and I went to day shift, things would progress further naturally."

Benjamin's eyes fell to my lips. "The day concierge isn't working out. The job is yours if you want it?" I closed my eyes and exhaled. The elevator doors opened, I ducked under Benjamin's arm and exited the confined area. "Holly," Benjamin stepped out after me, taking my arm. "It's the best I can offer. I'm sorry."

"So am I, Benjamin," I replied quietly. "It's too little, too late."

"Holly, please?" Benjamin raised his voice a little. "I'm trying here. I want things to go back to how they were between us. I want my staff to start working well with each other again."

"I guess that's the problem, Benjamin." I used my other hand to rescue my arm from his grasp. "I don't want things between us to go back to how they were. I want to date; I want you to take me home with you and make love to me, naked, in your bed. I want to sleep in your arms, wake and eat breakfast together before I go to work. I want to work towards marriage and babies and..." I took a breath. "I want more than a five-minute quickie in the office once a day."

Benjamin closed his eyes, and I knew I was asking for more than my commitment-phobic boss was willing to give. "Give me time, Holly," Benjamin requested.

"You've had two years. How much longer do you need?"

Benjamin looked at me. He stepped in to me and kissed me. He kissed me out in the open, where anyone could see us, and by the shocked gasp I heard, somebody did. Benjamin pulled my body tight to his and kissed me deeply. I felt that kiss all the way through to my toes. Butterfly's cyclones in my stomach, every nerve ending in my body sizzled with sensation. He pulled back slowly, his forehead resting against mine. "Six months, Holly. Give me six months to make this work?"

I nodded and stepped back. "I have to go home," I murmured and turned, walking away. Mia was standing by reception, pretending not to watch us, Jack, the new bellhop staring blatantly. I went into the office grabbing my purse and moving back out to the lobby. The bellhop was standing by a taxi outside.

"Mr Henderson instructed you were to use his card to pay for the taxi home, since you came into work on your night off," Jack explained.

I nodded and slid into the back seat. I knew how it looked. I was dressed up to the nines, here on my night off, exiting the elevator with my boss who just kissed me. Even if no one believed Colin before, they would now.

CHAPTER NINE

"Good evening, Holly," Terry greeted me as I arrived at work.

"Evening, Terry," I handed him an envelope.

"I'm pretty sure I don't want to accept that." Terry looked at the envelope like it was a bomb. "Have you really thought this through?"

"I have. I've been offered a better opportunity elsewhere, and I've accepted," I informed Terry. I held the envelope out for him to take. Terry took it reluctantly. "My months' notice. With my annual leave, that makes tonight my last shift."

Terry opened the letter of resignation, read it and sighed. "I'll let HR know to prepare an advertisement."

"I emailed them a copy before I left home," I informed him.

"And Benjamin?" Terry enquired.

"That's your job," I answered confidently.

Terry shifted uncomfortably. "I heard about last night."

I frowned. "I can't believe Colin stuffed up Zoe Jephson's request on purpose," I grumbled. "On the up-side," I shrugged it off, "I got to hang out with a movie star, watching films that haven't even been released yet, all night." I smiled. "Not a total waste of my night."

Terry's eyes widened. "I was referring to Benjamin kissing you in the elevator lobby this morning."

"Oh, that," I grimaced.

"Is that the reason for this?" Terry held up the envelope.

I took a breath. "Colin is the reason for my resignation. I can't work with him, and Benjamin made it clear this morning that working without Colin isn't an option."

"Benjamin told me he offered you the concierge position," Terry admitted.

"Yes, he informed me that wasn't working out," I sighed. "What Benjamin fails to realise is that the issue he's having with his staff, can all be directly connected to his new manager," I responded delicately. "I can't work with Colin on opposing shifts; I certainly couldn't work with him as my day-to-day boss."

Terry bowed his head in understanding. "Sadly, Colin is his brother, and Benjamin is determined to help his career. I suspect, he's being groomed for my job," Terry confessed.

"Well, Benjamin will lose everything for a brother who couldn't give two shits about him," I replied sadly. "I better get to work."

"I'll see you in the morning," Terry called as I moved to the staff corridor.

My last shift at Hotel Henderson was like any other. Instead of going for a swim on my break, I sat in the security office with Jarrett, enjoying a cup of tea and a farewell chat. "I thought you would be a lifer, Holly," Jarrett confessed, placing his teacup aside. "Though, I understand why you are leaving."

"You would be the only one."

Jarrett nodded to the monitors. "I've known since it started. Every morning before breakfast, Benjamin came in here and asked me about the night, but really, he came in here to watch you go about your morning rounds. Occasionally, he'd come in during the night too, after a night out, or when he couldn't sleep.

I exhaled. "I thought it was a secret, but it turns out, he was happy to let everyone know he was screwing the hired help."

Jarrett's eyebrows went up. "Come off it, Holly. You know that's not how it was with you."

"It doesn't matter now, Jarrett. It's over." I stood and packed up our tea cups. "I'll miss our chats."

"Me too," Jarrett gave me a sad smile. "Good luck with the new job."

The rest of my shift went without incident. Colin came in as I finished up my morning report. "Good night?" Colin asked with a frown.

"For the most part," I answered happily. "Why?"

"You're smiling," Colin pointed towards my face. "First time I've seen you smile in weeks."

"Well, I finish up in an hour, so I guess I have something to smile about."

Colin watched me confused, then his face cleared. "That's right; you start your holidays today." I looked at him and realised he hadn't heard I'd resigned yet. I decided not to spoil the surprise. "I also heard about you and Benjamin making a scene yesterday. I guess you two have patched things up?"

I smirked, Colin really didn't have a clue. Something occurred to me. "Is that why you hit on me?" I asked. "To cause issues between Benjamin and me?"

Colin shoved his hands in his pockets like a sullen schoolboy. "I hit on you because you're hot and I want to fuck you."

There was something more to it, I could tell by Colin's eyes. There was petty jealousy flaring deep within, but I had no idea what the catalyst was. I knew it wasn't me. I was just the by-product. I picked up my notes and moved to the door. "Let's get to breakfast," I suggested, needing out of this place.

Colin followed me into the staff room where we went through the typical morning debrief. Terry came in after ten minutes with Benjamin.

Benjamin's presence, while rare, wasn't unusual. We finished the debrief and as I closed my book and put the lid on my pen, I met Terry's eyes. He gave the slightest nod. I took a deep breath. "One more thing, or more of an announcement," I started. Benjamin sat forward interested. "As you all know, this was my last shift before I take a month's leave-"

"Hawaii, baby!" Katie danced in her seat, making us all laugh.

"Well, as it turns out, last night was my last shift for Henderson

Hotels." The laughter died instantly. Benjamin's fists clenched on the table. I met his unhappy eyes and tried to keep my composure. "Yesterday, I tendered my resignation, giving a months' notice. I won't be coming back after my holiday," I announced into the stunned silence. "It's been a pleasure working with you all over the years, and I want to thank all of you for making my time here one of the best experiences of my life. I wish you all the best for the future."

The silence was deafening as everyone looked between Benjamin and I. Colin looked absolutely floored. Benjamin cleared his throat. "You will definitely be missed, Holly. Have you got any idea where you will go next?"

I nodded. "Yes, I've accepted a staff management position with another hospitality firm."

"Staff Management?" Colin frowned.

"Yes, I'll be reporting to the owner directly in more of a consultation role, and managing all the staff for him. No more dealing with irate customers any hour of the day or night." I picked up my stuff to leave.

Katie was first out of her seat to come and give me a hug goodbye. "Good luck, Holly," Katie murmured. All the other managers followed suit. When Colin approached, I held out my hand for him to shakes, letting him know a hug wasn't an option.

"I'm sad to see you go, Holly," Colin admitted.

I truly believed he was. "You have the potential to be a good manager, Colin. You just need to get your head out of your own ass. If you can't do that, you need to be honest with yourself and Benjamin and get out. It's not your business you're destroying with your destructive behaviour."

Colin stared after me, his mouth hanging open, as I walked away without waiting for a response.

"Take care of yourself, Holly. I wish you all the best in your new job, though I know you'll be a wonderful manager," Terry smiled and pulled me into a hug. When he released me, I turned to say goodbye to Benjamin, but he wasn't here. Swallowing the disappointment, I walked to my locker and cleared out my stuff. Once I was ready to leave, I knocked on the Security office door to hand in my keys and pass.

Instead of Jarrett, Benjamin opened the door. "Jarrett is dealing with an issue. I'll take handover for you, Holly," Benjamin informed me as I stepped inside. "You promised me six months," Benjamin reminded me as soon as the door closed.

"I promised to give you six months to work out your commitment issues. I never said I'd stay working in a bad situation you refused to fix," I argued.

"You knew you were already taking this job?"

"I did," I sighed. "I think it's better for us if we do decide to enter a relationship. You can't be my boss any longer."

"We'll never see each other," Benjamin shook his head.

"I'll be working day shift. There is no reason we couldn't go on dates, spend the night with each other-"

"You'll be working for a competitor, so we won't be able to discuss business," Benjamin continued building roadblocks.

Taking a deep breath, I took Benjamin's hand and put my keys and pass tag in it. "You are making phantom excuses not to be with me, Benjamin. Just be honest and tell me you don't want a relationship, but don't lie to me, or yourself," I advised him. "I'll be gone a month. If you decide you want me for more than office sex, you have my number."

"Holly," Benjamin sounded like he was in pain. He slipped his hand behind my neck, thumb brushing along my collarbone. "You have always been more than office sex."

"Then I don't understand why the idea of dating me makes you spew bullshit excuses why we won't work?"

"Me neither," Benjamin breathed stepping closer.

"Benjamin-" The kiss was passionate, deep and searching. I fell into it, fell into him. Benjamin dropped my key pass as he stepped us back against the wall behind the door. He took my bag from my shoulder, dropping it to the floor as well.

I moaned as his body pressed to mine, his hands quickly scrunching the skirt of my dress up to get it out of the way. "Jesus, Holly, I've missed you," Benjamin growled.

His finger slipped under the side of my knickers and burrowed down to slip between my folds. There was no hesitation in Benjamin's touch or kiss. He was very adept at taking what he wanted and not over thinking it. He found my opening and thrust into me, pressing his mouth hard to mine to stop me crying out. I rocked my hips forward to meet the push of his hand. I was galloping towards orgasm already, desperate for his touch and kiss after weeks without. I felt Benjamin unzipping his pants and moaned. Benjamin smiled, pulling his finger free, pulled the gusset of my knickers to the side before grabbing my arse and lifting me. I wrapped my thighs around his waist while Benjamin aligned his body with mine. Once he was firmly niched against my opening, he grabbed my jaw harshly, forcing me to meet his eyes.

"Fuck, I'm going to miss you, Holly," he growled. I felt my breath catch in my throat. There was absolute anger staring back at me, as if I'd betrayed him somehow. I understood, with that look and his words, this was goodbye. I'd asked too much, broken the unwritten rules of our relationship, and now he was letting me go. I felt the tear escape before I could stop it. Benjamin's eyes softened, just a touch. He released my jaw to wipe the tear away. He moved his mouth to mine again, but hesitated, holding back, so our breath mingled, but our lips couldn't touch. "I don't want to let you go, Holly," he admitted.

"Then don't," I pleaded.

He kissed me, slowly and carefully. He moved into me with the same gentleness, so at odds with the look in his eyes only moments ago. Our fucking had always been hurried and to the point. The risk of someone walking in on us ensured we'd never taken our time. Today, knowing it was his last time with me, Benjamin wanted to make it last. He rocked his hips gently. I sighed and gasped with the intensity of my emotions. I wanted this to last, wanted him to tell me he'd date me when I came home, I wanted Benjamin. My brain told my heart to stop being foolish.

His hand found the zipper on the back of my dress and lowered it. My eyes sprang open; he'd never gone this far before. Benjamin slipped the top of my dress down enough that he could grope my breast through my bra. I moaned his name and held him tighter.

"Come upstairs with me. I don't want this to end here, not like this," Benjamin removed himself from me and righted his clothing. Collecting my key pass from the floor while I pulled my skirt down confused. Benjamin handed the card to me. "Come upstairs, Holly, let's do this properly for once."

I took the card, Benjamin walked out in front of me, leaving me against the wall. I stood there, my hand shaking where it held the card. He was finally willing to take me to his room and make love to me, but my feet weren't moving. I closed my eyes and breathed. He wasn't taking me as his lover, was he? He wanted me to sneak up there separately from him, and when I left later, I would be alone, facing the knowing eyes of all my former co-workers. I swallowed, opening my eyes, and stepped forward placing the card on Jarrett's desk. Turning my back on Benjamin's offer, I zipped my uniform and collected my bag.

Jarrett came in as I went to leave. "Everything sorted?" He asked with a kind smile.

My mouth moved, but nothing came out. I paused and tried again. "Could you tell Benjamin, if it's never going to happen again, I don't want it now?"

Jarrett frowned. "He'll know what you mean?"

"He'll know," I assured, my composure returning.

Jarrett nodded. "Good luck with everything, Holly."

"Thanks, Jarrett."

I walked out, shutting the door behind me. Benjamin and I were over. Hotel Henderson and I were over. As I stepped outside the autumn sunlight fell upon me, warming me on what started as a cold morning. Hawaii was beckoning. It was time to move forward and see what else life could offer me.

~To be continued...~

CASSIDY

Book 2: Hotel Series

EBONY OLSON

To all my readers,
who reached out to ask for this to be published. And Kate, who told me
Holly's story couldn't end with Henderson.

Thank you

CONTENTS

CHAPTER ONE

"You need to explain that rock on your finger," I demanded of Nichola, my eldest sister. She'd hidden it for most of the flight, but I managed to get a good look at it while she washed her hands in the bathroom.

"What rock?" Sadie asked sticking her face between us to take a gander. "Oh, my fucking God!"

"Sadie, you kiss your husband with that mouth?" Nichola chastised.

Sadie got a wicked glint in her eye. "My husband knows where my mouth has been; he doesn't care, as long as it's only kissing him these days."

"Back on subject. Where has your mouth been, that someone bought you this?"

Nichola blushed. "Holly, please." Raising a brow at her faux maiden behavior, I didn't give an inch. "Okay, fine," she snapped, a smile blooming on her face. "When I told Michael

I was coming on a girls-only holiday, he got a bit possessive. He insisted on putting that on my finger. We'll announce the engagement when I get back."

"You're marrying your boss?" The sigh I emitted sounding only vaguely jealous.

Nodding energetically, Nichola pulled Sadie and me into a hug. "You two will have to be my bridesmaids again, so no getting pregnant anytime this year." Nichola looked at Sadie.

"What, is it my fault my husband enjoys this body?" Sadie ran her hands over her voluptuous figure. Despite three children and a small tummy she never used to have, the woman still had a killer body.

"Make him enjoy it with a piece of rubber between you," Nichola warned as we waited for our luggage.

"Now that's kinky." Sadie and I chuckled when Nichola froze and turned scarlet red with embarrassment.

Our luggage arrived, and we found the shuttle bus that would take us to our hotel. After exchanging several prompting looks with Nichola, Sadie turned to me, "So who was he?"

"Who was who?"

"Hello! The guy who broke your heart," Sadie opened her hands like it was an obvious question.

"What makes you think...?"

"Na-uh," Nichola cut me off. "You phone us out of the blue to announce you are taking leave and would we like to come on a holiday with you. You're our little sister, Holly, we know you. You taking a sudden trip out of town is code for, 'I broke up with the love of my life and can't bear to risk running into him'."

"Remember Max in high school?" Sadie patted my hand. "You two were hot and heavy. When he cheated on you, you jumped a bus to grandma's house faster than little red riding hood."

"Or your fiancé Claus at university?" Nichola added. "When you found out he had that fetish that made your stomach turn, you dumped him. Then you went on exchange for six months so you wouldn't have to see him at university every day."

"So, I ask again, darling little runaway sister," Sadie raised a brow. "Who was he?"

"Okay, let's start smaller." Nichola took pity on me. "How long were you together?"

"Not together, just screwing each other brainless for the last two years."

"Two years? Come on, Holly, that's more than just sex," Sadie considered me. "So, you were in a non-committed relationship?"

"No, we didn't see others, but we weren't dating or anything either. Just an amazing quickie five days a week."

"How did you meet?" Nichola asked.

"We worked together." Knowing Nichola couldn't scold me for that now at least, I had no issue admitting it. "Actually, he was my boss."

"No fucking way!" Sadie looked ready to explode. "Tell me you weren't banging Benjamin Henderson?"

"Okay, I won't," I couldn't help laughing as both my sisters melted into a puddle of drool.

"So, fucking hot!" Sadie fanned herself. She met my eyes, "is he, you know, worth experiencing?"

"Sadie!" Nichola scolded.

"What? I'm married and have to live vicariously."

"He dumped her, give Holly a break," Nichola shoved Sadie's shoulder.

"Wait!" I looked at Nichola. "Why do you assume he dumped me?"

"Because it's Benjamin Henderson," Nichola 'duh'd' me. "Every girl wants to marry him; every girl gets their heart broken by him."

"I left him." Their jaws dropped open wide enough to showcase their tonsils. Sighing, I told them both the story. By the end of it, they were staring at me like I had two heads.

"You left Benjamin Henderson, the God of the sexy bachelors, waiting at his place, hard and ready for you?" Looking mortified, Sadie turned wide eyed to Nichola. "I've done three guys simultaneously, and am the queen of cum shots, and I'm speechless."

"A little louder, sis, the guys at the front of the bus haven't heard you're a You Tube cooking sensation." Rolling my eyes, I indicated the horrified faces of others on the bus near us.

Observing our surroundings, Sadie blew a kiss before turning back to Nichola. "Mum and dad were right about Holly."

"Really?"

Nodding in sympathy, a smirk pulling at the side of her lips, Nichola patted my shoulder. "Afraid so, Holly."

Slumping down in my seat, I huffed. "Why did I invite you guys along again?"

They hugged me from either side. "Because we love you no matter how big a disappointment you are to the family."

After a few breaths, Sadie gave me a side look and lifted a brow. "You know, John has a cousin, freshly divorced, since you're into older men."

"Oh my god!" I threw them both off me. "I am not dating a politician, lawyer, or banker. I am not moving back home, and I am not being set up with any relative or friend of one of my sibling's partners."

Nichola shook her head with a chuckle. "Mum and dad were so right about you."

Groaning, I covered my face.

———

WE FINALLY ARRIVED at the hotel, by lunchtime. We seemed to be the only three women not here with a partner or on their honeymoon. As soon as we alighted, it was something the valets, bellhop and concierge all paid attention to.

"Good afternoon, welcome to the Cassidy. My name is Henry and I'm the concierge. Do you have a reservation?"

"Yes, three rooms booked under Nichola Claire." Following the concierge to reception, he put us ahead of the line by using a spare terminal to check us in.

"I'm afraid only two of your reserved rooms are currently ready."

"Are they all the same room?" I asked. We could all go to one room for now if it meant a shower.

"Ah, yes, all deluxe rooms."

"Give my sisters the two available rooms; I can wait."

"Aren't you hungry?" Sadie asked surprised.

"Or dying for a shower?" Nichola queried.

"Aren't you?" I replied to both of them. "I can borrow one of your showers and then we can get some lunch before relaxing by the pool all afternoon?"

"If you check back with me after lunch, I'll let you know when your room is ready, Miss Claire."

After Nichola and Sadie checked in to their rooms, I went with Nichola to shower. Refreshed and dressed in a bikini with a sun dress over the top, I made my way back down to the lobby. While I waited for my sisters, I gathered pamphlets on tours, and places to eat.

"...will get that fixed up right away," a male voice assured a guest. The tall, gorgeous man caught my attention. Wearing the hotel uniform, he had sandy hair frosted by natural sun exposure. His caramel tan seemed more than likely natural, and his eyes were as blue as the ocean outside. He was Hawaii bottled into a man.

He turned from the receptionist he was helping and waved the concierge over. "Henry, why is room five-o-seven locked down? I need that room opened," the man asked the concierge as he passed the desk.

"Oh, the room is reserved, but wasn't ready for check-in. Once the cleaning crews finish, I need to find the guest and check her in," Henry explained.

"Well, it's clean, and I need it, so find the guest another room," the man decided, "unlock the room for me."

Henry moved closer to the desk. "Sean, that's the last deluxe room. If you take it, I'll need to upgrade the guest to a spa room for free. That's not good business."

Sean studied Henry. "How long is the guest staying for?"

Henry looked around a bit lost. "Four days." Both men looked at me surprised. "I'm staying four days, and, I'll take the free upgrade, thanks." My mischievous mind working. "For the inconvenience of giving my room away, and forcing me to wait longer, you can include breakfast."

Henry's mouth fell open a little; Sean was chewing the inside of his cheek. "How long is the wait on the spa room?" Sean asked the receptionist to his other side.

"Two hours," she replied after checking with housekeeping.

Sean exhaled, looked me over then turned to Henry. "Do it. Give her the upgrade and complimentary breakfast for the duration of her stay."

Sean called the shots, and worked during daylight; that made him the manager. Henry agreed, removed his hold on the now ready deluxe room and put a hold on the spa room. Sean instructed the receptionist he was standing next to, to check in the other couple.

"Ah, Sean, the spa room is only available two nights," Henry murmured, trying not to let me hear. I was pretending to read the pamphlet on volcano tours, but I'm pretty sure my lips twitched giving me away.

Sucking in a huge breath of annoyance, Sean moved over to Henry's computer. "Surely, you can find a room for the young lady, Henry."

"Currently, not without making her switch rooms halfway through her stay, I can't." Henry bit back politely, but with annoyance. Henry was searching through room by room to try and find one that was available.

"Oh, for the love of God!" Placing the pamphlets down as I stepped around the counter, I reached past a surprised Henry. Hitting the keyboard shortcut, I scanned the listings. "Here. Room seven fifteen is available for the next five days and is ready for check in. Will that suffice?" They both stared at me.

"That's a premier suite," Henry winced.

"Well, it suits me better than one of you sleeping on the couch so I could take the bed at your house, doesn't it?"

Sean raised a brow. I met the challenge with a smile. The side of Sean's mouth twitched. "Check our guest in, Henry," he directed.

Henry's eyes bulged. "Of course, Miss Claire, do you have your passport?" Sean waited long enough to catch my name, and then he headed off to deal with another problem.

Once I had my room key, I retrieved my bags from Nichola and stowed them in my room before we went to find food. After a very late lunch, we found three sun-beds by the pool, slathered on the sunscreen, and set ourselves up to rest. I took the sun bed in the shade; two years of night-shift does not give you a good UV tolerance.

Two hours later, Sadie stood up. "I'm going in for a dip," she declared and dived into the pool.

"I hate that she's had three kids and all it did was give her bigger boobs," Nichola grumbled to me.

"Mum kept her figure after having five kids."

"Mum is a politician's wife. It's eat like a rabbit or the media fat shames you," Nichola criticized.

We watched Sadie pull herself from the pool and Nichola scoffed. "I wish I had boobs like that."

As Sadie stood, a man walked up to her and whispered something in her ear before holding up his phone. Sadie smiled and shrugged and posed while the guy took a selfie with his tongue in her ear.

"Eww, I take it back, let her keep the tits," Nichola groaned in disgust.

"Is she famous?" I heard a woman ask her friend.

"Oh yeah, that's the You Tube chick who cooks and shit," her son answered.

It was like a bomb exploded. Everyone around us was trying to get a picture of themselves with Sadie. People started pushing and shoving each other. Sadie tried to calm them down, assuring they could get a group photo, but no one was listening.

"Shit," Nichola waded in, trying to help Sadie escape.

Looking around, I spied the lifeguard and waved him over. Once he was close enough, I signaled to use his whistle, which he did, as a fourth person fell into the pool.

"Everyone, your attention please." Pushing through the crowd with the lifeguard and another employee who had shown up. "Mrs. Fox is on holiday. But she will sign autographs and take selfies with polite fans who are willing to line up and take turns."

Grabbing Sadie's hand, I moved her away from the pool and over to a grassed area of the property. The other employee materialized a towel for Sadie. Everyone followed, forming a neat and polite line.

"As Mrs. Fox is doing this on her holiday, I hope you all respect there will only be one photo per person. Thank you." Leaving Sadie there, I turned to talk to the employee. "Can you manage this?"

"You're not her manager?" He asked surprised.

"No," I scrunched my brow in disgust, "I'm her sister, and I'm on holiday too. These are your guests. Get your manager or concierge to come deal with this shit." Walking off, I joined Nichola back by the sun-bed.

"Should we dress and go sit by the bar and drink cocktails?" Nichola asked.

"Hell, yes!"

Pulling our sun-dresses on, we moved to the bar. Passing Sean, who was making his way toward the impromptu signing, his eyes locked onto me. Assessing each other as we passed, we both turned our heads to keep eye contact until we couldn't. Then I looked over my shoulder to admire his backside as he walked away.

"What was that?" Nichola asked with a smirk.

"The manager."

"Really? I was thinking rebound," Nichola cocked an eyebrow at me.

I laughed. "Jesus, I'd need a rebound to rebound from the rebound if I went there. He's a dish."

"Best served hot and hard," Nichola finished for me. We both started laughing as we got to the bar.

I'd missed my sisters.

CHAPTER TWO

My ideas book was where I wrote all the things I'd ever considered for when I finally became manager of a hotel. Every idea I'd ever instigated at Henderson was in this book. Even more that wasn't because they didn't suit the Henderson style of hotel.

It wasn't always for me. Some of my ideas were how I would improve the place at which I was staying. Things I would never actually pass on to the managers, but I liked to write it down. My dad always thought I'd end up a hotel reviewer, but tried to encourage me into law or medicine. He'd been happy when I'd chosen a business school after I'd finished my arts degree. He hadn't been happy I'd dumped my lawyer boyfriend and chosen to work in a hotel. We hadn't talked much after that.

"I'm calling it a night," Nichola slurred a little as she tried to stand up.

"Me too," Sadie laughed. "Too much sun and alcohol."

"I'm going to stay up a little longer. I'll see you at breakfast in the morning."

While my sisters leaned on each other to go inside the hotel, I took my book and walked down near the beach. We'd watched the sunset while we downed cocktails. Sighing as I leaned against a tree where the path met the beach, I watched the waves roll in in the dark. The spring breeze was lovely on my skin after the heat of the day.

Footsteps crunching down the path towards the beach cottages, broke the serenity. Deciding that was my cue to leave, I turned and started back up the path. My steps hesitated when I came face to face with Sean, the manager.

"Miss Claire," he greeted surprised. Looking around, he raised that sexy brow at me. "Lost your friends?"

"My sisters had a bit too much sun and cocktails and retired early." Brushing past him, I wondered if he knew how sexy that brow could be.

Sean's eyes noted the book I clutched to my chest. "Are you a writer?"

Adjusting my stance, I shifted the book behind me. "No, it's where I write my thoughts."

Sean's brows lifted. "You wander around with your diary?"

His brow popped up a little higher, I laughed. "It's not like that either, no scandalous experiences or dear diary."

Sean smiled like he didn't believe me. He looked me over again. "So, Mrs. Fox, she's your biological sister?"

It wasn't the first-time people didn't believe it. None of us girls looked alike. "Yes, well, as far as our parents have told us. There are five of us, and all very different in appearance."

"So, you aren't in the same line of work as your sister?" Sean phrased the question with care.

"No, I'm afraid I'm not that good a cook," I laughed. Sean's smile dropped. His eyes flicked side to side, and brow grew heavy. "Oh, you mean...? No, and she doesn't do that anymore. Most of those people knew her for her cooking show, not her deep throat ability." Turning away while Sean still gaped at me for my openness, I took a step back up the path.

"Wait, you're angry?" Sean frowned at me.

Turning back around, I glared at him. "You insinuated I look like a porn actress. I'm allowed to be insulted. To clarify; I don't have an issue with my sister's former career. We all rebelled against our strict upbringing in our own way. Sadie was always comfortable in front of a camera, and she made a living from it. When she finished with it, she left with her dignity. There are actresses in Hollywood with their sex tapes who couldn't claim the same."

"I didn't mean..." Sean started. I raised a brow. He exhaled. "Okay, I was curious if the three of you were all taking a break from filming. Considering your age group, your sister's fame, and how hot all three of you are, it's a plausible conclusion."

He was right; I still wasn't flattered. "I'm five years younger than Sadie. When she became famous for fucking, I was still jail-bait." I enjoyed Sean's eyes bulging at my use of the F-word. "She finished with that world, married, and was pregnant with her first baby by the time I was legal. This is the first time anyone has ever implied my guilt by association. At least, it's the first time they had the balls to ask."

"Was that a compliment?" Sean chuckled.

Checking out his groin, I shrugged, then met his eyes again. "So that you know, my sister's lack of gag reflex isn't hereditary." Turning on my heel, I walked back to the hotel. I was in my room, running a bath when someone knocked at the door. "Who is it?"

"Room service," the female voice on the other side announced. Opening the door with care, my brows low with confusion. "Compliments of management." The woman smiled as she carried a tray in, placing it on the table for me. She handed me a small envelope on the way out. "Enjoy your evening, Miss Claire."

Closing the door after her, I opened the envelope to remove the business card. Embossed calligraphy showcased the name Sean Cassidy. Below his title of Hotel Manager, was his contact numbers and the Cassidy Hotel's emblem. On the back in a very neat script was handwriting.

I noticed you hadn't eaten dinner, so I saved you the best part. Please accept this as my apology for insulting you. Sean.

Lifting the lid exposed a banana crepe, smothered in Belgium chocolate. Smiling, I sat down to enjoy the gift. Once my sweet tooth was satisfied, I stripped and soaked in the tub big enough for two. Verging on sleep in the bath, I remembered sleeping there wasn't a safe option. Begrudgingly, I pulled the plug. Wrapping a towel around me before going to stand on the balcony, I looked out over the sea. It was a beautiful night.

Leaving the door open so I could listen to the waves, I removed the towel and crawled under the quilt naked. Reaching out, I turned off the light. The music of waves crashing to shore and the voices of nocturnal animals serenading me to sleep.

Knocking on my door disturbed a pleasant dream involving Belgium chocolate and nudity. "Who is it?"

"Room service, may I enter," a male voice called.

Remembering I negotiated breakfast, I didn't remember it being in the room. "Yes." I leaned up on my elbows to watch as the staff member carried a tray in and placed on the table. "I don't remember ordering breakfast," I told the attendant's back.

The staff member kept his back to me, which was good training. "For these rooms the in-room breakfast is complimentary, Miss Claire. Since you hadn't placed your order, Mr. Cassidy ordered for you."

"Should I ask?"

"Mr. Cassidy thought you were a bacon, eggs and waffles girl, I mean..."

"What kind of eggs?" I tried not to laugh at the attendant's faux pas.

"Scrambled, Miss Claire."

Smiling, I fell back into the bed. "Tell Mr. Cassidy he chose well, thank you." The attendant hesitated. Groaning, I pulled my quilt tight around me. "Wait, sorry, can you pass me my bag, I'm unable to go get it." The attendant located my bag, back-stepped to the bed and reached his arm back to me. "You can look, I've covered up."

The attendant, checked over his shoulder before he turned.

Removing some notes, I handed them to him. He smiled and bowed his head. "Very generous, Miss Claire."

I laughed. "You earned it for not even trying to sneak a peek."

"There are things you can't unsee, Miss Claire." Realizing what he'd said, the attendant tried to back pedal. "Not that I'd want to unsee you, Miss Claire, just..."

"Settle," I waved his defense down. "I've been in the industry six years. I know what you meant. I'm forever scared."

Exhaling in relief, the attendant smiled. "My worst so far was an overweight man with more hair on his body than head."

"A month ago, I got punched out trying to save a prostitute getting strangled to death by her fat bastard of a client. Both of them were naked, but the woman barely survived. The son of a bitch trashed the room."

The attendant's eyes were huge. "You win."

"Damn straight I do, I didn't even tell you the worst part." Sinking down into the comfort of my bed, I closed my eyes. The attendant took the hint and left. I lay there for a moment, letting the sound of the ocean wash away all my thoughts of Hotel Henderson. With an audible sigh, I pulled on a robe and followed the smell of coffee to the table. Breakfast filled the hole in my stomach, and the freshly squeezed juice woke me up. It was still early, so there was no chance my sisters would be awake yet. Slipping into my swimmers, I went downstairs to the pool, and did forty minutes worth of laps.

Not long after I finished my shower and dressed for the day, I met my sisters for the shopping tour. After a morning shopping, we enjoyed lunch at the Cheesecake Factory. The afternoon consisted of more shopping, before returning to the hotel.

"Are you sure you don't want to do the climb with us?" Nichola checked as we made our ways back to our rooms.

"Volcanoes aren't my thing, especially not climbing back down at dusk. I would be the person to trip and break something," I excused.

"You still have your Dante's Peak phobia, don't you?" Sadie teased.

"Totally!" Ever since that movie, the idea of climbing a volcano gave me the willies. "Plus, I worry how my sulfur allergy might react being that close to the top of a volcano."

"God, remember how sick she got in Rotorua when the family went to New Zealand for that holiday?" Nichola reminded us. "You ended up hospitalized because you couldn't breathe."

"That was bad," Sadie agreed, "you definitely shouldn't risk it."

"Cocktails in the bar again tonight?" Nichola suggested instead. We chorused our agreement then parted ways to stash our shopping. Since the girls weren't big on water sports, I'd organized to do some surfing while they flew over the volcano. I'd done lessons while on holidays in my teens and was confident I could pick it back up.

Packing my bag with my notebook, towel, and brush, I made my way down to the beach. Three hours later, I rode my final wave ashore and returned the board. Happy I'd not only remembered how to surf, but I felt I'd improved on my skill a little.

Showering under the beach shower, I dried off and brushed my hair up into a ponytail. I didn't put my dress back on for the walk back up to the hotel. Everyone else walked around in their bikinis. Years of swimming and yoga made me comfortable enough to do the same.

"You're a bit red, could I get you some aloe?" The female staff member who was serving drinks by the pool offered as I passed.

"That would be nice, thank you. How much?"

"Complimentary. We don't like our guests getting burnt and not being able to enjoy their stay." She came back with a cocktail and a bottle of aloe. "Aloe Vera juice and coconut water to cool and hydrate the inside, and the gel for the outside. Would you like Paulo to do your back for you? He's a masseuse, so you can double up and get a massage at the same time."

It was a good on-sell. Paulo wouldn't be free, but I could do with a massage. "If Paulo is available, I'd love it."

Led to a tent with a massage table, I took a seat and enjoyed my juice. Paulo arrived a few minutes later. He was a native Hawaiian and, momentarily, his height, and thick arms terrified me. He explained his pricing structure and asked which I'd prefer. I decided to go with the full body rub down, all with the aloe. Paulo may have looked intimidating, but his hands were soft. He knew all the right places to release my muscles.

Thirty minutes later, I felt relaxed, hydrated, and tired. Not wanting to sleep, I put my dress on and pulled out my notebook to write. After noting down my positive and negative experiences during the day, I then wrote a few ideas I could take back to the Holmes City Resort with me. I probably should have sat down to write, but I worried I'd sleep, so I was walking around.

"Hmpf," a male grunted as I slammed into a solid object, my book and bag falling to the ground.

"God, I'm sorry," I apologized, certain that was my fault.

Turning to see who had walked into him, Sean blinked at me. "Miss Claire?" He bent and collected my stuff for me. "Did you want to talk to me?"

"No, I wasn't watching where I was walking." Seeing that Sean was reading my notebook, I took it back and shoved it into my bag. "Sorry, I was writing and walking, trying to stay awake, and zoned out," I tried to excuse my silliness. Sean kept quiet, his eyes appraising me. "I did want to thank you for dessert last night, and breakfast this morning, I didn't realize how hungry I was."

Sean raised that eyebrow as someone behind him cacked themselves laughing. Forehead slapping myself, when I heard what I said, I tried again. "That came out wrong," I apologized again.

Sean's smile grew. "I'm glad you were satisfied," he teased, making me blush. Sean looked around. "I see you have lost your sisters again?"

"They are doing the sunset volcano tour."

"You didn't join them?" Sean moved us out of the way of his staff who were trying to get stuff done.

Removing my arm from his gentle grasp, I stepped another step away. "I don't do volcanoes. I went surfing instead."

"I thought the lessons ran in the morning?"

"They do, I didn't need lessons. I learned to surf years ago."

Sean smiled. "So, you are alone for dinner?"

"I am."

Sean turned around to one of the staff. "Gus, tell the others I'm taking my dinner break."

There was a murmur of affirmation behind him, then Sean placed his hand in the small of my back. "Come, Miss Claire, let's get you fed so you can get to bed early."

I laughed. "I'm meeting my sisters for cocktails when they get back, so I doubt that will happen."

Sean turned to meet my eyes, smile lines surrounding his humored blues. "Why didn't you take an afternoon nap then?"

"I was fine till I got the massage from Paulo. After that, the sun and surf caught up with me."

Sean looked ahead. "Paulo is very skilled with his hands."

"Every woman loves a man who is good with his hands," I responded with a cheeky smile. Sean's mouth twitched, but he didn't take the bait.

We stepped down into the Grotto restaurant. It was a beautiful rock pool haven that looked out over the beach and the sunset. "Table for two please, Monica," Sean greeted the hostess.

Monica grabbed two menus and led us to our table, which happened to be one of the best tables in the place. I guess Sean was the boss. We sat and browsed the menus, placed our orders, and then I watched the sun kiss the horizon. "Do you live here?" I sighed, mesmerized by the perfect sunset.

"The furthest beach villa is mine," Sean answered. I could feel his eyes on me.

"Must be nice to enjoy this daily."

"I admit, I still enjoy it after a decade. I work through it five days a week, so it still holds its beauty on the weekends for me," Sean answered. "You don't live near the beach I take it?"

"My apartment overlooks park lands, but I work and live in the city. I usually work weekends and miss the sunrise and sunset."

"You would have missed it tonight if you hadn't walked into me, correct?" Sean queried.

"I guess so." Considering how much I loved the sunset and sunrise, but rarely had time to see it, I frowned. Taking out my notebook, I jotted a note down. A simulated sunrise and sunset were a fantastic idea for business travelers.

"Miss Claire?" Looking up at Sean's coaxing, I saw him eying my notebook. "Put the book away. Stop working, and enjoy the sunset."

Embarrassment heated my cheeks. Closing my book, I slipped it back into my bag as our drinks arrived. Sipping my coconut water with pineapple juice, I watched the sun sink into the ocean. "I should have stayed longer," I sighed as night descended.

"Than four nights?"

"I only have three more sunsets before I jump the boat home."

"You're cruising back to Australia?" Sean asked surprised.

"Yes, a friend suggested it. I had a month. I should have stayed longer and caught a later ship."

"No boyfriend who would miss you?" Sean asked, failing to be casual about it.

A stone set in my stomach. I'd thought about Benjamin a lot, but I was trying not to. "No. I haven't had one of those in a long time," I admitted. "I've focused on my career since I left university and not had time for dating."

"No one has time for dating unless they make time," Sean lectured.

"I was seeing someone, but it wasn't serious, and we decided that needed to end."

"Wasn't serious for him or you?" Sean queried, seeming to see right through me.

"Either of us," I defended, "but I did think I meant more than it turned out."

Sean's eyes flicked over me then sat back as a waiter served our meals. He waited till the wait staff left. "Ten years ago, I came here on holiday with my girlfriend. A week after we got home to San Francisco, the lawyer she was also seeing proposed, and she left me. Everything reminded me of her and her cheating. I thought of the last place I was happy. I jumped on a plane and came here. Strange as it was, we barely spent any time together here, since we had different interests. So, this place didn't make me think of her. I stayed."

"Has there been anyone since?"

"I've dated, but nothing serious."

"Holiday flings?"

"Usually no, I rarely fraternize with guests," Sean negated my insinuation.

"Yet, you are having dinner with me?"

"Oh, this is business, Miss Claire. I worried you'd forget to eat again."

I smirked as I lifted my drink. "Well, here's to two people working and eating."

Sean raised a brow. "I thought you were on holiday, Miss Claire?"

Winking at him, I drank a sip of my hydration in a glass.

CHAPTER THREE

"...TOOK A MILLION PHOTOS. I'LL HAVE SOME DECENT ONES IN there somewhere," Sadie chattered.

We were two hours into cocktails, which translated to giggly and sarcastic. Nichola and Sadie were both sun-burnt. Tomorrow, Sadie would be brown, and Nichola would have freckles for the first time in years. After an afternoon of hydrating, I was a blush pink. I'd alternated real cocktails with nonalcoholic hydration cocktails.

"You ladies look to be having fun. Could I interest one of you in a dance?" A man somewhere around Nichola's age, who could have been attractive if his own ego wasn't in the way, inquired.

"I so would, but I'm married," Sadie flashed her ring.

"Same, but engaged," Nichola waved her ring.

The guy looked to me waiting. "Yeah, same, if I was even remotely interested, but I'm not." The guy smiled ready to move on, then actually heard what I said. You could see it on his face, trying to figure out if he'd heard me right.

Nichola and Sadie were wetting themselves trying not to laugh in the guy's face. He walked away still confused. "Jesus, you're mean," Nichola laughed. "That's the fifth guy you've sent off checking if his balls are still intact tonight, and he wasn't half bad."

"Which half? Were we looking at opposite ends?"

"You were," Sadie assured. "You were looking at his head, Nichola was looking at his balls. That's how she noticed they'd shriveled up."

We all started laughing again. "Ladies, enjoying your evening?" Sean approached us from the staff side of the bar.

"Are you working a double shift?" I asked with a raised brow.

"Covering so Daniel could have his break," Sean smiled. "I'll be finishing as soon as he comes back."

I didn't realize I was sitting there smiling at Sean till Nichola nudged me. "You going to introduce us, Holly?"

"Sean is the Manager of this fine establishment," I offered. "My sisters, Nichola, and Sadie."

"A pleasure," Sean smiled. "Refills?"

The girls ordered cocktails with the usual suggestive names. Sean laughed looking to me. "Guess?" I teased.

"That's dangerous," Sean teased back. "What about a Mountain Dew Me?"

Nichola had to cover her mouth to stop from spitting her drink on the bar. "Honey, with Holly, you'd have to give her a Leg

Spreader before you'd ever get anywhere with her," Sadie laughed.

"Really?" Sean lifted a brow at me.

"Or a Rowie, which is just vodka and lime," Nichola smiled. "I'm pretty sure that's what..."

"Say his name, and I swear you'll never see the sunrise," I warned.

"…got her drinking for her to let him take the big V," Nichola finished.

"I was sober losing my virginity," I assured Sean. "Possibly not when I said yes to the perv's marriage proposal, but definitely for that." My sisters kept laughing. Meeting Sean's eyes, I lifted my brow in challenge. "Surprise me. Let's see if you get this right?"

Sean grinned and started mixing. He served Nichola and Sadie first before mixing my drink. It was Friday night. Most of the young people had gone into town to go clubbing. The rest of the resort seemed to be heading to bed. Sean placed a pink drink in front of me. Taking a sip, I let the smooth delight coating my tongue light up my eyes.

"What does it taste like?" Sean asked.

My sisters hooted as I stood, grabbed his shirt to pull him forward across the bar and French kissed him. Happily surprised, Sean didn't pull away. Unlike when Daniel asked Nichola that question, I didn't pull away either.

When we parted, Sean licked his lips, his pupils dilated. "That was pretty nice," he murmured.

"What's it called?" I smiled, knowing he wasn't referring to the drink.

"Usually, Angel's Slit, but I'm renaming it Angel's kiss for tonight."

"Finally," Sadie patted me on the back, "well done, Holly." Sadie looked to Nichola. "Holly wins!"

Sean frowned when I threw my hands in the air. "I've walked into a bet, haven't I?"

"A dare," I corrected. "Winner got to choose tomorrow afternoons activity, and now it's snorkeling."

My sisters groaned in unison. "Come off it, Holly. You know we hate water sports," Sadie whined.

"Why don't I take you snorkeling, and you let your sisters do something you don't like to do?" Sean offered.

"Awesome idea," Sadie declared standing up. "You two should organize that now, while Nichola and I call it a night. See you in the morning."

Sadie and Nichola ran off, holding hands and giggling as they looked over their shoulders at us. I rolled my eyes. Sean chuckled. "Your sisters aren't subtle."

"No, but they are drunk enough to think they are," I smiled drinking the rest of my cocktail. "So, snorkeling?"

"Snorkeling." We sat there looking at each other until someone further around the bar cleared their throat. "Excuse me," Sean smiled then went to serve the man and his friend.

Finishing my drink, I stood up. The world was a little unstable. I sat back down. "You okay?" Sean asked coming back over.

"What was in that drink?" I tried to get the world to stabilize. "And why am I so hot?"

"Yeah, I should have explained where the drink got its name."

"Sean, I'm back," Daniel walked back in behind the bar, "thanks for covering."

"Not a problem," Sean called walking around and collecting my arm. "You're not a big drinker, are you?"

"Not really." Sean helped me back inside towards the elevators. "That last one kicked my arse." I stumbled as we stepped into the elevator, Sean reached out to catch me and ended up hugging me. "You smell delicious," I murmured breathing him in.

"Thank you, but that might be the drink talking," Sean informed me, setting me back on my feet. "There is an ingredient in that drink called Cupid's dart. It gives the drink that smooth texture on the tongue which is supposed to feel like a woman's..." Sean cleared his throat. "Anyway, this ingredient can cause an unusual allergic reaction. I guess you're one of the five percent of the world allergic to it," Sean cringed.

"In what way?" I asked, leaning in to get another whiff of him.

"It can be a very powerful aphrodisiac for those allergic." Sean's eyes transfixed on one of my legs.

Looking down, I realized I'd started running my hand up my thigh and lifted my sun-dress with it. I wanted to smack myself. Instead, I took Sean's hand and moved it to my thigh instead. "God, that feels good," I moaned.

"Holly, I don't sleep with my customers." Sean's hand reached the junction between my thighs.

"Okay, don't sleep with me," I murmured. It was like I was locked out of the control-room of my body while my doppelgänger took over. I'd think one thing, the right thing, and do exactly the fucking opposite. "Sean, help me." I meant for him to help me take back control, but the doppelgänger slipped his hand down the front of my knickers.

Sean's fingers immediately found my already swollen and tender clit. "Fuck, I should have taken you to my place." Sean was tapping out the distress signal in Morse code on my clit. Moaning, I gripped his wrist like it was my lifeline.

The elevator arrived at my floor. Sean stole his hand back just before the door opened and one of his staff smiled at him. "Everything okay, Sean?"

Forcing a smile, Sean nodded. "Miss Claire is reacting to something she drank and needs help getting to her room. Would you mind taking over for me? My shift finished an hour ago."

I could have kissed Sean at that moment for palming me off to a female staff member. The doppelgänger agreeing with that idea, stepped forward. Sean saved us both by turning me to the female. She caught me and frowned. "Does she need a doctor?"

"Just her bed will be enough, Deidre," Sean assured as Deidre helped me stumble down the corridor.

The elevator doors shut. I sighed with relief. "Thank you."

With no bisexual tendencies at all, this woman was not fueling my fire. She got me to my room and helped me inside. "Can I get you anything?"

Your bosses hand back on my... "I'm good, thank you." Crawling onto my bed with a groan, I fell face down. My arm pinned under me, so my fingers were already pressing my swollen bud.

"I hope you feel better in the morning," Deidre offered. "If you need anything please call."

Whimpering a thank you, I bit lip while my fingers pinched my clit. Giving me a sympathetic look, Deidre left. Lying there for several minutes, my climax tightrope walked the edge. I needed a guy to be doing this. I needed Benjamin. Tears filled my eyes remembering him. No, that wasn't going to work.

Reaching over to the bedside table, I grabbed Sean's business card. Picking up the phone, I called his mobile. "Sean Cassidy speaking."

"You need to talk dirty to me."

"Excuse me?"

"You gave me the damn drink, and I can't get off. Talk dirty to me."

"Holly?" Sean sounded surprised. "Shit, give me a minute."

My body reacted to his voice. "Actually, screw talking dirty; just talk. You have the deepest voice I've ever heard. It's a fucking turn on to hear it."

"You know you kissed me, right?" Sean reminded me. "I can't remember the last time someone kissed me like that."

"I love kissing, and you are a very good kisser," I breathed. "I wish you were kissing me right now."

"Only kissing you?"

"I didn't say where I wish you were kissing me," I wheezed. Oh god, the idea of Sean's tongue flicking my bean. "Fuck!" I panted, and came. I came harder than I ever had masturbating before, and probably more than I had during sex. Lying there getting my breathing under control, I felt so, very, relaxed.

Turning my head, ready to fall asleep, I saw the phone. Picking it up, I put it to my ear. "Sean?"

"Oh good, I worried you'd passed out," Sean teased.

"I'm about to. Sean?"

"Don't worry, Holly, I won't mention this ever happened."

"I was going to ask for some of that stuff," I murmured, half asleep. "That's the best orgasm I've ever had."

Sean was quiet for a minute. "Meet me by the jetty at one tomorrow afternoon. Goodnight, Holly."

Stretching to put the phone back in its cradle, I didn't stay awake long enough to know if I hung it up.

CHAPTER FOUR

YOU KNOW THE WORST PART ABOUT NOT BEING DRUNK WHEN you do shit? Remembering when you wake up. When room service arrived in the morning, I woke up feeling happy and tingly. Still dressed from yesterday, I could tip the staff member myself. It wasn't until I noticed the phone on the floor that I picked it up and wondered why it was there. That's when the elevator, the phone call, and that amazing orgasm, all came flooding back. Embarrassed didn't cover it. Mortified seemed a more suitable adjective.

Meeting my sisters for the tour to Pearl Harbor, I tried very hard not to remember those details. "Are you still snorkeling with Sean this afternoon?" Nichola prodded as we explored.

"At one."

"Did anything happen after we left last night?" Sadie shoulder bumped me from the other side.

"I went to bed, alone." I added the last to prevent any further investigation.

"Bugger," Nichola sighed, "I was sure he was into you."

Sadie agreed. "You should bang that guy, Holly, and tell us all about it."

"Should I ask why?"

"Because, Sadie's married, and I'm all but. "Since we can't shag that beautiful specimen, it all falls to you to enjoy what God created for women to enjoy."

"He might have a pin dick."

"With a voice that deep," Sadie laughed, "not a chance."

"He could be a selfish lay?"

"You are making excuses," Nichola scolded. "What's holding you back, Holly? You're single, hot, young. You are everything a guy like him wants for a few nights of fun. Get on it already and forget Benjamin Henderson ever existed."

"Oh my god!" I yelled. "This isn't going to happen. I'm not the sort of girl who meets a guy and jumps into bed with him. I don't do one-night stands or holiday fuck frenzies."

There was a static quiet all around us. Around us were either amused or appalled faces of other tourists. Was there a shade of embarrassment brighter than red?

"I'm sorry. Sisters, you know." Gesturing to my laughing sisters. Throwing my hands up in frustration, I stormed off. These sorts of walk around, touch nothing, sightseeing tours, never enthused me much. Only if it came with role-playing and popcorn.

When it came time to head back to the hotel, Nichola put her arm around my waist and rested her head against mine. "We care about you, Holly. If it's too soon, or too much, we understand."

"Because mum and dad were so right about you," Sadie teased.

Sighing, I looked at the two guys my age checking out a teenage girl. "See the blond to my left?" They looked at me, then Sadie and nodded. "Isn't she that porn star? Fox something?" Walking off, I let that play out.

"Holy shit, that's Fox Nastee!" one of them exclaimed. Sadie spent the bus ride with the two guys hitting on her and nearly taking it to the point of assault.

"You're evil when you're angry," Nichola murmured. "I saw you tell those boys who she was."

"Don't know what you mean," I responded, staring out the window.

An hour later I was sitting on the jetty waiting for Sean. "Good afternoon," he smiled down at me. Standing up, I brushed off my bottom. Sean assessed me. "Not a good afternoon?"

"Sisters spent the morning giving me a hard time about my life choices."

"Isn't that what siblings do?"

"I've been coping it from my parents and siblings all my life. There was a huge age difference when I was younger, so you expect it." I stepped towards him. "But, when one sister's perfect marriage ended up a front-page scandal. The other was infamous enough in the porn world that people still recognize her. You'd think that would give you a bit of acceptance." Sean just watched me. "I'm sorry, that was a bit of a rant."

"Actually, I'm wondering what you've done to still be at the bottom of the pecking order. Did you kill someone?"

"No."

"Drug addict?"

"I've never even smoked."

"Lesbian?"

"Deidre would be smiling this morning if I was even bi-curious," I teased.

Sean smirked, tried to swallow it and looked to the side. He'd promised never to mention last night. "We should get going." Nodding, I followed him out to the end of the jetty.

Opening a storage box, Sean removed the gear we'd need. Moving to the preparation point he pulled his shirt over his head. I stared. I mean, it was worth looking. He was no Benjamin with his gym, swim, run body, but Sean was the outdoors and active type.

"Something wrong?" Sean asked, frowning when I was just standing there.

"I was wondering how old you are?" Covering my perving, I moved forward to get myself ready.

"Thirty-five, is it important?"

"No, I picked you to be around Sadie's age. Just wasn't sure if I was right." Lifting my skater dress over my head to leave me in my bikini.

There was no response from Sean. When I turned, he blinked and looked away. "How old are you?" Sean countered.

"Twenty-eight."

"You look younger." Sean's eyes went to my boobs.

"Night shift causes limited sun exposure."

"Night shift? And you work weekends? According to the rumor amongst my staff, you work in the industry." Sean considered me as he handed me my flippers. "Are you a concierge?"

"I was, many years ago now. I've been working my way up for the past six years."

"Are you a hotel manager?"

"I was assistant manager till recently." My humor fading. Sean gave me that questioning look. "I was sexually harassed by a senior manager. When I reported it, the owner accused me of making it up because I wanted the manager's job. I had five years of leave accrued. I cashed it in, then handed in my resignation as I walked out the door."

Sean frowned and looked down at his feet. "So, you're between jobs?"

"No, I have a new job, but one dealing with only the staff instead of the clients now." I didn't want him worrying I was looking for his job here. I mean, he owns the place, his job is pretty safe. "Should we get some snorkeling done?" Picking up my mask, I walked to the jump point.

"You've done this before?" Sean asked as he came up beside me.

I set my mask in place. "Try and keep up," I teased, held my mask and jumped in.

Sean jumped in while I was airing my snorkel, then I led the way to the reef. We were down there for a while, enjoying the fish and colors. This side of the resort, the reef protected the beach, so it's where all the calm water activities occurred. The other side of the peninsula on which the Cassidy sat, was the true beach. The waves were good for surfing, and windsurfing. It was a great set up here.

Sean tapped me on the shoulder and gestured time to go back. Following him in, he helped me back up onto the jetty. We packed up quietly, drying ourselves with our towels before we walked towards land. "I'm this way," Sean gestured along the beach when we stepped off the jetty.

"Thank you, for taking me out. It was very kind of you."

"Well, I usually spend my weekends enjoying the islands, so it was my pleasure." Smiling, I went to walk back to the hotel. "Holly, would you like to have dinner with me tonight? There's this place, best sunset on the entire island."

"How can I turn down another amazing sunset?"

That made Sean grin. "Be ready in an hour. I'll meet you back here." Sean dashed away before I could question the meeting point. When I thought about it, he probably didn't want his staff to think he was fraternizing with a guest.

Back in my room, I showered and changed into a more anything-goes dress. Grabbing my cardigan and my bag, I headed back down the beach. Stopping for an aloe juice on the way, to help with hydration.

Sean was waiting on the jetty when I arrived. Smiling at me, he took my hand, walking me up the jetty to one of the small boats moored there. I didn't question it when he led me on board, untied the rope, and cruised us out and around the next peninsula.

Sean ran the boat ashore on a smaller beach which only had a forest. Collecting a hamper, Sean helped me climb forward to jump down onto the sand. Walking into the forest, then up some stone steps, we emerged on top of a cliff. We were above all the trees, able to look out to sea unhindered.

Setting down the hamper Sean unpacked it before taking a seat. "Let's eat," he encouraged. By the looks of it, the food was from the hotel kitchen. We sat and enjoyed still warm canapés, water, and mini cheesecakes for dessert. Sean brought wine, but when I declined after so much sun, Sean put the bottle away and poured water for both of us. We ate our entire meal in a comfortable silence, watching the sun sink below the horizon.

Before the light left us entirely, Sean packed up the hamper, pulled out a torch, and led the way back to the boat. When we got back to the jetty, he walked me up to the resort in silence. We'd barely said a word to each other the entire night.

Fare welling me in the lobby with a simple goodnight, Sean left the hamper with the front desk before he left. Yeah, the staff took note, but he hadn't kissed me or touched me, so it was something to intrigue them right now.

Up in my room and unable to sleep, I wandered out onto the balcony. I stood staring at the waves for a while before I wondered why I was doing it from such a disconnected location.

Making my way down to the beach, I drifted aimlessly,

enjoying the night and the peace. Finding a spot where the moon shone across the water perfectly, I stood there staring out. It had to be the most beautiful place on this side of the peninsula.

"I'll listen and not judge if you want to talk about it," Sean offered as he came to stand next to me. He stood beside me shirtless, a pair of cargo shorts hanging on his hips like he'd pulled them on in a hurry.

"Where did you come from?" Sean pointed out a dim light. I made out the silhouette of one of the beach cottages, the last one along this stretch of beach. It was set a bit apart from the others, nestled a bit deeper into the trees. "You've got the best view of the beach."

"I had my cottage built for this view, and a bit of privacy."

Sitting on the sand, I looked out over the water. "My father's a respected politician back home. We grew up around other prominent political families. When I was fourteen, I started dating the then Prime Minister's son. We were together for two years. It ended when I found out he'd slept with another girl." Fidgeting with the hem of my dress, still feeling a piece of that insecure teenager within me.

"The break up was quiet. I didn't even tell my parents. But the media used to make a big thing about us dating because our parents were opposing parties. So, when it became obvious, we'd broken up, the media sniffed out the reason. One Sunday I woke to my name and the words 'dumped for staying a virgin', scrawled across the front page."

Sean remained quiet.

"The article revealed I'd refused to have sex, so he went

elsewhere, and when I found out, he dumped me. My parents were angry at me. It was like I'd disappointed them for not giving into the pressure to have sex before I was ready. I was only sixteen. It got worse. Another paper placed pictures of Sadie and I side by side, the words, 'Exact Opposites' above it. They labeled me frigid, uptight, and various other nasty terms for respecting myself. I hated it. I wrote a letter to a better media outlet expressing my disappointment. In the media, in my parent's reaction, and in the prime minister's son for even talking about it. It got printed. I received a barrage of support from the public. My parents grounded me."

"That's a hard line to tow," Sean murmured.

"I decided that I didn't agree with my parent's values and chose to do an arts degree at university. My father was not happy. When I started dating a charming law student, my family acted like I was a lost child finally found. After we got engaged, my fiancé told me particular expectations of me as his future wife. Things that I was not down with doing. So, I ended the relationship. You can imagine how that went down."

"So, your acceptance with your parents revolves around the men you date? So why were your sisters paying you out about the past?"

"Oh, they weren't. It's..." I sighed. "When all the stuff in the media happened with the Prime Minister's son, I ran away to my grandmother's. My parents can't stand her. She sort of marches to her own tune. When they finally found me, both my parents yelled some stuff at me. My grandmother and my brothers and sisters heard everything. It gutted me, but for my siblings, it was water off a duck's back. They make fun of me now by referring to it. They say, 'Mum and dad were right about you', whenever I do something with which they don't agree. I know they are just taking the piss, but..."

"It reminds you how you've never been good enough?" Sean finished for me.

"Yeah." Standing up, I walked down to the water's edge. "After I broke off my engagement, I moved to Sydney to live my own life, dance to my own tune. I've never gone home again. Not for Christmas or anything," I confessed. "Last year, there was a big event on, my family were all together in the papers. Mr. and Mrs. Claire and their four children."

Moving up next to me, Sean took my hand. "Come on." He tugged me after him.

"Where are we going?" I asked as we walked back up the beach.

Sean looked back at me and winked.

CHAPTER FIVE

His cottage, that's where he took me. Into his inner sanctum where he insisted I sit on the lounge while he cooked up popcorn. "If you plan to do something kinky with that popcorn, I need to warn you that kink isn't my thing," I called into the kitchen.

Smirking at me, Sean pulled two bottles of soda out of the fridge. Opening them as he walked back into the lounge room, Sean placed one in front of me. "I told you, I don't fraternize with guests."

"I'm in your place," I pointed out, "this constitutes fraternizing."

Leaning down, Sean placed his hand on the couch behind me. "That's not fraternizing to me." His other hand dropped and trailed his cold bottle up my inner thigh, pushing my dress up.

"Sean!" Biting my lip, I grabbed his wrist to stop his progress.

"That was me fraternizing." Sean smiled before standing back up straight. "So, we're clear." He winked at me, lifted his drink to his mouth, and went back to the kitchen.

Grabbing my bottle, I drank from it. I needed to cool down because Sean half naked and teasing was a hell of a sensory experience. Coming back out with the popcorn, Sean dropped into the seat next to me on the lounge, and held the popcorn out to me. Taking it into my lap I grabbed a handful while he picked up the remote.

"Okay, nothing romantic, no sob stories..."

"No horror," I jibbed in.

Sean smirked. "Thrillers it is." Opening the Netflix page, Sean scanned through till he found a movie he wanted to watch and pressed play. He got up long enough to turn off the light before sitting back down.

Placing the popcorn between us, we both sank into the lounge watching the movie. After it finished, came another movie. It was a bit slower, and half-way through, I felt myself dozing. I turned to get comfortable and found Sean's shoulder. His arm wrapped around me and pulled me into him. I fell asleep.

I woke up in the middle of the night with my cheek resting on Sean's chest. He was lying on the lounge with me squeezed between his body and the back rest. When I tried to get up without waking him, Sean's arm tightened around my waist. "Stay, it's late."

"I should go." Sean released me. Managing to climb off him without falling and hurting either of us, I dropped a kiss to Sean's cheek. "Thank you for listening."

Sean grabbed my hand. "Spend the day with me?" His eyes slit enough to watch me.

"It's my last day..."

"I know, spend it with me?"

Considering him, I smiled. "We both need some more sleep first."

Groaning, Sean stood up, gave me a tired smile, and led me into his bedroom. He crawled onto his bed before turning to look at me, his hand gripping mine to force me to follow. I stared at the bed amazed. "Sean, I haven't shared a bed with anyone in eight years."

Sean tugged me down causing me to stumble forward into his arms. "Ten years for me. Go to sleep, Holly." Dismissing my worry, Sean fell straight back to sleep.

Smirking at how cute he was, I snuggled into him and drifted back to sleep as well. The next time I woke, I was alone. The sun was up, the scent of yummy food, like bacon and pancakes, and syrup filling the cottage. Scrambling out of bed to use the bathroom, I made myself decent before moving out to the open plan living area.

Sean was in the kitchen, still in only his cargo pants, but with the addition of an apron. When he turned and saw me approach, his smile lit up the room. "Good morning. I hope you're hungry?"

"I'm ravenous." Stalking toward the kitchen bench, I eyed the two plates of food. "Can I help?"

"Pour two glasses of juice and grab some cutlery for the table," Sean suggested.

Following his direction, I then stood in the dining room taking in his place in daylight. It was neat and tidy but still lived in.

There were photos of himself with a man who, by the similarity, had to be his dad on a bookshelf. Lifting the one from his graduation day to get a better look, I noticed a framed certificate behind it. A combined law and business degree certificate.

Swallowing the sudden ball of distaste in my mouth, I put the photo back. On the shelves below stood science fiction novels, adventure magazines, and cookbooks. He had more cookbooks than Mitchell, my yoga instructor. For a moment, I considered the option Sean was gay. Then I remembered the way he kissed me back at the bar two nights ago, and dismissed it.

"Come and eat," Sean whispered in my ear. Jumping, I spun, slamming back into the bookshelf. "Shit, are you okay?" Sean grasped my arms, just as wide-eyed as I was.

"Yes, sorry, I was lost in thought and you startled me."

"Really? I hadn't noticed." Sean physically moved me to the table and my seat. "Eat, ravenous one." Then took his seat.

We ate quietly for several minutes. I wasn't lying about being hungry, and the food was delicious. "Are you going to ask, or do you want me to pretend you didn't see my degree?" Sean eventually prompted.

"You sat the bar?"

"I did. I passed with flying colors."

"When you spoke about your ex, the way you spat his occupation, I wouldn't have considered you were one."

"That's because I'm not," Sean clarified. "I majored in corporate law. I interned, sat the bar, and had a starting position in a prominent law firm. Yet, I left it all behind a month after the woman I loved left me for a criminal attorney. He also happened to be my older brother."

My knife and fork froze in mid-air. Sean watched me. Picking up my juice, I took a sip. "You only have photos of your father?"

"My mother died when I was six months old; my father raised us both himself. With nannies of course, but still, he was there a lot," Sean revealed.

"He's a lawyer too?"

Sean's fingers gripped his cutlery. "He was. He gave it up to pursue other interests."

Recognizing a shut down when I saw one, I changed direction. Dad's work was a no-go topic. "Most of those photos are here, so he comes to visit?"

Sean relaxed a little, sympathy filling his eyes. "Yes. My father wasn't happy at first, but he could see how much happier I was here and supported my career change."

"Do you see your brother?"

"At family gatherings."

"Are they still together?"

Sean smirked. "Unhappily so." We met each other's eyes. Sean started laughing. "Okay, so he saved me from a bad marriage, but he was still my brother, and he was sleeping with my long-term girlfriend."

"I don't disagree with that sentiment," I shrugged, letting him know I didn't think he was a bad person.

Sean sat back. "You mentioned you were in a long-term casual thing?" I lifted my eyes to his. "Why did you do that when you are a person who doesn't do casual?"

"What makes you think I don't do casual?" I tried to avoid answering.

"A decade worth of experience of women trying to get in my pants. And, the fact that you announced it at Pearl Harbor to everyone on tour," Sean smirked.

My cheeks flushed with heat. "You heard about that?"

"Some of the other guests were discussing it on their return. That and the presence of a porn star in the hotel."

"You need to wipe that grin off your face," I warned him. "You knew why I was upset before you came down to go snorkeling, didn't you?"

"I knew you'd gotten upset; I didn't know to what extent."

I stood up. "Thanks for breakfast. I should go shower and change," I excused. I headed for the door to the path. "Anything specific I need for today?"

"Swimmers, a hat, sunscreen, and a smile," Sean informed me.

"Okay, I'll be back in an hour."

"Meet me in the lobby." Standing up, Sean took our plates to his sink and started cleaning up.

Nodding, I went back to the hotel. In my room, I stood in the shower considering my options. I had many. Sean was right. I'd been very upset last night over something so far in my past it shouldn't matter anymore. So why did it?

Back downstairs, I ran into Nichola in the lobby. "There you are, is everything alright?"

"Yes, I'm about to head out for the day," I explained.

Nichola frowned at me. She looked at my shorts and singlet over my bikini. "More water sports," she decided. "I don't know how you haven't burnt yourself with all your time in the water the last few days?"

"Lots of hydration and sunscreen."

"Well, Sadie and I are going on a horseback tour. Are you sure you don't want to join us?" Nichola checked.

Smiling, I kissed her cheek as I saw Sean enter the lobby. "I'm very sure. Have fun."

Moving away from her to meet Sean. "Everything okay?" He checked.

"Sure, let's go." Smiling, I let him lead the way. Peering over my shoulder at Nichola; she was smiling like a Cheshire watching me leave with Sean. Oh, if only my family knew.

CHAPTER SIX

It started in a helicopter. Not only did Sean take me on the aerial tour of the island, but he flew the helicopter himself. "I like to be in control," Sean confessed. Taking the stick in his hands, he lifted us off the helipad. Flying the route of the usual tour, he then showed me a few of his favorite sights.

Next, we went paddle boarding. Then it was lunch from Sean's favorite food outlet. In the afternoon, we went horseback riding. Not the trail rides my sisters had gone on in the morning, but a more intimate trail.

Sean saddled his horse himself, before helping me onto another horse. "This isn't part of the normal tour," Sean revealed as he led me down a steep path.

"I'm glad, or your insurance would be a killer." The track wouldn't pass a risk assessment back home.

"That's not why we don't bring anyone here. The locals want to keep it private."

Moments later, Sean pulled up into a clearing. Stopping next to him, my mouth to fall open in awe. Before us was a waterfall fed lagoon, isolated from the world by tall mountains and forest.

Dismounting, Sean tied the reins of his horse to a tree before helping me to dismount. He walked to the edge of the lagoon, pulled off his shirt, kicked his shoes off, and dived in.

Following suit, I stripped to my bikini and jumped in. The water was cool and clean. When I surfaced, I laughed. "This is amazing!" Sean smiled, his eyes focused on me. Treading water while I turned, taking it all in. "I've never seen anything this beautiful in person."

"Me neither," Sean murmured. Turning to face him, I realized his eyes were intent on me. He swam closer to me, and for a moment, I thought he was going to wrap me in his arms and kiss me. "Come on; you've got to experience it properly," he encouraged, as he swam by me.

I swam after him, towards the waterfall and then to the rocks to one side. "The current is too strong to get close to the fall," Sean explained. "It'd pummel you to death on the rocks beneath with the force of it." Climbing onto the rocks, Sean held out his hand to me. "But there is another way to get close."

Leading me across the rocks, we found around a tiny goat path. This led us in behind the curtain of water to a small eroded rock shelf hidden by the waterfall. It was darker here; the water shutting out most of the light, and the roar of the water making it hard to hear anything.

Standing back, Sean watched me take it in. Reaching out my hand to feel the water, I got the off-spray, not the direct fall.

Letting it fill my cupped hands, I drank the clean water. "What does it taste like?" Sean yelled over the roar of the water. There was a smile trying to escape his lips.

Slipping my hand into his hair, I pulled his mouth to mine. Our lips met, pinched, and opened. Sean's tongue delved into my mouth, tasting, dueling with my tongue. His hands feeling over the damp skin of my back and hips as our bodies pressed against each other.

We pulled back, our breathing a bit labored from the passionate kiss. Sean closed his eyes and leaned his forehead to mine. His mouth moved in the shape of words, talking to me, but I couldn't hear him over the water. Removing himself a moment later, he left me there.

Inhaling, I closed my eyes. Sean didn't fraternize with customers, and I took him to be a very moral man. I was sure that's what he'd reiterated after the kiss, that he couldn't do that with me. What was I thinking? I was leaving at lunchtime tomorrow to board a cruise ship and sail home. I should enjoy the day, say goodbye to him tonight, and go on my way tomorrow.

Exhaling, I opened my eyes and moved out from behind the curtain of water. Sean was swimming back across the lagoon to the horses. Slipping back into the water, I swam across the lagoon. Sean helped me out on the other side, then turned and pulled his shirt on.

"Thank you for showing me this place," I broke the silence between us. Starting to dress, I kept my back to Sean as I did. "It just topped my best five experiences."

"There's another place I want to show you," Sean offered as he mounted his horse.

"Thank you, but I've had enough for today. I'd like to have a rest before dinner." When I threw myself into the saddle, Sean's eyes dimmed with disappointment. "You don't have to return to the hotel with me; I can find my way back."

Shaking his head, Sean moved his horse forward onto the trail. "I'll see you back."

We arrived at the stables an hour later, and the staff took my horse from me. "Thank you again," I smiled at Sean, holding my hand out. Sean took it, his lips twitching with amusement. "We probably won't see each other again before I leave, so, it was nice meeting you."

"Have dinner with me?"

"I should spend some time with my sisters-"

"You're going to be stuck on a boat with them for the next week and a half," Sean cut in. "Have dinner with me? Please?" A small lilt in his voice revealing the subtle plea in the request.

"Where? What time?"

"Lobby at six," Sean decided, without even having to think about it.

"I'll see you then." Making my way back to my room, I showered and changed ready for dinner, then I collapsed on my bed for a nap.

The room phone woke me a little later. Opening my eyes, I saw the time and cursed. "Hello?" I answered, pulling myself from the heavy clutches of the bed.

"Am I being stood up?" Sean asked.

"No, God, I'm sorry, I fell asleep. I'll be down in a minute."

Sean chuckled. "Bring a jacket. I'll meet you out front."

Arriving out the front of the hotel, I found Sean sitting astride a motorbike. Peering down at the dress I wore, I looked back to him questioningly. "This is Hawaii, Holly," Sean answered my unspoken question, handing me a helmet.

Pulling my jacket on, I strapped on the helmet, and threw my leg over behind him. Gripping his waist, I tried not to squeal when he revved the engine and the bike shot forward. We rode to Sunset Point and sat there watching the sunset. Not a word said between us, and I found that silence was comfortable around Sean. After the sun dropped below the horizon, Sean rode us back to the resort. He took the scenic route which was beautiful at night.

When we got back to the resort, we ate dinner in the upscale restaurant. We discussed our favorite water sports and Sean's favorite things to do on his weekends. Afterwards, we went for a walk along the beach.

"How about you, Holly?" Sean asked. We'd run out of places and things to do in Hawaii. "What do you do for leisure at home?"

"I used to swim laps on my meal break when I was on night shift, and yoga on my days off."

"You never get out and travel? I've heard Australia is an amazing country for sight-seeing?" Sean challenged.

"I saw a lot of the cities growing up. My dad traveled a lot for work and the occasional family holiday. This is my first holiday in five years. I worked weekends till recently, so I haven't had time to do much else."

We stopped walking and looked out at the moon across the

water. It felt familiar. Searching for a landmark, I realized we were standing on the same spot of the beach as last night. Right outside Sean's beach cottage. The cool breeze blowing off the water reminded us that spring had only just arrived in this part of the world.

Stepping closer, Sean wrapped his arms around me to keep me warm. "Holly, I don't want you to leave tomorrow," Sean murmured to my hair. Exhaling, I closed my eyes. I felt the same. "Stay," Sean requested as he turned me to face him. "For the length of the cruise, for as long as you can. I'll pay your ticket home, but I want this time with you. Truthfully, I think you need a longer holiday."

I met Sean's eyes, so determined in what he was asking of me. "If I agree?"

"Well, there's this." Lowering his mouth, Sean kissed me. He was tender, tentative in his exploration of my lips. "There will be more sunsets," he whispered. He kissed a trail along my jaw to my ear. "We can explore more of Hawaii together. I'll take time off work to be with you," he assured. Dropping my head back, I enjoyed the wet trail his mouth created down the side of my neck. "Then at night..." Lifting his face above mine, Sean waited for me to open my eyes. When I met his gaze, my smile equaled the one in his eyes. "There will be movies and popcorn."

"Oh, you know how to woo a girl," I simpered.

"Is that a yes?"

Sobering, I withdrew from his affection. "You're suggesting a few more weeks. A holiday romance. At the end, I fly home and leave you as a happy memory?"

"I'm asking for a few more weeks, but at the end, the options will depend on both of us," Sean left it open.

"I'd love to, Sean, but this place is above my price range for that long a stay, even with you paying my ticket home."

"Holly, you'd still be checking out of the hotel tomorrow, and my bed doesn't cost you a thing," he dismissed my excuse. When I lifted a brow, Sean shook his head. "While I hope you want to do that, I don't expect it, Holly. We've shared a bed before."

"My sisters will have something to say about this. You know that, right?" I reminded him I wasn't alone on this trip.

Stepping back, taking my hand in his, Sean walked us to his cottage. "You're a grown woman, Holly. You've been making your own decisions for a long time now. They'll have to accept whatever you decide."

My sisters had never seen me as able to make my own decisions. Leading me into his cottage, the door clicked shut behind us. Removing my jacket, I kicked off my shoes as I stepped inside. Catching my shoulders in his hands, Sean pressed his body against my back, his breath tickling my ear. "Say you'll stay?"

"Two weeks," I murmured.

Sean's hot lips kissed down the side of my neck, his hands rubbing down my arms then encircling my waist. "You said you had a month's leave, Holly. That's three more weeks." His strong hands caressed over my abdomen. His lips pinched my neck as Sean's hands split. One traveling north, the other south.

"Two weeks is a respectable holiday fling, anything longer is more," I defended. A gasp escaped me as Sean's southern hand found the bare skin of my thigh.

Pulling back, Sean turned me to face him and cupped my face in his hands. "I want the more." His mouth captured mine in the kiss to end all kisses. Hard and passionate, he slid his tongue between my lips.

Butterflies swirled through my stomach. Muscles through my abdomen and pelvis contracted. Nerves fired down my legs till my toes curled and my body lurched forward to be closer to Sean.

Wrapping my arms around him, I pulled his body hard to mine. When his hands grabbed my arse, I jumped into his hold without a second thought.

Sean kissed me all the way to his bedroom. He refused to relinquish my mouth even when he lowered my legs to the ground and slid my knickers down my thighs.

My hands were tugging at his belt, shoving his clothes from his body. We broke the kiss to lift his shirt over his head, my dress and bra joining it on the floor a moment later. By the time Sean located my pearl and started tapping out his intentions, I was panting.

Sean moved us to lay on his bed. His fingers rubbed and stroked me, the hard pressure of his palm on my clit making me bite my lip. Spreading my thighs wider as the friction built a burning heat. When the tips of his fingers separated my moist folds, I arched and moaned as he made me crave more.

My fingers caressed over the hard lines of his tanned skin. Skimming the surface, I enjoyed the way Sean moaned in response. Brushing against his hardness, I felt the smooth length against the side of my hand. Turning my wrist, I grasped him, wrapping my fingers and twisting my hands over him. Sean grunted, his hips pushing forward with force. With a final kiss, Sean opened the drawer of his bedside table, ripped open a condom and rolled it on. He lowered himself between my welcoming thighs, and I helped guide him to my molten core.

Taking the invitation, Sean thrust forward. He took three goes to convince my body he needed more space than already on offer. Gripping his firm arse, I'm encouraged him while seeking something secure to hold me in this reality.

There was nothing hesitant in the way Sean delved into me, or in how I gave myself over to him. I was deeply attracted to him. And I was sick of denying myself what I wanted.

Sean lifted one of my legs up, bending it over his bicep so he could drive deeper. Throwing my head back, I gripped the bed-head to prevent scratching him up, my fingers gripping the wrought iron with all my strength. Capturing my mouth, Sean kissed me till I was breathless. Dropping his mouth to my breast, he changed the angle of his body. I bit my lip to prevent vocalizing how good it felt. Years of internalizing my pleasure and controlling my reactions natural to me now.

Sean lifted his head. Slowing his body, he turned his thrusts into circles, punctuated by a sharp push on the in, to reach as deep as he could. Clenching my jaw, I closed my eyes. Grunting, Sean put his hand to my mouth. "Open," he ordered.

Complying, I sucked his thumb into my mouth. Swearing, Sean thrust a little faster. Swelling inside me, his body demanded I open further to his need. I turned my head to hinder the moan that was building. As I pressed my lips together around his thumb, Sean used his hand to force my mouth open and drove his hips forward. I moaned audibly, a tension I hadn't even recognized I was holding escaping into the room. God, it felt good to let it out.

"That's more like it, Holly. You don't have to be quiet here. I want to hear you."

When I moaned again, Sean grinned and kissed me. Moving his mouth to my breast, I was climaxing for him seconds later. Opening my lips, I let Sean know how hard I was cumming. Years of pent up restriction and fear flying free and leaving me limp, and the most relaxed I'd been in two years. Clenching his eyes and gritting his jaw, Sean's entire body seized. Grunting with each thrust, Sean forced his body to finish what it started. Drawing the pleasure out longer for both of us.

When he collapsed beside me, we took a minute to catch our breaths while staring at the ceiling. "Three weeks," Sean choked, clearing his throat. "I want the three weeks."

Rolling to my side I kissed his chest. The smile on my face hurting my cheeks, using muscles it felt like I hadn't activated since I was a child. I couldn't remember being this happy for a long time. Tucking me under his arm, Sean waited for my reply. Having just had the best orgasm of my life, was I going to say no?

"I best go book my flight."

CHAPTER SEVEN

GRUMBLING, I HID MY HEAD UNDER THE PILLOW TO DROWN OUT the sound of the phone ringing. "Hello?" Sean's voice answered sleepily. "That's okay, Henry, my alarm will go off shortly. Is there a problem?" Sean ran a hand down my naked back, over my rear, and between my thighs to caress me. "No, she's not missing. Miss Claire was inquiring about the best places to watch the sunrise from yesterday. She intended to set out early to take advantage of her last morning as a guest of the Cassidy Resort."

I bit my lip on a moan as Sean's fingers sunk into me to massage my good spot. "Assure her sister that if Miss Claire hasn't surfaced by the end of breakfast, we'll go looking for her. Thanks, Henry." Sean hung up.

"Lier," I accused from beneath my pillow.

"Not at all. From where you are lying, you have an amazing view of the sunrise." The bedside table drawer opened and closed. The distinct sound of a foil wrapper tearing filled the silence.

Lifting the pillow, I peeked out at the window. I blinked once, twice, then lifted my head to watch the sky changing color. It was beautiful. The gray light of dawn growing lighter over the ocean outside.

Sean shifted between my thighs behind me. "Beautiful isn't it?" He kissed across my shoulders. "Just like you." He kissed my cheek and nibbled my ear.

Pressing himself into me, Sean moved like the tide, surging deeper and deeper with each wave. Gold light lit up the horizon, marbling the gray sky with blues and pinks. Gripping the bed, I closed my eyes a moment, lifting my hips to feel more of Sean.

"Watch it, it's beautiful," Sean breathed in my ear.

"You're not watching it."

"I've seen it for ten years. The beauty of you cumming in the morning, that's something new, but equally as captivating."

Withdrawing, Sean surged forward again, still not reaching full tide. The sky was sapphire on gold. The gold was melting, bleeding into the sapphire, blending to aquamarine. As the morning broke free of the night's clutches, Sean filled me. His strokes deep and not so purposeful as he lost himself to the brilliance of my dawning.

"Let me hear it, Holly," Sean demanded when I fell into the habit of keeping quiet.

Opening my mouth, I sang along with the birds outside,

praising the sunrise. Swept up by the wave of pleasure, Sean surged through the ocean of climax to crash upon my back breathless. He kissed me deeply before he removed himself to dispose of the condom, then returned to lie beside me.

"That was the best sunrise I've seen in ten years," Sean declared. "I want to start every morning like that."

Chuckling, I turned my head to watch him. Sean turned his face to me, and his lips turned up into a smile.

"You know what I've liked most about last night and this morning?" I challenged. Sean's smile faded a little at my tone, and he rolled his body towards me. "We were both naked, and we did it in bed." Smiling, I closed my eyes, snuggling into the comfort. "It's been eight years since I've had sex naked, in a bed."

When I opened my eyes, Sean considered me with raised brows. "How have you been doing it with your casual liaison?"

"Fully dressed, and quickly, against the wall, or the desk," I admitted.

"You were having sex at work?"

"Yes, but never during my shift."

"So, the sexual harassment...?"

"My new manager found out and tried to blackmail me into extending him the same courtesy." Watching Sean, I wondered if my admission changed his impression of me. "Do you still want me to stay?"

Sean caressed my face. "You think I'm going to throw you out of my bed because your former boss was too stupid to treat you right?"

I jolted back from his reach. "How did you know it was my boss?"

Sean looked guilty. "I overheard your sisters discussing it. Something about what a scandal it would be if it came out. They felt the media would be all over it if they found out, and they were deciding if they should let your parents know."

I jumped up from the bed. "They what?"

"I guess your boss is someone important in your country. Your sisters worried about the backlash." Sitting up, Sean observed my reaction.

"He's the son of someone, and a perpetual bachelor," I groaned. "That I was in a two-year long affair with him would be front-page news. It's the longest relationship he's ever had." Pacing, annoyed with my sisters, and worried Sean would judge me for getting involved with my boss.

"It probably lasted as long as it did because it was secret," Sean suggested. "You were also a subordinate who he could take advantage of, and manipulate. If you asked for something more serious, you could be made redundant. He could get rid of you without the grit of a relationship ending."

"You make it sound like he was using me."

Sean raised a brow. "You said it yourself; you thought you meant more than it appears he did. You had to quit your job, Holly."

I stopped pacing and swiped at the moisture leaking onto my cheek. Closing my eyes, I steadied myself. "He wouldn't have let it end, if I'd stayed. He didn't want the affair to end, but he didn't want a relationship with me either. If I didn't leave, he would have seduced me again, and I wanted to date and have a relationship. I've craved what you've given me in the last twenty-four hours for a decade. I didn't even realize how badly I wanted it till I met you."

Throwing the sheet back, Sean stood, taking me in his arms. "Strangely enough, I didn't realize how much I missed it until you walked into my hotel and smiled at me."

Meeting Sean's eyes, I stepped back fearfully. "You can't look at me like that, Sean. Three weeks. That's all I agreed too."

Sean reeled me back into his grasp, his hands caressing my hair, forcing me to meet his eyes. "You agreed to three weeks and to see where it goes from there," Sean reminded me. "A lot can happen in three weeks, Holly."

"My world fell apart in a day, Sean. I'm uncertain I'm up for any more change right now."

Sean rested his forehead against mine. His alarm started shrieking across the room. With a huff, Sean released me and silenced the alarm. "I'm going for a surf before work. Did you want to join me?"

"My swimmers are at the hotel. I should go and pack, and spend the morning with my sisters." Sean look away rejected. "Tomorrow morning, definitely."

Sean's lips twitched in a smile. Tugging me toward him, he kissed me deeply. "Check out, then bring your stuff down here." Opening the drawer next to his bed, Sean handed me a key on a key ring.

I held it up. "You keep a spare for your flings?"

"I had it cut yesterday while you slept," Sean countered. "I decided after the waterfall, that I couldn't let you leave today. I planned, hopeful that you'd give this a chance."

"My sister considers you a rebound." In my head, I worried how intensely I already felt about Sean.

"Officially, you would be my rebound also," Sean offered.

Meeting his eyes, fear clenched my stomach in its irrepressible fist. "This might hurt."

Nodding, Sean took my face in his hands. "I'm betting it will." He kissed me slowly, emotionally. Sean didn't bother with surfing. Our bodies fell back to the bed, where we expressed our emotions to each other physically.

As we walked back to the resort together, Sean took my hand. It felt nice to walk connected like that. I tried to drop his hand before entering the lobby, not wanting his staff to see. Sean held it tighter.

"They are going to know in a matter of days you're staying with me, Holly. There's no point playing denial games."

He was right. When we walked inside and his staff noticed with wide eyes and wider mouths, I felt way too self-conscious. Sean cleared his throat as we passed to the elevator, and everyone snapped out of it, returning to their work.

"You're going to be the gossip today," I warned.

"I'm a single man who doesn't indulge in illicit affairs with women who hit on me," Sean declared. "I'm gossiped about already."

"It's about to be so much worse," I warned humored.

Sean grinned releasing me into the elevator. "Go pack your stuff and say goodbye to your sisters, Holly. I'm going to make the rumor mill burn with my plans for you."

I blushed as the elevator doors closed, separating me from Sean. Nervous and excited all at once, I had what my mother used to call the jitters. My nerves were on edge, the thought of eating made my stomach turn, and I couldn't stop smiling. The next three weeks could be a great adventure I'd remember for the rest of my life fondly. Or, it would be my biggest heartbreak.

Was I stupid for hoping for an amazing three weeks that I could walk away from with a smile and fond memories? Probably. Still, it was the about time I took what I'd waited two years for with Benjamin.

———

"YOU WHAT?" Sadie screeched across the breakfast table.

"Calm down," I shushed her.

"Calm down? Overnight you've decided overnight to cancel your cruise home and go island jumping. By yourself."

"I'm a grown adult, Sadie. I can go on holiday by myself," I dismissed her concerns.

Sadie made a noise that made it obvious she disagreed. "Sadie," Nichola shook her head. Her eyes turned to me, so like our mother. "Are you sure about this, Holly? You can't get your money back on the cruise this late."

"Well, I was crashing in your room and didn't pay for the

accommodation only boarding. So, the company was happy to reimburse me. That will pay for my flight home instead."

Sean purchased my ticket home before I contacted my friend who I'd booked the cruise through. I was over the moon she got me a refund, as that was my spending money for the next three weeks.

"This is stupid, just get on the boat," Sadie decided.

"You're not hearing me. I've already booked a flight home and canceled my cruise. They wouldn't let me on the boat home if I tried," I clarified the situation for them. "I've enjoyed spending time with you both, but it might be years before I take another holiday like this again. I want to see the rest of Hawaii, enjoy more of the recreation, and I don't know, live, for the rest of my holiday."

"You're reckless, stupid, and immature," Sadie lectured.

"Yeah, well, I guess mum and dad were right about me," I snapped. "I can't believe you have the gall to call me reckless."

"I'm your older sister," Sadie scolded.

"And such a great role model. There's a guy over there who looks like he needs a blow-job. Why don't you let him and his friends fuck your every orifice and film it? Nothing reckless about that." I stormed off leaving Sadie and Nichola staring after me mouths wide open.

Muttering to myself angrily all the way back to my room, I was there two minutes before someone knocked at the door. "Who is it?"

"Sean Cassidy, the manager," he sounded like he was laughing.

I opened the door sheepishly. "I noticed you stormed out of the restaurant. Was there a problem with breakfast?" Sean asked professionally, a smile tugging at the side of his lips.

Grabbing him by the collar, I pulled him into my room. The door slam shut as I pushed Sean against the wall and started kissing him heatedly. Sean's hands were all over me. He undressed me while I pulled his clothes free from his outdoorsman physique.

"Jesus, Holly," Sean breathed. "I'm working. I just came to make sure you're okay?"

"I'm not okay," I murmured. "I need you inside me."

Sean didn't waste another word arguing. "Condom?" Sean requested as we maneuvered through the lounge to the bed.

"Fuck," I muttered, breaking away for a second in annoyance.

"Holly?"

"I'm not used to needing them."

"Because rushed office sex doesn't allow for practicing safe sex," Sean nodded understanding.

"I'm clean, and I'm on birth control."

Sean took my face in his hands. "I'm clean, and I'm sensible." Sean kissed me, deep, but quick, then collected his clothes and dressed.

"Wait, so that means we're not doing this?" I asked surprised.

"Not right now, no. You're upset and angry. You are not in the state to make wise decisions about unsafe practices."

"Excuse me?"

Sean sighed, righting his uniform. Collecting my clothes, he walked towards me. "You have nothing but my word that I'm clean, Holly. What happens if, for some reason or another, your contraception didn't work?" Sean caressed my cheek. "Major life choices made for five minutes of angry sex."

Taking my clothes, I turned my back to redress. "Why does everyone have the ability to make me feel like a stupid child?"

"I'm older than you, Holly. The same with your siblings. I guess your former boss was older still," Sean spoke carefully. "I've seen people's lives turned upside down by one thoughtless moment. While I'm all for spontaneity, I'd prefer you not to leave here with a life-altering regret."

Turning me around to face him, Sean wiped the wetness from my cheeks with his thumb and kissed me. "Go settle in at my place, enjoy your afternoon, and come up to the resort and have dinner with me. Tonight, I promise I'll fuck you so hard you'll struggle to walk tomorrow."

"You better," I grumbled.

Sean smirked. "We wouldn't want to prove your sister right about you being reckless."

I gapped at him. "How did you know that?"

Sean chuckled. "My staff called me to deal with a loud dispute in the restaurant. I was on my way to your table to calm the fight down when you suggested your sister start a gang-bang and stormed out."

Embarrassed, I sat on the bed. I'd become one of those guests. "I didn't realize we were that loud. I apologize."

Combing his fingers through my hair, Sean used my hair to tilt my head up for his lips. "You can make it up to me tonight."

My eyes dropped to the still obvious erection in his pants. Grabbing his pants, I yanked him closer as I freed his hard-on to my lips. "I'd rather do it now."

CHAPTER EIGHT

"Are you sure?" Nichola asked as we stood in the lobby waiting for Sadie so they could catch the shuttle to the port.

"I'm sure. I want to stay for a few more weeks and experience as much as I can."

Nichola's eyes went over my shoulder. Turning to see that Sean was at the front desk talking to his staff, I blushed. "Well, I can't say that it's not worth experiencing," Nichola sighed.

When I met Nichola's eyes, we laughed. "I swear, I am going to be Island hopping and seeing as much as I can." Nichola raised a brow. "I didn't say I'd be doing it alone."

Nichola pulled me into a hug. "Be safe, Holly. Call me when you get home, and we'll organize Bridesmaids dresses."

"Again?" I whined.

"You're my sister, Holly, you have to be my bridesmaid," Nichola insisted.

She released me from the hug as Sadie stomped into the lobby and glared at me. "Try not to be stupid," she scowled, then walked out to get on the shuttle bus.

Nichola gave me a side hug. "You're not stupid, Holly. Never have been. Enjoy the holiday."

Nichola went to join Sadie, scolding her when she took the seat next to her. Sadie held up her hand to gesture she wasn't listening and turned her attention to the window. Yeah, Sadie had serious middle child syndrome.

Waving as the bus pulled away, I collected my bag and headed down the path for the beach cottages. Letting myself into Sean's place, hung my dress from the symphony in his wardrobe so it wouldn't crease. I'd packed it in for the formal dinner on the cruise. Heading to the beach, I wanted the ocean to wash away my cares. Renting a board, I surfed the morning away.

After a shower at Sean's, I went to Sean's favorite beach shack for lunch. Back at the hotel, I went to the lobby to organize what else I would see or do this week. "Afternoon, Miss Claire, I didn't realize you were still here?"

Looking up, I smiled at the concierge. "Afternoon, Henry. Yes, I decided to stay for a few more weeks to fully experience this wonderful place."

Henry looked surprised. "But you checked out of your room?"

He had a very valid point. "I did." I wasn't exactly comfortable pointing out I was staying with his boss. "I'm staying in one of the cottages with a friend." Henry's brow frowned, no doubt aware of everyone staying in the cottages. "Not permanently.

Just a couple of days here to explore this island, and then I'll be island hopping."

"Oh!" Henry looked unsure. His eyes told me he was trying to work out with which guest I was staying. "Well, is there something I can assist you with?"

Holding up one of the brochures, I grinned. "A booking on the north shore zip line for tomorrow please?"

Henry took the brochure. "Morning or afternoon?"

"Whenever there is availability."

"I'll give them a call for you, Miss Claire. If you tell me which cottage you are in, I'll call you with the time."

It was a good try. "I'm going to Waikiki to do the bicycle tour, so let me know when I come up for dinner."

Henry almost huffed in annoyance. Winking at him, I turned to leave when he blushed. Sean was standing smiling at us. "Everything alright, Henry?"

"Of course, Sean, just helping Miss Claire make a booking."

"I'll take over. I need you to visit Mr. Harrington and see to his most recent request please." Sean handed Henry a folded piece of paper.

"Yes, Sean." Henry swapped Sean the brochure for the piece of paper. "Miss Claire would like to do the zip line at some stage tomorrow."

Nodding, Sean waited for Henry to walk away. "So, the zip line?"

"I didn't know how quickly you'd be able to organize leave. So, I thought I would spend the next few days doing all the local stuff." My eyes drinking in the gorgeous man who was keeping a respectable distance from me.

"I've informed my staff I'll be on leave from Wednesday." Reaching over the desk, Sean took the other brochures from me, letting his hand linger on mine a minute as he did. "Is this everything you want to do?"

"So far. I'm sure you'll have plenty more ideas of how best to spend my three weeks here?"

Sean gave me a lopsided grin. "I have an idea about tonight, that's for sure."

"Movie marathon?"

Sean leaned toward me. "I thought that was your sister's thing? But, if you want me to film it, I won't object to having a way to reflect on our time together."

"Never going to happen."

Sean pouted. "Okay, well, then no movies," he winked. "I'll book you into these, and I'll book us into a few more." He waved the brochures standing straight and moving to the phone.

"Henry wants to know where I'm staying now." Sean lifted a brow. "I told him I'm staying with a friend in the cottages."

"As sweet as it is that you're trying to protect my reputation, I'm pretty sure our arrival this morning let that cat out of the bag."

"Really?" I smirked stepping closer.

Meeting my eyes, Sean looked a bit frightened. "You look very dangerous right now, Holly."

"I want to kiss you."

Sean's eyes lit up. "As much as I want that too, while I'm working, I prefer to conduct myself professionally." Sean smiled watching me. "But you knew that?"

Nodding, I took a step back. "I do," I assured, taking another step back, still smiling at Sean. Over his shoulder, I spotted Henry approaching. "Well, I'm off to go bike riding, I'll see you at dinner?"

"I'll meet you here at six."

"Thank you, Mr. Cassidy," I farewelled sweetly.

Sean got this humored look on his face with my formal farewell. Then Henry was beside him and understanding dawned. Winking, I went out to catch a ride into Honolulu.

———

THE GUIDED bicycle tour was an eight-mile cruise through Waikiki culture and history. The route took us through green parks, past white-sand beaches, and into the heart of Honolulu.

We started by heading along a car-free path toward Kahi Hali'a Aloha. A burial mound holding skeletons dug up during various Waikiki construction projects. We rode along a waterfront path to the Waikiki Aquarium. The second-oldest aquarium in the United States. We rode by the Waikiki Natatorium War Memorial swimming pool. It was built on Kaimana Beach to honor the men and women who served in World War I.

After cruising along the beach, the tour headed to Kapiolani

Park. The largest and oldest public park in Hawaii, it is a popular meeting point for parades and festivals. Next, we rolled by the Honolulu Zoo and stopped for a delicious soft-serve ice cream.

We rounded off the tour by heading past Fort DeRussy, the Hawaii Army Museum, Cassidy's Point, and Ala Wai Harbor. Finally, we rode the car-free path, past the Ala Wai golf course and along Kapahulu Avenue to where the tour began.

It was a well thought out tour, and beat the usual stand and shuffle tours that my sisters seemed to enjoy. I jumped on the shuttle bus back to the resort and went for a shower and rest before dinner. After a full day of exercise, my legs were telling me about it, but I was happy.

Arriving in the lobby right on six, I took a seat. Sean wasn't in the lobby, and, knowing what managing a hotel consisted of, I decided to wait until he was free to eat. "Miss Claire," Henry greeted. "Can I help you with something?"

"No, thank you, Henry. I'm waiting for my dinner date."

"Did Sean give you the information about the zip line tomorrow?"

"Not yet. Mr. Cassidy told me he'd give that to me when I came up for dinner tonight," I assured, before looking out the window. "I might sit by the pool to watch the sunset. Could you let Mr. Cassidy know where to find me?"

"Of course. And, your dinner date?"

I resisted a chuckle. Henry's eyes told me he knew with whom I was having dinner. "Him too." I walked off before he could press for me to confirm his suspicions.

Finding a seat overlooking the beach, I watched the colors start to change ready for sunset. "Can I get you something?" The poolside waitress asked.

"Hydration in a glass would be wonderful please."

"Of course, what room should I charge it to?"

Crap. "I'll pay cash." Pulling out a few bills, I handed it to the waitress. Laying back, I watched the sun's descent, my eyelids racing it.

"There you are." The waitress placed the drink on the table next to me, my change with it.

"Thank you." Sitting a bit straighter, I tipped the waitress, and started drinking. My drink was gone by the time the sun disappeared from the sky, and my stomach was complaining. Realizing it was an hour and a half past the time Sean said to meet him, I decided I was going solo for dinner tonight. Whatever the issue he was dealing with must be serious.

Making my way to the outdoor bar, I found a table and browsed the menu. The bar served more casual meals than the restaurant, and with how hungry I was, that would do if it meant it was fast.

"Can I get you another drink, Miss Claire?"

I smiled up at the waitress. Her name tag read Bee. "Is that your real name?"

She smiled, observing her name tag. "Short for Beatrice. I hate people calling me by my full name."

"I hate people using my surname. Anything connecting me to my family's fame is unwelcome. Call me Holly?"

Bee smiled. "Can I get you something, Holly?"

"I'd love the Bird and Brie burger with battered beer fries and a Coke please."

"Aioli?"

"Definitely." I smiled handing her my card. "Credit please."

Bee took my card and order and walked away. She returned with my Coke and card a few minutes later. Sean took the seat opposite me as she did. "I'm sorry, Holly," Sean sounded as exhausted as I felt. "Drink up, and we'll go get dinner."

"I've ordered. I was starving."

Instead of annoyance, Sean lifted his eyes to Bee, who seemed frozen on the spot. "Double bacon and beef meal please, Bee. Charge our meals to me please."

"Holly has already paid for her meal, Mr. Cassidy." Bee squirmed. There is no better word for it. The pretty waitress smitten for her boss.

"Has she?" Sean raised a brow at me.

"I agreed to stay, I didn't say you could support me while I'm here."

Bee's eyes widened. "Coke for your drink, Mr. Cassidy?"

"Beer please, Bee. I'm in serious need of beer," Sean answered, unbuttoning his collar and removing his blazer.

"Yes, Mr. Cassidy."

I waited till we were alone. "That girl has a serious crush on you. If she doesn't spit in my food, I'll be surprised."

Sean ignored my comment. "I'm sorry; we had an incident."

"I gathered," I shrugged off his concern. "I've worked the industry long enough to know how it goes, Sean, don't fret. Are you finished for the night?"

"Hell, yes," Sean stifled a yawn. He looked at me; then his eyes went to the bar. "Back in a second," he excused as he stood and went to the bar. He came back with his beer and took his seat. "I've asked for our meals to be takeaway. I want to go home and change. Then we are going to sit and watch some crappy movie that requires no brain function from me."

"Go have a shower. I'll bring dinner down when it's ready."

Sean threw back his beer, sculling it. When it was empty, he sighed and met my eyes. "Can't leave the bar with any drinks," he explained before standing. "Thank you for being understanding." Leaning across the table, Sean threaded his hand into my hair and kissed me passionately. It was a short, but intent kiss that left me wanting more. Sean pulled back. "I'll see you in a few minutes."

Sean grab up his blazer and walked to the bar. He gave the staff instruction before he made his way toward the beach. The staff all smiled at me, eyes insinuating enough to make me blush. Well, that was that.

CHAPTER NINE

THE ZIP LINE WAS EXHILARATING. THE ECO-ADVENTURE started with a four-wheel-drive down a rugged dirt road. While we walked along an elevated platform in the trees, the guide shared tips for getting the most out of the experience.

All seven lines of the course we're dual lines, so many on tour raced their friends to the end. Since I was by myself, I enjoyed the spectacular surroundings as I glided over the forest floor below. The views looked out at fields of tropical fruit and to the white sands and azure waters of the coast.

There were various rope challenges as well. I had a ball climbing, rappelling, and crossing rope bridges between platforms. On top of this morning's wake up with Sean, followed by a surf, my body was sore by the end of the afternoon tour.

When I arrived at the lobby for dinner, I found the first available seat and damn well planted my tired arse in it. "You look wiped," Sean chuckled as he dropped into the seat beside me.

"Yep, you'll be doing all the work in bed tonight." I leaned against him. "I'm going to lie back and think of England."

Sean laughed. "England?"

"I come from a British colony, Sean. Sex was a husband's right, but women weren't to enjoy it. Oh, no, we women were to lay back and think of England or pray to the Virgin Mary."

"Well, that explains the praying you do," Sean teased. I tickled his side and he jolted away. "No, seriously, Holly, you make sex a devoted spiritual experience." He moved his mouth to my ear. "Especially when you stop biting your lip and let me hear you."

Blushing like a Hawaiian sunset, I tried to hide in my shoulders. "I like what you do to me."

Sean smiled and moved his face a little closer. "I enjoy the way you react to me. You are sort of zero to a hundred in one caress."

"Years of quickies train your body that if you're going to get off, it needs to get there fast," I confessed. "Though, the way you work me seems to make getting there way more intense."

Sean adjusted the way he was sitting. "If I weren't still on shift for another three hours, I'd be suggesting we skip dinner and get room service later."

Biting my lip, I closed my eyes as I imagined racing back to Sean's place and stripping him. My thighs ached as I squeezed them and my hands hurt where I gripped my skirt. Damn clinging to ropes half the day. "Holly?"

I opened one eye to peek at Sean. "I'm a little sore, so as lovely as that sounds, dinner and a rest sound better."

Sean took my hand in his. "Then let's eat before someone decides to O.D. again."

I let Sean lead me to the dining room. "Is that what happened last night?"

Sean looked at me. "Yeah, though I shouldn't have told you that."

"Please, who am I going to tell?"

Sean smiled. "Good point." He kissed the top of my head as we walked. "We have an American celebrity staying with us. Yesterday, they partied a little hard. Their manager called for help, but wouldn't let us call an ambulance," Sean revealed. "This celebrity has a reputation that drugs and whoring would jeopardize. So, I had to call a friend for a favor. She's a private doctor here and is very good at keeping her mouth shut. She saved the client, and once they were stable, presented the manager with the bill. They weren't impressed with her charges and tried to insist we cover the fee."

"Ouch!" I cringed. "Please tell me you didn't?"

"God, no. That's a staff member's annual wage. I'd have to let someone go, and I'm very happy with my staff, so no," Sean answered. "I'd warned the manager that she was expensive. They said they didn't care. I told the manager they could sort it out with the doctor. Bells, my friend, told the manager they could accept the bill, or she could call the police."

"Which means public knowledge, so they won't do that," I acknowledged.

"That's right," Sean agreed. In the restaurant, we were led to our table and shown the specials.

"So, everything got sorted in the end?"

"In the end, yes," Sean nodded.

We placed our orders. I went for high protein to counteract the day's activities. "When I get back, I'm going to spend every weekend out and doing something, even if it's bike riding around Centennial Park."

Sean smirked. "Feel a little unfit, do we? Cause you don't look it." Sean's eyes indulged in the view down my sun-dress.

"No, it's the after ache that's killing me." Clasping my hands behind my chair, I stretched. "But the endorphins from exercising, they should take my mind off the lack of sex."

"Lack of sex?" Sean cocked a brow, looking trapped between offended and humored.

"Yeah, because I can't deny I'm going to miss you when I get home. My body especially will, but I'm not going to be rushing into anything, so I'll need to burn the energy off somehow." I considered my cutlery. "Maybe I can convince Roger to let me use the hotel pool either before or after my shift every day for laps." Lifting my eyes to Sean, I appraised his broad shoulders. "Maybe twice a day."

"Roger?" Sean asked with a chuckle.

"My new boss. Sweet guy. You know what I like about him most?" Sean frowned shaking his head. "His wife. She's wonderful and pregnant with child number three. It's so obvious they adore each other, so I'll never have to worry about him trying to bend me over my desk." I said the last with a little too much venom, and a little louder than needed for Sean to hear.

Sean's eyebrows were in his hair. He cleared his throat and the waiter, whose brows were equally as high, placed our entrees on the table. "Sorry, I got a bit carried away."

Sean waited for us to be alone again. "So, you're working for another hotel?"

I blinked, surprised that's what Sean wanted to discuss. "Yes, where else would I work?"

"Well, I thought you might be working as a reviewer," Sean mentioned carefully. "I saw some of the stuff you'd written about your initial impression of my resort here. The things you felt needed fixing, what worked and what didn't."

I continued to blink at Sean. "You got all that off one glance when I dropped my book at your feet?"

"I can see a lot with a quick glimpse," Sean admitted. "You've also been writing about your experiences each day at my place. You don't write like a travel diary, you write like a reviewer. The good, the bad, the downright horrible."

"I'm not a reviewer. At least, I don't earn my keep by reviewing. The first entry in that book was when I was nine. My family traveled a lot. I loved seeing new places, seeing how different places did things. For Christmas one year, I got that notebook. It was intended to be a diary, but I started writing about my travel experiences. I've been doing it ever since."

Sean considered me. "Could I read it?"

"No. I consider it just as private as if it was a personal diary."

"I'd love to know what you think I need to fix here, Holly," Sean pushed.

"That's not a good idea," I muttered, and started eating.

Sean watched me, dropped his head and started on his meal. "Can you tell me about your new job? Are you managing a hotel?"

"No. I'm a staff manager. I'm playing intermediary between the owner and the hotel staff. He doesn't have hospitality experience, despite his family's big name in it. He went his own way and started a business which services the hospitality industry. He started this hotel as a bet with his father."

"So, you will be the general manager?" Sean assessed.

"That and a sort of personal assistant." I didn't even consider I'd jumped two roles forward. No wonder Colin had been pissed when I'd explained my new role. The others probably picked it up right away. Even now, Sean stopped eating, looking a little perturbed.

"Did I say something wrong?"

Sean shook his head. "I saw you light up in a way I haven't yet. You love your job."

"Don't you?"

"Yes, I do, I just didn't realize you were so passionate about yours," Sean defended.

"I love being self-sufficient," I informed him. "I've spent years working my way to the position I've wanted since I was nine years old, Sean. I'm finally there. Of course, I'm going to be happy about it."

Sean nodded as our mains arrived. "So, you should," he acquiesced.

It was my turn to wait till we were alone. "You seem a little annoyed?"

Meeting my eyes, Sean shook his head and picked up his knife and fork. "I'm just not ready to think about you going home."

Reaching across the table I touched his wrist. "In case you've missed it, I'm a verifiable mess when it comes to relationships, Sean. I inevitably fuck them up. Give it three weeks, and you'll be happy to see the back of me."

Sean smirked wickedly. "Holly, I already do enjoy seeing the back of you. Or did you miss that in my kitchen this morning?"

Hot heat burnt my cheeks and I suddenly felt shy. Sean laughed, but I was already planning how to greet him when he came home this evening. First, I was stashing condoms around the cottage, so he didn't have to stop to find one.

CHAPTER TEN

"Condom," Sean panted. He went to pull away from where he knelt over me on the couch.

"Wait." I grabbed his balls to hold him in my mouth.

"I'm going to cum, Holly," Sean grunted. Searching under the cushion for the condom, I ripped it open. Sean's grip in my hair tightened as he pulled out, my saliva dripping from his tip. "Where did that come from?"

Smirking, I enjoyed his groan as I rolled it over him. "I was prepared."

Standing me up, Sean stripped me down, not that my knickers weren't already flung across the room. Sean spun me around and had me kneel on the lounge. He pushed me forward, then gave my sweet spot another licking for good measure.

"I love how you taste, Holly," Sean rumbled. He stepped in behind me. "I love your arse," he growled, dropping a quick smack to the mentioned anatomy. "Your back." He dropped kisses up my spine, teasing my entrance with his engorged head. He reached around and groped my breasts. "I had so much trouble keeping my eyes above deck that first day we met. These were bursting out of your dress and bikini top." He gripped my hair to turn my head. "And I love this pouty little mouth," he muttered, before crushing my lips in a kiss that made my knees go weak.

Releasing me, Sean jerked my hips back and thrust forward, ramming all the way home on the first stroke. I cried out, fingernails digging into the back of his couch. Moaning with every high-friction stroke of his body in mine, I was coming five thrusts later. Sean hot on my tail. Literally.

I was still gasping for breath, eyes wide as Sean grew large and throbbed inside me. On his next thrust, I heard a popping sound, his stroke after that felt like heaven. Sean swore and pulled out as he came all over my bum and spine. "What the?"

"It was a bit too much, and the condom broke," Sean panted. He looked pained.

His cock was swollen and dripping, the remainder of the condom acting like a tourniquet. Sean rolled it off, gasping somewhere between pleasure and pain as he did. His release started dribbling down my back. Pushing him away, I raced to the bathroom, turning on the shower.

"Holly?" Sean came through the door. "Are you okay?" Sean frowned at me. "That water is cold, Holly. It's just sperm. It's nothing to freak about."

"I'm not freaking about it, I just didn't want to make a mess on your lounge," I sighed. The hot water kicked in, and I could relax.

Sean stepped into the shower with me, caressing my arms. "Are you sure that's all it is because you ran out of there pretty fast?"

My cheeks heated, Sean tipped my chin up to force me to meet his eyes. "It's silly," I murmured.

"Try me," Sean soothed.

Swallowing, my chest and neck were growing as hot as my cheeks and getting worse by the minute. "You got my arse."

Sean looked at me like I was telling an unusual joke. "You freaked out because I came on your arse?"

"No, it ran back down the crack and into my arse." I covered my face embarrassed. "It felt different."

"I take it that's a first for you?" I nodded. "You've never let a guy fuck you there?" I shook my head. "And never had a guy blow on you and felt the trickle effect?" Again, I shook my head, face still hidden in my hands. "Well, that's surprising," Sean snickered.

"Excuse me?" I dropped my hands and glared.

"Well, you've been pretty happy with everything I've done so far, even when I've got a little rough. I assumed we weren't covering new ground." Swallowing, I looked away. Sean stopped. "Wait, Holly, you've been spanked and had your hair pulled and shit before, haven't you?"

Biting my lip, I shook my head. "Actually, no. I mean I've had the thrusting hard and fast, but not the other stuff."

Sean looked me over. "But you were so into it when I grabbed your hair at the restaurant?"

"I've read books about it, and always wanted to have a guy dominate me like that, but you're the first guy who's done it."

Sean looked gobsmacked. "Did you like it?"

Stepping closer, I wrapped my arms around his neck and pulled him closer. "A little too much."

"But you didn't like my spunk going in your backend?"

"I didn't say that. I just wasn't expecting it, and it felt different," I clarified. "It was more the shock of the condom breaking that freaked me, that's all." I reached between us and stroked his flaccid member tenderly. "Did it hurt? It looked like it hurt."

"Hurt?" Sean murmured, starting to grow in my hand. "No, not physically. It was the effort of acknowledging it broke and pulling out. Especially, when what I wanted to do was cum deep inside you."

Closing my eyes, I hung my head back. "God, that makes me so horny," I admitted, pressing my thighs together.

"Me too," Sean whispered against my neck. "Can I tie you up?"

"Yes."

"Can I fuck you and then cum all over your breasts?"

"God, yes," I breathed, gasping as his finger found my clit and threw me into overdrive.

"Not tonight," Sean susurrated against my lips.

I whimpered. "Tonight, is a perfect time. I'm too tired to ride you, so tying me up is a great idea."

Sean chuckled and kissed me. "What was the movie you were watching?"

"No idea," I breathed as his free hand tugged my nipple. In truth, I didn't pay it much attention. When Sean got home, I jumped him as he came in the door. He'd managed to laugh something about me being exhausted, before he'd yanked my underwear off, laid me back on the lounge, and gone to town on my-

"You're right," Sean muttered, breaking through my recall as he reached full hardness in my hand again. "Tonight's a good night to have you tied to my bed."

———

I STRETCHED like a contented cat when Sean's alarm went off. It wasn't till I tried to roll over that I realized my legs were wide apart. "What the...?"

Sean chuckled as he slipped between my thighs. I didn't get to question anything further. My breath rushed out in a moan as Sean shoved into me. Afterwards, I watched him dress for his morning surf. "You coming?" Sean asked, smiling at me.

"Twice already today, I can take a break," I sighed.

"I meant for a surf?"

"I can barely move," I moaned. "My arms feel like lead, my thighs were already sore before you kept them in the air last night, and now I'm pleasurably sore in my lady bits. I'm staying in bed." Sean came towards me. "Na ah," I shook my head. "If you want it tonight, my bat cave needs rest time."

Sean stopped. "Bat cave?"

"Dark and damp, when penetrated it makes winged things cyclone through my stomach, and for weird, unearthly sounds to come out my mouth," I educated.

Sean blinked, then knelt over me laughing. "Okay," he kissed me. "You have nothing on this morning anyway. Get some more sleep. I'll see you for breakfast." Sean kissed me again, and then he was gone, out into the early dawn and the waiting waves. I put my head down and missed breakfast entirely.

Sean left a print out with the itinerary for the next two weeks of island-hopping adventures. Today was his last day of work until he'd be joining me, but once he did, he'd booked us in for something nearly every day. Everything I'd asked to see plus much more. Week three, however, just stated, 'you and me'.

Biting my lip on a blush, I turned my focus back to today. Swimming with dolphins followed by a hike up the Diamond Head Crater. Both took an hour, but with travel time, wouldn't get me back until just before dinner time again. I had a distinct impression that I might not be able to stand tonight.

In swimmers, shorts, a t-shirt, and enough sun cream to protect a rhino from getting burnt, I headed to the sea life park. My dolphin experience consisted of a fin shake, cheek kiss, drag across the pool, and then the dolphins made me fly. Not literally. It was a move called the foot push, but my god, it was amazing.

Still in a buzz and my wet hair pulled back in a ponytail, I was then bused to Diamond Head Crater. The tour included a forty-five-minute hike to the top. Here we walked through a narrow tunnel to climb a spiral staircase to the summit. The view from the top was spectacular. A beautiful panorama of Waikiki, it's emerald hills, and the azure waters of the Pacific Ocean.

Again, my entire body was aching by the time I returned to the hotel. My legs from the hike, and my arms from holding onto the Dolphins. Sean was in the lobby when I came in dragging my feet. "Do I get to tie you up again tonight?" He whispered after he changed direction to intercept me.

"Only if it leads to you massaging my feet and legs." I put my head on his shoulder pretending to sleep. "Maybe my arms too, and my back, and head, and bum."

"Have you stretched?" Sean asked, moving me away to arms distance, then he turned and walked me to the path that led down to the cottages.

"Not yet. I'll do some yoga before my shower."

"Don't come back up for dinner. Just order room service when you are ready."

"Are you sure?" Not that I objected to the idea, I loved it. I just didn't want to miss spending time with him.

"Go rest," Sean smiled. "I'll see you when I get home." He kissed the crown of my head and gave me a covert smack on the bum to send me on the way.

At the cottage, I stripped down to my swimmers, and stepped out onto the white sand in front of Sean's place. Moving through a yoga sequence, I held positions longer to get a more effective stretch.

By the time I finished, I was able to sit and watch the blue disappear from the sky. The daylight washed away by currents of pink, red, orange, and purple, before shifting into the deep blue of tropical twilight.

Finishing my open-eyed meditation, I took myself inside and showered. I already felt more mobile, but the hot shower left me feeling alive again. I left my towel in the bathroom intending to dress and order something to eat, but I only made it as far as the bed.

I woke up to total darkness outside, but the light on in the kitchen. "Sean?" I called, hearing movement out in the lounge room. "God, please let it be Sean," I prayed quietly to myself.

"You're awake?" Sean smiled coming into the room. He was bare chested, just his pants slung low on his hips.

"I fell asleep," I yawned and looked at the clock. It was nearly eleven.

Sean dropped his pants, causing my breath to catch at the sight of him naked. I squirmed in reaction. The bed dipped under Sean's weight and he settled himself above me. "You did, but I needed the time to make some preparations for tomorrow anyway." Sean rubbed my nose with his playfully. "Do you still want that massage?" He ducked his head to my neck and pinched along my carotid.

"I think I'm okay, but I won't say no to a rub down," I breathed.

Sean smiled and moved his hand between my legs. "I could rub down here?"

"Perfect," I moaned and opened my legs for him.

A phone started ringing. I groaned. Sean looked over at the display. "I'll call him back," Sean assured, then he disappeared between my legs.

CHAPTER ELEVEN

"Dad, you called?" Sean spoke on the phone after we'd both cleaned up and showered. "When?" Sean got up and went into the kitchen. "Can you come a couple of days later? I'm going to be away."

I packed up my things while he spoke to his dad arranging dates and times for his visit. It didn't take me long to pack my clothes for the next two weeks of island hopping. Since Sean was still on the phone, I called Trish.

"Aren't you on a boat?" She answered.

"I didn't go on the cruise. I was ready to kill one of my sisters and decided to stay in Hawaii and see more of it."

"Sadie?"

"How'd you guess?"

"Because she's always needed to bring you down to try and make herself feel better about herself. Probably stems from being the former whore in the family."

"Probably."

"So, when will you be back?"

"Not for a couple of weeks. I'm island hopping for the next two weeks, so I might be out of contact at times," I explained. "If you need to get hold of me, just email me."

"Oh, okay," Trish waited a minute. "Send me a photo of him when you hang up."

"Who?"

Trish laughed. "The guy who you stayed behind for."

"How could you possibly know?"

"Come on, how long have we been friends? As if I don't know your 'I met a guy' voice by now. How do you think I knew about Benjamin? Prick. So, who is he?"

"The manager of the hotel we were staying in."

"When they say girls have a type...," Trish teased. "So, is he a worthwhile rebound?"

"Started out rebound, is now a holiday fling."

"Oh god!"

"What?" I asked, worried something had happened.

"Holly, you went away to get over a broken heart, not to break it twice."

"I wasn't in love with Benjamin."

"And I'm a white chick with a skinny arse from England."

Trish was South American. She had a gorgeous figure, despite her focus on her arse, it wasn't sizable. Air hostesses' uniforms only went to a certain size to encourage them to stay svelte. Trish could gain twenty pounds and still wear her work dress.

"You're hot, and you know it. At least you can tan."

"You missed my point."

"No, I ignored it." Sean walked back into the room. He sat on the end of the bed and started massaging one of my feet.

"Just keep reminding yourself it's only sex."

"Only sex. Right. Got it." I winked at Sean. "You have to stop doing that," I told him, "Trish tells me I'm only allowed to use you for sex."

"Just sex?" Sean smirked. "What about tour guide?"

"I'll ask."

"Oh my god," Trish groaned. "It's too late. I'll start preparing the broken heart recovery party now."

"You are such a pessimist," I teased.

"Holly, he lives there, you live here, you must know it's never going to work out?"

"Three weeks, Trish," I assured. "I'll be home in three weeks."

"Sure." Trish hung up.

"Another sister?" Sean asked.

"Flatmate and best friend," I advised. "Your dad is coming to visit?"

"Yeah," Sean frowned a little. "His visit will cross over with your being here, but I've explained I'll be busy and he'll have to enjoy my company on occasion until I go back to work."

"You didn't tell your dad about me?"

Sean smirked. "He guessed I had a woman. I told him I'd let him meet you if he promised to be on good behavior."

Taking my foot out of his grasp, I squirmed a little. "Do you think I should? I mean, I'll be leaving a few days after he gets here, so what's the point?"

"I guess the point would be to be polite. It's two weeks away, Holly, there is a lot of room for growth in that time."

"Growth into what?" I asked confused. Sean stood up, putting his back to me as he stacked our two bags by the door. "Sean, this is a holiday fling. I have a job and life to go back to in Australia. I can't afford to become emotionally invested in a guy who lives ten hours away by plane. Hell, I can't afford the commute to be able to see you on a regular basis. This thing would fizzle and die for you before I even set foot on the Tarmac in Sydney."

"Do you know the biggest problem with our jobs, Holly?" Sean huffed.

I frowned, confused by the change of topic. "No."

"We are always anticipating problems and trying to prevent them, or solve them ahead of time." Sean came back to the bed. "We tend to forget that you can't do that with everything, and relationships is one of those things. You are very good at your job, Holly. I saw that the day we met with the way you solved your room issue. I've seen it in the way you observe my staff and what happens at my hotel." He smiled sadly. "You suck at relationships, and now I know why."

"I do not suck at them. The guys I date fuck them up, just like you are doing by acting like this is one when we agreed it wasn't."

"I agreed to see where this went," Sean clarified. He moved forward on the bed, to be hovering in front of me.

"I can't, Sean. I'm just getting over being fucked over by a guy. I can't…"

"Holly!" Sean snapped calmly. "Stop over analyzing the situation. We enjoy each other's company. You promised me three weeks. Let's take this as it comes."

I met his eyes, thrown by how intent they were on me. "If you make me fall in love with you, I'm going to hate you for it."

Sean caressed my face. "If you make me fall in love with you and leave me, I'm going to come find you, Holly."

"No, you won't."

Sean smiled. "You're right because if I fall in love with you, I'm never going to let you go." He kissed me before I could respond, forcing me back on the bed beneath him.

He kissed me, taking my mind off our different opinions, and tuning it into something more real. Like his firm body pressing mine to his bed. My hands crept across his back and shoulders, tangling my fingers in his hair.

Sean's phone started ringing again. Sean broke away from the kiss and looked at the screen. "Hold that thought," he excused answering the phone. "Dad?" Sean slipped his hand beneath my top to caress me. "Can you email that to me? Will see you then." Sean hung up. "Now, what were we talking about?"

"Fucking," I answered. "Definitely fucking."

CHAPTER TWELVE

THE EARLY DAWN FOUND US BOARDING A DECENT SIZED motorized yacht. "It's mine, and I rent it out for guests to use," Sean explained as we stowed our bags in the bedroom.

"Do I need to use a fluoroscope to check the bed?"

Sean smiled. "It gets professionally cleaned after each hire. It's our home for the next two weeks," he informed me and went back upstairs to the cockpit.

Stowing my gear, I followed him up as he started the engine. "Can I help?"

"Release the lines."

"Um, before I do that," I hesitated. "Do I keep the ropes, or leave them on the jetty?"

Sean chuckled and took me to the first line, showing me how to do it properly. "You get the one at the port bow," Sean directed. I stood there blinking at him. Sean smirked and pointed as he headed back to the cockpit. "Front of the boat."

Releasing the line by myself, I coiled the rope as he had done, then made my way to the cockpit. Sean was already motoring us out from the mooring and carefully past the reef. Once we were out a bit, Sean moved the stick - which I was guessing was the throttle or accelerator - forward. We started speeding through the water north.

"Why not fly?"

"By the time we drove to the airport, caught a charter to the island, drove to another hotel and checked in, we'll be there. Besides, this way we come and go on our timetable, not the airlines." Sean hesitated for a second. "You don't get motion sickness, do you?"

"No, I love boats."

Placing his arm around my waist, Sean pulled me close to him. He kissed me tenderly. His eyes hungry when he pulled away. "I should have hired a skipper," he sighed. "I could have spent time below deck ravishing you."

"You could teach me to drive instead," I suggested. "That way if you get pulled overboard by a shark, I can escape."

Sean looked at me bewildered. "Pulled overboard by a shark?"

"Yeah."

"Does that often happen in your country?" Sean chuckled.

"More than you want to know. Especially when couples go out alone together on the eve of one applying for a divorce."

"Ah, I see."

"I don't think you do," I corrected as he moved my body in front of his and placed my hands on the wheel. "I come from a country where every animal wants to kill you. All the fauna is deadly. Psychopaths creeping through bush, sea, and your own home in some cases."

Sean put his hands around my waist. "That's right, world's most deadly spiders and snakes, right?"

"Don't forget kangaroos, koalas, platypus, sea snakes, blue ring octopus, white pointers, bull sharks - who come into the fresh water - crocodiles, and the drop bears are the worst."

"Drop bears?"

"The worst! The number of campers killed by those... I was terrified of tents as a child by the time my brothers got through warning me about drop bears."

"You're pulling my leg, right?" Sean chuckled. "I mean, don't you ride kangaroos to school as kids?"

"Oh, yeah, sure, but you wouldn't approach someone else's kangaroo. Especially not a wild one. They have claws longer than my hand and can gut someone. Koalas are just as dangerous. We have professionals whose sole job is to keep them off the harbor bridge and opera house. Little bastards climb all over the city buildings and take chunks out of them. They leave huge gouges in the glass and stone. Very dangerous if they get you alone after dark."

Sean was quiet behind me for a moment. I was struggling to keep the smile off my face and my voice serious.

"You know I'm looking this up when we reach port right?" Sean whispered in my ear. "If you are bullshitting me, I'm going to spank you till your bum cheeks match the sunset."

I squirmed against him. "Now I wish I'd lied and told you they were cute and cuddly."

Sean's fingers gripped my waist as his body reacted to my bum rubbing against his groin. "Lord, have mercy. Let's focus on you driving the boat."

Sean taught me to slow the boat, stop it, and start it again during the three hours to the island Kauai. Our first stop was the Wailua Marina where we were only stopping for the afternoon. We joined the afternoon kayak tour to secret falls. Sean and I shared a tandem kayak up the Wailua River. He sat in the back as the strongest of us and insisted on taking photos of me paddling. He also started a water fight with me halfway up the river by 'accidentally' splashing me.

We left the kayaks and hiked to secret falls where we swam beneath the fall with the rest of the group. Sean and I frolicking and flirting like horny teenagers. By the time we returned to our boat, it was approaching sunset. We cruised down to Lihue and docked there for the night.

We ate dinner on the wharf before taking an evening stroll along the coastline. "We have an early morning tomorrow," Sean murmured in my ear as we lay intertwined in bed later. "We should think about sleeping."

I panted something like yes, before Sean gently circled his hips again. We were both covered in sweat, enjoying a slow, intimate session. Sean was taking his sweet time, making me praise him and God repeatedly for the last hour or so.

Sean's smile beamed in the low light of our cabin. "I want to cum, but I'm enjoying being here, inside of you too much."

It had been a long day, but I knew exactly what he meant. "I want you to sleep inside me. I want you to cum, then put it back inside me bare, and sleep there."

Sean closed his eyes, Adam's apple bobbing, neck muscles straining. Sucking his earlobe into my mouth, I bit down a little till he groaned and thrust deeper. I smiled releasing his ear. "Pin me down and fuck me, Sean."

Needing no further encouragement, Sean pinned my hands above my head and pounded me hard and deep. I was breathless, pleasure racking my body, making me arch and beg for him to fill me with his cum.

Sean obliged me, growing significantly in girth, my eyes bulging at the feel as he hammered me. A moment later Sean cried out, his hips jolting with each heaving spurt of climax. It felt amazing, so much so, that my own body reacted and I came for him again.

Holding himself trembling above me, Sean opened his eyes and looked down at me. His eyes glittered in the night, thoughts racing. I could see it, see that he wanted to say something to me. My own heart was beating double time. "That was amazing."

Sean smiled, dropped a kiss to my lips and he fell beside me breathless. He went to the bathroom, then came back and snuggled in behind me. "I washed," he soothed as he slid his still semi-hard cock back inside me and wrapped me in his arms.

I didn't care. I was on birth control, and I believed Sean when he told me he was clean. It would do no physical harm. "Did you use condoms with her," I asked half asleep.

"I loved her," he replied, casually, as if that answered everything.

It made me think about that sentiment and what it meant to me. Was I in love with Benjamin? Was that why I was happy to forgo protection with him? I know condoms didn't mean anything to him but an inconvenience. I was so caught up in his interest in me, it hadn't bothered me.

I'd only been with my fiancé before Benjamin, and we'd always used protection out of my fear of getting knocked up. "I've only had unprotected sex with Ben," I whispered. "That doesn't mean I loved him."

Sean's breathing, which had been heavy, changed for a moment. His arm tightened his hold on me. "I only claim what I intend to keep." I frowned at his words, not awake enough to process it.

"Get some sleep, Holly," he urged. The kiss on my shoulder made me smile. Bare naked sex didn't mean love to me, but Sean's kisses were starting to mean something.

CHAPTER THIRTEEN

AT TEN THE NEXT MORNING WE WERE ON TOUR IN THE KAUAI backcountry on a zip line adventure. We flew above the lush tropical rainforest canopy, zipped across valleys and gullies, and soared over streams.

We followed that up with a trip to the enchanting Hali'i waterfall to enjoy a picnic lunch and swim. We'd found a space of our own beside the tiered waterfall, enjoying a walk through the rainforest to get there. We sat watching the splendor of the falls and just enjoying being with each other. "Hali'i, in Hawaiian, means to cover like a blanket," Sean murmured as he covered my body with his on the bank.

I smiled up at him as he moved his hand down my waist to shift the gusset of my swimsuit aside. "Is this an appropriate place?"

Sean smiled as he unzipped himself, eyes looking around to make sure we were still alone. "It's a magnificent place."

He kissed my mouth heatedly as he pressed into me. I gasped

feeling how turned on he was. Lifting my hips, I encouraged both of us to get there sooner. Any of the others on tour could decide a walk in the rainforest would be good.

I couldn't believe that the sex with Sean just kept on getting better and better each day. When my body tightened with delight, I bit Sean's shoulder to prevent anyone else hearing me find paradise.

Sean grunted in my ear and quickly pulled back, letting his release fertilize the earth. Sitting up, I righted my clothing and watched his seed soak into the soil. "You just seeded the earth," I teased.

Sean grinned fixing himself up and collapsed into my lap. "Next time we come here, there might be a tree with juicy, delicious fruit on it."

I laughed. "It will be rather popular, possibly the world's best aphrodisiac."

Sean lifted a brow. "World's best?"

I blushed. "Well, the best in my world, so far."

"Hmm. I might have to up my game, ensure I keep the world's best title for the rest of your days."

I smiled at him. He smiled back, caressing my cheek. "You blush so easily, Holly."

"Its new for me. You started it."

The happiness reached Sean's eyes as he pulled my mouth to his. "So, you blush only for me."

"You have that effect on me."

Something serious flashed in Sean's eyes as he brushed his lips over mine. He pulled me to him, and I went willingly. Lying in his arms, kissing in paradise.

That afternoon, we took our last walk through Lihue. We enjoyed a casual meal before retiring to the yacht for the night. Watching a movie in each other's arms, we fell asleep much the same way.

Sean woke me early in the morning, his body hard and eager for me. I knew I was going to miss this when I went home, but it was an experience I needed.

"You need to stop lying there grinning and get ready for the day. Our tour leaves at nine," Sean teased as he stepped out of the shower with just a towel around him.

Eying him up, I grabbed the towel pulling him onto the bed. "That's still plenty of time for more of you."

Sean laughed as he covered my body with his. The towel flung across the room as he gave me a second helping of holiday lust. I was giddy and grinning madly as we raced to the tour office, barely making our ride.

After being fitted with gloves, a helmet and headlamp, we climbed into a four-wheel drive and headed inland. We crossed old sugar cane fields as the guide explained the history of the plantation.

"Around eighteen seventy a series of ditches were hand-dug by Chinese laborers to deliver water from the rainforest to the sugar cane fields. This land is privately owned and only recently been accessible to the public after the closure of the plantation," the guide educated us. He then went on to tell us about the lives of the workers.

The car stopped for a photo op at a lookout that gave the best view of Waialeale Crater away from a helicopter tour. A few minutes later, we arrived at the start of the narrow man-made channel and were provided with a safety demonstration.

"It's a pity we can't share," Sean whispered before he climbed into his tube and prepared for the ride.

"I could sit on your lap the entire way, but I'm worried it could get dangerous."

"True, the spectators may get jealous." Sean's eyes went to the group of young men standing in line. I smiled shaking my head and dropping into my tube.

It was a cross between mild white water rafting and a lazy river ride. The water was knee deep in most places, and the current moved us along fast enough that no paddling was required.

Every opportunity Sean could, he caught my hand and held it. We floated in and out of tunnels, one of which was almost one and a half kilometers long. We glided hand in hand with only dim headlamps to light our way through. My fear of never emerging was only dampened by Sean's hand in mine.

At the end of the tubing adventure, the guides served up a picnic lunch at a beautiful, natural swimming hole. Sean and I sat hand in hand while we ate, then we splashed and hugged as we swam with the other tourists.

On the way back to the tour office, we sat side by side. My head rested on Sean's muscular chest, his arm firmly around my shoulders. "Thank you for insisting I stay." Smiling, I linked fingers with his free hand. "It's already been an experience I won't soon forget."

Sean kissed the top of my head, his arm wrapping me tighter to him. He didn't need to say anything in response. I found the silence between us to be more comfortable then I could ever imagine.

Returning to the boat after lunchtime, we headed to our next destination. The far side of the Kauai island. We arrived at the Na Pali coast in the late afternoon. The sun casting a dramatic light upon the majestic cliffs.

"It's considered to be the Jewel of Kauai." Sean wrapping me in his arms as we observed the breathtaking beauty of it.

"I can see why."

"Those cliffs are close to three thousand feet."

"I live in the metric world," I teased. Lifting my camera, I stepped free to take photos.

Sean steered the boat while I took photos of the green valleys, hidden beaches, and magnificent secluded waterfalls that dropped from hanging valleys into the ocean below. It was absolutely breathtaking.

"I want to get a photo of you," I told Sean.

Stopping the boat, he came to me. "You can have one of the both of us." He took the camera and held it away from us as he took me in his arms. Taking out my phone, I connected remotely to the camera to line up the shot then posed and tapped my screen to take the photo. The camera clicked.

"Keep tapping," Sean whispered as he turned his face to mine and kissed me.

When he pulled back, I knew my happiness was shining out from my insides. It was the happiest I could ever remember being.

We ate dinner on the deck watching the sun begin to set. Before it became too dark, Sean took to the wheel and cruised us toward our destination for the night. Twenty minutes south.

That night, the heat between us was remarkable. Sean took me slow and deep, making me wait for my release. Every touch and kiss was intense. I had to believe it was an enchantment of this place, this paradise on earth.

I fell asleep in Sean's arms, drawing randomly through the sheen of perspiration on his skin. We both needed showers but couldn't bear to disturb what just happened between us.

"I wish this holiday never had to end," I whispered when his breathing grew heavy. "I've never had a more perfect week than this."

————

"SEAN," a deep voice called as heavy footsteps thumped above deck. "Cassidy, you in there?" A big fist thumped on the hatch above the room.

Sean muttered a curse and rolled out of bed pulling his shorts on as the banging started again. "Give it a break, Tama. I'm not alone."

"Crap, sorry, Sean."

Sean opened the door and made his way above deck while I grumbled and tried to find my clothes with my eyes closed. I finally managed to pull knickers and a dress on, then went to find out if we were being pirated or something.

As I came above deck, I blinked into the early dawn light. Sean stood at the back of the boat talking to a man twice his breadth and of Polynesian descent. He was bulk muscle and the sort of guy if you met in the dark, you'd wet yourself.

His eyes came to me over Sean's shoulder, and his lips pulled up on one side. "Girlfriend?" The man tilted his head towards me.

Sean turned and put his arm out towards me. "Not yet. Tama, meet Holly, she's on holiday, and I'm showing her the best of Hawaii."

"And you brought her to meet me. I'm flattered," Tama smiled and pulled me into a hug. "It's nice to meet you, Holly. Where do you come from?"

"Australia," I muffled a yawn. Sean smirked and tucked me into his side to kiss the top of my head.

"Australia?" Tama's brows jumped. "Well, that's a bit away."

"Holly is in the hotel business as well," Sean informed his friend. "Tama runs my resort and tour company here in Waimea."

I felt my brows lift but didn't comment on the news that he owned more than one resort. "And he's here at the crack of dawn to give you his report?" I grumbled instead.

Tama chuckled. "Business happens via email. No, I heard Sean was on holiday and saw the yacht moored here. I thought I'd drag Sean out for a spot of fishing. Do you like fishing, Holly?"

"Not as much as I like sleeping, Tama," I tried to hide another yawn.

Sean's body shook with restrained laughter beside me. "I might pass, Tama. I'm taking Holly to Ni'ihau in a few hours for snorkeling and then heading back to O'ahu for the night before continuing to Maui."

"Will you be stopping in Moloka'i?" Tama lifted a curious brow.

Sean shrugged a shoulder. "We'll spend a couple of days there before we head back."

Sean's answer surprised Tama. He looked me over this time, from head to toe. "Well, I won't keep you. You're going to be traveling a fair distance the next few days. Promise me you'll visit again soon for a fish."

Sean smiled. "I'll be here for our usual catch up."

Tama smiled at me. "Will you be joining us on that visit, Holly?"

I shook my head. "No, I'm heading home in a little over two weeks."

Tama looked to Sean whose mouth lifted on one side like I'd told a cute joke. Tama shook his head. "Well, it was nice meeting you, Holly. Keep your eyes open on the crossing to the island. There are lots of dolphins and whales this time of year. I'll see you in three weeks, Sean."

Tama left us shaking his head and laughing softly to himself. Sean turned me to him and kissed me. The kiss was gentle and tentative. When Sean pulled back, there was a crease in his brows. I used my thumb to iron it out. "Something wrong?"

Sean inhaled deeply. "Last night, the two of us."

I smiled. "That was pretty intense. Those cliffs definitely had an effect."

"Oh, it was the cliffs?" Sean queried humored.

"Absolutely. I'd say it was the best sex of my life." I stopped and thought about it. "Yep, definitely the best. I doubt you could repeat or improve upon last night."

"I believe that's a challenge, Miss Claire."

I smirked backing up. "Oh, you think you could top that?"

"Absolutely." Sean stalked towards me. His eyes twinkled.

I squeaked and ran below deck for the cabin. Sean was right behind me. He tackled me in the narrow aisle and pinned me to the wall. His hands were under my dress relieving me of my underwear, his mouth searching mine for submission.

My hands shoved Sean's shorts to the floor; then I pressed my feet against the opposite wall to lift myself for him. Sean groaned as I slipped him between my folds and he found my moist core.

Sean pulled back, tilting my face so I could look down into his lust filled eyes. "You make me wild for you, Holly. Make me want to throw caution to the wind, to lose control, but I hate not cumming in you."

I bit my lip at the hunger in his eyes. He searched my face, looking for an answer to a secret question. I forced his mouth to mine and kissed him heatedly. Sean moaned and gripped my bum. He turned towards the cabin, holding me above him as he walked.

In the cabin, he dropped me on the bed and quickly collected a condom while I yanked my dress over my head. Sean crawled into the bed with me, his hunger raw in his eyes. I knew what he wanted, but as I turned to lay on my stomach and lift my hips for him, I worried there was more to his hunger than lust.

As he pressed me into the bed, I gripped the sheets and closed my eyes. There was something between Sean and I that went beyond physical desire. I knew that from the moment we met. I thought it was like what I had with Benjamin, but as I thought back, I realized, it had always been more than that.

"Fuck," I moaned, realizing I was entering dangerous waters with Sean, but I couldn't walk away now. I didn't want to. I wanted my three weeks of paradise. My heart would need to barricade itself against anything more. My head and body needed this.

Sean circled his hips inward, plunging into my depths, reaching for a part of me I couldn't risk him reaching. I whimpered and moaned, wondering if he was already farther in than I knew.

My body seized on the awareness, and I cried out helpless, surrendering my body to the effect Sean had on me. As we lay panting, I buried my face in the pillow and cursed at myself. Suddenly, that three-week deadline couldn't come fast enough and was too soon all at once.

Huffing, I sagged into the mattress. I wasn't going to give up my dream job for a man I met on holiday. I was determined. Sex and fun. That's all this could be. No matter what, I was going home at the end of three weeks.

CHAPTER FOURTEEN

"Where are we going?" I asked Sean as he carried my bag away from the boat.

"It's a surprise."

Smiling, I walked beside him to the road where a taxi was waiting. "If I remember correctly, the itinerary stated today and tomorrow were Molokai. But it didn't state what we were doing here."

"You sound suspicious."

"I am. I'm ready to bum around on the beach and read a book. This island looks like the hiking and extreme sports kind of place."

Sean held the door for me to hop in the taxi. He caught my mouth as I stepped up to him. "It's a surprise."

Taking the hint, I enjoyed the scenic drive from the harbor around the shore and up into the mountains. The taxi dropped us at a cottage and Sean led the way inside. Buggered - not in the sodomized sense, just tired - I followed. So far, we'd spent every day on all the adventure tours I wanted to do, plus extra that Sean declared necessary. There was nothing left on my list to do.

I walked through the neatly decorated cottage to the back deck. This part of the cottage sat on poles over the forest canopy below. In awe, I stepped outside and took in the view. Across the ocean, I could see a city skyline on a distant shore. "Is that Maui?"

"Sure, is." Sean wrapped his arms around me from behind. "Beautiful isn't it?"

"Not even close to the right adjective," I breathed.

"This is my place here. My hide away from the world. I've always come here alone. But, this time, I wanted to bring you here, Holly." Flattered, I gazed out into the distance, still in awe of the raw natural beauty before me. "Holly, I've grown to like you very much these past few weeks. I'd like you to consider staying longer."

Frowning, coming back to the here and now, I tried to comprehend what Sean was asking. "I thought we were staying two nights? Don't you have to get back to your dad?"

Sean turned me to face him, keeping me close. "We are, and we can come back here whenever you want, if you stay. Don't go home, yet."

My mouth moved, my brain scrambling to find something to say. Nothing came out.

"I know I'm asking a lot, but there is something more than a fling between us, Holly. Something worth pursuing long term." Sean swept my hair back from my face. "Don't answer today.

We have two days here with nothing to distract us, and we're stuck in each other's pocket. What I'd like you to keep in the back of your mind, is if you want to leave without exploring what could be us."

I took a deep breath. Sean pressed his finger to my lips. "I said don't answer today. Just keep the idea in the back of your mind."

Waiting till Sean took his finger away, I licked my lips and nodded. I'd think about it, but I knew my answer. Sean smiled. "I'll go unpack our bags and make us some lunch."

"You have food here?".

"I have a housekeeper. She stocks the fridge for me when I let her know I'm coming."

"So, what is our plan for the rest of the day?" I asked, following him back inside.

"No plans. The next two days are carefree us time."

"Huh," I replied nonchalantly. I lifted myself to sit on the kitchen counter. "So, if I just want to lay around reading?"

Sean lifted a brow. "I have a few books to read too. Happy to lay around with you."

———

I WOKE up in Sean's arms two mornings later. Sean's question front and center of my mind. To say the last two days were bliss would be an understatement. Sean and I seemed to fit without either of us trying. We sat around reading; we were intimate, we cooked and laughed together as we got to know each other better.

We would be leaving this place of peace today to return to Oahu and life. These two days were going to stay entrenched in my memory for the rest of my life above any other over the last two weeks. The moment where my eyes fluttered open, my heart rippled in the happiness of the moment, and I realized I was in love.

I wanted to forehead slap myself, but I couldn't get the smile off my face. It was a collision of happiness and misery, and neither emotion was willing to give an inch. I was flying home in four days. Home. To my friends and the job, I'd always aspired to have. But, to leave meant I gave up the best relationship of my life. Sean could be the one. Could I walk away from him, board a plane, and continue with my life without regretting it?

It was the fork in the road. The one people always remembered. The choice of two futures, either choice you win and lose. My career, or love? Could it remain heaven? I wasn't stupid enough to think that there wouldn't be ups and downs, but it could be close to perfect.

As if hearing my thoughts, Sean woke up, or, a very hard part of him woke and tapped my bum cheek. By the time I rolled to face him, Sean's eyes were open, his mouth smiling at me. His eyes observed mine, and for a moment he hesitated. He searched my eyes, and then a smile bloomed across his face.

"It will be worth it, Holly." His mouth brushed mine, his hand skimmed over my waist. "I'll make a few calls about jobs that are available for you when I get back today. That way, you'll know the opportunity you are giving up to be with me, will still exist with me."

"I'm considering it; it's not set in stone, Sean. I'll still need to go home and get my stuff, and I can't just leave Trisha high and dry."

Sean pulled me closer. "I'll come with you. I've always wanted to visit Australia."

"You want to make sure I don't change my mind once I get home," I teased.

"It's a hard decision to make, Holly. I understand what you are giving up to try being with me. I also know how influential friends can be. They use fear to talk sense into you, rather than encouraging you to follow your heart."

"Don't make me regret this, Sean. Tell me anything now you think may be a problem for us?"

Sean opened his mouth just as his phone started ringing. The curse that came out directed at his phone was impressive. "Hello?" He answered rolling away. "What happened?" Sean scrubbed his hand through his hair while he listened. "Damn it! Okay. I'll call and organize a car. I'll be back at the resort by nine and will sort that out when I get there."

Sean hung up his phone and turned to look at me. "Work could be a problem. Then there is my father."

"What about him?"

Sean sighed. "You'll understand when you meet him, which, is going to be sooner than later. He's landed at the airport, five hours earlier than expected and I need to organize a car to collect him since I'd booked one for later. We need to get back. Two weeks without a major incident was asking too much."

"Another celebrity?" I asked climbing out of bed.

"Cheating spouse. Got busted by the other partner and the

husband threw punches at the other guy," Sean explained. "Unfortunately, that other guy is one of my employees."

"Ouch!"

"Tell me about it. The police are there. Just the sort of shit I needed." Sean scrubbed his head again and started scrolling his phone for a number. "You shower first. I'll join you once I've at least got one problem sorted."

An hour later we arrived at the marina and boarded Sean's boat. It took us a little over two hours to get back to the Cassidy resort. We took our luggage back to Sean's and then Sean left me there to deal with his business. I started looking into visa applications.

After realizing what a pain moving to Hawaii was going to be just in getting a visa. I sighed and collapsed on the lounge. I found my phone and called home. Trisha didn't answer, telling me she was either asleep or working. "Hey, you're going to hate me. Sean's asked me to stay longer, and I think I want to try. I've never connected with a guy like this. What if I never meet another guy who gets me like this one? It's worth trying, isn't it? I'll speak with you soon. Love you."

With nothing else to do, I changed, grabbed Sean's board and went for a surf. The weather wasn't fantastic. The waves were breaking a bit close to shore, but I still managed to enjoy myself. We'd had some rain while away. Sean wouldn't let that stop us from doing whatever he planned that day. Every day for the past two and a half weeks had been fantastic.

By lunchtime, I showered and dressed and was back to trying to work out the logistics of moving my life to Hawaii. This time, I was on the phone to the American consulate about the best visa for which I could apply. Sean came home and sat beside me, looking over all the information I'd scribbled down on a notepad. "Okay, thank you," I hung up.

"That's rather a heavy sigh?" Sean smirked.

"I think you'll have to find someone to run your resort and move to Australia to keep dating me. Fewer hoops to jump through." Pushing the list of what he would have to do to move to Australia next to the one for me to move here.

"You looked up what I needed to do?" Sean chuckled. "Well, at least I know you are serious about being with me, and it's not the venue making this decision for you."

"Absolutely not. Beautiful as it is here, I love my country." I pushed the lists away. "Has your dad arrived?"

"Yes. He's settling into his room."

"And the police?"

"Sorted. The guests involved have left, albeit separately. My former employee has decided not to press charges and resigned."

"You didn't fire him?"

"I would have. But, by resigning he gets paid out his leave. Since he was working while injured, his insurance will cover his medical fees."

"You gave him a choice, didn't you?"

"He assured me the affair occurred while he was off shift, but the man accosted him during his shift. It's fair." Sean took my hand and stood. "I'm not officially back at work, so we have the afternoon to ourselves. How about we go back to bed and wake up properly?"

Smirking, I stood, placing my bum on the table. "There is a perfectly good table right here."

Sean's lips twitched on the side. He moved between my thighs, arms wrapping around my waist. "I want to cum in you, Holly. The condoms are in the bedroom."

Butterflies took flight in my stomach. I met his ocean blue eyes, and I never wanted to stop staring at them. "We can start here, finish there."

Sean cupped my cheek in his hand. "We will start here and continue in the bedroom." His mouth brushed mine, his body moving forward to press me back on the table till he hovered over me. Staring into my eyes, his eyes became serious. "I never intend to finish with you, Holly."

CHAPTER FIFTEEN

"You look nervous," Sean smirked as he pulled my chair out for dinner.

"I'm about to meet your dad after knowing you for three weeks. It's insane."

"Relax, Holly. He's just my dad," Sean chuckled. "And if it helps, he met my mother one day and proposed the next. My father is a big believer in love at first sight."

My eyes watched Sean as he took the seat next to me. "Do you?"

"I wouldn't have sent you the dessert that first night if I didn't," Sean revealed. "You already twisted my arm into a suite with free breakfast. I own three resorts, Holly. I'm not usually that bad at business."

"You thought I was a porn star."

"Not when we first met. When I ran into you on the path, I was deep in thought wondering how I would handle it if you were. Thankfully, that wasn't the case. So, dessert." He winked at me. His eyes moved to the entry, and he stood again. I recognized his father walking towards us and rose as well.

"Sean," his dad grinned and hugged him.

"Dad, this is Holly Claire. Holly, my father Raymond Cassidy," Sean introduced.

I put my hand out. Raymond shook it firmly. "Lovely to meet you, Holly. Any relation to Nathan Claire?"

My tongue felt too big for my mouth. "Do you think Claire is that uncommon a surname in Australia?"

"Sean told me your father was in politics. I made the connection," Raymond defended politely.

"He's my father."

"Ah," Raymond looked intrigued. He took his seat, and I sat back down. "So, how long have you two been seeing each other?"

"Three weeks," Sean replied taking my hand in his. "Best three weeks of my life. So far."

"Do you live locally, Holly?"

"No, I am on holidays."

Raymond raised a brow. "Oh, when do you go home?"

"Sunday," I answered.

"And what do you do for work?" Raymond inquired.

"I'm effectively a general manager for a resort."

Raymond smiled. "So, you come here regularly to check in on the Hawaiian branch of your resort?"

My brows furrowed. "Ah, no. I was here on holiday with my sisters."

Raymond looked confused; he tilted his head in question at Sean. Sean put his hand over mine. "Holly stayed on three extra weeks to be with me. Her older sisters cruised back. I'm trying to convince Holly to stay on permanently."

"Oh, I see," Raymond smiled in relief. "And is he succeeding, Holly?"

"He was until I saw the criteria for my getting a visa. I've suggested Sean moving to Australia would be easier."

"You expect him to give up his life, everything he has built here to follow you?" Raymond accused.

I raised a brow. "If it didn't work out, Sean would still have his resorts here and return to his home. He would possibly gain by opening a new resort in Australia, giving his brand an overseas market. If I move here, I give up my dream job, my apartment, my friends and my life. If it doesn't work out, I've got nothing to go home to, Raymond. You think that is the fairer option?"

Raymond sat back. "I suppose not." Raymond looked at his son. "Are you considering moving to Australia?"

"No, dad. I couldn't return to a busy city lifestyle after ten years here. Currently, the plan is for Holly to relocate here. If visas become an issue, we will discuss other options then."

Raymond seemed satisfied with this answer and opened his menu to browse. Sean lifted my hand off the table and kissed my palm. When I met his eyes, he winked at me. "So, how are negotiations going for that place in Ko Olina?" Raymond asked.

"Stalled currently. I made an offer, but the owner is trying to get someone to outbid me. I've told them if they don't accept by Monday, I'll rescind my offer."

"Do you think they will take it?" Raymond raised a brow.

"If they don't, they will struggle to find someone who will offer even close to what I have and risk bankruptcy."

"Well, if that goes well, you could offer Holly your role here while you get the new resort operational."

Sean squeezed my hand gently. "Dad, you know I have a code about relationships with my staff. Holly also needs to have her independence. There are plenty of opportunities for her here."

Raymond turned to me with raised brows. "He's very headstrong, Holly. Are you sure you are capable of enduring him?"

"That's what we are going to find out, Raymond."

Raymond's eyes glinted. After we ordered our meals, Raymond turned his attention back to Sean. They discussed golf, the weather, the new president-elect, issues of state, and issues in Hawaiian politics. Truthfully, the political talk was getting the best of me by the time dessert came.

"Are you planning on relaxing while here, Raymond? Or are you like Sean and need to be doing something while the sun is up?"

The men laughed. "Well, you figured us out already," Raymond conceded. "I'm booked into the sunrise hike. Sean won't pass up his morning surf to come with me. Maybe you would like to make the trek with me, Holly?"

"Holly surfs with me in the morning, dad."

"She can do that anytime," Raymond objected. "I only make it over here once a year. She should spend time with me. Get to know the old bastard you're going to grow into."

"You look too young and fit for anyone to be calling you an old bastard, Raymond," I laughed. "And I'd love to do the Sunrise hike with you. You can start telling me all the embarrassing youth stories about Sean."

Raymond smiled. Sean shook his head, but his lips pulled up. He was happy I was making an effort. That night, when we got back to his place, he showed me how glad he was.

———

THE NEXT MORNING found me hiking alongside Raymond and six others. The weather was muggy, and I was sticky with sweat by the time we reached the peak to watch the sunrise.

"Worth the effort?" Raymond inquired with a smile.

"Anything worth having, usually is," I murmured. Closing my eyes, the sun blanketed me in its golden rays. The group fell quiet as we all enjoyed the peace of the moment. That first impact of sunlight for the day was always magical for me. I couldn't explain why. It just was.

The sun lifted and released its hold on me. I felt energized. Opening my eyes, I found Raymond observing me with a smile. "Has Sean told you much about his mother?"

"Just that she died while he was young," I sympathized. "And, that you loved her a lot."

Raymond smiled. "More than life." He walked away from the group a little, so I followed. "I met her at a charity function when I was twenty-two. I had just started as a junior in my father's law firm, and she was the assistant event manager for the function. It was her first big gig, and she wanted to make an impression. That meant it had to go perfectly," Raymond reminisced.

"Did it all go to hell?".

Raymond guffawed. "With Beth at the helm? Not likely. That woman was as determined as they come. No, the night went without a glitch. I watched her all night. I admired the way she handled the staff, and how she solved major problems without incident. Especially, how damned beautiful she was."

Raymond turned his head to meet my eyes. "She wasn't what would be considered beautiful by today's standards. But in the sixties, she could outshine Marilyn Monroe."

I smiled, getting a picture of the woman. Raymond turned his eyes back to the sunset. "The night was over, and people starting to leave, when she came up to me. Collecting a champagne glass and sipping it she asked me my name." Raymond's eyes twinkled. "We chatted about the evening. Eventually, she huffed and asked if I thought I might ask her to dance before the band stopped playing. I did. We danced. Then I walked her to the bus stop for her to get home. The last bus was pulling away as we turned the corner."

"So, you offered her a ride home?" I asked trying to guess the story.

"God, no. I was drunk," Raymond admitted. "My father drummed the whole drink driving thing into us boys before it was even a thing."

"Rather pioneering," I complimented.

"No, I took her home with me," Raymond smirked. "She wasn't as easy as she was forward. We stayed out on the back patio talking all night. Our hopes and dreams, ambitions and hesitations, our desires and needs." Raymond turned to face me. "But it wasn't until the sun rose and shined upon her face, that I saw the real woman hidden beneath. She closed her eyes and absorbed the first rays of light. The true meaning of peace revealed itself to me at that moment."

"Ah," I smiled understanding. "You came on this hike to be with your wife."

Raymond chuckled. "I am always with her, Holly." He tapped his left chest. "She's always with me. There has been no other since that day. When she opened her eyes again, I got down on one knee and asked her to marry me. She smiled, looked at the time and told me she needed to get home."

"So, she didn't say yes?"

"Not immediately. I drove her home, and she introduced me to her dad. So, I did the proper thing and asked him for her hand. He had four daughters. He was glad to be rid of one," Raymond laughed.

"That's not as sweet as I was expecting."

Raymond met my eyes. "Back in those days, women were expected to keep house, Holly. Beth told me straight up she was keeping her career, and she did. She was punished for it when she got pregnant the first time, effectively told by her boss to go home and be a proper wife. It took her a year to get her career back on track after that, only for her to fall pregnant again." Raymond studied my eyes. "I was sure she would resent me, her sons, for making her dreams harder to reach, but she didn't. She loved her boys, and she loved showing everyone she could be a good wife and mother and still have her dreams too."

I looked out at the horizon. "You are telling me the sacrifice to be with Sean will be worth it."

Raymond's eyes sparkled. "Sean has my spirit and drive, but he has his mother's determination. If you love him, Holly. He will support your dreams, and do what he can to see you fulfill them. All he will ever ask is for your love and devotion."

"I'm not exactly a religious girl, Raymond. But, if it's fidelity you worry about, that's never been an issue. I am loyal for as long as he is."

Raymond nodded. "Good. Should we head back? I was thinking of a surf myself this morning."

"If you don't object, I'll join you."

Raymond was pleasantly surprised. "You don't have to hang out with me, Holly. Neither Sean nor I will think bad of you."

"Oh, trust me, I'm not doing this to be nice," I snickered. "I'm still waiting for all those embarrassing stories you promised last night."

Raymond chortled. "You're gorgeous. Okay, let's start with my favorite…"

CHAPTER SIXTEEN

WALKING INTO THE RESTAURANT, I WENT UP ON MY TIPPY TOES to find my dinner companions. Raymond and Sean sat at Sean's usual table. Smiling, I made my way to join them. They were talking pretty intently and didn't notice me approach.

I was just a table away when Henry walked the opposite way. "Evening, Miss Claire."

"Evening, Henry."

Sean's head snapped up. "We'll discuss it later, dad," Sean ended their conversation. He stood, giving me a genuine smile and welcoming hug. His lips brushed my cheek, and he lingered a little as he inhaled my hair. "How did it go?" Sean inquired as I took the seat beside him.

"Good. It's only a maternity relief position, but it's twelve months of paid work, and they would be willing to sponsor me."

"So, you accepted the role?" Raymond asked enthusiastically.

"Well, no, they haven't offered it yet. Kerry said she would get back to me by tomorrow evening, so I have time to make arrangements before I fly home."

Raymond turned to Sean. "Are you flying out Sunday as well?"

"I can't. I've just taken two weeks of leave," Sean advised. "Holly is flying home alone. She will make arrangements from there, and once her visa is approved, I will fly over. We'll spend a week in Australia finalizing everything before we come home."

"Sounds like you have it all planned out. Hopefully, the visa won't take too long."

I forced a smile. One of the things I needed to take care of when I got home, was telling Roger I wasn't accepting my dream job. I had no hesitation moving country to be with Sean, but I hated the idea of giving up that position. Roger and Sammy were great, and I'd been looking forward to working with them.

"Everything okay, Holly?" Sean asked as his dad excused himself, answering his phone.

"Yeah, just haven't heard from Trisha. She normally gets back to me within two days." It had been three days since I left the message. I didn't want to arrive back to a tirade, or worse, a room full of my sisters and an intervention.

"Maybe she needs time to process the news?" Sean suggested.

"Possibly."

After dessert Raymond excused himself for the fifth phone call since I joined them. "Your dad is popular tonight," I queried Sean.

Sean nodded and threw his napkin on the table. "And it looks like I'm about to get as busy." I followed Sean's eyes to the doorway, where Henry was signaling Sean. Sean stood up, bending down to kiss my head. "I'll see you back home."

Taking his hand, I stopped him leaving. "I thought you weren't back at work until Monday?"

Sean gave me a frustrated look. Nearly every day since we got back, he'd spent hours disappearing to deal with work. "I'm sorry, Holly. This isn't just a job to me. It's my business." He squeezed my hand and walked off.

Looking around, I noticed Raymond had wandered out by the pool. Giving up, I placed my napkin on the table and made my way back to the cottage. Changing into exercise gear, I spent an hour doing a flowing vinyasa yoga on the beach.

When I came back inside, Sean still wasn't home. After showering, I checked my phone. I'd missed a call from Trisha while I'd been on the beach.

"Are you insane?" Trisha answered when I called her back. "You've known the guy four weeks, Holly. Four weeks! You have taken this rebound thing too far. Now, listen to me. You need to say goodbye to his gorgeous arse, get on a plane, and come home."

I waited to make sure she finished. "I'm in love with him."

The silence stretched out. Finally, Trisha exhaled. "Well, damn! I guess I need to apply for a job with Hawaiian airlines. If you are moving your skinny white arse to paradise, so am I."

My mouth fell open. "Really?"

"Yes! And, we are going to live together. You are going to date this guy for a proper length of time. Then, when I deem it true love, he can propose. You'll have a proper engagement, wedding, etc., and then I will let you move in with him," Trisha lectured. "I'm not letting you rush into this, Holly. That heart of yours is too fragile for this spontaneous love shit. You need to step back a few meters, and do this thing properly."

"You're going to move to Hawaii with me?" I asked getting excited.

"Hell, yes! I meant what I said, Holly. We'll get our own place. Deal?"

My smile stretched across my face. "You are the bestest friend in the world. I am going to give you the biggest hug when I see you Monday."

"What time do you land?" Trisha asked, her happiness evident in her voice.

"Seven at night," I answered.

Trisha huffed. "I'll be halfway to New Zealand by then. I'll see you Tuesday morning, and we can work out all the details over breakfast."

"Sounds good to me." It was the best outcome. "Thank you for understanding, Trisha."

"Moving countries doesn't bother me, Holly. Sticking with the best friend I've ever had is important. Plus, I love Hawaii. Why wouldn't I want to live there?"

"Are you sure?"

"If you are sure you've fallen in love with this guy. Enough that you would give up everything to be with him. Then, it's an experience worth being in the front row to see. Besides, finding a guy in Sydney has been a massive fail for me. Maybe I'll have more luck over there."

Snickering, I asked Trisha about her life and guys. We laughed about the few dates she'd had while I'd been away, then said goodnight till Tuesday. With time to spare, I packed most of my bag, then jumped online looking for an idea about places Trisha and I could rent. If we were going to live here, it needed to be by the beach. Residing with Sean had spoiled me for morning surfs and afternoon beach yoga.

CHAPTER SEVENTEEN

Sean looked over his shoulder and smiled at me. Heat filling my cheeks, I focused on the track through the trees. Ensuring the horse's footing was sure on this track, was more important than how sexy Sean looked on a horse.

We were on our way to the waterfall Sean brought me to on what should have been my last day three weeks ago. We rode in silence. I'd fallen asleep before Sean came home last night. This morning, our interaction had been about affection, not talking.

We made our way down the steep, narrow trail until we reached the bottom and dismounted.

"You're happier today," Sean observed as I pulled my dress overhead.

"Trisha called. She's decided to move here with me, and we are going to live together."

"Wait, my place is only two bedrooms."

It made me laugh. "Trisha and I are getting our own place. She will support this madness but wants me to do it properly. So, dating and everything first." Sean looked unsettled. "What's wrong?"

Pulling me close to him, Sean's naked chest warm against my bare stomach made things clench down below. "I intended for you to be moving in with me, Holly. It doesn't make sense to get another place when you are spending most nights with me anyway."

"Because our work schedules will mean we only get to see each other at night during the week?" I clarified.

"Basically, yes. We'll at least have weekends together."

"And what about Ko Olina? When you go there to ensure your new resort gets on its feet, you'll be staying there during the week for months, right? And if I'm here, already traveling over two hours to work and back each day?"

"Ko Olina is closer to Waikiki," Sean debated. "So, you can stay there with me, and it shortens your drive to work."

"Exactly," I smiled tapping his chest. "And it's only half an hour from the airport for Trisha. I was looking at this last night, as well as places to rent. My thinking is that Trisha and I will get a place near Ko Olina. You can stay with me during the week when you are working on the new resort, and I can come North with you for weekends."

Sean didn't seem to like that idea. "What happens when I'm not at the west coast resort for the week?"

"I have to drive further to see you a couple of nights a week." With a shrug, I moved towards the water.

"Only a couple?"

"We can't live in each other's pocket, Sean. We need time out from each other, time with friends, time alone to process things. Trisha is right," I breathed, feeling more at ease with this plan. "We need to do this right. We need to date, get to know each other over the long term, not the short-term intense passion of something new."

Sean turned me to face him. "This isn't going to wane for me, Holly. I already know you are the love of my life. But, you're right. Slow and steady is best. So, if it makes you happier to find your own place, and for us to date, I'm okay with that." My smile beamed up at him. His eyes sparkled as his hand dropped to take mine. "But I don't want to wait years for you to be my wife, Holly." Sean dug something out of his pocket and dropped to one knee. "We can have a year-long engagement, a traditional length. But I want everyone to know you are going to be my wife."

Sean produced a beautiful diamond ring. My breath rushed out of my chest, my stomach clenched and my eyes pricked with tears.

"Take this ring as my promise that I will marry you, Holly. That I will be your loving husband, and my oath to always be there for you, in whatever way you need me. Let me plan my future, my family, with you."

"Sean!" I exhaled, a tear escaping.

"Will you be my wife, Holly? Will you promise to reserve the job of devoted husband for me only?"

I couldn't say no. I didn't want to. I knew Sean and I would work. "No sooner than a year?"

With a smirk, Sean slipped the ring on my finger. "As long as you need. All I ask is that you promise to come back to me."

"I will," I smiled through unshed tears. Trisha was going to flip.

Rising to standing, Sean embraced me. We kissed heatedly, the passion building. Sean dropped his mouth to my ear. "How about a skinny dip?"

Chuckling, I stepped back from him. Sean's grin lit up his face as I pulled the tie on my bikini top and tossed it aside. Sean opened his boardshorts and dropped them to the ground, his body hard and beautiful to observe. Hooking my thumbs on the side of my bottoms, I pushed them down. Sean's pupils dilated.

"Catch me," I challenged. I dove into the clear waters. Sean's splash sounded while I was still under the water, swimming towards the fall. Catching my ankle, he dragged me back through the water to him.

Surfacing, I caught a breath only to have him steal it away with the intensity of his kiss. Wrapping my thighs around his waist, I held tight as Sean moved us to the rocky outcrop near the base of the falls. The spray of water showered us as my back pressed against the stone. Sean using one arm to encircle my waist, the other to hold the rock, so we didn't sink.

Reaching between us, I slipped the hard yearning of Sean into my velvet heat. As Sean pushed in, the friction made me pant his name and drag my nails across his back.

"I'm yours, Holly," Sean breathed in my ear. My teeth found his shoulder. "I promise I will love you right," he grunted as he thrust into me. "To always support you," he moaned as he withdrew and then punctuated it with another thrust. "We will be happy, Holly. I promise, I won't let you down."

Closing my eyes, happiness flooded me at his words. Taking his face in my hands, I forced his pacific eyes to lock with mine. "No secrets, Sean. No lies, and no secrets. Absolute honesty. That's all I ask. No nasty surprises."

Sean groaned hard, his face dropped to my shoulder and his arm at my waist tightening as if he worried I'd slip away. "Always," he moaned. "As soon as we get back, I will tell you everything."

I clutched him to me in every way. "I love you," I confessed, my voice a mere breath by his ear.

Sean's entire body tensed. His next thrust was hard and deep. The sound of his groan was so primal it ripped into my core and demanded my body concede to my feelings for him. I threw my head back as my body exploded into a million stars of hot fiery pleasure.

Sean cursed and thrust harder and deeper, driving me further out of my body and out of my mind. "Jesus, Holly." Sean pushed me hard into the rock behind me. His teeth gripped my shoulder, then he yelled his ecstasy into my flesh as he claimed my body for him.

My eyes widened with shock. With Sean pulsing inside of me, I understood how intimate sex without protection was. That from this moment onwards, it would always mean so much more for me.

Sean lifted his face, his eyes glassy with pleasure and happiness. "I love you, Holly Claire."

"I love you too."

The sun was radiating joy as we made our way back to the resort. The ring on my finger sparkling in the sunlight, Sean's eyes much the same. We kept looking over at each other, smiling, and my cheeks would heat every time, which made Sean laugh.

As we walked back to the main resort, I noticed a bunch of news vans parked out front. "What's going on?"

Sean's smile dropped a little. "An American senator is staying with us. There was some debacle yesterday on the mainland. He's holding a press conference today to give his opinion on how that will affect his state." As we approached the doors, Sean's steps slowed. "I'm going to duck in to check how it is going. How about you head home and shower."

Smiling, I went up on tiptoes to kiss him. It was a little more than appropriate for public, but it matched the intensity of my feelings.

Sean chuckled to himself when a valet wolf whistled. "I'll see you in an hour." Stepping inside, Sean collected some clothes from Henry to change. Possibly so he wasn't greeting the senator as the manager in a pair of boardshorts and shirt.

With a smile and no interest in politics, I started skipping to the side entrance to head back to the cottage. Passing by one of the news vans, the screen on the open side of it caught my attention. I stopped dead, confused as Raymond stood addressing the press.

Blinking rapidly, I approached the van. Inside a man was pressing buttons and adjusting volumes. He looked at me with a frown. "Mind if I watch a little?"

"That's fine. Here, you can listen as well. He pulled the cord of his headphones, and Raymond's voice filled the van. Raymond was discussing a shooting at a shopping center. Looking disgusted as he tallied the dead, Raymond shook his head. "America needs to learn from places like Australia. We need to look to countries which have introduced gun laws successfully. We need to take steps to protect our people against the modernism that our amendments were never written to consider..."

"Who is that?" My stomach was tensing.

"Senator Raymond Cassidy. He's the sitting rep for San Francisco, so the majority of his constituents support his stance on gun laws.

"How long has he been senator for?" I asked, my hands clenching my dress.

"About eight years now. Cassidy's a good man, but a typical lawyer and politician, if you know what I mean?"

I certainly did. Four days and not once did Raymond or Sean tell me he was in politics, and Sean knew how I felt about political families. My stomach dropped as Raymond called his conference about gun control to an end. He smiled calling Sean up on stage. Sean didn't look happy, but he took the spot beside his father.

"You all know my son, Sean. I've been trying to encourage him to run for office locally. When I told him, he should get into politics, he told me he'd think about it. I didn't expect him to take that to mean start dating the daughter of someone holding office."

My throat constricted, fists clenching the skirt of my dress. Sean's jaw clenching while the reporters laughed. "I am proud to say that Holly Claire, the daughter of Australian Prime Minister Nathan Claire, has agreed to marry my son."

"Are you okay?" The man in the van asked.

I couldn't unclench my fists to wipe the tears streaking down my cheeks. "Is this local?" I inquired, trying to hold myself together.

"No, it's national. Why?"

"When will it go to air?" I knew my father's cabinet monitored American politics closely. There is no way they would miss this.

"It's live."

I nearly screamed. So much so, I had to cover my mouth, the dress still clenched in my fist, to stop it coming out. When I resisted that urge, my next instinct was to vomit.

"Hey, you don't look well. Should I call someone?" The man asked turning the sound off so he could focus on me. Raymond was still talking, Sean standing there, playing the part of the perfect son. I knew that look. I'd played that part half my life, watched my brothers and sisters play it during my father's campaign. I hated it.

"I'm fine. I need to go." I was anything but fine. Pulling out my phone, I headed back to the cottage.

My father's people would be all over this in a matter of minutes if it were live. The Australian people barely knew there was a third daughter; I doubt the Americans did. Raymond had made me a public figure just by putting my name in the same sentence as my father's. Australian tabloids would be all over this, digging up the old scandal. Every journalist would want to find the dirty details of my estrangement from my family.

Thirty minutes later, I was carrying my bag back to the front of the hotel when my phone started ringing again. Ignoring it, I stopped by the door and spoke to a taxi driver, giving him my bag before I stepped inside. Spotting Henry, I waved to get his attention.

"Miss Claire, I hear congratulations are in order?" Henry greeted.

Taking a deep breath so not to burst into tears, I held my emotions in check. "Do you know where Sean is, Henry? The taxi is waiting to take me to the airport."

Henry frowned. "I'll find him for you." Walking to the concierge desk, Henry picked up the phone. "Sean, its Henry. Holly is waiting at the front door for you." Taking a breath, Henry's eyes flicked over me. "Ah, to say goodbye. Her taxi is waiting." Henry looked at the phone surprised and hung it up. "Um, he's on his way."

"Thanks, Henry. Goodbye."

"Goodbye, Miss Claire. Have a safe travel home."

Stepping outside, I waited by the taxi. Sean came running out the door a minute later, just as my phone started ringing again. Checking it, I pressed the silent button. "What's going on?" Sean asked, worried. When his eyes met mine, his shoulders sagged. "Holly..."

My phone started ringing again. "My father's press secretary has tried to call me twenty times in twenty minutes." Pressing silent again, I felt the first tear escape. "Had I not watched your father's broadcast, I would have answered the first call.

But I did. So, I know exactly what has his boxers wedged up his arse to have him calling for the first time in years."

Sean's face dropped. "Holly, I can explain."

"It's too late!" I met Sean's eyes. "I asked you straight out if there was anything I needed to know, anything that could be an issue for us. You didn't tell me."

"I know how you feel about father's in politics. You made that very clear, Holly. I was going to tell you in Molokai, but we got interrupted. I was going to tell you when we got back just now. It doesn't matter. What my father does shouldn't impact us," Sean argued angrily.

Henry and the valets raising brows as they pretended not to listen.

"I agree, it shouldn't have. Had you told me in Molokai that it could be an issue, I could have prepared myself for it." Silencing my phone again, I shook my head. "At the falls, when I asked for truth, you still had a chance. But the moment your father made me a public figure, by putting my name right beside my father's, it affected us."

"I didn't know he was going to do that," Sean pleaded.

"But you stood there and let him. You told him not to tell me he was a politician, right? Before I met him, you warned him, didn't you?" Sean bowed his head. "So, you deceived me on purpose."

"Holly, please? It was new and I didn't want you not to give us a chance because my father is a senator. How is it fair to judge me because of his career choice?"

"Jesus, Sean! Do you understand the media storm your dad

caused for me? I'm not just the prime minister's daughter. I'm his estranged daughter. To a tabloid that spells family disgrace, or horrible family secret." I swiped at the angry emotions spilling down my face. "You should have told me about your dad, and you should have told your dad to keep me out of it."

Slipping the engagement ring off my finger, I put it in his hand. "I love you, Sean. I would have been faithful to you in every way. But, I will not stand in the background smiling and used for someone's political gain. That boat sailed years ago, and I'm not getting back on board ever again." Kissing his cheek, I turned to climb into the taxi.

"No!" Sean growled, grabbing my wrist, his eyes pleading as he turned me to face him. "You promised to come back."

"You lied to me. Even when we came back, you still didn't tell me this was about your father."

My phone started ringing a different tone. This time my father's face flashed on the screen above DAD. Sean watched the screen as I pressed the decline button.

"I'm sorry, Holly. I wanted to tell you. But, I knew how you felt about these things, about the way your father judges you because of your boyfriends. I didn't want to lose you over something irrelevant." My phone went off again. Sean took it from my hand and turned it off before handing it back to me. "Stay. Let me protect you from this?"

Irate and struggling to stay calm, I was beyond angry that one sentence could turn my life upside down. "God, you should have told me. Even this morning, it would have changed everything right now. But you deceived me, Sean. How do I trust you again now?"

"I will never lie to you, Holly. My father was the only thing I've kept from you?"

"I never lied at all." Stepping into Sean, I kissed his lips lightly. "I wanted you to be different." Stepping towards the taxi again, I found those steps the hardest I'd ever taken in my life. "I have to go. I moved my flight forward. Goodbye, Sean."

CHAPTER EIGHTEEN

Arriving home was a sweet relief, and a painful acceptance. Sean let me leave. He didn't turn up at the airport and sweep me off my feet with a passionate kiss and promises never to break my heart again. My life wasn't a movie; it was cold harsh reality.

Stopping at the phone store on the way home, I told them I needed a new unlisted number. Explaining to the salesman I was receiving harassing phone calls got me very fast service.

Messaging Trisha, Mitch and Roger the number, I told them I was home. Collapsing on my lounge, I contemplated checking the news.

Eventually, I unpacked my bags and settled for crying into my pillow. "So, I guess we're not moving to Hawaii?" Trisha queried at the door.

"Aren't you meant to be at work?"

"Yeah, but then I saw the news. Something about the Prime

Minister's estranged daughter getting engaged. Then your message arrived with a new number, and I kinda figured shit might have gone down. So, I developed a stomach bug." Trisha kicked off her work shoes and came to sit on my bed. "What happened, Holly?"

Giving Trisha the summary, she huffed and collapsed on the bed next to me. "He should have told you. That's a huge deal considering your past. Did he know?"

"Yes."

"Then he fucked up, and he needs to own that." We lay there staring at the ceiling for several minutes before Trisha sighed. "He better get on a plane and chase after you."

"If he doesn't?"

"Then it wasn't true love."

There was loud knocking at the door. We both sat up and looked at each other. No one ever knocked on our door like that. A moment later there was a crashing sound out on my balcony.

"What the hell?" Jumping to my feet as loud cursing came from the balcony. Pulling back my blind, I found Mitchell trying to right the pot plants he'd knocked over.

"Holly, there are some serious looking dudes at your door. Did you blow something up?" Mitchell whispered. "Don't answer that. Here, I'll throw you onto my balcony, and you can hide next door till they are gone."

Groaning, I opened the sliding door. "Not necessary. I'm not under arrest." Turning back to Trisha, I huffed. "This is going to get ugly."

"I'll brew the coffee. You get changed. You can't stand up for yourself with a tear streaked face and pussycat pajamas."

"I'll help with the coffee." Mitchell hugged me on the way through my room. "There is a tonne of reporters downstairs too."

"Argh, we are going to have to move," I complained.

After changing, and many more bangs at the door telling me they knew I was home, I opened the door to my father. Well, his bodyguard's chest. His security came in first and ensured no potential assassins lay in wait. Why they discounted me, was beyond me, but they asked Mitchell and Trisha to leave.

"Get stuffed! This is my house and my friend. I'm not leaving her alone in a room full of strange armed men." Trisha tapped her toe.

"I'm her father." Dad rolled his eyes.

"As I said," Trisha shrugged. Picking up her coffee, Trisha sat her curvy behind on the couch. I tried very hard not to laugh.

My father glared daggers at us. "It's okay. I doubt she's dangerous," Dad dismissed his security. Waiting till the door closed, he removed his jacket. "Don't I get a hug?"

"No. What do you want?"

Dad cleared his throat. "I hear congratulations are in order?"

"Oh, you heard about my new job? Thanks, yes, I'm very excited," I smiled leaning against the kitchen counter. "Didn't think you would be interested."

"I meant your engagement."

Frowning, I looked at Trisha, she shrugged, I looked back to my father and picked up my coffee. "No idea what you are talking about, Nathan, or is it Mr. Prime Minister?"

"Dad still works."

"Never has before. Anyway, I'm single like always, so I don't know what poor information you've received." I took a mouthful of my coffee.

"U.S. Senator Cassidy announced you were engaged to his son only twenty-four hours ago in Hawaii. A country I happen to know you only arrived back from this morning," Dad argued.

"Would you like some coffee?" I offered.

"No, thank you. I would like a straight answer."

"Are you sure, because Trisha makes the best coffee."

"I'm sure. Are you engaged to Sean Cassidy?"

"It's the best coffee in the Southern Hemisphere. You're missing out."

"Forget the damn coffee, are you engaged?" Nathan finally yelled.

The room went silent. I glared at my father. "No. When I realized he was a senator's son, I remembered my experience dating a prime minister's son. I decided not to repeat history."

"You broke up with him?"

"Yes."

"Because his father is a senator?"

"Because his father didn't announce his son's engagement to me. He announced Sean's engagement to your daughter! It shouldn't have mattered who my father was. But, in this case, considering the nature of our relationship..."

Nathan studied his polished shoes. "Were you in love with him?"

"What does it matter, Nathan? You don't care, you never have. Your interest has always been the same as Raymond Cassidy's. 'What does that connection gain you?' Well, there is no connection anymore, so if that's all you are here for, there is the door."

Dad took a deep breath, counting to ten under his breath. "What is your new job?"

"I'm the general manager of a hotel," I answered with only half the pride I felt.

"You finally got your dream job? Well, done. It's good to know that screwing your boss got you somewhere."

My coffee mug smashed against the wall beside him. "Get the fuck out!" I yelled at him. Trisha was beside me pulling me towards my bedroom as security burst in to see what the hell happened.

"Get out and never come back. I hate you! Get out!" I screamed at him. "You're a shit dad. Do you know that? That's why you have a son with a drug problem, a porn star daughter, and another who doesn't want anything to do with you. Because you're an asshole and you don't deserve a minute of my time. Now, get out!"

"Come on, Holly. Go take a breather." Trisha shoved me into my room and shut the door. "Seriously?!" She scolded my father. "The girl's heartbroken because she's a blood relation to you, and all you can do is criticize her. I agree, get out. She's too good to be your daughter. Was she adopted?"

"I've never understood that girl. She gives up the men in her life for the most illogical reasons."

"Freud says it all comes back to the parents. Maybe take a look in the mirror and figure out why you caused your daughter to give up the love of her life?"

"I'll show myself out."

"You can't help yourself, can you? The new job, had nothing to do with her ex. She got it because she's that good at her job. If you knew anything about her, you'd know that," Trisha responded. "I can't believe Holly's related to you because she's actually got a heart."

The door closed. Trisha exhaled hard. "Okay, honey. Daddy jerkyl has left the building."

Sighing, I got control of my emotions. "I'm sorry about the coffee mug."

Opening the door, Trisha dropped onto my bed next to me. "Forget the mug. That was bloody good coffee you wasted on that arse."

"Sorry."

Putting her arm around me, Trisha rested her head against mine. "What happens now, Holly?"

"Life."

~To be continued …~

HOLMES

Book 3: Hotel Series

EBONY OLSON

CONTENTS

CHAPTER ONE

"Good morning, Holly," Michelle greeted as I moved through the cafe to my table. "Usual?"

"Yes, please." Sliding into my usual morning seat, I pulled out my notebook, my laptop, and started work.

"Here you go, Holly." Placing a hot chocolate and a croissant with honey on the table, Michelle looked at the door. "Is Roger running late?"

"No, I'm early this morning."

"So you are. Trouble sleeping?"

"Too much to do to sleep properly." Scanning the project list for items that I still needed to complete, I tore off a piece of the croissant and started eating.

"Well, don't make a habit of it," Michelle counseled and went back to serving her customers.

After marking off everything done yesterday, I added to the project list and then started checking my emails. "You look stressed, Holly." Hesitating at the sound of that voice, I lifted my gaze, taking in the tailored suit, broad shoulders, dark hair, and tired green eyes. My chest tightened. Benjamin hadn't changed a bit in the seven months since I'd last seen him. Except for the eyes. I'd never seen him look tired like this before.

"Benjamin," I greeted politely, closing my laptop and sitting back to sip my hot chocolate. "How's business?"

"Still doing well," Benjamin forced a smile. He fell quiet waiting for me to say something. I honestly didn't know what he expected me to say, so I continued drinking my hot chocolate. After the silence grew awkward, Benjamin frowned. "You're working with Roger Holmes?"

"Yes."

"So that was a job interview I walked in on here that day?"

"No, the interview happened at the hotel. What you walked in on was my meeting Sammy so that I felt confident Roger wasn't going to try fucking me over my desk."

Michelle was just leaning in to collect my empty plate. Her eyes bulged, but she didn't say anything.

Exhaling roughly, Benjamin took the seat opposite me. "You promised me six months to get used to the idea of us trying a relationship."

Sitting straighter, I pressed my lips together to resist blurting an impolite response and focused instead on keeping things civil. "It's been seven. The offer expired."

"Was that before or after you got engaged to Sean Cassidy?"

My chest restricted. Well, fuck! Thanks for bringing that heartache up.

"I saw the news, Holly. Followed the media hounding you about your engagement, the breakup, how your father was involved somehow, and that you aren't talking to any of your family since it happened. With how quiet you like to live your life, that was a circus for you."

Sitting forward, I placed my mug back on the table. "At least Sean was willing to have a relationship, Benjamin. He didn't treat me like a scandalous secret of which he was ashamed." I reopened my laptop to keep working.

Benjamin pressed it closed again and sighed. "I was at your sister's wedding last month."

"Why?" I asked shifting in my seat.

"I'm friends with the groom," Benjamin explained as if that was obvious. "Why weren't you there?"

"My estrangement from my parents has spread to include my family in general." I hadn't spoken to my sisters since I'd found out they told my father about Benjamin. They didn't have my new number for them to reach out to me, and I'd moved after my father's visit. That's how angry the verbal backslap from my father had made me. "How was it?"

Benjamin considered me. "Nowhere near as fun as it could have been if you were there, Holly."

"Trust me, Benjamin, even by last month the chance you had with me had already expired. You lost your chance with me the moment you invited me upstairs for a farewell tumble between the sheets, instead of something lasting."

Benjamin frowned. "I see."

"Do you really, Benjamin? Because there was a hell of a lot you missed last time we were together."

Benjamin's jaw tensed. "You're stressed and tired; this wasn't a good time." Standing up he pushed in his chair and turned to walk away. Taking three steps, he turned back around, coming back to the table. "Go on a date with me?"

"No," I replied casually, not even looking up as I opened my laptop. "I've had my heart broken enough this year, thanks. You can apply again next year."

"Holly?"

"Benjamin!" I lifted a brow as I met his eyes with sincerity. "You were right. It's not a good time. I am neck deep in work, and I don't have time to try and coordinate dating right now."

Taking a deep breath, Benjamin put his hands in his pockets. "I know better than anyone what you are like when focused, Holly." He leaned across the table and kissed my cheek, then went to the counter to collect his order.

Just what I needed.

"Glaring daggers at his back won't actually throw them," Roger broke my stare as he sat beside me.

"Still satisfying, but without the mess and jail time."

Smirking, Roger got Michelle's attention, and once she'd noticed him, he pointed to my computer. "Let's start."

After going through our usual day to day stuff, I pulled up the plans for the conference. "We've sold out for the conference and the pre-conference cocktail bash. I'll print out the list of attendees for you when I get into the office today."

Roger was scanning through the names on my screen. "I don't see your name there, Holly."

"The pre-conference cocktails are for hotel owners to schmooze and compare the size of your portfolios. No one is bringing their general manager."

"You've pulled all this together. You should be there."

"I'm good with not going."

"Is that because of two particular names on the list?" Roger quirked a brow, tapping the screen next to the name which may have been causing my sleepless nights of late.

An email popped up on screen giving me an excuse to close the spreadsheet. "Damn. Helena had to fire a bell boy last night."

"Why?" Roger peered over my shoulder.

"He got caught stealing from a guest." Picking up my pen, I wrote a note to check in with Helena about how that affected the roster for the front of house staff, and to see if we still had any names on the candidate list from the last round of interviews.

"Holly. Do you want to talk about why you don't look like you've slept all week?"

"There is so much to get right before the guests start arriving on Friday," I disregarded his concern. What he wanted to know is if I wanted to talk about that name on the list. I didn't. I most certainly didn't want to go to the cocktails night on Friday and have to see him. At least at the conference, I could avoid everyone.

"Stop stressing. You have it all under control. The list is there to prove it," Roger pointed to the project list. "It will all go off without a hitch. Oh, and you are coming on Friday night. Sammy insists."

I groaned.

Sammy was Roger's heavily pregnant wife and a world-renowned hotel reviewer. She was also impossible to refuse once she decided something. Honestly, I loved the tiny blond cannonball. But, I'd learned quickly that saying no to Samantha Holmes was not something any sane person did.

Roger chuckled. "She will drag you there kicking and screaming, so you may as well come along peacefully."

"Can't. I'm booked to have my appendix burst and rushed to the hospital for emergency surgery."

Roger reminded me a little of Mutley with that laugh of his. "How the hell can you plan to have your appendix burst?"

"Research the signs and symptoms and act the hell out of it. Either way, sorry, won't make it," I replied genuinely as I scribbled notes.

"I'll be sure to let Sammy know," Roger shook his head humored. We both knew Sammy would probably drag me out of the operating theatre while anesthetized.

"Good." Ripping off the page I'd been writing on, I put it in front of him. "Your to-do list."

Roger frowned. "That's a long list."

"You wanted to host this international conference to show off your new hotel. Welcome to the legwork that only you can do."

"A welcoming speech?" Roger groaned. "Two of them?"

"One for the cocktails on Friday, the other for the conference opening."

"What's this degustation discussion?"

"You are discussing your in-house menu over breakfast on Sunday with a few select owners who have shown an interest in your international cuisine choice."

"But the rotation of national food dishes was your idea."

"And the degustation item on the agenda was Sammy's. You don't want to do it, go argue with her."

Roger deflated. "You know; I'm starting to suspect you two plot behind my back."

"Don't be ridiculous," I smirked as I packed up my stuff. "We do it to your face."

Roger smiled knowing it was the truth. "Where are you going? Breakfast meetings require eating breakfast."

"I've eaten, and I have to go sort out this bell boy mess."

"How?"

"Eligibility list with any luck. Otherwise, I need permission to interview this afternoon. We can't afford to be short staffed for the conference."

"How are you going to find candidates to interview in a matter of hours?" Roger asked, exasperated.

"This isn't the first hotel for which I've worked. There is always front of house staff looking for extra shifts."

"You're going to poach other companies staff?"

"Just offer them some extra shifts for the weekend, that's all." With a wink, I left Roger sitting there groaning. He was such an honorable man. A simple thing like borrowing someone else's staff seemed horrific to him, but it was smart business. I had enough on my plate with this conference; I didn't need a staffing shortage as well.

My phone rang as I crossed the street to the Holmes resort. Even from the outside, it looked like a tropical oasis in the middle of the concrete jungle. Roger and Sammy had done a great job setting it up. "Holly Claire, speaking."

"Hey, I just landed and am needing sleep so give me the quick rundown?" Trisha, my best friend, and roommate greeted.

"Bellhop got caught stealing so need to find a replacement A-sap; Benjamin Henderson asked me on a date this morning, and Sean Cassidy is going to be at the conference this weekend. My weeks been smashing. Yours?"

"Hold up. Are you shitting me?"

"Sadly, no."

"Okay, stuff sleep. You need good coffee and immediate best friend attention. I'll be at your restaurant in thirty minutes. Coffee and breakfast better be ready when I get there."

Tears welling in my eyes from exhaustion and relief for my best friend, I smiled. "You're the best."

"Please, any excuse to come eat at your place for free."

"Free?"

"You love me!" Trisha cooed and hung up.

Chuckling, I went in to order a second breakfast. I seriously needed my best friend to get me through this weekend.

CHAPTER TWO

"So, what am I going to wear on Friday?" Trisha asked as we rode the elevator to Mitchell's apartment that night.

"Where are you going on Friday?" We'd been discussing her latest fling five seconds ago.

"The cocktail thing with you."

"Why would you want to go to that? I don't even want to go to it."

"Please. You want to know what Sean is going to say after all this time. It's been six months. Don't you want to know why he didn't chase after you and declare his undying love?"

"No."

"Bullshit! I want to know, so you sure as hell want to know. On top of that, Benjamin Henderson is going to be all over you, especially when he sees Sean there, and I'd pay to see that."

"Sorry, it's sold out."

"Hire me as a waitress. I can carry a tray like no one's business."

"Trisha."

"You have to go," she insisted as the elevator opened.

"No, I don't." I stepped into the hall. "They both had their chance. They blew it."

"But you need to know why?" Trisha knocked on the door.

"I don't care. It happened. Let it go."

"No. Sean didn't come to see you, and he should have. I want to know why he let you go."

The door opened. Tony smiling as his eyes passed us over. "If I were a straight man, I'd think I died and went to heaven." He pulled me into a hug. "Our dates are here."

In the kitchen, Mitchell smiled from where he was tying the laces on his shoes. His smile dropped. "What happened?"

"Sean's going to be in town this weekend, and Holly is planning to avoid him."

"Good," Tony chimed.

"Hell, no!" Mitchell responded simultaneously.

They looked at each other. "Sean didn't come to see her. He doesn't deserve a second of her time," Tony defended me.

"She needs to know why!" Mitchell and Trisha replied in stereo.

"You need to go, Holly. If only to prove to yourself you can stand in the same room as those two bastards and survive," Trisha encouraged.

Both men raised their eyebrows. "Two?"

Covering her mouth, Trisha faux whispered. "Benjamin will be there too."

"I'm coming!" Mitchell suddenly decided. "I'll be your date."

"No. I'm going. I'm her best friend, and I could potentially score at this event."

"Guys…" I groaned.

"Well, I will focus on being her friend and not picking up."

"Hey! This is my work. My job and an event I've been working my arse off to pull together. It is not a circus attraction called 'the ghosts of Holly's love life.' I'm not selling tickets for you guys to play fly on the wall to one of the hardest nights I'm probably going to endure this year."

Trisha and Mitchell looked sufficiently embarrassed. "Shame on you two." Placing a gentle hand to the small of my back, Tony walked to the door and held it for me. "So, since it's a working event, what horrific illness are you conjuring to get out of it?"

Our favorite restaurant and nightclub was more accessible by public transport from Mitchell and Tony's place. It was the one downside to moving when that media storm hit. The bonus was that Trisha and I lived near the beach now and I surfed regularly.

"Appendicitis."

"Ooh," Tony shook his head scrunching his face. "Too severe and the recovery time is weeks. Tonsillitis would be better. Quick recovery and it will dampen your gag reflex."

"Sadie is not my role model."

"You should respect your sister more. Sadie managed to be a porn star and cleaned her image up enough to become a lawyer's well-respected wife. She's now a YouTube cooking sensation. Not many can pull that off."

"Argh, I've seen videos of what my sister pulled off, it wasn't always handsome."

"Only the girls have to be hot in porn. Guys are judged by their huge-"

"I noticed," I rolled my eyes.

"One would ask what you were doing watching your sister's porn movies anyway," Tony assessed me.

"I wasn't. My college boyfriend owned the entire collection. Though, in his defense, he had those movies before he knew she was my sister."

"Was that meeting awkward?"

"Only because of the size of the tent in his pants. He'd never gotten that hard for me before." I looked over my shoulder. "Where are our dates?"

"Plotting, I think." Tony put his arm around my shoulder all fatherly. "You've not had the best luck with men, Hols. Maybe you should find out why."

As the older, wiser one of the two, Tony was fatherly, while Mitchell was best friend material. "You think I should go now?"

"Give him a moment to find out why he let you leave. If you

don't like the answer, nothing is going to stop you from leaving again."

"It could break my heart all over."

The elevator arrived, and we stepped inside. "It will never be as hard as the first time. Who knows, maybe Sean was in a car crash when he chased you to the airport."

"A bit far-fetched."

"But it does happen, Hols." He pushed the button for the ground floor, then held the keep doors open button. "Do yourself a favor. Find out. If he let you go, you can move on knowing he is a dipstick. If something stopped him, maybe you need to find out what."

Pressing my lips together, I closed my eyes, took a deep breath, and told myself it couldn't hurt to know. Trisha and Mitch stepped onto the elevator. "Okay, hear us out. You know we have your best interest at heart, Hols, but-"

"I'll go."

"Really?" Trisha asked astounded.

"Really! But I'm going because it's my job to be there, so I'll be going alone."

"Holly…" Mitchell glanced at Tony before eyeing me with concern.

"I can handle it. Just make sure the fridge is stocked with something potent when I get home. I have a feeling I'm going to need it."

Walking off the elevator without them, Tony started organizing my team. "Okay, Trisha, you're in charge of stocking the ice cream. Mitchell, you'll stock the bar. I'll organize the late night delivery of Hols' favorite."

"Double bacon and cheese pizza," Mitchell smiled. "Plan made."

"What happens if she doesn't come home?" Trisha considered.

"Oh, that's not going to happen. Now that I know there is pizza waiting for me, I'll be coming home for sure."

"She just may not be alone," Mitchell winked at Trisha.

"Seriously, you'll be in a luxury hotel. Get a room."

"Are we eating and dancing, or complaining about wall-banging? Because I could bring up that guy from the pet store that you brought home like a lost dog last fortnight."

Eyes opening wide, Trisha blushed profusely as she covered my mouth.

"Pet shop guy?" Tony's manicured brows bunched. "Not Jeremy?"

"He is so not your type," Mitchell folded his arms.

"I know. It was a total pity fuck. His girlfriend dumped him, he started crying, so I showed him my rack to cheer him up. Next thing I know, we're in my room, and he's licking peanut butter off me like a hungry puppy."

Mitchell and Tony recoiled. "Peanut butter?"

Trisha shrugged putting her arm through mine. "It's a thing. Come on."

"Isn't he only sixteen?" Tony teased.

"Twenty. Legal and lots of lead in his pencil. And it was quite a thick pencil."

I covered my ears. "No, no, no. You'll ruin my pet shop chi putting that stuff in my head. Only cute puppy and kitten thoughts allowed."

"That's your concern? I thought Trisha hated peanut butter?"

"She does. It's why she's my perfect housemate. I never have to share my-" I looked at Trisha horrified. "No, you didn't?"

Trisha cackled. "I seriously have a new found respect for peanut butter." I glared daggers. Trisha rolled her eyes. "Oh relax, I'll buy you an untainted jar tomorrow."

"Damn straight you will. And for good measure, you can leave me instructions on exactly what Jeremy did with the peanut butter. Just in case Friday goes well."

Trisha laughed and shoved my shoulder. "Now I'm hungry."

"It's like Mary Magdalene living with the Virgin Mary," Tony commented behind us.

Trisha swung around. "Hey now, don't be comparing Holly to our lady of grace. That poor lass got seduced by a god. And don't go knocking on the other Mary. Jesus loved her, that's why he hung around with her."

Mitchell was laughing. "There was probably an excellent reason why Jesus and his apostles let her into their circle too, and I've seen Benjamin Henderson. Holly got seduced by a god. Trust me."

Cheeks heating at the memory of my first time with Benjamin and all the times after, I sighed. Trisha was otherwise focused. "Don't you go dissing my religion, Mitch. I could be the whore of Babylon, and as long as I repent, they'll forgive me. You two sinners of the flesh, however..."

Tony lifted a brow. "I still go to church."

Mitchell smiled. "Yeah, and they've been trying to hook you up with that divorcee for how long now?"

"You're only welcome because you look too buff and manly for them to realize where you play hide your sausage at night. Wait. Is that why you always ask Holly and me to go out dancing with you? So if you get seen in public, they think you're tapping hot young honey like us instead of each other?"

Mitchell and Tony looked like a deer in the headlights. Stopping, I shook my head. "Seriously? I thought you two were out?"

"I am," Mitchell stated proudly. "But, only Tony's close friends and family know."

"As a teacher at a prestigious religious school, it's harder to be male and gay, than female and gay. I could lose my job."

"That sucks," Trisha huffed. "Okay, you can be my sugar daddy." Wrapping her arm through Tony's, Trisha cuddled in, then we started walking to the bus stop again.

Thunder cracked loud above us, and we all looked at each other panicked. A moment later we were all running to the bus stop as the rain started pelting down on us.

It was Spring and the nights hadn't quite found the warmth of the sun yet, so I was shivering like crazy when we got to the restaurant. Trisha wasn't fairing much better herself.

We were chatting, waiting for the hostess to find our reservation when a body-warmed suit jacket fell over my shoulders. Turning, I blinked with wide eyes to see Benjamin smiling at me.

"I saw you come in." He folded up his sleeves, exposing the muscled forearms that had held me up against a wall in my old office like I was a feather. My body was suddenly hot. "Warm up. You can give it back when you are ready." Walking away, Benjamin spared a nod for my friends.

"Okay, twice in one day," Mitchell whistled. "If that's not fate-"

Glaring at Benjamin's retreating behind, Trisha scowled. "It's stalking. Seriously, what are the odds?"

Picking up our menus, the Hostess lifted a brow at Trisha. "Considering he owns the restaurant and conducts a lot of business here; they're pretty high. If you'll follow me?"

My friends all looked at me, Tony's brown furrowing. "Did you know he owned this place?"

"No. I ran Benjamin's hotel, not his business affairs."

"I think you were the queen of his business affairs," Trisha whispered so the hostess couldn't hear.

My entire body heated under the force of those memories. Taking off the jacket, I handed it to the hostess as we reached our table. "Thank Mr. Henderson for me."

"You can return it yourself. He's eating by himself tonight." Placing the jacket back in my arms, she winked before she walked away.

"Damn."

CHAPTER THREE

BENJAMIN SMILED AS I APPROACHED HIS TABLE. THERE WAS paperwork spread all over it, and I recognized one of the reports from the template I created while I worked for him. At least I knew where he came for an office now. "All warmed up?"

"Yes, thank you." I folded the jacket neatly over the back of the chair in front of me.

"Are you sure?" Benjamin's eyes went to my chest.

Looking down, I realized I was still smuggling smarties. Uncomfortable, I folded my arms across my chest, the sensation against my sensitive nipples making me bite my lip. "I'm good."

"Oh, I know you're good, Holly. I asked if you were warm. You can keep the jacket longer if you need it. I only got here a short time ago. I won't be leaving anytime soon." His eyes were intent, and I got the sense he wasn't talking about his presence in the restaurant.

"I should get back to my friends." When I turned to look at them, I found them all watching us like a bunch of gawkers. Turning back, Benjamin's smirk had grown as he noted our captive audience. "Thank you for the thoughtfulness."

"You have never left my thoughts for a minute, Holly."

"Don't do that. Don't be charming. It's too late for that, and it's not going to fool me again."

Benjamin sat forward placing his elbows on the table. "Holly, I'm sorry you feel I purposefully fooled you during our relationship, but I never made you any promises of anything beyond what we had."

"I know. That's why you lost me." Dropping my arms from my chest, I went to step away. "Oh, by the way, how's Colin enjoying the night manager's role?"

Benjamin's jaw tense. "How did you hear about that?"

"I made friends while I worked there, Benjamin, and just because I left doesn't mean those friendships stopped. I heard you begged Betty to come back from her maternity leave early to sort out the mess Colin made."

"Did you want to say you told me so?"

"No. I truly am sorry that it didn't work out as you hoped. I'm even more sorry that you still seem to think I'm some malicious bitch. Goodbye, Benjamin."

Benjamin stood quickly. "Holly, I'm sorry, that's not what I meant." His hand wrapped around my bicep to prevent me from turning away from him.

My teeth pressed into my lip to stop from saying something

horrible. Benjamin probably still didn't believe Colin propositioned me and tried to blackmail me.

Benjamin's face fell. "I made a range of mistakes when it came to you, the first of which was complacency. I can't undo that. But, if you give me a second chance, I won't make the same mistakes again."

Lifting my arm out of his grasp pointedly, I considered him. "Neither will I."

Closing his eyes, Benjamin swore under his breath. "One more chance, Holly. That's all I'm asking."

"I'll think about it." With all the nonchalance I could muster, I walked away to join my friends.

"Look at you all confident and shit," Mitchell praised as I took my seat. "Benjamin couldn't look away."

Peering over the top of her menu, Trisha raised a mocking brow. "Did he ask you for a second chance?"

"Yes."

"Did you tell him to kiss your arse?"

Winking at Trisha, I considered the menu.

"He looks lonely sitting there by himself," Tony sighed.

Meeting his boyfriend's eyes, Mitch smiled. "It must be hard being famous and rich and having to guard against gold diggers constantly."

"Good evening, I'm Pete. I'll be your waiter this evening. Can I start you with some drinks?"

"Pete, has Mr. Henderson eaten yet tonight?" Tony asked the waiter.

My eyes jumped up from the menu. "What are you doing?"

"No, sir, he hasn't."

"Tony, no!"

"Thank you. I'll be back in a minute. Mitchell, you order for me."

"No."

As Tony stood, I tried to rise also, but Mitchell put his hand on my shoulder and pressed me back down into my chair. "You'll be safe."

"Oh my god," Trisha covered her mouth with her menu to hide her glee. "Holly will kill you both in your sleep."

Watching Tony approach Benjamin while Mitchell ordered drinks and starters; kill wasn't the right word. When Benjamin smiled and stood packing away the work in front of him, the words slow, painful, violent, and horrific were painting red through my mind.

Staring in morbid fascination, my heart beat frantically as Tony returned to the table and took his seat beside Trisha. The guys always sat opposite one another. Now I knew why.

Leaving his gear at the other table, Benjamin carried his scotch to join us. The waiter added another chair at Tony's end of the table, which thankfully, put Benjamin away from me.

"Good evening. Thank you for the invitation to join your group. Nice to see you again, Mitchell." They shook hands. His eyes went to Trisha. "Trisha. So, what's the event?"

"No event," Tony replied. "We normally do dinner on Friday or Saturday nights depending on Trisha's roster. With Holly working this weekend, we decided to have dinner early this week."

"We also missed last weekend because Trisha was working," Mitchell clarified.

"Oh, so the four of you are quite close?"

"You seem surprised," Trisha challenged.

"Well, I knew you were Holly's best friend, but the first time I met Mitchell I got the impression they were on a date."

Smiling at his tactic the first time Benjamin approached us out, Mitchell folded his menu closed. "That's the impression I wanted you to have. Though, my insinuation we were intimate wasn't so much for your benefit; I already knew you were into Holly. I just wanted to know if she was into you too. But, when she told me you were her boss, well, that changed everything."

Benjamin considered the group. "So, you all know about us."

Smirk growing at Benjamin's discomfort, Mitchell almost gloated. "Oh, yes. We know all about it."

"And we know you are trying to get under her skirt again," Trisha accused.

Sitting back, Benjamin took a deep breath, potentially regretting accepting the offer to join us. He looked at Tony in question as the waiter placed our drinks on the table and left again. Tony lifted his beer in the air. "Welcome to your trial by fire, Mr. Henderson."

When Benjamin turned wide eyes to me, I shrugged, a small smile pulling at the side of my mouth. We all sat there watching him for a moment. Benjamin looked very uncomfortable under our gazes.

"I'll start," Trisha offered. "That night at the opera. What did you hope to achieve finger fucking that chick in front of Holly?"

Choking, Benjamin quickly took a drink of his scotch.

"Are you ready to order mains?"

"Ah, yes, I think so," Benjamin took advantage of the interruption and ordered without even looking at the menu. We all followed suit. "Another drink for me too, please, Pete."

"Yes, Mr. Henderson."

Silence descended over the table after the waiter left and Benjamin realized we were still waiting for an answer. Exhaling hard, Benjamin sat up straight.

"It was never my intention for that to happen. I didn't want to show up solo in case Holly took a date. The woman in question was quite sexually aggressive and placed my hand between her legs. I didn't want to offend her, and Holly's coldness to me had angered me. I wanted to make her jealous after she ended our affair."

"I ended it? I'm pretty sure you're the one who told me it was over right after you accused me of being malicious because you passed me over for promotion."

"Holly, look at it from my perspective. What was I meant to think?" Benjamin argued.

"That your brother was an asshole molester and sexual predator," Trisha grumbled.

Silence descended again as both Benjamin and I took large mouthfuls of our drinks avoiding looking at each other. When the entrees were set on the table for us to share, Tony picked one up, his eyes intent on Benjamin. "What did you think about the media circus to do with Sean Cassidy?"

"I didn't believe it at first. I mean, it had only been a month since Holly left and now she was supposedly engaged. It didn't make sense. Then I saw the interview of Cassidy when the media caught up to him at the airport in Hawaii two weeks later. He looked like shit as he admitted that the relationship was over." Benjamin met my eyes. "I recognized the same forlorn look in him that I'd seen on my face since you left. That's when I knew it was true."

We were all silent for a moment, the Mitchell cleared his throat. "The last question for now. What was it like to lose the best thing that was ever going to happen to you, and know it was all your doing?"

Sitting back in his seat, Benjamin huffed as his tired eyes lifted to mine. "Shit. Fucking shit." Taking a long pull of his drink, Benjamin put the glass down empty. "I have a lot of work to get done tonight, so I might take a rain check on joining you." He stood up. "For what it's worth, Holly. You were right to leave me."

"Benjamin, I didn't leave you any more than someone leaves a one night stand after the lust has fled. What we had, came to an end and left the opening for more or less. We walked off on different paths wanting different things. That's not leaving someone. That's being true to yourself and acknowledging you're worth more than a fling."

Shoulders stiffening and jaw tensed, Benjamin nodded his

head. "Enjoy your evening." Then he retreated to his work table.

"Ouch," Mitchell murmured. "Is it bad that I feel sorry for him?"

Scowling across the table, Trisha huffed. "Yes. He fucked our friend over, so I don't care if he's hurting. He got what he deserved. Frankly, a little bit of resistance to winning her back will be a good thing."

Nodding his head, Tony set his gaze on me. "Trisha is right. It will make him appreciate Holly more if she does give him a second chance later."

Mitchell sighed. "I want to invite him dancing after dinner just to see him move." The other two shrugged and agreed silently.

"You can't be serious?"

Mitchell patted my hand. "We'll leave it up to you. If you can resist those sad eyes when we leave here tonight, we'll leave him behind too."

Glancing over that side of the restaurant I found Benjamin watching us from his table. Mitchell was right. There was a world of melancholy in Benjamin's sea green eyes. He messed his dark hair with a frustrated hand and returned his focus to his paperwork.

Damn it. I hated seeing people hurt, especially when I could make them smile again. When we finished dinner, all of us laughing about one of Mitchell's yoga experiences, I looked over to see Benjamin leaning over his paperwork, hand in hair, looking exhausted.

"Holly?" Mitchell called when I didn't follow them to leave. Benjamin lifted his head to watch me.

"I'll catch up in a minute." As I walked over to Benjamin's table, he sat back. Everything about his posture said he was expecting me to tell him to get lost.

"Look, Holly, I know-"

"We're going dancing. You're welcome to join us if you can accept it as just a night out with friends."

CHAPTER FOUR

Benjamin was a good boss and a good lay. He was not a good dancer. At least not in the nightclub scene. So, Benjamin and Tony were holding up the bar together, watching Mitchell play bump and grind with Trisha and me on the dance floor.

It stopped things from being awkward because I could effectively pretend Benjamin wasn't there. We danced, we flirted with the guys checking us out, and we had a good time.

Honestly, knowing Benjamin was watching, I might have flirted a little bit more than I usually did. Something Mitchell noticed and acknowledged with no more than a knowing smile and shake of his head. Trisha was a little less subtle.

"Holy Mary, Hols. I've never seen you get your flirt on like that. We should bring Benjamin out more often," Trisha teased as we made our way back to the bar. "I think you left half the floor hard."

Raising a brow, Mitchell scoffed. "Only half? I thought I was at a campsite with the number of tents pitched."

"Yeah, yeah, whatever!" We reached the bar only for Benjamin to turn those green eyes on me - hot and smoky and surveying my body like it was cheesecake. "God, I want cheesecake right now."

Winking at me understanding that's not what I meant, Trisha started laughing. "I could go some cheesecake."

"I know a place that does late night desserts. The cheesecake is to die for."

I knew the place Benjamin was talking about. I'd discovered it when I was a concierge and had a client who liked gourmet desserts close to midnight.

Chuckling, Mitchell clapped his hands and rubbed them together. "Sounds good to me. Let's go get cheesecake."

Heading up to the street level where it was cold and wet outside, Benjamin pulled out his phone and put it to his ear. "I need a car to pick me up at the GPO." He hung up. "Our ride will be here in a few minutes," Benjamin advised.

"You didn't have too. We're used to roughing these conditions."

Benjamin raised a brow. "You've already been cold and shivering once tonight. I don't want you getting sick before your big event this weekend."

We waited patiently undercover of the federation building until Benjamin's phone buzzed. Checking the screen, he then looked up the road. "This will be our ride."

We all looked up to see a taxi driving up the street with it's light on, and a nice shiny town car right behind it. Suddenly stepping out, Tony waved down the cab. "We're going to call it a night; watching me dance winds him up. Nice meeting you again, Benjamin," Mitchell fare-welled before hugging me. "Sorry, totally Tony's doing." He dashed through the rain. Waving goodbye, Tony yelled his apologies as he climbed into the cab.

Placing his hand on my lower back, Benjamin walked us out to the waiting car. Just as we got to it, Trisha hugged me. "I've decided to catch a ride with the boys. I'll see you at home." Before I could react, she ran over to jump in the cab with the guys.

The cab pulled away while I was staring at them shocked. "Bastards!" Slipping into the luxury car, I pulled on my seatbelt. When Benjamin joined me, he was smiling broadly. "Did you pay them to disappear?"

"Not at all. Your friends started scheming the moment you mentioned cheesecake. Entirely their doing. Not that I object."

"I bet."

"I will be a perfect gentleman, Holly."

"I'm pretty sure you were a perfect gentleman the first time you put me against the wall."

Benjamin smirked. "Is that an offer?"

"Nope." Benjamin just smiled. "Why are you so tired? I've never seen you look exhausted before."

Benjamin raised a brow. "Let's just say I haven't been sleeping well for the past few months. Guilty conscience, or something like that."

"What are you feeling guilty about?"

"Some months ago I was in the fortunate position to get rid of a competitor, so I did."

"And that has left you sleepless?"

"No. That didn't make me feel bad at all. Entirely self-serving, but important for my goals. Business is business, as my dad always says. Recently, this competitor came back. Not locally, but still, it could affect my plans. I'm concerned it's about to become personal."

"Why?" How the hotel business could suddenly become personal, I had no clue, but I'm sure there are grudges in every industry

"Because they are very determined, and so am I."

"You always have been when it came to your business."

Smiling, Benjamin caressed the fingers of my hand on the seat then covered it entirely. "I think I can honestly say you are the only female who truly knows me, Holly. We were colleagues and friends before we became more. I think that's why I never tired of you."

The sting of his words made me flinch my hand away. "Was that meant to be a compliment? Because all I heard was that I was the only female to waste two years trying to do things your way. I was the only one too stupid not to demand more from you when things should have progressed beyond office sex."

Benjamin shook his head. "Don't you see? The fact you didn't is the reason I developed feelings for you. You knew what would scare me off and you gave me the time I needed." Benjamin turned to face me. "I fucked it up, Holly. You told me you needed more to make you stay, and I backed away instead of admitting the way I felt about you. You know me. I don't make the same mistake twice."

"Sadly for you, neither do I."

Benjamin smirked. Not the reaction I was expecting. "Which is why it won't be the same this time, Holly. I'm going to date you and win you over, the way I should have years ago. This time, when you tell me you're ready for more, I'll make sure I'm ready too."

"What are you saying, Benjamin?" I worried at the look in his eyes.

"I'm saying I'm turning forty this year and I've spent twenty years focused on making my business successful. It's time I considered a wife and kids as my next items of focus."

I sat blinking at Benjamin. "And you want that with me?"

"I've never even been inclined to with anyone else, Holly. You're perfect for me, and I know I could make you happy."

"Wait!" I tried to jumble through what Benjamin was saying. "Are you proposing?"

Benjamin laughed. "No. Not yet. I'm old fashioned and believe in dating for several months before taking the next step." I exhaled in relief. "I just wanted you to know where we are heading. If you are willing to give me a second chance?"

"Ah, I thought we were heading for cheesecake. Let's not overcomplicate dessert," I changed the subject back to something I could handle.

Benjamin smiled. "Silly me. This was more steak and wine conversation." His smile stayed put through dessert and the drive to my place in Coogee. It was close to midnight when we pulled up at my home. Stepping out of the car, Benjamin considered the apartment building.

"Thank you for dessert," I fare-welled as he approached. His hands in his pockets, looking devilishly handsome.

"My pleasure. I was grateful you invited me along." Benjamin swept a strand of hair back behind my ear. "Have dinner with me tomorrow night."

"I'm flat out with work and-"

"Just dinner, Holly. If you give me a curfew, I'll make sure you are in bed by it."

"I'm pretty sure you left yourself an opening there, so I'm going to decline and say goodnight instead."

Benjamin smirked. "I'll behave."

"I doubt you know the meaning."

"I promise, Holly. Dinner and talking. I won't press my luck."

Was I seriously thinking this was a good idea? I shook my head. "Not this week. I'll see you at the cocktail event on Friday."

Benjamin studied his shoes. "Be my date?"

"On Friday?" I watched him nod his head. "It's a work event. I'll be there in a professional capacity, not for fun. So again, no thanks."

"Holly-"

"Benjamin, don't rush this! You hurt me. I need more than your charm and cheesecake to move past that. I need patience and a sense of security. Let's just keep this informal for now.

When we see each other, we can talk. Let's see where that leads."

Taking a deep breath, Benjamin acceded. "Okay, Holly, but I don't give up on something I want as badly as I want you."

Stepping into me, Benjamin planted his lips against mine. His arms wrapped around me and pulled me tight against him. Moaning, I fell into his embrace, opening my mouth to taste the scotch on his tongue. The heat of him was searing through my body, removing any goosebumps from the cold weather.

Slowly, Benjamin pulled back. His eyes glimmered like the Emerald city of Oz. Pure satisfaction and delight lighting up the night. Releasing me gently, he stepped away. "You know how to reach me if you change your mind about dinner tomorrow night." Benjamin grinned like a Cheshire.

"You are too cheeky." Still, I couldn't keep my lips from tilting up in amusement; I blame the wine. Six months of celibacy can die a quick death with one good kiss. Walking to the door of my apartment building, I pressed in the code. Once the door shut behind me, Benjamin slipped back into the warmth of his car and it drove off into the night.

"So?" Trisha stepped out of the kitchen with warm milk for me as I entered the apartment.

"He kissed me."

"Expected."

"He wants to date."

"Also expected."

"His end goal is marriage and babies." Eyes wide, I blinked twice then shook my head.

Trisha hesitated. "Was he abducted by aliens?"

"Possibly?"

"Maybe Benjamin's been possessed. You know, by some demon who wants to spread his spawn on the earth."

"Also possible."

Trisha clicked her fingers in excitement. "Fuck, he's probably been possessed by the devil. It makes sense. He's so good looking and suave and rich. Maybe the devil is going to use his body to impregnate you with the antichrist."

"So, I should avoid him then?"

"Oh hell no! If that's Lucifer, he's going to be amazing in bed. You should seriously tap that. Just make sure your pill is up to date and enjoy the ride."

"Trisha…" I sighed, hugging her. "You need help, honey."

"Yeah, but you know I'm right," she hugged me back. "That's why you kept boning him when you knew it wasn't right. It was too good a ride."

"Yeah, he was good," I agreed, sadness filling me. "Sean was better."

CHAPTER FIVE

"Morning, Michelle." Walking into the coffee shop, I headed for my usual table.

Noting I was early again, Michelle looked me over. "Still not sleeping?"

"Only a few more days and this thing will be out of my hands. Then I might take a few days off and sleep for two days straight."

"I'll get your order." With a smile, Michelle headed into the kitchen.

"You shouldn't run yourself into the ground."

Looking up, Benjamin came to stand by my table with his take away coffee in hand. He must have been at the counter when I walked in.

"I think that's a pot calling a kettle black, comment."

Smirking, Benjamin took the seat opposite.

"Benjamin, I've got work to do. This cafe is where I start my workday."

"At seven o'clock? What sort of hours is that?"

"The sort of hours a general manager works. Just ask Terry. He probably works longer hours for you. You should consider hiring a general manager international. With how big you've grown your company, there is more than enough work for a manager here in Australia and another overseas," I offered offhandedly.

"What a good idea. Do you want the job?"

His ease of acceptance and offer made me chuckle. "Makes it hard to date me if I'm overseas eleven months of the year."

"I meant the Domestic general manager's role. Terry is using his frequent flyer points to take his wife overseas with him now that the kids are all out of the home. He'd kill me if I took his wife's reward for doing without him all these years away." Studying Benjamin to see if he was serious, I was surprised when the glint in his eye told me he was deadly serious. "I'd offer it to Betty, but with a newborn and plans for more, I can't see her wanting to travel around the country regularly."

Tilting my head, I considered last night Benjamin was talking marriage and babies, and today he was offering me a role that I would have to give up to have children. "Maybe you should offer it to Colin. Isn't that who you were grooming for Terry's role?"

Benjamin gritted his teeth a moment. "Colin still has a lot to learn."

"Like not trying to blackmail staff into sleeping with him?

You're right. He needs to hone seducing them into it and being able to keep them on tap for years to come."

Benjamin exhaled hard as his coffee cup hit the table a little too hard. "You make it sound like I do that regularly, Holly. You are the only employee I have ever seduced."

"At least you admit you did that. I notice you glossed right over what Colin did. In fact, you've not once apologized for putting me in that situation by telling him about us, or for not believing me when I told you it happened, or-" The annoyance on Benjamin's face stopped me in my tracks. "Oh my god! You still don't believe he did that to me?"

Realization dawning, I looked away. All my energy immediately escaped my body and left me feeling drained and used all over again. "You can leave." Taking out my laptop ready to hide my depression in my work as I had for seven months now, I set it on the table.

"Holly, he's my brother. You don't truly expect me to believe he's like that?"

"I expect you to get the fuck away from me. If you don't believe me now, what's going to stop Colin doing it again when I'm your girlfriend or wife? Do you even understand what it's like for someone to abuse you like that? For someone who is your superior to abuse his position? He didn't try and blackmail me when he was a concierge. He waited until he was my supervisor. That tells you the kind of man he is."

Sitting there glaring at me, Benjamin didn't want to believe that about his brother. It was easier to think I was the problem. "Just get lost, Benjamin. I don't want to see you again."

Opening my laptop, I quickly swiped at the tears about to

escape my eyes. God, I'd come so close to falling for his charm again last night, I would have missed that he still thought I lied.

Rising out of his chair, Benjamin looked down at me, his jaw tense and eyes angry. I didn't look up at him, but there was no missing the clench of his fists as he watched me wipe away the tears again.

"Holly, is everything okay?" Michelle asked as she put my drink and food on the table.

"Fine, thank you, Michelle. Mr. Henderson was just leaving."

Removing his handkerchief, Benjamin put it on the table beside my laptop. "I'm sorry you're upset." He then handed Michelle a twenty. "Holly's breakfast is on me." Grabbing up his coffee, Benjamin left.

Sitting beside me with concern, Michelle squeezed my shoulder. "Holly, what happened?"

"Nothing worth discussing." Collecting the handkerchief, I dried my eyes. "I'll be fine."

Not looking convinced, Michelle patted my back until I set the handkerchief aside. With a thankful simper, I squeezed Michelle's hand and shooed her back to her customers while I focused on my work.

By seven thirty, Roger was sliding into the seat next to me. Checking the time, I blinked at him. "You're early?"

"Michelle called and told me you were upset by another customer this morning. She was worried considering the gentleman normally comes and goes, but this morning he waited for you to arrive." Swallowing around the lump in my throat, I turned my eyes back to the laptop. "Benjamin Henderson, I take it?"

When I didn't answer Roger exhaled roughly. "I like Benjamin. He's a good businessman, but everyone knows he's the stereotypical playboy billionaire. How the hell did a smart girl like you get involved with a man like that?"

"He's just one of those guys you can't say no to. Now he's talking marriage and babies and wanting me to be his GM, but he can't even accept the truth about the sexual harassment issue."

Roger's brow lifted. "Oh, the hell with that! If he thinks he can lure you back to work for him with the promise of a wedding, he's insane. There is no way you would fall for that shit."

"What?"

"Remember, Holly? You were his ideas person. All those brilliant concepts you came up with are what made Henderson hotel what it is today. Do you think maybe now the dust has settled, Benjamin realized he'd lost more than his gal Friday?"

The thought hadn't even occurred to me. Considering how business orientated Benjamin was, I couldn't believe I hadn't considered that Benjamin's interest may be more than missing me as a lover. "I don't know, Roger. I've never seen him this tired and stressed. Still, I can assure you I won't be returning to work for him. I love my job with Holmes resorts too much."

"Good! I can't compete by offering marriage and kids as Henderson can. It would have made the bidding war to keep you on staff awkward."

Despite the disappointment over Benjamin's refusal to believe my accusations against Colin, I laughed. Roger was one of those people who did that, which is why he and Sammy worked together. "Well, since you are here." I opened up my project sheet. "Should we start?"

Three hours later I was sitting in my office going over the plans for the conference when my phone rang. "Holly Claire speaking."

"Holly, its Lance. Our old boss is here to see you?" Lance had been a bellhop at Henderson that I had nominated for the concierge program. He got fired just before finishing training for having sex with clients during work hours. Or, perhaps it was because Benjamin witnessed Lance flirting with me. Either way, he's the reason I landed the job with Holmes, and he'd been a fantastic concierge since he started.

"Tell him to go away."

Lance chuckled. "Are you sure that's the expression you meant?"

"No, but let's rise above our emotions and be cordial and professional. It will rub it in Benjamin's face that he fired you."

"Will do."

Hanging up, I sat back to stare at the ceiling while I counted down from ten. At two my phone rang again, just as I expected. "Sorry, Holly. He's refusing to leave till he sees you."

"He's trespassing, so threaten to call the police."

"Yeah, I think he preempted that response. He's checking into a suite as we talk."

"That makes him Monica's problem as the day manager. Tell her to deal with him."

"Holly, he looks like he got in a fight. I've seriously never seen him look this messy."

Picturing Benjamin all disheveled, I raised a brow. "I have."

"I bet."

Forehead slapping myself, I groaned. "You knew?"

"There was a reason I never hit on you."

"Tell her I'm in room seventeen twenty-three. I'm not leaving till she sees me."

"Yes, sir. Welcome to Holmes resort. Please let me know if there is anything you need."

"I just did. Make it happen, Petts."

Taking a deep breath, Lance waited. "I'm not sure what you did, Holly, but he is very determined."

"I mixed business with pleasure. I'll deal with it, Lance. Thanks." Hanging up the phone, I went back to my project sheet. I would deal with Benjamin later, but that was personal so he could wait for me to finish work for the day before he got my attention again. Then I'd tell him where to stick his plans for the future and job offer.

First things, first. Deal with the catering staff about our billionaire gluten-free diet attendees. It didn't escape my notice that the majority of gluten-free diets were for females. I was starting to wonder if it was a chromosome disorder or just a diet fad. Either way, much more appealing to deal with than a tall, green-eyed billionaire with commitment issues.

CHAPTER SIX

"Dᴵᴅ ʏᴏᴜ ꜰᴏʀɢᴇᴛ ꜱᴏᴍᴇᴛʜɪɴɢ ʟᴀꜱᴛ ɴɪɢʜᴛ?" Lᴀɴᴄᴇ ᴀꜱᴋᴇᴅ ᴍᴇ as I walked into work Thursday morning.

"I don't know? Did I? I thought I got everything on my list." Frowning, I tried to think of what I'd missed.

"Let me give you a hint. Room seventeen twenty-three."

Concentrating on why that room should mean something to me, I bit my lip when green eyes flashed before me.

Lance laughed this time. "He was mega pissed when he found out you left without seeing him. Stormed out of here even more pissed than when he came in."

"So he left?"

"For a while. Probably had to take care of business. Benjamin came back late with a change of clothes and his laptop bag. Told me to tell you he's found a new workspace and he'll be waiting."

Groaning, I started walking to the elevator; Lance's laugh mocking me as I went. I was too stressed for this shit. Benjamin would have to wait until I had my day under control.

Going about my usual morning routine, checking in with managers and ensuring everything was right before I checked final preparations for the cocktail event tomorrow evening.

When that was all done, I decided to get something to eat on my way back to my office. "Holly, the usual?" The chef asked when I entered the restaurant.

"Yes please, Havier." Giving him a smile, I stepped aside to wait and look over the menu. I always checked it to see what the specials were. Happy with it, I lifted my eyes to the video wall, which showed the sun high over turtle bay in Hawaii. The picture was crystal clear for those eating in here; it could have been a window to the outside. One of the ideas I'd had in Hawaii that I brought home and gave to Roger. A way to bring the unique resort experience into the city.

"Holly, are you meant to be meeting someone?" Havier asked as he handed me my toasted sandwich.

"No, why?"

"There is a man who has been sitting with his arms crossed glaring at you since you came in."

Wincing, I closed my eyes. "Dark hair, green eyes in a suit?"

"Yep."

"Which way do I need to walk to avoid him?"

Havier smirked. "Jump over the waterfall."

"Fine, but, if my sandwich gets wet-" I complained.

Havier shook his head at my joke. "That desperate, hey? Must be an ex-husband. Go through the kitchen, but do not touch anything or I will throw your dead body over the waterfall."

Havier never let anyone but his staff in his kitchen. Kissing his cheek, I escaped through the kitchen under Havier's supervision.

Unfortunately, Benjamin wasn't stupid and was waiting for me at the other exit. "Finished playing cat and mouse?" He asked when I nearly ran over him coming out the door. His hands grabbed my biceps to stop me falling.

"I've been busy. I work here, remember?"

Benjamin looked at the plate in my hand. "Well, it's your lunch break. Spare me the time it takes to eat that sandwich." Taking my free hand, he led me towards the elevator.

"Where are we going?"

"My room so we can talk privately."

"I don't want to be in Private with you."

Hitting the call button on the elevator, Benjamin's eyes seemed worried as they took me in. "Are you scared of me? I'm not my brother, Holly."

My eyes filled with tears wishing that was the reason I didn't want to be alone with him. "Why couldn't you have believed me the first time? You fucked everything up. It's all your fault."

"My fault?"

"Yes! Your fault. You are to blame for everything that came

after. You were the turning point where it all changed. You are the catalyst for the best and worst experience of my life. You, Benjamin." Shoving the plate into his hands, I stepped out of reach. "Here, I'm not hungry anymore." Pushing through the fire-exit door, I ran up the stairs.

"Holly!"

Exiting the next level up, I stormed into my office. Benjamin changed everything. He started the chain of events which led to Hawaii and my first experience of love. Real love. Not teenage love, or expectant romance where you date the person everyone expects you should, nor the kind curtained by lust and temptation that Benjamin was to me.

Sean was real love. He was everything I'd ever wanted. Sean was kind, and understanding and considerate, and a fantastic lover. The way he looked at me, touched me, had no expectations of me. I was willing to move countries for him. But, I would never have gone to Hawaii, never have met Sean, and never had my heart broken so publicly, if it hadn't been for Benjamin not believing me about Colin.

My door opened. Benjamin stepped in, still holding my sandwich, watching me cry. Taking a deep breath, he shut the door, placing the sandwich on my table. A moment later I was in his arms being held tightly against his chest. He hugged me till my crying calmed down, then he lifted my face and wiped my cheeks.

"I keep making you cry when what I want is to see you smile at me like you used to. You're right. I'm the one who fucked us up, and I've missed you every day since."

His lips pressed against mine, determined, intent. Closing my eyes, I kissed him back. It had been a long six months. Mitchell had been telling me I needed a rebound. Somewhere familiar and the one who caused it all could be the perfect place to throw me back from my heartache. Anything to stop thinking about Sean Cassidy.

Deepening the kiss, Benjamin moved me back a step to my desk. A moment later his hands were sliding my skirt up and rubbing me over my knickers. "Benjamin, wait." I didn't want it to be like before; I couldn't handle this.

He kept kissing me as his hands grasped the back of my thighs and pulled them open to press his pelvis right to the junction of mine.

"Benjamin, stop!" I shoved him away. "You need to go."

He frowned at me, confused, eyes glazed in his lust high. Then his eyes went to my door. Stepping back, Benjamin straightened his tie. Turning my head, I found my heavily pregnant boss's wife glaring at Benjamin. "Sammy?" I choked, quickly righting my skirt.

"I believe Holly asked you to leave, Benjamin," Sammy declared sternly, opening the door wider and stepping aside to clear the doorway.

Breathing deeply through his nose, Benjamin turned his eyes to me. "Call me. Please." He left.

Shutting the door, Sammy looked me over. "You okay?"

"Yes. No. Fuck, I don't know what okay even is anymore," I mourned sinking into my seat.

"Which pretty much tells you-you're not okay." Sammy did

that awkward pregnant sitting thing across in the other chair. "Roger told me Benjamin has been seeking you out. Lance told me he'd camped himself here. I came up to see if I needed to throw him out. Apparently, I did. Though, sooner might have worked better."

"I'm sorry about that. He followed me in here. I didn't intend for that to happen." In all the years Benjamin and I had fucked, no one busted us even once. Pretty telling it wasn't meant to happen now if you ask me.

Sammy considered me. "You are damn good at your job, Holly. I could have walked in to find a guy balls deep in you and, as long as it wasn't my husband, I wouldn't fire you. I may suggest you lock the door next time, but I'm not going to get huffy over the need to get off taking you? With how stressed you are right now pulling the conference together, you probably need to blow off the steam. Hell, this," she pointed to her belly, "is a result of me needing to vent and climbing on my husband without thinking. Trust me; I would have understood."

A little relieved, I relaxed.

"However, speaking from experience. Unless both you and he are on the same page about casual sex, exes are not a good place to vent."

"Argh, I don't think we've ever been on the same page since it started." Dropping my head on the desk, I sulked. "I just need to get through this weekend. Then I can get my head together and decide if having Benjamin back in my life is something I want."

"I would say let's go get a drink, but you're working, and I'm not drinking for another year yet."

Sammy was a white, blond, shorter version of Trisha, and always made me smile. "Well, if I go missing tomorrow night, come check and see if I'm passed out with a bottle of vodka under my desk. With two exes in the same room, I think it's bound to require alcohol."

"Pfft," Sammy waved her hand. "I'll have an ex, two one night stands, and a weekend fuck fest in that room with me tomorrow." When I raised a brow, Sammy smirked. "I've been making the rounds of hotels long before I met Roger. I've had my fun on the job."

"Did they know they were the job?"

"God, no. None of them even know I'm a reviewer still. They all still think I'm a consultant. Even Benjamin."

My mouth dropped open. "Um!" By the fire of embarrassment surging up my neck and cheeks, I was sure I turned bright red.

Sammy laughed. "Yeah, I know why you went there. That man is smooth as baileys over ice and a player if ever I met one. That's why he lasted the weekend." Covering my face to hide in my hands, Sammy tsked. "I'm not judging, Holly. What Benjamin Henderson wants, Benjamin Henderson gets. You should be asking yourself why you have been his repeat for such a long term? And why he is desperate to get you back? Because seriously, Holly, everyone who knows him will tell you, Benjamin only thinks about himself and his business."

"Sammy, please don't take this the wrong way, but both you and Roger have a vested interest in my not going back to him. No matter if I get involved with him, I won't be working for him again."

"I agree. Roger and I do. Roger has also been friends with Benjamin all his life. Their fathers were good friends. Roger knows Benjamin best, and he is worried about you, Holly. Not from a business perspective, but because Roger is the sort of guy who cares. Even if Benjamin is serious about marriage, do you think that will change the way he operates?"

"You think he would marry me and still live his playboy life?"

"No, Holly," Sammy shook her head. "I'm worried he'd treat you as another holding that needs to be managed and controlled, not loved and adored. If you are unsure, look at his mother and father. Benjamin is just like his dad. Singularly minded and focused. Everything else, including Graham's wife and kids, was just another investment in his portfolio."

Fidgeting with the bottom of my dress while I considered Sammy's advice, I tried to imagine my life as Mrs. Benjamin Henderson. Other than the sex, it wasn't coming to me.

Eventually, I exhaled and shook my head. "I don't have the headspace for this right now. I just need to make this weekend go off without a hitch. Next week, I can deal with Benjamin and his reasons for being back in my life."

Sammy nodded in understanding. "Can I ask you to keep one thing in your mind while you consider all of this?"

"I love this job, Sammy. I promise he won't lure me away."

"That's good. But I want you to ask yourself why Benjamin waited until now? It's over half a year. Has it taken him that long to figure out you meant more to him? Did he think you would come back to him maybe? Or, did something happen that suddenly made him take action?"

Interested to hear her theory, I sat forward. "Do you know something that I don't?"

Smiling, Sammy pushed herself up to stand. "I'm a reviewer, honey. I always know more than the general public." Waddling over, she put her hand on my shoulder. "Stay by me tomorrow night. Benjamin is terrified of me."

CHAPTER SEVEN

"You've done a great job with the place," Roger Holmes Senior praised his son. "The sunscape in the restaurant is probably my favorite, though, the underfloor river through the lobby is pretty amazing."

It was the first time Roger's dad had come to see what his son had created. By the sound of it, he was impressed. "I can't take all the credit. Holly came up with the sunscape."

At his son's words, Roger senior turned his eyes to me. "You look familiar." He clicked his fingers. "Prime Minister's estranged daughter, right? You were engaged to an American senator's son, and your dad caused an issue."

"Dad!" Roger scolded as I took half a step back. "Did you want a spoon to stab her with?"

"Mr. Holmes," Benjamin suddenly appeared beside me. "Been a long time."

"Ben, how are you?"

Lifting my eyes to the sky, I cursed inwardly. Roger frowned as Ben put his hand into the middle of my back as if we were there together. Closing my eyes, I counted to ten while Benjamin and Holmes Senior caught up. Opening my eyes, I spotted Sammy across the room talking to one of the caterers. "Excuse me, I need to check on something." Stepping away, I made my way towards Sammy.

A glimpse of sandy hair and caramel tan made my heart race. Angling my head just enough, I spied Sean Cassidy talking to a circle of hotel owners; his ocean blue eyes bright as he smiled at the attractive woman his age with him. Snapping my eyes away, I bit my lip as the need to cry came upon me.

"Holly?" Sammy worried, grabbing my arm as I tried to pass. "What happened?"

Glancing back to Sean and the woman touching his forearm flirtatiously while they spoke, I choked on the emotions suffocating me. Sammy followed my gaze.

"Oh, that's Amber Miles. She's the daughter of Donald Miles. Owner of the Miles vacation rentals worldwide. She's not here with Sean, I can assure you."

The binds on my emotional straitjacket eased a notch. "You're sure?"

"Trust me, I've met her enough times. That woman is so far up herself, she wears her vagina as a hat."

When I blinked at the description, Sammy just shrugged one shoulder and sipped her cranberry juice. I burst out laughing. "Oh my god, Sammy, I've never heard that. I love it?"

Sammy smirked. "I assure you, if Sean Cassidy went for you, he wouldn't go near that woman at all. They are just people in the same profession conversing. They are probably discussing his recent acquisition."

"The one at Ko Olina? That should be ready by now." The laugh Sammy gave me was fleeting. Turning my back on Sean, not wanting him to look up and see me, I fidgeted. I shouldn't have come tonight.

"Shouldn't the food be out by now?" Sammy complained.

"I'll chase it up," I volunteered. The opportunity got me out of the cocktail lounge which attached to the restaurant. The sun was setting on the Sunscape as I went to the kitchen and rang the bell.

"Holly, you look delicious," Havier appraised my cocktail dress. "You could make a man unfaithful dressed like that."

"I wouldn't be interested in a married man. The way I'm going, I expect I may never be interested in a man again."

Havier lifted a brow at the overshare but politely waited for me to get to my reason for being there.

"Are the canapés ready? Sammy is going to eat someone's arm off in a minute."

Havier laughed. "They will be ready in a minute."

"You made ones that she can eat right?" I'd chosen food with ingredients that a pregnant woman could eat.

"Have I ever let you down, Holly?"

"No, Havier."

"Good. I'll do my job, and you do yours." Returning to the kitchen, he started barking orders.

Gazing back at the sunscape wall, I watched the sun set slowly. The jewel colors were reflecting across the ocean, spilling pinks and reds like watercolor paintings, the darkness of night creeping up on the fading sunlight.

It took me back to the restaurant at Cassidy resort. For a moment, I allowed myself to be back there, Sean sitting across from me, smiling and making me the happiest I'd ever been. When I opened my eyes, the moon was waxing into the sky.

Dabbing at the tears in the corner of my eyes, I settled myself. It had been six months. I needed to get over this. I thought I had until I saw Sean's name on the guest list. Damn, but I was still in love with him.

"Isn't the gig in the other room?" Lance came up beside me.

"Yeah, I was just chasing up the food," I smiled, my professional mask slipping back into place.

Placing a slip of paper on the sill, Lance rang the bell. "Are you sure you're not hiding out here?"

"Honestly, I love coming in here to watch the sunset. It reminds me that happiness, can be fleeting, but the memories will last a lifetime."

"Are you about to jump off the waterfall or something? Because that was kind of sad, and if you are thinking of topping yourself can I have the opportunity to change your mind? I can get a room and remind you how to smile?"

"Lance," I shook my head, "not appropriate."

"Is this about our former boss?"

"The manwhore of Sydney? Not really?"

Lance frowned. "Look, I know something went down between you. Rumor says it was his brother that caused the issue, but I worked there a few years on night shift too. Do you know how I knew when you too started sleeping together?"

I shook my head.

"His door was a frigging revolving door of women. I damn envied the guy. Then, it stopped. From one night to the next. Over. The same time that happened, you started coming in to work early on Wednesday nights and eating dinner with the boss in his place." Lance considered me. "Up until I left, from the moment you started the Wednesday night *'ideas dinner'* thing, he didn't bring another woman upstairs with him."

Peering down at my toes, I sighed. "I know. Well, I didn't know for sure, but I was confident that was the case."

"Trust me, from a manwhore's perspective; we don't give up our harem overnight unless it's something we need more in our lives. Benjamin fucked up promoting Colin over you, but he was a good boss until that moment, and he cared about losing you enough to give up all others."

"It's a pity Benjamin never showed me that or told me that personally."

Lance huffed. "Yeah, well, if you see me getting serious about a girl, remind me not to subconsciously fuck it up out of fear of allowing myself to get hurt. Benjamin has looked like shit since you left Henderson's. I think it would have hurt less to be honest in the first instance."

Trying not to laugh at the irony, I raised a brow. "Well, if at least one person learned something valuable from that mess… it still was fucking shit to go through."

Lance smiled. "Well, you chose the perfect revenge. That dress is going to make him jealous of any guy looking at you. You should get back in there and flirt with everything rich and handsome. It will drive him berserk."

"Thanks, Lance."

Lance smirked as a covered plate slid onto the serving sill. "I need to get this to the Halversteen widow." He grabbed the dish and left.

Taking a breath, I realized I'd been gone from the event nearly an hour. I considered how I was feeling and recognized I did feel better. Maybe Benjamin deserved that second chance. We'd never dated or been in a relationship properly. If we dated, I could determine if there was a side to him worth loving.

I was just about to walk back in when I remembered Benjamin wasn't the only heartache in there. Rubbing the sore spot on my chest, I grimaced as a mean thought of using Benjamin for my purposes tonight flashed through my mind. Scolding myself internally, I shook my head and braved the party.

Stepping back into the event, I made my way to the side and picked up a glass of wine. Red, to fit with my mood. For several minutes, I stood watching the networking occurring. Sean had moved on to another group. Benjamin was talking to another.

Slipping around the edge of the crowd, I focused on reaching Sammy and Roger, who were discussing Roger's other business in the hospitality industry. It was one of the main reasons our meetings took place at a cafe. I liaised heavily with his personal assistant to ensure he was where he needed to be for the resort.

Just before I reached them, Benjamin stepped in my way. "Can we please talk?"

Swallowing the lump of guilt over the plea in his voice, I gulped a deep breath and moved over to the corner of the room, stealing a canapé from a passing waiter as I walked. Stopping by the window that looked over the foyer and river below, I turned to face Benjamin.

"I confronted Colin. He admitted he tried to coerce you into sleeping with him. I fired him."

"I heard you punched him?"

Benjamin inhaled unhappily. "It came to blows, yes. He cost me one of my best employees, and, he took something I'd shared with him and used it to manipulate someone important to me. It was unprofessional, unethical, and just an asshole thing to do."

Sucking in a large sip of my wine to avoid saying anything equally unprofessional, I waited patiently.

"I'm sorry I didn't believe you. Colin's my baby brother, and I wanted to believe he couldn't be that kind of person. It was easier to believe you were malicious than accept he was that big an asshole."

"Would you have ever made us more?"

Benjamin met my eyes. "Probably not. Not until you asked for it."

"You would have dumped me a heartbeat later."

"Yes, but I would have done it gently, so there were no hard feelings. I wouldn't have wanted you to feel uncomfortable about continuing to work for me. And then, given enough time, I would have tried to start over with you, just as I'm doing now. I would have realized you were different, Holly. You are important to me, and I need you in my life."

Moving closer, Benjamin placed his free hand on my face, caressing in front of my ear. "Give me a chance to show how much you mean to me, Holly. I promise you won't regret it."

"Benjamin-"

"Excuse me," a deep voice interrupted.

My heart started beating double time as I turned to take in the ruggedly handsome appearance of Sean Cassidy, in a tux. Damn it! My knickers were instantly wet. Benjamin's hand dropped away, and we faced Sean.

"I'm sorry to interrupt, but I was hoping to have a word with Holly," Sean requested politely.

"I'm sorry to be rude, but, no. Holly's at work and this isn't the place. Frankly, she shouldn't give you the time of day if you should enquire."

I lifted my brows shocked at Benjamin's attitude. "Benjamin."

"He hurt you, Holly. He needs to leave you alone." There's that pot calling the kettle black again.

Sean lifted a brow. "I'm only asking for five minutes, Holly. We can stay right here if your friend wants to watch and supervise." His voice was still polite and gentle. "Is he a relative?"

"I'm sorry. Benjamin Henderson, this is Sean Cassidy. Sean this is Benjamin, my former boss."

"We've met," Benjamin dismissed the introduction.

"When?"

"Twice now," Sean's brows pinched as he considered us. "This is the boss you were having an affair with?" The tension was collecting on his shoulders. I didn't have to answer; the shame in my eyes gave it away. Sean half laughed. "You son of a bitch."

"Watch yourself," Benjamin warned.

"Here I was thinking you were protecting her, but you were serving your self-interest. Why don't you tell her how we know each other, Benjamin?"

"You need to step away and cool down," Benjamin warned, keeping his voice quiet as those around us started paying attention.

"Guys, maybe we should take this into the other room?" I suggested.

"You're not going anywhere with him," Benjamin ordered.

"He was at your sister's-" Sean began to tell me.

Benjamin turned and swung clocking Sean on the cheek. I blinked, then they were brawling on the floor.

"What. The. Hell?"

CHAPTER EIGHT

"You're home early," Trisha called after the door slammed behind me. "Did something happen?" Walking into the lounge room, I looked over Trisha and Mitch sitting on the couch drinking wine.

"Ah, crap!" Trisha stood up and walked over to me. "I'll get the vodka. Sit down and tell us what happened."

Dropping on the lounge, Mitch pulling me into his side for a hug, I frowned still trying to puzzle it out. "I'm not sure what happened. Benjamin was there. He confronted Colin and fired him. He was saying something about how much I mean to him and that I'm important to him when Sean came up and asked to talk to me."

Returning with the vodka, Trisha placed a shot glass full in my hand. I threw it back. "Did you speak to him?" Trisha topped up the shot glass and sat back with her wine.

"No." My mouth turned down at the sadness in my voice. Did I want to speak to Sean? I was confused as shit. Throwing back the next shot, I watched the chaos of my evening play over in my head while Mitch topped up the glass this time.

"Why not?" Trisha looked disappointed.

"Benjamin got all protective and wouldn't let him near me. They knew each other, but Sean didn't know Benjamin was my ex. Then Sean was pissed. He started to talk to me, and Benjamin just lost it and punched him."

Mitchell looked like a kid in the candy shop. "Seriously? That would have been so hot!"

"No, it wasn't! We are at a professional work function, and they start brawling over me like cavemen. That's not hot, it's pathetic. It's embarrassing. My boss was there, and he knows about my affair. It would have taken Roger five seconds to know I caused that mess at his first big event."

Mitchell sulked but squeezed my shoulder to let me know he understood. "So what happened next?"

"It snowballed from there. I got shoved out of the way by others getting in to separate them. That's all I saw."

"You didn't ask Benjamin why he went all Tarzan?" Trisha asked concerned.

"No, I just left while they were still reenacting planet of the apes. I didn't want to speak to either of them. I just wanted to get out of there."

"You just left?" Trisha checked.

"Yes."

"You didn't tell anyone you were going? Kick Benjamin in the shins? Nothing?"

"Yep."

Trisha took the shot out of my hand and drank it herself. "You're my idol," she gritted afterward. Once she recovered from the vodka hit, she perked up. "So, ice cream?"

———

"HARRY, that is not your designated table," I scolded one of the merchants for the conference.

"Come on, Holly. This table has the best position."

"I know. That's why it's an A table. You were too stingy to pay for an A table and elected a B table. This space is designated to Jenkins so pack your stuff and haul your arse to your set table, or I'll pack your stuff and security can haul your arse out altogether."

"Why are you so angry today? You are normally sweeter than this?"

"I'm sick of putting up with men wanting more than they are willing to commit too. Move it!"

Sulking, Harry started packing his display back up. Mr. Jenkins, who let me know about the mix up stood smiling at me. "Thanks, Holly." Smiling politely, I walked up to the kitchen to check on the progress of the catering.

In the Daintree restaurant foyer, I found myself looking at Sean. A bruise covering his left cheek the only sign of last night as he waited for a seat for breakfast. Planning to leave unnoticed, I just back stepped three paces when Havier made that impossible. "Holly, are you checking up on me or eating?" Havier called from the kitchen.

Sean's head turned and his ocean blue eyes locked with mine. "Holly," he murmured my name. His eyes dulled as if sadness washed over him. "Please, just five minutes?"

Swallowing despite the constriction in my throat, I moved my eyes to Havier. "Breakfast, Havier. For two." Eyeing Sean, I moved towards him. "You can eat with me." Not waiting, I walked into the restaurant.

There was a table near the kitchen that was always kept aside for management. In other words, it was Sammy and Roger's seat that the other managers and I used when eating. Seating myself so I could see the sunrise, Sean blinked at the wall-long screen before sitting. "That's the view from my beach."

"I know. The videographer used your house as his marking point. I gave him several points of reference. In the end, we ended up with ten different scenes that we use on rotation. That way our customers never get the same scene twice in a week."

"Can I ask what points of reference?"

"You could, but it would eat into your five minutes. Havier is making my breakfast to go."

Pressing his lips together, Sean met my eyes. "I'm sorry I hid that I'm the son of a senator from you. I shouldn't have deceived you. I just wanted you to choose me before something I knew was a big deal for you scared you away."

"I understand that. I still hate the way I found out, but I get why you did it. It doesn't change what your father did or how it made a mess of things for me."

Sean exhaled. "I saw, and I experienced. The media were like bloodhounds who caught the scent of scandal." Sean sat back.

"From the moment I landed in Sydney till I flew out again they hounded me."

"I had to move because I couldn't even leave my building."

"Is that why you changed your phone number?"

"No, I did that as soon as I landed. My dad wasn't going to let up."

"I saw that he came to your house. The American tabloids decided that visit marked the end of our relationship. They decided your dad told you to end it."

"He didn't. He just wanted to know if it was true. I told him to get lost."

Sean sat watching me. "I missed you every second after you left. I wish you would have given me a chance to explain before you jumped that plane."

Licking my lips, I avoided his eyes. "How is your new resort coming along in Ko Olina?" I asked to change the topic.

Sean tilted his head as if it was the last thing he expected I would ask. He fidgeted with the cutlery. "Good. I went there when I got back from Sydney and focused all my attention there to try and avoid hating myself for letting you go. It was up and running in record time."

I would have smiled politely and said great, or something equally as polite, but that would suggest I was happy he got over me. We sat in uncomfortable silence for a moment. Sean suddenly sat forward, resting his forearms on the table. "Are you with Benjamin Henderson?"

"What?"

"Are you dating him, seeing him, in a relationship with him?"

"No. Why on earth would you think that?"

"Last night he was pawing you every time I looked at you. I was waiting to get you alone, but from the moment I walked in he was all over you. I decided to try asking to speak to you." Touching his bruised cheek, Sean winced a little. "That didn't work either."

"I do not see Benjamin in any way."

"Does he know that?"

I sighed. "Benjamin's trying to change my mind about seeing him, but I've been too busy even to consider dating."

Sean's eyes brightened somewhat. His face was trying to smile, but he was resisting. "Good to know."

"Here you go, Holly," Havier placed my egg and bacon roll with Monterey Jack cheese and barbecue sauce on the table. "And don't you dare ask about the welcome nibbles."

Grinning, I stood up grabbing my breakfast. "Thanks, Havier. My friend here will have Roger's favorite."

"Of course, Holly," Havier offered me his cheek, and I gave it a peck. "Remember to breathe out there."

"Bye, Sean," I farewelled sadly.

"Holly?" Sean stood up. "I'm here for the weekend. Can we do dinner, or drinks, or-" Sean shrugged his shoulders as if lost. "Please?"

Lifting a brow, Havier pursed his lips, rocking back onto his heels and twiddling his thumbs as he watched us. "I'm working all weekend, Sean."

"I know, but, the conference ends at six. I've never stayed in Sydney any longer than I had to be here. I wouldn't even know where to eat. Surely, you could spare me another meal. I mean, you do eat, right?"

My heart was in my throat making breathing hard. Tears filled my eyes. Six months. Was it rising exes in Scorpio or something? Why now? "I'm sorry, Sean." Walking out, I tried hard to get the heart tearing in Sean's eyes out of my head as I made my way back to the conference room; the conversation playing over in my head.

I was halfway to the conference room when Sean's words stopped me in my tracks. Spinning around, I stormed back to the restaurant, bypassing the waiting line to reach Sean at the table I'd left him. He looked up as I approached, despair in the depth of his ocean eyes. "When did you come to Sydney?"

Sean sat back. "Didn't you watch the media coverage?"

"No. I barely watch television anymore."

Fist clenching on the table, Sean sighed. "The first time was a day after you left me. It took that long to organize someone to watch my business and a flight here. I stayed for two weeks trying to find you. Your number was disconnected, and I never got your address or where you worked. The second time was for your sister's wedding. I stalked the entrance to the church waiting for you to show up. Your sister had your dad's security escort me out. Your media filmed it all."

My legs felt weak. "You came after me?" I whispered.

Sean lifted a brow. "I've never stopped coming after you, Holly. That's why I'm here now. I was going to throw your name around till I found which hotel you worked at, and then I was coming to find you."

My jaw felt lax. Reaching out, Sean touched my hand. Just a brush of his fingers, but it may as well have been a stun gun for the way my body seized in reaction. Stepping back out of reach as the tears escaped my eyes, I turned on my heel and left.

CHAPTER NINE

"Holly?" Roger knocked gently on my office door as his head peaked around to find me. "I've barely seen you all weekend."

"Is there a problem? I thought everything was running smoothly?" I worried standing up. Wiping my face quickly, I tried to look like I had my shit together. The truth is, I didn't. I'd hidden behind the scenes for the last two days, going out of my way to avoid everyone I didn't have to deal with, and when I got time to myself, I spent it doing work to prevent analyzing that conversation with Sean yesterday morning.

"Everything is good. Or, at least, out there it is. I'm not so sure about in here."

"No, everything's fine. I've been getting ahead on those plans for the rock climbing wall we discussed."

"I meant the fact you look like shit, Holly. Have you slept at all this weekend?"

Patting my hair to make sure it wasn't sticking out weirdly, I fidgeted with my blouse. "Ah, not really."

Shoving his hands into his pockets, Roger assessed me. Stalking forward, he closed my laptop. "Go home. Eat something delicious and fattening. Drink something volatile. Sleep. Don't do work. Don't think about work. Don't do anything but sleep."

"If I can't?"

"Don't come into work tomorrow. Call it a stress day, or time in lieu, or whatever you need to call it. Just take the day for you. They'll both be gone tomorrow. Hopefully, Henderson got the message you aren't interested and will leave you alone."

Alone. What a word to use.

Roger pulled me into a hug. "You did a great job pulling this all together. Everyone is raving about it. Now, go take some you time and do what you need to do to get yourself sorted." As Roger walked out, I went to open my laptop. Roger stuck his head back inside. "Now, Holly, or I'll sic Sammy on you."

"Okay! I'm going." Grabbing my bag and jacket, I stepped out locking my office door.

"I've got to go be present for the last few talks. Enjoy your afternoon."

"I'll see you on Tuesday." I was exhausted, emotionally wrung, and heartbroken all over again. Catching the train home, I changed into pants and t-shirt before heading to walk along the beach. It was only spring, and while it was warm, it wasn't quite shorts weather yet.

Sitting on the beach for a while, I watched the waves roll in.

'Didn't you watch the media coverage?'

Frowning, I pulled out my phone googling Sean Cassidy and Holly Claire. Article after article and lots of images popped up. Searching through, tears falling as I watched Sean escorted by my father's security away from the wedding. The editorial also showed a photo of Nichola yelling at Sean outside the church.

My stomach dropped. I expected Sadie to have been the one to dismiss him. The older photos had Sean leaving a building angry, the captions stating my family circled the wagons and wouldn't let him near me.

Observing the building he was leaving, I recognized Nichola's house. My jaw tensed as I realized where he had gone to find me when he first came to Sydney. Nichola knew where to find me in those first few days. The last photo was Sean arriving back at Honolulu airport looking completely heartbroken. There was a video of Raymond Cassidy that came up in the search. Taking a breath, I clicked on it.

"Senator Raymond Cassidy has confirmed his son's engagement is off. The senator only announced Sean's engagement to Holly Claire, youngest daughter of the Australian Prime Minister, weeks ago, but has confirmed today that only hours after he made the announcement, it was over," the news host advised.

The camera snapped to Raymond standing in front of the media. "Senator, is it true that your son's engagement is off?" A reporter asked.

"It is," he mourned.

"Can you tell us why it ended only hours after you announced it?"

Raymond sighed. "Sadly, I wasn't aware of Holly's situation with her family when I made the announcement. My understanding is that Holly's father contacted her, and not much longer after that she ended her relationship with my son and flew home. Sean did try to fix things between them, but Holly's family have ensured Sean can't get near Holly to even talk with her. I sincerely regret that my pride and sharing the happy news publicly, has caused both my son and Miss Claire such heartache."

The camera went back to the news reporter. "This announcement comes after weeks of speculation on the relationship." Photos of Sean looking heartbroken and of me sitting by myself at the bus stop or on the park bench where I go to eat my lunch started flashing on the screen. "Reports suggest that Holly was told by her father to end the relationship, and was confirmed by Holly's flatmate only days after the media frenzy in Australia began.

Footage of Trisha leaving for work started showing as she tried to push through the media to reach her taxi.

"Are you Holly Claire's flatmate? Can you confirm she's engaged to Sean Cassidy? Is Holly truly estranged from her father?" Reporters called after her. Trisha turned and glared at the reporter.

"All I have to say is the Prime Minister is a jerk who only cares about his self-image and doesn't give a shit how that affects his daughter. I can't blame Holly for not wanting anything to do with that asshole."

The reporter came on the screen again. "Prime Minister

Claire's only statement has been to request the media respect his daughter's privacy. In other news-"

The video cut out. I caught a glimpse of a headline about Sean Cassidy opening his new resort and all the articles after that seemed to focus back in on his business ventures. Shoving my phone away in my pocket, I wiped my eyes dry.

Gazing out at the waves rolling in, all I could see was Sean looking like hell as he returned home after trying to follow me. He'd kept his promise. It took him six months, but he'd finally found me. Wasn't it too late though?

Heading home, I slumped down on the sofa and watched a few shows. I painted my nails, fingers, and toes. I completed five Sudoku puzzles, and through all of it, I remembered Sean and the sadness in his eyes when I walked away from him yesterday.

Going to my jewelry box to change my earrings, I spied Sean's business card that he gave me that first night in Hawaii. It had his private mobile number written on it. I considered it all the way back to the lounge.

Sitting there with a glass of wine I stared at the card as if it might come to life on its own, or maybe, I wanted Sean to appear in front of me magically. With a huff, I picked up my phone and pressed call. The conference finished thirty minutes ago, and I wasn't sure if he was flying home tonight, but in case he wasn't going to try again, I needed to hear him out. He'd earned that by coming looking for me.

"Sean Cassidy," Sean answered on the fourth ring. I hesitated at the sound of his voice. My stomach clenching, and heart pounding. "Hello?"

"It's Holly," I rushed so he didn't hang up.

"Holly," Sean breathed my name.

Closing my eyes on the way my stomach clenched around that sound. We both sat there in silence for a moment.

"Holly? Is there something you want?" Sean asked, his voice strained.

"The truth," I whispered, blinking away tears.

"Where can I meet you?"

Giving him the address of a restaurant, I could hear Sean tapping away on his phone. "I'm twenty minutes away."

"I'll see you then," I sighed with relief. Hanging up, I bit my lip. Was I doing the right thing? Looking down at what I was wearing, I swore. Racing to the bedroom to change out of my lounge pants and baggy top, I put a pair of jeans and a cute top on.

Walking the block and a half to the restaurant, I was just a few meters away when a taxi pulled up. Sean jumped out, grabbing out his bag and hefting it to his shoulder before he paid the driver. Sean turned to look at the restaurant as I walked those final steps to meet him.

"Hi," Sean greeted, a hesitant smile trying to breach the fear in his eyes. I wondered if I looked as scared as he did.

"Hey, thanks for coming." I eyed the luggage. "You'd already checked out?"

"I was on my way to the airport."

"When is your flight?"

"Nine," he answered checking his watch.

I checked mine. We had an hour till Sean needed to be there to check in for an international flight. "The airport is only fifteen minutes away."

"I'm guessing Trisha appreciates that?" Sean turned to take in the view of the beach. "You live close by?"

Pointing to my building. "I'm up there. Fifth floor."

Sean took in the building. "Well, now I know where to find you away from work."

"Let's get a table," I suggested, not ready to think about Sean starting to turn up randomly like Benjamin. We found an empty seat outside and waited until the waiter took our drinks order to meet each other's eyes.

"So, do you enjoy working for Roger Holmes?"

"Yes. It's the best job I've ever had."

"Really? Because you've looked better?" Sean criticized.

"So have you. It's not the job. Though, I'm surprised I still have one after that shit on Friday night."

Sean nodded in understanding. "I'm sorry about what happened with Henderson. I wasn't expecting to get decked asking to speak to you." Sean rubbed at his bruised cheek.

The waiter placed our drinks on the table. Taking a large mouthful of mine, I fidgeted with the glass.

Sean watched me. "Holly, I never wanted to hurt you. I was going to tell you right after my dad left. When you called me downstairs to say goodbye, I was arguing with him about the announcement. I don't want my life publicized any more than you do."

"You stand behind him at his media broadcasts."

"Rarely," Sean huffed. He met my eyes. "It's good for business. I have very wealthy politicians, and celebrities stay at my resorts just because I stand behind my father and smile whenever he visits. It's not always press conferences. That wasn't even supposed to happen, but he needed to respond to that shooting. Most of the time its pictures of the two of us bonding on the golf course, or on the beach. It's a symbiotic relationship. We both get quality time with each other, but he also gets the family values shots, and I get free publicity."

Staring at my drink so many thoughts rushing through my head.

"I'd already told my father you wouldn't be part of those photos unless you wanted to be. That you were even more protective of your privacy than me. I was already angry about the announcement without my consent, but then you left," Sean cut off, his eyes glassy. Turning his face away, he took deep breaths.

My eyes filled with tears, my chest tight from restraining my emotions. Catching the waiters eye, I signaled for the bill. I couldn't stay here and do this. We needed privacy to discuss these things. I could take him for a walk down the beach.

"I searched for you for weeks, Holly. I tried to use the media to find you when your family wouldn't help me, but they never aired it."

"What did you say?"

Sean met my eyes, the depth of the ocean of sadness in his eyes almost drowning me. "I love you. I'm sorry."

My stomach flattened against my spine, my heart rate picked up, and those tears I'd been holding back so far surged forth. Standing up as the waiter placed the bill in front of Sean, I started to walk away. "Holly?"

Stopping, I watched him throw a twenty down for a ten-dollar bill as he turned to face me. I waited, heart racing in my chest.

"Holly, I love you. I'm sorry," Sean repeated. People at other tables stopped to watch as Sean stepped towards me again. "I'm sorry I didn't tell you the truth when it was important. I'm sorry I broke your trust." He kept walking towards me. "I'm sorry I let you get in that taxi and leave." He stopped right in front of me. "The biggest fuck up I made was letting you leave without hearing me; without hearing that I was sorry, but I love you." Sean cupped my cheek. "I'm sorry, but I love you still."

My insides were goo. Melted and liquefied, swishing around inside me as Sean's eyes let me see how much he meant those words. Stepping into him, I wrapped my arms around his neck and kissed him so hard it hurt.

CHAPTER TEN

THE APPLAUSE AND CHEERS STARTLED US APART. WIPING THE tears from my hot cheeks, I bit my lip. Clearing his throat, Sean grabbed his bag and took my hand. "I'll walk you home."

We walked hand-in-hand up the street to my building. "Did you want to come up?" I asked looking at the time. "You still have thirty minutes till you need to leave."

We continued to hold hands in the elevator; my spirits soaring as we rose to the fifth floor. When we emerged into the corridor, I walked us to my door, Sean taking note of the apartment number.

"Coffee?"

"Sure." Sean looked around the lounge room, the photos catching his eye. "You and Trisha have traveled a lot."

"Every time she's home for the weekend we try and get away for a few days and do something. That was the long weekend in June. I took the Friday off, we flew to Melbourne, drove the

Great Ocean Road to Adelaide, and then we flew home. That photo is in front of the Twelve Apostles."

"Twelve?"

"The limestone stacks were caused by erosion. It's eroding by a few centimeters each year," I explained, walking Sean's coffee to him. "There are only eight stacks still standing; the ninth collapsed in two-thousand and five. They expect the existing headlands to become stacks in the future eventually."

Sipping his coffee, Sean nodded appreciatively and moved on to another photo.

"Cradle Mountain in Tasmania. We wanted to be there while it snowed. Trisha got the hiking bug and wants to do Kakadu after the wet season."

Sean smiled. "You caught the adventure bug in Hawaii and passed it on."

"Oh, I think Trisha had it before me. That's why she's an air hostess," I smirked going to the lounge; Sean following and sitting beside me.

"I need to know where I stand before I leave, Holly. If you need time, I can give you that. If you want to date, take this slow this time, I'm good for that too, but if it's positively over, no chance of you ever feeling the same for me again, I need to know, so I know where to start with you."

"How does that work? Starting with me when it's over for good?"

"I'm a very determined man, Holly. I know you loved me. I just need to know how hard it's going to be to make you love me again."

Considering him, I set my coffee down on the coffee table. "I won't deny I love you, Sean. There is nothing past-tense in that emotion. I will also admit I love working with Roger Holmes. I have my dream job, and I'm not willing to give it up for you. I can't move to Hawaii to be with you, and dating across the Pacific is never going to work."

Sean looked confused for a moment, his brows furrowed as he considered my answer. Eventually, he put his coffee cup down and looked at me.

"What if I was closer to you? If I moved here to Australia?"

"But, your businesses?"

"I've already hired managers, and I've taken a more general manager role over all my resorts. I'm traveling a lot more, but I could promise to be here every weekend. You just have to say the word."

"How would that work long term?"

Sean picked up his coffee, took a mouthful and put the cup back down. "Like you, I love my work, Holly. If dating leads to marriage and babies, I'll adjust my travel time to spend more time at home with you and our kids. You tell me where you want to live, I'll buy us a place, and we can raise our family there. Until then, we make it work between our careers. That's the best I can offer for now."

Looking at my knees, the pessimist in me started listing all the complications of that arrangement. "What if you get sick of the ten-hour flight back and forth? I don't want to get my hopes up again just to have you break my heart when you get bored."

Sean took my hand. "I fly business class, and I fly by night if I can. I've already been doing it for months now. I've handled it. It will just make it worth it to have you waiting for me to return." His hand cupped my cheek, his mouth moving closer to mine. "I'll always come back for you, Holly."

Our lips touched, light but sensual. Circling his nose around mine, Sean brushed his lips against mine again. Latching on this time, I pinched his lips with mine, starving for his taste. Sean's arm wrapped around me and pulled me close to his side, but it wasn't close enough.

Throwing a leg over his lap, I straddled him, pressing him back into the lounge as I kissed him hungrily, Sean reciprocating. His hands held me, his mouth wandered along my jaw, down my neck, nibbling. Groaning, Sean lifted his glazed eyes to meet mine. "I've missed you, Holly, but I can't do this if I'm going to catch my plane."

Turning my head to see the clock, I noted the time and that Sean needed to leave. Closing my eyes, I held onto him just a moment longer. I wasn't sure if I could handle letting go of him a second time. Sean stroked my hair back from my face. "I'll be passing through Sydney next Sunday. Can we do dinner before my connecting flight?"

"Why are you connecting in Sydney?"

"I've got business up north."

"What sort of business?" I asked taking my seat back beside him.

"I purchased a private resort on an island in Queensland. I've been over here for three weeks now overseeing the renovations, but I need to fly home and check on my other hotels this week. I'll head north again next week for two weeks. I've already booked flights for next weekend, but I could fly down to see you the following weekend?"

I sat there blinking. "You own a resort in Australia?"

"Yes. I realized once you started your job here, you were never going to give that up to come back to me. Not after I saw the fire in your eyes when you spoke about your work. I met the former owner of this resort on my flight over for your sister's wedding. He was getting divorced and needed to sell to pay his wife out. I saw it as a sign. So, when I left Sydney after the wedding, I flew to the island and checked it out. It was a good investment, so I bought it."

'Some months ago I was in the fortunate position to get rid of a competitor, so I did - this competitor came back, not locally, but still it could have an effect. I'm concerned it's about to become personal.' Benjamin's words played over in my head making me shift uncomfortably.

Sean stood up. "I should get going. Can we do dinner next Sunday? I'll be here overnight and fly north early the next morning."

"Okay."

Sean watched me with concern. "Holly, is something wrong?"

Shaking my head, I stood to show him out. Benjamin's words were playing over in my head. Collecting the coffee cups, I took them to the sink.

"I'm already booked in at a hotel, Holly, so if you are worried about me rushing things again, don't be."

"No, that's not it," I dismissed his worry. I turned back to face him. "How did you meet Benjamin Henderson?"

Sean took a deep breath. "Are you going to date him, Holly? Is that your hesitation, that you have already agreed to give him a second chance?"

Watching Sean for a minute, I didn't answer. His jaw clenched. "I see." Staring at the door, Sean schooled his features before looking back to me. "Ask Benjamin how we met. Let's see if he will be honest with you," Sean opened the door as he collected his luggage.

"Sean, wait," I stepped to the door after him. "I want the truth from you."

Sean turned to consider me. "Next Sunday, dinner. I want that second chance too. Email me the time and place. I'll answer any questions you have then." Sean looked hurt and annoyed. "I'm sorry, Holly, I have to go."

Walking down the hall to the elevator, Sean turned to watch me while he waited for it to arrive. The doors opened, and he stepped inside. And like that, Sean Cassidy was gone again from my life.

Inside, I shut my door before running to the balcony to watch Sean wait for the taxi. Once he slipped inside and drove off, I realized how cold it was outside.

Back inside, I curled up on my lounge in a ball and put on The Longest Ride. I don't care that I was crying before anyone died. I needed to cry, and Nicholas Sparks obviously owned shares in a tissue company. If you needed to cry, his movies were guaranteed to aid your need, at the very least, it gave you a good cover story for answering the door with tear infested eyes.

What was I doing? Was I giving Benjamin a second chance? What about Sean? Jesus, why wasn't Trisha home when I needed her?

Picking up my phone, I dialed Mitchell. "Hey, it's me."

"Hey, Me, how did the weekend go?"

"Avoidance is the best tactic. Which is why I need my girlfriend, and ice cream, and a sounding wall."

"Give me a second. Babe, I'm going to see Holly. She's hit the wall."

"Remind her that punching things in anger never does any good," Tony called.

"No, not literally hit the…forget it, I'll be back later. Jesus, he can be such a guy. I'll be there with ice cream soon."

"Thank you."

"Don't thank me yet. You're going to get fat eating all this ice cream."

"I've got the day off, so I'll come to yoga tomorrow morning."

"Good answer."

Five hours, two pints of Ben and Jerry's, half a bottle of vodka, and two more tear-jerking movies later, Mitchell caught a taxi home. Standing out on the balcony, I tried to remember what it was like to not be an emotional mess. Mitchell wanted me to date them both. To let them both do their best to win me over, but I wasn't that sort of girl. Still, it wouldn't hurt to give them both a one date chance, right? At least, that was my reasoning when I picked up the phone and texted Benjamin.

CHAPTER ELEVEN

Benjamin looked a million dollars, topped off by the car he leaned against waiting for me which cost more than my annual paycheck. I'd never seen Benjamin's collection of sports cars. I'd heard about them, but never seen them. Tonight, I was getting a ride in a black Ferrari.

Striding out of my apartment gate, I smiled up at Benjamin. He was the epitome of all those billionaire romance novels as his eyes roamed over me.

"Evening. You look stunning."

"You said to dress up. I hope this is okay?"

Benjamin stepped towards me, his hands circling my waist. "Perfect." His mouth dropped to mine, placing a chaste kiss on my lips. Pivoting, he opened the passenger door for me, guiding me forward. Benjamin ensured I was in, then shut the door before going to the driver's side. "Ever been to a tango club?"

Blinking, I smiled at the surprise. "No. Can you tango?"

"Can't you?" Benjamin teased.

"No."

Benjamin smiled. "Don't worry, I'll take care of you." His hand rubbed my thigh through my dress in a soothing manner, then with a pat, he put his hands back on the steering wheel and pulled onto the road.

The club was in an industrial space. From the outside, it looked like an empty warehouse, if you bypassed all the expensive cars in the car park. A security guard checked Benjamin's name off a list. "Your number is twelve tonight, Mr. Henderson. Your meal booking is for nine."

"Thank you, Samuel." Tipping the guard, Benjamin drove through the gate. After leaving the Ferrari in car park number twelve, Benjamin walked me to the door.

"This place has some high profile clientele. It's an unspoken rule that you can't speak about anything you see here. Very famous people come here to get away, politicians meet their mistresses here, nothing sordid, just an off the books place where high profile personalities can come out for a good night and not worry about photos of them ending up all over the Internet."

"Okay. Is that why you like the place?"

"I like the atmosphere, but I thought you would prefer it rather than seeing another video of your private life on YouTube."

Unsure what he meant, I frowned. He read my befuddlement. "I'm referring to your rather public makeup scene with Sean

Cassidy on Sunday." When my confusion didn't clear, Benjamin's smile dropped. "You weren't aware?"

Mouth falling open, I shook my head. "Someone filmed us talking at the restaurant?"

"Just where he apologized loudly, and you kissed him for it," Benjamin muttered. The bouncer at the door greeted us and let us inside. "I was surprised to hear from you after I saw that, but I'm grateful I did."

A heavily made-up woman smiled as we approached her at the end of a velvet-curtained hallway. "Benjamin, welcome back." Her eyes appraised me. "Miss Claire, correct?" I hesitated at her knowing who I was. She gave me a kind smile. "Don't worry, no one will mention you ever being here, or who you were with." Her eyes returned to Benjamin. "You are vouching for her. She's your responsibility."

"I'm aware, Tilda."

As Tilda swept the curtain open the muted sounds of the club encroached on the peace. Taking my hand, Benjamin led me into another hall with a glass wall that overlooked an old-school dancehall set up.

In the middle of the space was a large dance floor, on which, many couples were dancing. Around that were lots of tables and booths. Not all of them occupied, but there were some with people talking in them. There was a live band with a female singer, and waiters moving around the space from the bar.

My eyes drifted to people entering another glass-walled room on the other side, Benjamin noticing put his mouth to my ear. "The smoke room. If you want to light up, be it regular cigarettes, or something more illegal, you must go to the smoking room."

"They have pot?"

"Amongst other illegal substances," Benjamin smirked at my shock. "But it all has to happen in the smoke room. Rules of the club, the dance hall and the dining rooms stay clean."

We reached the end of the walk. There were two doors. The door out to the dance floor, and another into a hall signposted as the dining area. Pushing open the door to the dance floor, Benjamin led me along the line of booths until he found the one marked with a twelve in Roman numerals. I was starting to understand the number at the gate. It gave you your carpark, your table, and probably your seat in the dining room too.

A waiter approached and placed a jug of sangria on the table. Tipping him a twenty, Benjamin asked for a scotch. The waiter nodded and walked away. Pouring me a glass of the cocktail, Benjamin placed it in front of me as he shuffled around the booth so he could watch the floor while we talk, but I noticed he took the opportunity to place his hand on my leg.

"The idea is for the staff to interact with patrons as little as possible. They have a cocktail for the night available by the jug. You can drink that or order spirits, but the staff won't ask you what you want. They just give the standard and walk away. Same with food. You have the choice of three set menus when you book. There are tapas, dessert, or a cheese and wine menu."

"Which are we having?"

"You seemed partial to dessert."

My mouth mirrored Benjamin's smirk, letting him know he'd chosen well. The waiter placed Benjamin's drink on the table almost stealthily - if I'd blinked, I'd have missed him – then we both sat quietly enjoying the atmosphere and drink for a few moments.

After a long sip of his scotch, Benjamin sat back, observing me. "I'm going to make the assumption, since you made amends with Cassidy, that we are both getting a second chance. Am I correct?"

"I'm giving you both a date each. I'm not sure if it's a second chance yet. You are both pursuing me, and I need to figure out if forgiving either of you is an option for me. You both hurt me in very different ways, but the outcome was the same. You broke my trust, and trust to me is everything."

Benjamin considered my words carefully as he finished his scotch. Setting his empty glass on the table, Benjamin used a finger on my chin to turn my gaze to meet his. "I can't apologize for the way I messed things up anymore, Holly. My approach is to move on and start fresh." He offered me his hand. "Come dance with me."

I couldn't argue with him. He'd apologized, and admitted his mistake. I hated when people kept harping on as if saying sorry a million times would fix things. It's one of the things I'd always liked about Benjamin. He said his piece then he let it go. Of course, usually, he said it with a finality that made you know it was to happen how he wanted. Taking his hand, Benjamin led me to the floor.

I was conscious of anyone watching me, but no one even turned our way other than to nod at Benjamin or appraise the way I looked. Swinging me into him, Benjamin braced us, his hand on mine, placing my other on his shoulder, his other to my back with his palm parallel to the floor. Stepping me into the dance, Benjamin used his hands and pelvis to lead me.

I'd never danced the tango; I'd never danced anything formal except ballet. In Benjamin's arms, you wouldn't know I'd never taken a lesson. The song finished, and a more aggressive tango dance came on. I recognized it from a musical I'd watched when I was younger. Benjamin smiled, he adjusted his hands and moved us into it.

The strength in his frame reflected the heavy beat of the music, his hand caressing across my ribs before pressing me into a turn under his arm, turning me this way and that, laying me back on his knee and brushing his knuckle down my sternum lightly before pulling me up and quickening his pace. He was so into it I was sucked into the drama of the music right with him.

We weren't the only couple on the floor but stuffed if I noticed another soul in the room for the next hour as Benjamin controlled my body in that dance. The tango was seduction, and it was working. The heat was pooling between my thighs, my breath short over the rapid beating of my heart. My eyelids were heavy with every sensual but chaste caress.

Nothing in the way Benjamin touched me on that dance floor would be inappropriate in front of a church crowd, and yet, it was sinful and erotic and masterful in its duplicity. As the band announced they were taking a break, Benjamin met my eyes. Heat blazed in his as I was sure it did in mine. "Thirsty?"

"Very." My tongue flicking across my lips to wet them.

Leading me back to our table, Benjamin filled my glass.

Signaling the waiter, he left a twenty on the table as he took the seat next to me.

"I never realized what good stamina you had, Holly. I should have. You swam laps for an hour straight every night you worked, and I saw you and Trisha on that dance floor last week, but still, I'm impressed. You didn't once stumble or lose your breath out there."

"Well, I know your morning workout, so I was never in doubt of your stamina, Benjamin." When I winked, he smirked but didn't say anything. The waiter put his drink on the table and took the twenty. We sat there, drinking and smiling at each other.

When the band came back, Benjamin checked his watch. "We have another fifteen minutes till dinner. Would you like to have another dance?" He offered me his hand.

It was a much slower dance. The music would speed up and slow down, enabling Benjamin to take his time moving his hands around my ribs, his thumb dragging just beneath my bust. He bent me back over his arm, holding me there, then let his free hand grab a firm hold of my arse before slowly trailing down the back of my thigh to lift my knee to his hip.

My lashes fluttered, my breath rushed out, then Benjamin lifted me and quickly spun me to match the sudden upbeat. As he pulled me close, pressing our pelvises hard against each other before stepping us backward, I realized, just like the first time he pinned me to the wall in my office, he had perfect control of me. His seduction was masterful.

The music changed, Benjamin brushed my lips with his. "Let's eat."

CHAPTER TWELVE

THE DINING ROOM WASN'T THE RESTAURANT TYPE OF SPACE I imagined. Room twelve was a small intimate space with a large ottoman in the center. There was a beautiful tray sitting in the middle of the cushioned table, on which lay two large plates holding various samples of desserts, two bowls of ice cream, a bowl of strawberries, a bowl of honey, and a bowl of cream.

Next to the ottoman was a small table that held an ice bucket with a dessert wine and two glasses. Against the wall was a stand with a drawer and a music player on top. On the far wall was a full-screen video from the first-person perspective walking along a beach at sunset.

Suddenly nervous, I swallowed. It was beautiful, but it was also so heavy on the seduction side of things that I felt uncomfortable.

"I know, it's a bit much," Benjamin chuckled. "It's just how they do things here. As I said earlier, some important people use the club to see their mistresses and the set up was originally for that intention. Since then, others have just used it as a place to have peace from the paparazzi. I've only known about it for a year. It will adapt to the user's needs."

Moving to the music player, Benjamin touched a screen then scrolled through a menu. The video changed to be aerial views of places all over the world. The music turned to easy listening music. "This is my favorite video of the ones available. I've been trying to go and see each of these places in person since coming across it."

Moving to the ottoman, Benjamin poured the wine, offering me a glass before he sat on the ottoman. Something with his ease and the way he was talking about the video made me relax slightly. Benjamin kicked off his shoes and sat cross-legged on the ottoman watching the video. It was the most relaxed I'd ever seen him.

Pointing to the screen, Benjamin smiled at me. "Victoria Falls. One of my favorites. Absolutely amazing." Selecting a strawberry, he dipped it in the honey and popped it in his mouth. Closing his eyes, Benjamin moaned. "You have to try this honey. They've spiced it with something that makes your taste buds come alive."

Kicking off my heels, I joined Benjamin on the ottoman. Picking another strawberry, Benjamin dipped it in the honey and looked at me. "Cream or no cream?"

"No, cream, thank you."

Smirking, Benjamin offered me the berry to bite. Sinking my teeth in, I closed my eyes as fireworks of delicious flavors exploded in my mouth. Moaning, I nodded in appreciation. "That's amazing!"

"Now, drink the wine." Benjamin lifted his glass to his lips, his eyes sparkling as he appreciated the taste. When he licked his lips, I was tempted to taste it from his mouth. I didn't. Sipping my own wine, I behaved. Strawberries burst on my tongue, followed by hints of cinnamon and caramel.

"God, it's a foodgasm!"

Benjamin laughed before picking up a bowl of ice cream and handing it to me. Setting the wine down, I scooped a mouthful of the salted caramel and brandy ice cream into my mouth. Benjamin sat eating his. The scenery changed. "Kakadu in the wet season. I went at the wrong time, but it was still amazing. I nearly got eaten by a crocodile. Gave me a bit of a reality check."

Chuckling, I lifted a brow. "When was that?"

"About three months ago. I stopped over on my way back from a conference in Dubai." His eyes were watching the screen mesmerized. "I have to go back after the wet season and see the other part of its beauty."

Liking this side of Benjamin, I smiled. He'd never even discussed his love of traveling in the years I'd known him. It was always business. "Trisha and I are going to go together. It's on our list."

Turning his face to mine as he set his ice cream aside, Benjamin took another sip of his wine. "What other places do you have on your list?"

We sat there eating desserts, comparing our bucket list of places we wanted to travel. We discussed places we had already been and what we loved and hated. I avoided talking about

Hawaii; Benjamin didn't mention it either, even though I knew he had been there several times.

"Kathmandu is the last on this video," Benjamin explained as he took the slice of peach from the top of the last piece of peach and raspberry cheesecake and handed me the cheesecake. "I haven't made it there yet."

"Are you going to climb?" Sipping my third glass of wine, the flavor explosion washed over me.

"No, I like all my fingers and toes. I just want to go and see the area, go to a monastery in Tibet, and spend a few days experiencing the way they live."

"Really?" My eyebrows lifted, trying not to laugh at the image of Benjamin as a monk.

Benjamin smirked. "Really. I don't live my life by my dick, Holly."

"I gathered that."

Benjamin looked at the demolished tray of food and the empty bottle of wine. "So, what did you think?"

"Heavenly. Every dessert was picked to compliment the various flavors in the wine. Every sip after every morsel revealed all the fruity notes and sweetness. It's the best meal I've ever eaten."

"Confession. It's what I love about this place. I've been coming here once a week by myself since I discovered it and just enjoying the food experience and the scenery." Picking up the tray, Benjamin moved it to the side table. When he came back, he laid back on the ottoman.

"And who do you dance with, Benjamin?"

"I told you this place originally catered to affairs? They have escorts available to hire. I've never hired one, but for solo parties, they will dance with you for free if they don't have a client at the time. I've never shared this part of the experience with anyone before."

Pressing my lips together, I considered this was a special place for him. "I'm the first person you've brought here?"

"Don't look so surprised, Holly. This place exists on anonymity. You have to be careful who you bring in with you because you are responsible if they blab anything they see." Sitting up to lean on his elbow, Benjamin stroked my cheek, and I turned my face into his touch. "I know you can keep your tongue still, Holly. I also knew, after all the media attention you've had this year, that you could appreciate what this place is about for me."

"I do."

When he traced my lips with his thumb, I opened my mouth and pulled his thumb inside to suck and wrap my tongue around. Benjamin used his thumb to bring my face to his. He kissed me, and just as he did on the dance floor, Benjamin used his body to turn me and lay me back on the ottoman smoothly.

His kiss was slow, tender, filled with want, but holding the leash of his desire tight. An inferno of lust raged through me, my body hot and ready for devouring. Opening my eyes, I found the room spinning above me, and I groaned. Benjamin pulled back and smiled at me. Hand caressing over my ribs, he didn't press for anything more.

"I never realized how much I needed you till you weren't there, Holly. I'm not just talking about my business. You were always important to me there, but I never realized how much I'd come to look forward to seeing you every morning, how much I enjoyed eating a meal with you on Wednesday nights."

Benjamin watched me; his eyes seemed so honest and open. Scanning me, Benjamin looked around the room then he sat up and helped me to stand. "I think we possibly overdid it on the alcohol."

"Yes, though I usually can drink a lot more without it affecting me this hard. You can't drive us home, can you?

"I only had the two scotches and a glass of the wine. Over the four hours we've been here, I'm still under the limit. You have work tomorrow; I better get you home." Helping me with my shoes first, Benjamin then got his on before standing. He wrapped an arm around my waist to walk me out. "Come here with me again next week? I want to make this our new Wednesday night thing together."

The world spun anticlockwise. Benjamin steadied me. "Shit, I haven't been this drunk this easy in years."

Studying my eyes, Benjamin frowned. "That wine was a pretty high alcohol content."

"If we do this again, I can't get this drunk. I need to crawl out of my grave in the morning, and Thursdays are busy days."

"Okay, I'll monitor your intake next time." Plopping me down in his car, Benjamin shut the door. Relaxing my head back on the headrest, I closed my eyes.

"Holly, where are your keys?"

Opening my eyes, I found myself standing at the gate to my apartment. Wait, was I upright? No, Benjamin was carrying me. Blinking at the keypad, I struggled to press the pin code. The gate buzzed, and Benjamin carried me through. I managed to get my keys out of my handbag before we got to the main door. "You can put me down."

"You said that when I got you out of the car, then proceeded to pass out again. I think it's safer just to carry you." He helped me unlock the door then carried me to the lift where I rested my head on his shoulder as we ascended.

The scent of warm amber made the bellows of longing churn in my abdomen. "I miss your smell. I used to go home with the smell of you on me and curl into bed with it. I convinced myself you cared for me. That you were falling in love with me."

"I loved going through my day with the smell of you on me," Benjamin echoed. Jolting awake again, Benjamin holding me upright while he tried to unlock the door to my apartment. He got it open and walked me in. "Is Trisha home?"

"No, she's back tomorrow morning." Though, I'm not sure it came out as words. "Argh, I was fine till I laid down."

"Which one is your room?"

Pointing to the door, I tried to stay conscious as he took me inside. Lowering me to the bed, Benjamin started taking off my shoes. "Not the ending I was expecting to the night."

"You were planning to get laid."

Benjamin smirked. "I wasn't planning it. I was hoping, but it wasn't a set plan."

Cupping his face in my hands, my smile melted as he looked up at me. The room stabilized as I focused on his lips. "I hate that you lied to me. I never know if I can trust you now."

"I'm a businessman, Holly. We don't lie; we just omit the truth. You were an employee, and I needed to manage a situation. I couldn't interview you for the role because you were more qualified than the preferred candidate. I managed an HR issue. It just happened to impact our relationship. That was something I had hoped to avoid but had weighed as a possible risk."

"You were willing to risk losing me?"

"As a lover, yes. Not as my employee. I never considered you leaving your job as an option." Smoothing his hands over my thighs, Benjamin instigated an eruption of lust beneath my skin. "I don't think I would have lost you if Colin wouldn't have pulled that shit. It wasn't a factor I'd accounted for."

"And you account for everything?"

"Yes. I usually do."

"Did you account for a condom tonight?"

Smirking, Benjamin retrieved two from his suit pocket. Planting my lips on his, I kissed him heatedly, trying to transfer the heat inside me to him. Rising above me, Benjamin laid me back, his body pressed to mine, and the temperature inside me grew to a boiling point.

"I'm going to spontaneously combust." I worried, wrapping my legs around his calves.

"Fuck, Holly, I've missed you." His lips kissing the rise of my breasts as he unzipped my dress. Head too heavy to lift, I closed my eyes to enjoy his lips and touch. Damn, I drank too much.

CHAPTER THIRTEEN

Feeling happy and tingly, I smiled to myself as I remembered feeling the same way in Hawaii. Inhaling the melted aroma of male cologne on my skin, I frowned as the scent didn't match the one of Sean in my memory. My breath stopped in my chest.

Flashes of last night came back, but the second half of the dining experience was static. I couldn't even remember getting home. The most I remembered from last night was kissing Benjamin, feeling extremely hot, very horny, and out of control of myself, but that was it.

Feeling between my legs, there was no evidence of sex, but that didn't mean we didn't use condoms. Lifting my head, I found Benjamin still sound asleep, naked in bed beside me. Pressing my lips together on a sob at the sight of him, I cursed the way fate worked. Waking up with Benjamin was a first for me. I just wished I wasn't too busy freaking about what happened to enjoy it.

Slipping from the bed, I pulled a jumper and knickers on, found my phone, and went out to the lounge room as I made a call I was probably going to regret.

"Holly? I'm at work, is something wrong?"

"I just need a minute, Sean. I had an experience last night and the way I feel this morning isn't right." I licked my lips, trying to phrase my question the right way. "I was drinking and was tipsy, but not enough to be that far gone. It reminded me of when I was in Hawaii, and you made me that drink."

"The angel's kiss? I remember."

"What was the ingredient I reacted too?"

"Cupid's Dart," Sean exhaled.

"Do you know if it's in any other kind of drinks? Like a sangria or wine?" I was biting my fingernails, something I'd never done.

"Not in those, no. It is in a few fancy cocktails, but you would know by that smooth texture over your tongue. Did you drink something like that?"

"No, just the Sangria and the wine."

"Holly… did something happen last night? You sound distressed."

"I don't know. I don't remember much after the desserts, just flashes and being so hot and horny and kissing."

"Dessert?"

"Yes. It was one of those things where each item of food brings out the various notes in the wine you are drinking. It was wonderful. I loved it, and I drank a bit, but I've drunk more than that and never lost control." Sean was quiet. "You hate me?"

"No, I'm googling what other recipes contain Cupid's dart. Apparently, it is used for its aphrodisiac qualities in honeyed strawberries, and also in a massage oil which can have the same effect. For regular people, it gives them a slight tickle, but for those who react, it's reported to have the same effect as a date rape drug."

I sat staring at my blank television screen. "Strawberries dipped in honey?"

"I'm guessing that was on the menu?"

"Thanks, Sean. I need to go deal with this."

"Holly, I'm sorry this happened to you again."

"It's no one's fault, Sean. You didn't know I reacted; the service staff couldn't have known either. It's just bad luck. I know going forward to avoid honey dipped strawberries unless I'm with the man I'm dating."

"You didn't tell anyone about it?"

"No," I shook my head. "I mean I did, the next morning, but all I told them was the drink gave my libido quite the kick. I didn't mention the ingredient or how I reacted like a drunk sex-crazed lunatic."

Sean was quiet for a long moment. "I see. Have you spoken to Henderson yet about how we met?"

"No, not yet. You still don't want to tell me?"

"The first time we met was at Nichola's house when I went to try and find you. He's very close to your sister and her husband. I'll tell you the rest when I see you on Sunday."

"You still want to see me?"

"Holly, you wouldn't have called me if you purposefully slept with another guy. You would have just used the Cupid dart excuse, or reminded me we aren't together and you can sleep with who you like. I could hear that you were upset calling. That means if something happened, it wasn't your doing."

"I don't know if something happened. I need to find that out first. Bye, Sean."

"Call me if you need me," Sean farewelled before he hung up.

Glancing at my bedroom door, I exhaled hard. In the kitchen, I made coffee before taking both cups into my bedroom. Benjamin was awake, checking emails on his phone. His eyes lifted to me as I handed him the coffee. "Morning," he greeted with a smile as he took the coffee.

"Morning. Benjamin, about last night-"

"It was a nice night, but, on our next date, I'm not going to let you drink so much that you pass out on me."

I blinked. "I passed out?"

"Just after you came on my tongue. Do you know how long it's been for me? I got you off, and by the time I had the condom on, you were out to it. You can check the bin in your bathroom if you like. The condom got thrown away unused. Well, it's not filled with anything."

A flash of Benjamin kneeling between my thighs as he tongued me and the way my back arched as I came hard had heat filling my cheeks and neck. "Oh!"

Benjamin laughed, pulling me towards him. "I've still got another if you want to make it up to me?" He kissed me.

Placing my hand on his chest, I stretched away, licking the taste of him from my lips. "Benjamin, can you call the club and ask what the spice was in the honey last night? I have a feeling, based on my reaction last night and a previous similar experience, that they have used a spice to which I react. I just need to clarify that is the case."

"A spice you react to?" Benjamin repeated brows furrowing as he set his coffee aside.

"Yes. It causes an amatory response when I'm sober, but when I'm drinking, it can be closer to Rohypnol."

"The date-rape drug?" Benjamin watched me swallow and look away. Using his fingers on my chin, Benjamin forced my eyes back to his with a gentle grip. "Wait, are you suggesting I drugged you last night?"

"No. Of course not. How could you have known? I only found out earlier this year that I react to it. Apparently, I'm one of five percent of the world's population that it affects so aggressively, so it's not anyone's fault if that is the case. I'd just like to know if it was so I know to avoid honey dipped strawberries from now on."

Combing a hand through his hair, Benjamin shook his head in annoyance and typed a text on his phone. "So, this spice is why you went from happy tipsy to pass out drunk?"

"Yes."

"And what's the spice you suspect?"

"It's called cupids dart."

Benjamin swore under his breath. Standing up, he pulled his pants on roughly, looking all sorts of pissed off.

"I'm not upset, Benjamin. I just recognize the symptoms and want it clarified."

Benjamin turned to face me; his eyes were angry and worried. "It still makes me feel like shit, Holly. I would have had sex with you last night if you hadn't passed out, and you would have woken up feeling dirty about the experience. Fuck, I went to sleep frustrated but relieved we were passed what happened. Now, I'm waking up to find that's not the case, and you probably freaked out waking up to even find me here."

"Benjamin, I never said I was over what happened. Is that what you thought? That we would have sex, and all would be forgiven?"

"No, I just know you wouldn't have sex with me if you weren't considering getting serious with me. You're not the sort of girl who does casual sex." When his phone started ringing, Benjamin turned away to answer it. "Tilda, thank you for getting back to me so quickly."

Benjamin found his shirt and started dressing. I wasn't sure how to feel about everything. I couldn't blame him for the honey, but I didn't plan on sleeping with him before I made a firm decision between him and Sean, or remaining single and opening myself to something new altogether. I mean, I was horny, but I was happy. I didn't need a guy to fulfill my life, but it'd be nice.

"Yes, I understand it was a standard recipe. I'm not claiming the club is at fault. My date reacted to something she ingested last night. She just wants to clarify if this particular spice was the cause, so she knows to avoid it in the future." Benjamin took a breath. "I'm aware, Tilda. She is not upset; she just recognized her reaction. I'm more upset about how the night ended than she is, so can you please just confirm if a spice called cupid's dart was in the ingredients?"

Benjamin waited for a second, pinching the bridge of his nose and closing his eyes as he listened to whatever was said. I finished my coffee worried he was going to get in trouble at the club. I didn't want his place of peace taken away from him.

"Thank you," Benjamin finally lifted his head and looked out my balcony door. "No, I wasn't aware she would react. I'll be sure to pass that along. Thank you, Tilda." Hanging up, Benjamin put his phone in his pocket as he turned to face me. "It was in the honey as you suspected. It's what gives it that impact when combined with the strawberries. It is an old recipe used specifically for seduction. The club passes along their apologies and hopes you are not put off attending again because of this one instance. Tilda asked me to assure you that if you wish to go again, you can give notification of any food allergies to avoid a reoccurrence."

"Thank you." I meant it, sincerely. It's nice to have that reassurance that your out of character behavior was justified. I'd not been upset when it happened with Sean because I had nothing to regret in the morning, but I could have this morning. "I have to get ready for work."

Striding towards me, Benjamin took my hands in his. "Can we go out again this weekend? Tomorrow night?" He requested gently.

"I have plans with Trisha this weekend. Next Wednesday is the earliest I'll be available."

Benjamin smirked. "So, you are willing to tango again?"

"I am. But maybe the tapas might be the way to go this time."

Benjamin stroked my cheek. "Okay. Suits me." His lips brushed mine. He hesitated, then he folded me in his arms and kissed me harder. He pulled away with a growl. "You are lucky we both have to work, or I'd be demanding a repeat of you sitting on my face so I could tongue that juicy pussy of yours."

"You're so romantic."

CHAPTER FOURTEEN

MY PHONE STARTED RINGING AS I WAS PACKING MY LUGGAGE. I considered Sean's name on the screen and picked it up hesitantly. "Isn't it late over there?"

"It is. I was worried about you all day and wanted to talk to you before I go to sleep."

"Nothing happened," I sighed sitting on my bed next to my suitcase. "I don't understand why it was worse than the first time. I still recall everything that happened between us in the elevator and the phone call. Last night, my memory was a little sketchy over the details. I wouldn't be anywhere near as upset if I could remember it."

"I've spent the day reading up on it. My understanding is that it gets worse on each subsequent exposure and can turn into an allergic reaction, which will require medical intervention. From what I've researched of the Amorous Honey recipe - that's what it's called - the quantity is nearly three times more than what I used in the drink, so it would have hit you harder and faster as well."

I exhaled. "Good to know for the future. Wait, you looked up the recipe?"

"Of course I did. If you google Cupid's Dart several recipes come up under it. Funnily enough, the cocktail I made you also comes up with that listing."

"I should get a copy of that listing to ensure I never consume it again."

Sean was quiet for a moment. "Are you sure you are okay, Holly? I can bring my flight forward and be there in twenty-four hours."

"No, I'm fine, really. I'm going away with my friends this weekend. We are doing a biking wine tour in the Hunter Valley."

"A biking wine tour?"

"We ride push bikes between wineries," I explained, happy to focus on something else. "They have a minibus that meets us at each vineyard. The bus carries any purchases for us and delivers us safely back to our hotel later."

"Sounds like a great way to spend your weekend. Will I see you Sunday night or would you prefer to wait until I'm passing through Sydney next? I'm booked to head back to Hawaii in three weeks, but I could fly down next weekend to see you."

"This Sunday will be fine. The riding tour is all day Saturday, so I'll be home in time Sunday. Why don't you meet me at my apartment? I'd love for you to meet Trisha."

"That sounds good. I'll message when I've booked into my

hotel to give you an idea of what time to expect me," Sean organized.

"I'll see you then. And, Sean. Thanks for calling to check on me."

"I couldn't sleep not knowing you were okay, Holly. I'd call you nightly if I didn't worry that was overstepping the bounds of what you want right now."

Stomach twisting, I pressed my lips together. I'd love to hear Sean's voice every night, but I wasn't ready to move that quickly yet either. "Goodnight, Sean."

"Night, Holly."

Staring at my darkened phone, I was both happy to be talking to Sean again, and tortured by the inability to see a relationship working between us. I sat there, tormenting myself until the front door closed. "Bring on the wine!" Trisha called.

"God, I hope I remember how to ride a bike," Mitchell laughed. Smiling, I went out to get a hug from my friends.

"Oh, what happened?" Seeing me, Trisha pushed her carry-on luggage from work aside, she pulled me into her arms. "Do I need to kill that gorgeous ex-boss of yours?"

"Not yet. Make me one of your coffee's, and I'll spill all about our date last night." While Trisha walked into the kitchen, I turned my eyes to Mitchell and frowned. "What are you doing here?"

"Ah, I want the goss from last night too. I made Trisha message me her arrival time so I could make sure she didn't get any dirty details without me," Mitchell groused manhandling me to the lounge and forcing me to sit. "So, spill, did you ride his big dick all night long?"

I burst into tears.

———

"WHO'S silly idea was it to drink and ride?" All but falling off his bike at the last winery on our tour, Mitchell crumpled to the grass lawn area and laid himself out as if he was dead. "Tony, mouth to mouth, babe. I need it, stat!"

Dismounting my bike, I handed it off to the tour operator for the return. "I know why they left this one until last. That hill was a killer." Turning around, I rolled my eyes at Tony and Mitchell macking on the front lawn of the winery. Trisha pulled out her camera and took photos of the soft porn show.

"Selfie!" Getting out her selfie stick, Trisha pulled me into a photo with her. Laughing when Mitchell photobombed the picture. The hilarity continued when Trisha set up a makeshift photo shoot with all four of us.

"Okay, enough posing," Tony declared after fifteen minutes. "More wine and cheese."

"Did we miss lunch?" Mitchell frowned, rubbing his growling belly. "I don't remember lunch."

"We had that picnic at the other winery that the tour provided," Trisha reminded.

"That wasn't lunch. It was more food sampling. Let's go get food." Mitchell put his arm around my shoulders, and the guys walked us into the restaurant attached to the winery. Food sounded like an excellent idea. We ordered mains, and the guys ordered bread to soak up all the wine they'd been drinking.

"We still have the tasting to do here," Trish reminded.

"Hence the bread," Tony agreed. "I could barely ride straight coming here."

"I think that was your fitness, not the alcohol," Trisha teased.

"I'm fighting fit, thank you." Tony's eyes came to me. "You've been rather quiet today, Holly. Something bothering you?"

"Like Mitchell didn't spill his guts Thursday night," I rolled my eyes.

"What Mitchell spills on me would get you girls pregnant," Tony slurred a little. It made us girls chuckle. Tony was rarely ever vulgar.

Moving the breadbasket in front of his boyfriend, Mitchell kissed his temple. "You need more bread, babe, and to stop talking,"

Trisha prodded Mitchell across the table. "I hope you are both super vigilant about safety?"

Mitchell rolled his eyes. "We've been together eight years, now. We get caught up in the moment occasionally, you know."

"There goes your ability to lecture me constantly."

"Again. Together eight years," Mitchell gestured between him and Tony. Then fluttered his hand at Trisha. "Not eight minutes, Miss mile high club's first-class floozy."

"Damn straight, it's only first class, buster!" Trisha flicked her hair over her shoulder. "Not giving it away to someone who can't afford the perfection of this awesomeness."

When I smirked shaking my head, Tony caught my eye and raised his brow at me. Exhaling dynamically, I focused on the menu. I didn't want to discuss this anymore. I'd had a great day being with my friends and not focusing on my disaster of a love life.

"You should call your sister, Holly," Tony announced. "The nice one, and find out what she knows."

Blinking at the change of subject, I looked up to find everyone watching me and realized the conversation about me had continued without my input. "Nichola?"

"If the guys met at her house, she would know the story, and her side of it is unlikely to be biased towards either of them."

"Unless she was screwing Benjamin when Sean showed up," Mitchell offered.

"Nichola has more class than that," Trisha dismissed. "Plus, she married Benjamin's best friend, it's too much risk to cheat on your boss and husband with his best mate."

"Especially one as notorious as Benjamin who is often stalked by random tabloids for gossip." Tony's eyes came back to me. "Finding out the deal with their meeting may help you make a choice, Holly."

"I've been thinking about that all day. I'm happy as I am. Single, hanging with my friends. They've both hurt me. I'm better off just discarding this shit and enjoying my singledom."

"Fuck, no!" Trisha scoffed. "You are a miserable wreck. You need to sort this mess out, not run away from it."

"Agreed," Mitchell piped in. "You need to admit you gave up

on a good thing when you ran home from Hawaii, and you need to fix that shit."

Trisha smacked Mitchell's elbow. "No direction, remember? We agreed; her choice."

"Right! Sort your mess, and stop running from it."

Tony forehead slapped himself. Taking a breath, he met my surprised eyes. "What these other two are trying to say in their poor drunken state, is that you've been miserable since you came home from Hawaii, Holly. Yes, you were unhappy leaving, but you were heartbroken coming home. Try as you have to pretend you were over it, you haven't fooled us for one second. Now, none of us is going to tell you how to live your life-"

"Yes, I fucking will if she picks wrong," Trisha muttered.

"-but, we can't stand back and let you trip yourself up when it's the prime opportunity to set this right. If you don't want either of them, either because you don't love them or are unable to forgive them, then we accept that. You need to choose what's right for you, but you can't just give up and run because it's too hard."

Sniffling, I swiped at my watery eyes. I wasn't crying, not yet. Sucking in a deep breath, I nodded at Tony. Giving me a fatherly smile, Tony filled my glass with the wine they'd ordered.

"Just to clarify, she loves Sean, right?"

"Mitchell, jeez!" Trisha groaned. She covered her eyes.

"Drink your wine and concentrate on what I'm going to do to you back at our hotel, babe."

"Deets, please," Trisha requested enthusiastically.

"Perv," Tony grumbled.

"Definitely! I'm living vicariously, so spill all your dirty deets so I can fantasize about it later tonight when I'm by myself."

"You are a seriously disturbed and sick individual, Trisha Martinez."

"Yeah, but your boyfriend loves it."

"Yes, I do!" Mitchell agreed with a boisterous laugh. "I seriously do."

CHAPTER FIFTEEN

The door buzzer rang. My head and two others turned to look at the intercom, then the other two swiveled back to watch me. "Do you want me to answer it?"

Shaking my head at Trisha, I went to the intercom. Sandy blond hair, caramel tan, and ocean blue eyes showed on the screen. My heart pounded, and my arms bloomed in goosebumps. Gripping my stomach, I tried to stop the tornado of butterflies as they spiraled and surged upwards into my throat.

"Hi," I choked out when I pressed the buzzer, followed quickly by hitting the unlock button. "Come on up. Do you remember the number?"

Sean smirked. "I've spent months looking for you, Holly. I don't plan to lose you again so quickly. I'll be up there in a minute." As Sean stepped through the doors, I hit disconnect.

"I like him already," Mitchell mock-whispered to Trisha.

"Stop. This isn't a game."

Trisha hugged me from the side. "Definitely not. It's more a romance novel, and we are 'shipping' the couple we think should be together."

"He lives hours away by plane. I'm not even sure this is viable. I'm just having dinner with him and talking. We might walk away from this night as nothing more than friends. So, let's not get our hopes up." The look on my best friend's faces was a mixture of sympathy and disbelief.

When the knock came at the door, I jumped a little. Inhaling, I gave my friends a clear 'behave' glare and opened the door, but I should have taken a more substantial breath. The sight of Sean standing there in his jeans and button-down forced all the air out of my lungs in a rush.

Sean smiled down at me, ocean blue eyes taking me in, glassy with excitement. He was dressed to go out to a fancy restaurant, and I was hypnotized by how good he looked in his suit. Glancing down at the beach dress I was wearing, I shook my head.

Sean's lips slowly turned down. "Holly?"

"Dinner was my choice, right?"

"Of course. It's easy enough to take the jacket off and dress down, but most women given the choice of a venue, choose a nice restaurant."

"I'm not most women."

"I know, but I wanted to be prepared just in case." He lifted a freezer bag. "I know flowers are customary, but I thought this was a much better gift?"

Eyeing him as I took the bag, I checked the weight. "Is someone's head in here?"

Sean's dimples came out on full display. "No," he laughed. "It's Dole Whip. I ordered it when I went home and had them send it to Australia for me to pick up in Duty-Free. I know how much-"

"I'll take that!" Trisha jumped in and stole the bag, quickly disappearing into our kitchen again.

"-you love it," Sean finished, giving the entryway a bizarre look.

"That was Trisha. She also loves Dole Whip, to the extent that I doubt she'll leave me any. Come in. My best friends want to meet you."

Moving into the open living area, we found Mitchell and Trisha huddled over the pineapple ice cream, spoons digging into the tub. They looked up at me and blinked innocently. Sean chuckled softly beside me. Mitchell looked Sean over and drooled.

"Sean, meet Trisha and Mitchell."

Mitchell swapped his spoon to his left hand to shake hands with Sean. "Nice to finally meet you. The cameras didn't do you justice."

"Wait!" I held up a hand. "You saw him on television when he came looking for me?"

"Well, yeah." Mitchell withdrew a little his shoulders folding forward like a shield. "We didn't tell you because you were already a mess and we figured you'd seen the news and chose to ignore it. I mean, I asked you several times if you'd seen the news, and you kept glaring at me, so I assumed that was a yes, and don't dare ask about it."

Clenching my teeth and fist to stop from swearing and strangling Mitchell, I inhaled forcefully and went to the lounge to grab my purse. Would it have made a difference? Who the hell knows? You can't change the past, only the future. I turned to look at Sean. Did we have a future? "Ready to go?"

Sean loosened his tie and removed it. "Can I leave this here?"

Reaching out for it, I placed it neatly on the back of the bar stool. Trisha abandoned the ice cream to come over and hug me. "I have to head off in two hours, so I'll see you in two days." I hugged her back, butterflies shifting their swarm pattern in my stomach. "Stop stressing. He's not asking you to marry him tonight. Just have fun," Trisha whispered.

Keeping my mouth closed, I stepped to the door. "It was nice meeting you both." Sean waited until we got to the elevator to speak again. "Can I ask where we are going?"

"Music by the sea. A string quartet performs on the beach once a month. A restaurant across the road caters. I've gone every month since I moved here. It's a nice relaxing evening."

Sean raised his brows, peering at his shoes. "Did I steal someone else's ticket?"

"No, I normally go alone. I called up and booked an extra bean bag for you."

Sean's mouth lift on one side with a tentative smile. "Beanbag?" He shook his head when I nodded. "Well, this should be a first date I won't quickly forget." Sean's laughter lightened my mood.

When the elevator doors opened, I found myself smiling as I alighted the lift with him. So much so, when Sean took my hand in his, I found it comfortable, a surge of happiness chasing away my anxiety.

"How are you handling the travel?"

"Hard, but I put myself in for it, so I'll see it through." Sean sent a side glance my way. "For now at least. If I get sick of it, I'll hire a GM, and they can do the traveling. Have you given any thought to how you will handle the travel when Roger expands?"

"I'm not officially a general manager. I'm his staff manager. I won't be required to travel if he does expand unless it's to hire the first staff."

"So, you have a guaranteed fixed abode?"

"I do."

Sean met my eyes briefly, causing a small pang of guilt to curl in my stomach. He'd had that and given it up on a chance meeting while chasing me across the ocean. The knowledge tarnished the joy of the evening. Heartbreak led Sean and I both to this place separately, and yet, here he was, still trying to see if a future that included the two of us together could exist.

We reached the beach and crossed the road to a makeshift stage and an area of sand that had been roped off for the night. Bean bags, beach chairs, and mini tables set around the stage. "I like to sit facing the water. The quartet is the background to the music Mother Nature already provides. That's how they intend it, and the performers encourage you to watch the waves instead of them."

"Sounds, relaxing."

Considering the smile on Sean's face, I felt a lightness in my chest and my lips pulling higher. At the entrance, we were shown to our two beanbags and given the wine list. Slipping off my shoes, I scrunched my feet in the sand.

Watching with a humored expression, Sean appraised his dress shoes. "Am I expected to go sans shoes too?"

"It adds to the experience."

Chuckling, Sean shifted to remove his shoes and socks. When the waitress came to take our drink order, I ordered a glass of wine and a jug of water. Usually, I spoiled myself with a few glasses of wine here, but tonight, I would only have the one. I didn't need another drunken regret moment like last week.

"There doesn't seem to be a lot of chairs. Is it not a popular event?" Sean asked, looking around.

"Limited numbers due to council regulations. Plus, classical music by the beach isn't exactly going to draw the young crowd."

"Only the cultured?" Sean was grinning.

Blowing out a breath, I sagged in my bean bag. "You hate classical music, don't you?"

"I'm not enamored, but you may be the one person to sway me."

"Why?"

Sean turned his gaze to mine, his smile lighting up his ocean eyes as they focused intently on mine. "Well, how could I not enjoy classical music when it's combined with the beach and sand, and..." Sean's eyes traversed my body, finishing his sentence for him. My breath caught with his heated look speeding my heart and setting fire to my ovaries, or something in that general area. "Bean bags." Wiggling his body, Sean settled himself better in his seat. "The kid in me loves bean bags."

I was laughing before I realized it. Sean's humor mimicking mine relaxed me into this evening, and I let my anxiety go. I would treat tonight like a night out with a good friend. Not a date; especially not with an ex. If I didn't put any pressure on myself, then I could enjoy the night and Sean's company.

We ate, we drank, and we listened to the quartet play along to the ocean. As the sun fell, Sean placed his drink aside and put his hand out to me. "Dance with me?"

My laughter died in my throat, my eyes casting around to find no one else dancing. "Let's start the trend."

Scooping my hand, Sean pulled me up from the bean bag. He walked us to the side where we wouldn't trip on anyone, or block their view, and took my hand and waist in his firm hold.

"I'll lead." Sean drew me closer, till my body was pressed to his, and started dancing us around in the sand.

The sun died, Venus glimmered in the sky, and then the curtain of night was pulled back to expose to the magical expanse of stars and space. Lifting my face to the twilight, my lips soft in happiness as we shuffled our feet in the sand.

"I want to undress you, lay you down and make love to you with that smile on your face, Holly. I want you in my arms when the sunrises."

Lowering my face to meet his eyes, my chest tightened with mixed emotions.

"My heart has been aching since you left me, Holly. I already know your answer, it's been on your face since I arrived tonight, in your voice since we spoke on Thursday. I lost you because I didn't tell you something about another person, and then I failed to protect you when it mattered. You're not going to sacrifice anything else for me, and I've bent as far as I can to be with you, but it's not enough, is it?"

The splinter in my chest pushed deeper into my heart, making breathing all the more painful. "No, it's not. I don't want a long distance relationship; to be a port you stop at between your homes. I want to be your home, and I want you to be there every night to hold me while I sleep, but I can't give up a job I love for a relationship that has already hurt me so much."

Sean's eyes were glassy. Mine were blurry from the surging tide of heartache inside me. Holding me tighter, Sean put his lips to my forehead. "Give me the night to say goodbye?"

Dropping my face to his chest, gravity drew my emotions down my cheeks. I wiped my face on Sean's jacket before I met his eyes again. "Remember that first night at your place?"

"Movies and popcorn?"

"I have Netflix, and we always have popcorn." Offering the most I could give at this time.

Sean's cheeks lifted in the saddest smile he'd ever given me. The movement broke the dam in his eyes, and a single tear cascaded down his cheek. I caressed my fingers in the hair behind his head, urging him to look down. Sean gave me an inch, I placed my lips on his heated cheek and drank his salty tears.

"I still love you, Holly." His eyes met mine, pleading with me to tell him there was a chance. "How did we end up here? How did one sentence destroy us so easily?"

Stepping back, I kept Sean's hand in mine. "Here, I'll lead on the way back."

Guiding Sean to our seats, we collected our shoes, and then I led him back to my place.

We watched movies, we ate popcorn, we laughed, but every time I met Sean's haunted eyes, I wanted to cry. I didn't want to sleep. I didn't want to have to say goodbye because we both knew this time it was for good. I couldn't let this end like this. I didn't want my last memory of Sean to be hollow.

I needed just one more night of his love.

CHAPTER SIXTEEN

A CLICK BURST MY BUBBLE. THE SOUND WASN'T A MOMENT OF fear that jolted me awake, but the door locking yanked me from my deep sleep more effectively than any alarm. Becoming aware of my surroundings, my body felt soft and listless, my naked skin sensitive against my sheets. That was the best night's sleep I'd had since I left Hawaii, leaving my heart smashed open like a coconut.

Blinking my eyes open, the first rays of dawn reaching across my bed, blurred fingers of reality coming to steal my last moment of happiness.

Stretching out to touch the space beside me, the warmth of Sean's body was still there, his scent surrounding me in a lingering seduction of happiness, lust, and pleasure.

Grasping the scroll of paper held within the circlet of a diamond ring. My heart stuttered at the sight of that familiar delicate metal. Gently easing it from the rolled up piece of notepaper, I unrolled the note already knowing these words would come down on my heart like a hammer to a glass table.

Holly,

Thank you for the last night of happiness with you. I know I wanted to be with you when the sun rose, but I feared if I stayed till your eyes were on me, I'd never be able to walk out the door, and I couldn't bear to see regret in your eyes in the morning.

The ring is yours. I bought it for you, and it was my promise to you. The pledge of my heart forever, and that if you left, I would come for you. I kept my promise, Holly. The ring is a reminder to you that no matter what tore us apart, it wasn't a broken promise.

My lungs restricted in my chest, the floodgates opened in my eyes, and my next breath rushed out in a sob.

I want you to be happy, Holly. If I have to give you up for you to have that happiness, then I will. I must. Nothing would hurt me more than looking in your eyes a year from now and seeing resentment that you gave up your dreams for me. You have my number. If you need me, I'll be there, if I can.

I love you, Holly. Always.

Sean.

My heart shattered into a billion pieces, never to be whole again.

———

"HOLLY?" Roger called across the table gently.

Lifting my eyes to him, then to Havier, who was holding my usual breakfast wrap. "Oh, Thanks, Havier."

"Are you going to eat this one, or are you going to throw it in the bin on the way out as you have for the last two weeks?" Havier held my wrap hostage.

"I've eaten as much as I can every time, Havier. I have a lot on my plate."

Havier looked at Roger. Roger's eyes stayed focused on me. "Apparently so, Havier. That was why she can't take the time to have a relaxed morning at our usual cafe in the morning now. Holly tells me she needs to be here first thing because she has too much to do."

"Hire her an assistant. She needs time to eat and sleep, or you'll need to replace her entirely when she dies in a week." Slamming my wrap on the table, Havier stormed off to the kitchen.

Exhaling, I turned my eyes back to my notebook. "The rock climbing wall has come in over budget, but if I cut back on some of Sammy's ideas for the room additions, then I can get us the money back immediately."

"Holly…"

"I know Sammy was keen to see those services offered, but if we hold back on them until after we complete installation of the rock climbing wall, we won't have to touch the contingency fund."

Taking the pen out of my hand midway through me taking notes on the email that just came through, Roger shut my laptop and moved it to the seat beside him. I sat blinking at him, not sure what was wrong. "Holly, just stop long enough to eat your breakfast while it is hot."

When I went to open my mouth to object, Roger placed the wrap in front of me and stared me down. Exhaling in annoyance, I picked up my breakfast, peeled back the paper and took a small bite.

My stomach grumbled as I swallowed that tiny bit of food, but it tasted bland just the same. Pushing his empty plate to the side, Roger observed me as he picked up his coffee and took a mouthful.

Taking another tasteless bite, I grimaced, putting the wrap aside. "Can I have my pen back to finish my notes, please?"

"In a moment," Roger assured over the rim of his hot beverage. "I'm going to ask you three questions. If you don't answer them truthfully and without bullshit, I'm going to fire you, Holly. For your health's sake."

My mouth fell open. I'd worked my arse off for Roger and his resort. These last two weeks, I was in the office before seven, and here long after that. What had I done wrong to lose my job?

"Did we stop meeting at the cafe so you could avoid Benjamin Henderson seeking you out?" My mouth closed, shoulders pulling back. Roger raised a finger. "One lie, Holly, and I'll fire you on the spot. I want a straightforward, honest answer."

My throat convulsed. Looking away, I searched the dining room for Mousetrap. I'd been working here seven months, and that python still scared me. I'd only been working here for a week when I'd felt him sliver across my foot and wrap around my ankle on his way to the kitchen. I'd released a squeal like a cat getting its tail pulled.

"Yes," I answered unemotionally, focusing on spotting the snake. Now is when I needed the slithering mouse eater to try and strangle me.

Roger tilted his head in my peripheral vision. "Is Benjamin the reason you're not sleeping and eating, or is it Sean?"

Giving up on that damned reptile, I started praying for the kitchen to catch fire. Glancing at Roger, I flinched at the sympathy in his eyes and stared at my hands in my lap, fidgeting with the nakedness of my ring finger.

"Sean. We said goodbye for good. He wouldn't give up his work for me, I wouldn't give up this job to be with him, and I didn't want a long distance romance which would lose its appeal too quickly."

Roger nodded as if he knew that was the case. "Holly, are you sure this is what you want? I'd hate to lose you, but right now, I'd prefer you to walk out that door and be happy with the man you love than have to organize an intervention."

A fire burned in my stomach. "I'm not giving up my dream job for a guy who lied to me, Roger. I want to be here."

Sighing, Roger finished his coffee and put it down. "Then I need you to stop burying yourself in work. I know there is a lot to do, but you weren't burning the candle at both ends previously to get it done. Cut back, Holly. Start taking care of yourself, or I'll sick Sammy on you."

"I'll try," I pouted. Sammy was cranky of late. This baby was looking to be their biggest so far, and she was over feeling like a stuffed goose, especially with her youngest still breastfeeding. Glaring at the kitchen, I was annoyed there were no flames in sight. Fate wasn't helping me out of this conversation.

Roger eyed me. "I need you to do more than try. Sammy is due in a matter of weeks, which means I'm going to need you to take on extra duties."

The last time I'd taken on extra duties for my boss, I'd had my brains fucked out on my desk. I knew that's not what Roger meant, but it was the distraction I needed at this moment.

"Roger, I'm not taking Sammy's place in your bed while she's recovering. You'll just have to suffer cold showers like the rest of us."

Roger blinked wide eyes at me. He noticed the corners of my mouth lift, and he chuckled, shaking his head. "I like my appendage firmly attached, thank you. Sammy would barbecue it if I even let another woman look at it."

Opening his bag, Roger pulled out a pamphlet. "I'm investing in another resort. I was meant to fly up there between Christmas and new year to look at the island and the facilities, see if it was worth what they are asking. With Sammy due at any moment, I'm not flying anywhere. Sammy and I discussed it. We trust you to inspect the resort for us."

"Me? What about work here?"

"Holly, you are organized, I have no doubt the Hotel will cope for a week in your absence." Roger slid the pamphlet in front of me. "It's a private island, containing two resorts; the rest is all a protected reserve. One resort is an adults-only retreat, a place for couples to get away for a luxury island holiday, a week there is your pay for a month."

"I hope you're paying for this vacay then," I choked.

"All expenses. But that's not the place you'll be there to inspect. At the southern end of that island is a high-end family getaway. Bungalows on the beach, a smallish resort, and lots of activities for kids. That's the place you'll be staying and checking out for me. I want to make sure that just because it's family orientated, it still caters to childless couples."

"Or singles?"

"And singles. A Holmes resort always caters to everyone." Roger slid plane tickets and a credit card with my name on it across the table. "No one knows you're coming for anything more than a holiday, Holly. The credit card is a company card, so I trust you not to go wild. I've booked you a villa on the beach for a week. I want you to suss it out, do the activities that appeal to you, go to the spa, everything and anything. I also want you to visit the other resort for a day. Check it out for me, find out if they interact nicely with their neighbors. The hotels share a helipad and a jetty for boats. I don't want to buy a place that has issues getting its clientele there and back."

Taking in the pamphlet, the plane ticket, the card, I lifted my eyes to Roger. "I'm not going to turn down a free island getaway, but are you sure you can spare me?"

The side of Roger's mouth twitched. "Positive. Check it out for me. If I need to make staff changes, note down names for me. Everything you can think of, Holly, and I know you can think of more than I will. You're probably the better person to do this anyway."

Lifting my eyebrows, I gathered everything into my notebook. Putting it all aside, I couldn't help thinking the holiday was perfect timing. "Christmas at home, and then I fly up north on Boxing Day?" It was perfect for getting my mind focused back on work, and away from the sacrifices I made to have my dream job.

"You don't spend Christmas with your family?"

"No, they all head down to Canberra for a fancy family get together. I haven't been since I moved to Sydney." I wasn't bothered by it. I'd worked every Christmas since, happy for the extra pay double time provided. It was better than being singled out as the black sheep in the family and nagged for not conforming.

"What about Trisha and your friends? Do you all get together?"

"Trisha spends three weeks at home with her family every Christmas. She flew out yesterday. The boys have their families to visit."

Roger's brows drew down. "Well, I don't even have to ask Sammy because I know her answer. You'll be spending Christmas lunch with us. My family is flying in, and my dad took to you at the conference. He'd love a chance to pick your brain."

"Are you sure?"

"Very sure. Just don't give my dad anything brilliant. We may have the same name on our resorts, but we are still competitors."

It made me laugh for the first time since Sean vanished from my bed. Picking up my wrap, I took a bite, suddenly famished.

"So," I asked between bites, "what names have you picked out for the youngest of your spawn?"

We hadn't talked about anything but work for two weeks. The perfection of Roger's happy, and horny marriage was a reminder of what I didn't have. Not that Roger talked about their bedroom action, but Sammy didn't hold back on telling me how randy pregnancy makes her, and how she was sure Roger kept getting her pregnant on purpose just for the nonstop sexathons. Considering her admission about how baby three came to be, I can only assume that their sex life wasn't exactly suffering before her uterus hung the occupied sign.

Chuckling, Roger hailed the waitress for another coffee. His shoulders dropped, and his eyes cleared. If I didn't know better, I'd say he was relieved.

CHAPTER SEVENTEEN

"Holly."

Stopping at the gate to my apartment, I turned to see Benjamin getting out of his car. He was dressed in a suit and looked like he just finished a meeting. Roger had made sure I left work at a decent time today, personally escorting me from the building. So, for the first time in weeks, I was home before sunset. "Benjamin, what are you doing here?"

"Well, you stood me up, you won't return my calls, and you go straight from home to work and back again. There was minimal opportunity for me to orchestrate a chance meeting with you, so I figured I should just show up and find out why I got blacklisted this time?"

Benjamin was the epitome of the sexy businessman. He was the playboy billionaire women drooled over in romance novels. The handsome face that dominated the social pages unwillingly, and the most eligible bachelor in town. He stood there in his suit, the very image of the man I once worshipped and hoped to be good enough for, and I didn't feel a thing.

"You didn't do anything."

Benjamin tilted his head, stepping closer. "Then why did you stand me up."

He was talking about our Wednesday date, the week after Sean left. "I've been busy at work."

Benjamin lifted a brow. "So Roger told me when I asked him."

"What else did Roger tell you?"

"That you needed space, which I've given you, but it's driving me crazy not seeing you or knowing why you're not talking to me." Benjamin waited, hands in his pockets. He wasn't being forceful, pushy, or demanding. He was standing there asking me genuinely why he got dumped for no reason.

Exhaling, I looked up at my empty apartment. Turning my gaze down the street, I gestured he followed me. "Let's get a drink." Benjamin's brows furrowed, but he stepped in beside me and walked with me to the restaurant and bar I liked on the corner.

"When you passed me over for promotion for a family member, that hurt, Benjamin. I mean, yeah, he was your brother, but I'd not only proven myself a good manager, but we'd also been sleeping together for two years, and you dismissed me without a thought to how I would feel. You made me feel used and dirty."

"I'm sorry, Holly. That wasn't my intention."

"When you wouldn't hear me about the sexual assault, it destroyed any trust left between us. It took me a few days to realize it, and by then you'd ended things anyway. I realized immediately that our professional relationship also ended the moment you dismissed my concern for my reputation and wellbeing as maliciousness. You could have got down on one knee and proposed to me that day in the security room, and it wouldn't have changed my leaving, Benjamin. You lost my trust as my boss, and you'll never get that back."

Benjamin shoved his hands in his pockets. "I see."

"Good, it will save you from making the same mistake with any other female employees in the future."

We walked a few steps in silence.

"So, you won't ever work for me again. Why did I lose my second chance at a personal relationship?" Benjamin sulking was kind of cute, especially with that pout.

"Because I fell in love, but not with you."

"Cassidy," Benjamin ground out the name. "I was told he didn't fare any better winning you back."

"His life is elsewhere; mine is here. Neither of us would give up what we already had, so we gave each other up instead."

Arriving at the restaurant, I faced Benjamin, meeting his eyes. "It took meeting Sean to realize I'd been in awe of you, Benjamin, but I'd never fallen for you. I was with Sean for a month, but I'd fallen for him before we ever stepped into a bedroom or been intimate. Sean didn't betray me; he just didn't warn me about his dad. It wasn't till he found me, and left me, that he broke my heart."

Benjamin's face changed, his eyes on mine keenly. "You still love him, and I lost to him even though he left?"

"You're an amazing man, Benjamin. In the professional and intimate contexts. But, I don't love you, and I don't trust you to have my best interests at heart. I'm sorry, but I can't date you."

Benjamin bowed his head. "There is nothing I can do to persuade you? Maybe you just need more time. I can wait, Holly. Six months, a year, however long you need."

It made me smile. "Benjamin, I've seen you when you set your sights on something, but I'm not a business acquisition. If it's my professional skills you're scared of losing, I'll offer my services as a consultant."

Benjamin's head jumped up, his pupils dilated. "A consultant?"

It made me sad. Sammy and Roger had been right; Benjamin always put his business first. "Yes. We'll work out a schedule. I'll stay at your hotel and assess things for you over a week, and then offer some solutions."

"I can work with that." The side of his mouth turned up, eyes glimmering with evil intent. "Can you also be in my bed for that week?"

It made me laugh. "Let's keep it professional for now. I'm going to charge you for this."

"Tax deductible, and you're worth the cost." Benjamin stepped forward, the back of his knuckles grazing my cheek. "You're worth a lot more than you give yourself credit for, Holly." We stood there, staring into each other's eyes. "I'd like to propose another option."

"Go ahead."

"Friends. Maybe at some stage more, but even if that never eventuates, I've missed how we talked, Holly. We became friends in those years together, even if we never labeled it as such. I want to be able to sit down and have a drink with you and talk about whatever we need to talk about."

Taking a deep breath, I stepped towards the door of the restaurant. "Let's do that." Signaling the waiter, he found us a cozy table in the back, the windows open to let the fresh breeze blowing in from the ocean outside. We sat, we talked about work and our industry, we laughed about our friends and their antics, and after a few hours, we walked back to my place, bid each other goodbye and agreed to catch up again soon.

As I rode the elevator, I wasn't relieved or happy or fooled. Benjamin wasn't giving up; he was just taking a different approach. The one he used first to lure me into his charm. It wouldn't work this time, but perhaps our friendship could.

As I dropped onto the sofa after a shower, I picked up my phone and pulled up a photo of Sean and me together on his boat. The ache in my chest hadn't eased at all in the last two weeks. Even as I felt better having the trip to do for work, it didn't diminish how much I missed the man I'd come to love.

Opening the messaging app, I typed out the same three words I typed out every night. Putting the phone aside, I pulled out the pamphlet on the resort I would be inspecting. Roger was right; it was very family orientated. Opening my laptop to look at their website, and flipping open my notebook, I started researching this resort. When I finished with their website, I went to Trip Advisor and read the reviews, making notes of the praise and the critiques.

By the time I finished my notes, it was midnight. Closing everything down, I crawled into bed. Picking up my phone, I looked at those words I couldn't bring myself to send. Not for fear of saying them, but concern how Sean would react. Benjamin was right; there was more to our relationship than sex. It was the same with Sean. Perhaps, we didn't need to give it all up.

I pressed send.

Snuggling down staring at the screen, I bit my lip. In the darkness of my room, my phone was the beacon. As the minutes ticked by, my heartbeat filled my ears. Until I looked at the time and cursed. Hawaii was twenty hours behind us. It was four in the morning, of course, he wasn't going to answer if he was there.

With a sigh, I set my phone on the nightstand and stared into the darkness. Thinking about Sean and our time together, I remembered the time at his private hideaway and how he'd been about to tell me something important before his phone rang. Recalling the look of absolute sorrow in his eyes in the Daintree restaurant after I walked out, refusing to give him a second chance.

Rolling onto my side, I faced the nightstand and collected the diamond engagement ring he'd slipped on my finger. How did one sentence destroy what we had? Too damn easily. That's how.

Hating my alarm when it rang in the morning, I reached out blindly and banged around till my hand found my phone and silenced it. Rolling onto my back, I opened my eyes begrudgingly to see daylight and groaned. I hadn't been surfing in weeks. Since I didn't need to be at work until eight, I could fit in a surf this morning. Picking up my phone to check my notifications, I froze at Sean's name in my message alerts.

I miss you too. I'm sorry I left the way I did.

Exhaling, I set the phone aside. Climbing out of bed, I readied myself for the surf. Just before I left, I sent another message, one that needed saying more than anything else.

I forgive you.

For more than just the morning after letter. I know Sean tried to tell me about his dad, and I didn't doubt for a second he'd had nothing to do with his father's announcement. I had to let it go, just as we'd let each other go. If we had any chance of remaining some version of friends, we needed the air between us clean.

The surf felt terrific this morning. Feeling lighter and more accepting as I rode the lift back to my apartment, I showered and dressed for work then went to meet Roger for the first time in weeks without feeling like I was dragging myself through the mud to get there.

By Friday, my anticipation for the trip was growing. I'd sat down with Roger and gone through all the issues I could already foresee based on reviews and the website. We'd discussed strategies and ideas and decided to go ahead with the trip. When lunchtime came around, I was kind of excited at the prospect.

"Is that a smile?" Sammy asked from the door.

Looking up from my work, my smile grew at the sight of the vivacious blonde. "Do you get excited before you go to a new place to do a review?"

Sammy shrugged one shoulder. "Not since it started taking me away from my family. Let's go eat; I'm starving."

Following Sammy down to the restaurant, we took up our usual table, Sammy taking a bit more effort to get in the seat. "I swear its twins. The sonographer assures me it's just the one, but I think they are lying to save Roger's life." It made me grin. I don't think Sammy would ever harm him. "So, you're looking better. Did you get laid?"

Blood rushed to my cheeks. "No. It's nothing like that. I had drinks with Benjamin Monday evening, and we agreed to be friends."

"You know Benjamin's idea of friends with a female will still include clothes on the floor and legs in the air, right?" Sammy raised a brow. "Not that I frown upon such a thing. God knows his friendship leaves a grin on your face. Just so long as you know that going in."

I'm sure my cheeks were tomato red. "Just friends. He wants my brain more than sex."

Sammy sighed wistfully. "Words no woman before has ever uttered about Benjamin Henderson, and likely never will again. Sadly, I believe you in this instance. Losing you was bad for business, and that is Benjamin's priority over sex."

"Ladies," Roger joined us, kissing Sammy's upturned cheek before dropping his face and kissing the large belly. "Including this little lady."

"Nothing little about her," Sammy complained.

Smirking, Roger took his seat, looking over the lunch menu for today. "What does the doctor say?"

"If you wanted to know, you should have come to the appointment."

"Honey, I couldn't reschedule that meeting. It was a two-million-dollar international deal."

Sammy rolled her eyes. "Did you get the contract?"

"Yes, Honey."

"Then, you better buy me something worthy of my forgiveness." Sammy put the menu aside. "He's opened the conversation about a cesarean. He wants to book me in next week. The doctor's concern is that she's too big to come out the way she got in."

"What did you say?" Roger asked carefully.

"What the fuck do you think I said? I told him to book me in tomorrow. I want this baby out already."

"So, we've set a date?" Roger asked excitedly.

Sammy recomposed herself. "Monday morning. I've already let the nanny know and made arrangements with your assistant for you to be free." Sammy lifted her eyes to me. "Sorry, Holly, you'll have to do without my husband's company for breakfast on Monday."

My face split into a grin. "Oh, the hardship. I guess I'll make do with Lance."

"Lance?" Sammy and Roger asked in unison.

"Are you tapping that hot toy boy?" Sammy accused. "Is that the reason you're smiling again?"

My laughter filled the silence. "No, but I've already set up a meeting with Lance for the performance reviews. I'll be sure to add the boss's wife thinks he's hot to his achievements and give him an exceeds expectations."

Sammy blushed while Roger shook his head. "Damn lucky that I'm a secure man, or that boy would be out on his ear." Stopping to consider the menu, his eyes flashed up to mine. "Shit, that's why Benjamin fired him, isn't it? Lance hit on you, and Benjamin found out."

Biting my lip, I shifted in my seat. "Lance has always been a flirt. He just took it too far for Benjamin's liking."

Roger's jaw clicked as he turned to Sammy. Sammy raised a brow at him, and Roger returned to studying the menu.

"What was that?"

"Nothing," Sammy sighed. "Just putting my husband in his place before he can get out of it."

Roger's mouth twitched. If there was something I'd learned about these two, is that they loved stirring each other up. Again, the little spark of jealousy snaked around my stomach. One of the reasons Benjamin didn't stand a chance with me anymore, is because I'd seen this marriage. It wasn't perfect, but it was ideal for them, and it set my goals higher for what I expected in any future relationship.

"Holly," Lance walked over to the table carrying a parcel. "This just arrived for you. It said it needed to be refrigerated immediately."

Taking the parcel, I frowned at the beautiful gift wrapping. "Thanks, Lance." Opening the envelope, I pulled out the card.

Holly,

This one is all for you.

I forgive you too.

Sean

MY HEART POUNDED in my ears as I unwrapped the parcel to find a tub of Dole Whip. The pineapple ice cream he'd brought me for our date. A drop of moisture fell from my cheek onto the lid of the container. He forgave me, for breaking my promise and not coming back. Looking up, Lance, Sammy, and Roger watched me, their faces full of genuine sympathy and expectation.

"So, Christmas Day, there will be three kids," I forced my mind to something more exciting. "Best I go find a present for the new princess." Standing up, I forgot about lunch, my mind solely intent on getting away before anyone asked any questions.

When I got home that night, I changed and curled up on the lounge with my favorite romance movie and the tub of Dole Whip. I don't know why people put themselves out there after their first heartbreak. If I'd learned anything this year, it was a disturbing truth. Love sucked.

CHAPTER EIGHTEEN

THE HELICOPTER WAS THANKFULLY AIR CONDITIONED BECAUSE outside was hot and humid. There were three couples on the flight along with one family. The others didn't look impressed with the two kids talking excitedly.

"Are you staying at the Hideaway?" The woman opposite me queried. She asked politely, but the look on her face was displeased. Possibly because her husband kept licking his lips while looking at my legs.

"No, I'm staying at the Retreat Resort on the other side of the island."

This revelation got the attention of the other couples. "There's more than one resort on this island?"

"Two. The Hideaway is adults only on one side, the Retreat is a small family friendly resort of the other side. They share the helicopter service."

The couples seemed relieved by that information, and they

stopped giving the kids dirty looks. "Why are you staying at the Retreat if you don't have a family?" The first woman questioned. Perhaps she thought I chased wealthy married men.

"Honey, that's the prime minister's daughter," the man with her murmured. "She might be meeting her family out here, where they can have a private holiday."

The woman's eyebrows jumped. "Oh, that's why you are familiar. Are your family here?" Her husband rolled his eyes and went back to licking his lips while eyeing my legs.

Smiling politely, I ignored the question and turned my gaze back to the window. The guy made me uncomfortable, so I was glad to be staying on the other side of the island from him. Yesterday, Mr. Holmes Senior suggested I become a professional consultant after I told Roger the agreement I made with Benjamin. Roger warned his dad to stop trying to steal his best employee, but the idea was still churning. My favorite part of my job was solving problems and thinking up plans to make a Hotel better.

The children started talking louder and pointing out the window as the island came into view on the far side. It looked like we were sweeping around the island to approach the helipad.

"Ladies and gentlemen, we are approaching your destination. Usually, we fly directly across the island and give you an aerial view of your playground. However, there was a bad storm overnight, and they have repairs taking place at some of the island activities. If we fly over we will cause more damage," the pilot announced.

Flying around the island, a one-story large building with

wraparound verandah sat nestled in the trees surrounded by smaller cottages. The picture matched the one in my pamphlet, telling me it was the Retreat Resort that I was here to appraise. Two large lagoon style pools sat front and back of the main building, connecting by waterfalls and creeks either side, giving the island within an island impression. A tennis court and other activities visible from the air.

We coasted up the east coast of the island, where the bushland dominated again and then moved inland to a large clearing and helipad. After two flights, I was glad to know I'd finished with the travel. Two men stood waiting to help unload the helicopter, and two women wore different uniforms waving.

"Guests of the Hideaway, please follow me," the first directed.

"And those for the Retreat Resort, are with me," the second called, leading the way to a waiting electric vehicle; the troop carrier version of a golf cart. "Your luggage will be transferred and waiting in your room by the time you check in."

Stepping onto the cart, I listened to the quick tour provided and focused on learning as much about this resort as possible. If I was lucky, I might even be able to spend the last few days relaxing. After check-in, I was shown to my beachfront one-bedroom villa and left to settle in. Keen to keep busy, I changed and went out to see what this resort offered.

———

"...I'VE nearly filled my notebook with ideas and issues. I've only been here two days."

"Anything glaringly obvious that would put you off the sale?"

A gurgle in the background told me Roger was nursing the latest addition to the Holmes household. Little Nina.

"No. To be honest, it is a luxury resort with all the trimmings of a high-end family resort. It doesn't cater to singles and couples though. We'd need to address that if you are going to compete with your neighbors."

"Have you been over there yet?"

"I've been busy experiencing everything this side has to offer. It does seem like the Retreat is on good terms with the Hideaway. All the staff know each other, and they share island facilities. Hiking trails, the zip lines, the island explorer boat, are all timetabled between the resorts."

Walking to the window, I watched the rain pouring down outside. The storm hit just after dinner, and a warning was issued for severe weather overnight. "Check out the other place tomorrow. It might give you some ideas of what standard we need to set." The sky lit up, and thunder roared. "What's that noise?"

"Tropical storm. Looks fierce, but the staff assured the resorts here were designed for the worst of the weather to pass by without impact." Both resorts stood in natural coves with ranges behind them, which sheltered them from the ocean and its monster storms. "I should get off the line since it's getting pretty close now."

"Okay, promise me you'll check out the Hideaway tomorrow."

"Well, I've already booked into the spa, which is at the Hideaway, so that's the plan."

"The spa is a shared resource?"

"No, it belongs to the Hideaway, but they allow guests from here to book there too."

"One less expense to maintain."

"One less income to your resort too. If you have a falling out with the Hideaway owner, you will lose a fair few resources. They own the helicopter and the boat. You wouldn't be able to get your guests here."

Roger was quiet. "Well, that's a negative."

Lightning flashed down the beach just before a loud crack filled the air, causing me to jump. "Okay, the storm is here, I'm going now." Thunder rumbled, reminding me how small and fragile I was in the face of nature's fury. The lights in the bathroom flickered, and I swear the building trembled in fear.

"Call me Friday," Roger farewelled and hung up.

Moving next to the bed, I dropped my phone on the bedside table. Gathering up all my research and notebook, I packed it neatly in my bag. I didn't want housekeeping to stumble across it. I knew how staff gossiped.

The wind howled around the building. Picking up my phone, I walked to the window and took a photo of lightning branching across the sky, lighting up the beach like daylight.

Pausing as I caught a flash of beach chairs flung across the sand, I bit my lip. These weren't just your standard beach chairs. They were bulky wooden seats meant to stay put during a storm. Another flash, my eyes widened as a chair hurtled towards my building.

"Fuck!" Dropping to the ground, I knelt with my hands over my head.

The foundations shook, breaking tiles and splitting wood filled my ears, and the storm stopped being muffled by the building. The tempest no longer outside as rain whipped me where I knelt trembling.

Lifting my head when the noise stopped, I took stock of everything. I wasn't hit. I wasn't hurt. The beach chair had hit the roof and now it, and most of the roof structure, were on the bed. I cursed till my nana rolled over in her grave.

———

"CAN I get you anything else, Miss Claire?" The manager offered as he handed me a cup of hot chocolate. He wasn't in uniform since he'd been pulled out of bed himself by the incident. His slacks and t-shirt were still better than my drowned rat appearance.

"No, thank you." Accepting the steaming-hot drink in my hands, I sipped. We were sitting in his office, having called the concierge when my shelter stopped protecting me. Wrapped in a blanket, I was evacuated to the main building and checked by the nurse while the manager went to assess the damage. I think he'd taken one look at my room and realized, had I been in bed, they'd be in an awful situation. The storm had passed, but there was no way I was returning to my room tonight.

"We are fully booked out, so I can't offer you another room, Miss Claire. I've had my front desk call the Hideaway. They have a vacancy. If you wish to continue your holiday, they have kindly offered for us to transfer you there and you will maintain free access to all the amenities here. As it is, you will need to spend at least tonight there."

"Yes, thank you, I'm happy to do that." Snuggling the blanket tighter around me and my skimpy nightdress. Not exactly the outfit I planned to be wearing to visit the Hideaway, but with my belongings currently pinned beneath the wreckage in my cottage, I had no choice.

The manager picked up the phone. "Hi, it's Daniel. Our guest has accepted your hospitality; I'll have her brought over now. Yes, of course, her name is Miss Holly Claire." The manager blinked at me. "Ah, yes, as in that, Holly Claire." The manager's eyes widened a little, and he turned his back to me. "I just remembered about all that mess. If it's an issue? Ah, no, she's by herself. No injuries, just a bit shook up by the ordeal, and all her belongings are inaccessible currently."

There was a moment's silence where I was left to wonder why my name was such a big deal, and then I remembered the media storm about my relationship with my father.

"Okay, thank you." Hanging up, the manager turned, his eyes reassessing me. "They are coming over to pick you up. Once we can gain access to the cottage, we will have your things brought over to you."

"Thank you, Mr. Spicks. I'm sure glad I'd already booked some time at the spa tomorrow," I tried to ease his concern.

"Yes, I suspect you'll need it." The manager dropped his face to his chest. "And possibly a bottle of vodka by the time tonight's over," he muttered, my ears having to strain to hear him.

"Pardon?"

He cleared his throat. "Are you sure I can't get you anything stronger? That was a very close call."

"Ah, no, I'm good, thank you."

The manager's eyes went to my trembling hands. "I might just duck out and check on things," Mr. Spicks excused and left, closing the door behind him.

Exhaling, I focused on finishing the hot chocolate without slopping it all over me. My eyes drifting to the clock to note it was nearly midnight. Closing my eyes for a moment, I felt the exhaustion of the last few months deep in my bones. Maybe I could just spend all day in bed tomorrow.

I had just placed the mug on the desk when the door opened. "She's just in here, boss."

Standing up, I tucked the blanket tighter and turned to see Hawaii in a bottle stride into the room. "Sean?"

"Jesus, Holly." I was still standing blinking when he pulled me into his arms and planted his lips on mine. Melting against the warmth of him, I opened my mouth to his urging and clung to his shoulders desperately.

The clearing of a throat drew us back to ourselves, and our location. Tucking me in tight to the side of him, Sean turned to face Mr. Spicks. "Thanks, Daniel. I'll look after Miss Claire for the rest of her stay."

The manager of the Retreat smirked slightly, pulled it in, and nodded. "I'm grateful. Miss Claire, if you need anything." He offered me his business card.

"Thank you, Mr. Spicks."

Sean eased me forward; I went with him. "When did you arrive?" Sean asked once we were in a golf buggy.

"Tuesday."

"When do you head home?"

"Wednesday."

"Stay with me till you go?"

"Yes." I didn't have to consider it. Fate must have thrown that beach chair at the building I was in for a reason. I wasn't naive to the fact that only my accommodations were damaged. Mr. Spicks told me it was their first incident since the resort opened ten years ago. Fate couldn't have sent the message any clearer then if there was a neon sign in the sky.

Lightning branched across the darkness.

'Okay, I got the message.'

CHAPTER NINETEEN

"Are you okay?" Sean yawned behind me.

His arms wrapped around me, holding me and kissing my shoulder. We didn't have sex last night. Sean brought me back to his villa in the staff section of the resort and held me till I fell asleep. "You look gorgeous standing here. Were you wearing that when they pulled you out of the room?"

Glancing down at the sheer, royal blue, summer night dress, heat raced to my cheeks. Thank god I'd kept on my knickers. "Ah, yes. The first thing the concierge did was give me his jacket. They replaced that with a blanket when we got to the main building."

Sean kissed my shoulder again. "Talk to me." Turning me in his arms, Sean took my hand and led me back to bed. Sinking down onto the bed, I let Sean pull me into his side and rest my head on his chest. "I'm trying to figure out how this is going to work."

"The rest of your holiday with me?"

"The rest of my life with you."

Sean's hand stopped rubbing my arm. "Do you mean that?"

"I've been miserable without you. Seeing you come through that door last night, lit up my insides like Christmas at the Griswold's. I don't want to walk away from you again." Lifting onto my elbow so I could see Sean's reaction, I stared into his ocean eyes. "If you still want me, I'm yours."

Sean's fingers threaded through my hair. "Holly, I've wanted you from the moment you walked into my resort. I've never stopped wanting you. Leaving you a month ago was the hardest thing I've ever done in my life, and I nearly couldn't do it." Sean's eyes flicked back and forth on mine. "What about your dream job?"

Stroking his stubble, I felt a surge of happiness rush through me, like I swallowed a shot of pure, undiluted joy. "I'm not giving up my dream, it's been changing this last month, and now, I'm making room for you in it. I don't know how the logistics will work, I'll need to go home next week to figure it all out, but I will keep my promise to return to you because I love you."

A smile bloomed across Sean's handsome face. Crunching up, he snatched my lips in his, pulling me down to his body, not relinquishing his hold on me.

I jerked back. "No more leaving me in the dark. I want you always to tell me the truth, even if you think it's going to hurt me. I don't want any nasty surprises."

"I promise I will never keep anything from you again." He moved to kiss me again, but I kept my arm braced between us to stop him.

"In the interest of full disclosure, I need to tell you something." I pressed away to sitting, biting my lip, wondering how to phrase this.

Sean's brow furrowed. "Did you sleep with Henderson?"

"What? No. I mean technically, yes, but, we didn't have sex. Well, we nearly did, but I was under the influence and-"

"Holly, I get it. He was the Cupid's dart guy." Sean propped himself up on the bed head. "Whatever it is, Holly, I'm not going to change my mind. I love you. I'm not giving you up a second time."

My stomach was in knots. "Well, the first thing you need to know is I've agreed to work as an advisor for Benjamin Henderson." Sean gritted his teeth. "And, off the back of that, I'm considering doing that for a few other hotels as a side business."

"How does Roger feel about that?"

"I haven't quite discussed it with him yet, but his father wants to hire me, so potentially, I could service Holmes Resorts, and Henderson Hotels and be content with that."

"You can add Cassidy resorts to that list too. I want to see that ideas book of yours if they are all getting a look at it."

"You already did. Did you use it?"

Sean lifted a brow. "I instigated one or two of the ideas you left me. I would have preferred a note telling me you love me, than a list of things that might improve my resort."

My heart trembled in my chest for a moment, then I inhaled deeply, trying to keep calm and be in the present.

"Anything else?" Sean checked.

"This isn't home." I'd been here all of five minutes, but as beautiful as it was, this would never be home to me. I already knew that.

Sean scratched the stubble at his chin. "Are you asking me to move permanently to Sydney?"

"No, I understand you have your business to run, I'm just telling you, I already know this isn't going to be the place I call home, last night's encounter aside."

"My home will be wherever you are, Holly. This place is my work."

My mind calmed with his words. Sean eased me down to lie with him, his touch subduing my body.

"Let's start small. Speak to Roger. Decide how you can be with me and still manage your career. Once you know the answer to that, we can work out the living arrangements." Soft lips kissed my forehead firmly. "I still want to marry you, Holly, but after the media storm about our engagement, can I humbly suggest we elope and marry in Hawaii or here? Somewhere the media will find it hard to crash. I saw the turnout at your sister's wedding."

"Speaking of which, do you want to fill me in on what happened with Benjamin?"

Sean's chest vibrated on a grumble. "That first time I came looking for you, he was the one who answered the door at your sister's place. Nichola wasn't there, just her fiancé and Henderson. He told me to leave you alone, that you didn't want to see me, and slammed the door in my face. I stuck around, trying to find you for two weeks, but had to go home when I couldn't even use the media to bring you to me. I don't understand why they would interview me, but they never aired what I said."

"Benjamin's dad is the media in this country." So seven months ago, Benjamin had started blocking Sean in readiness to win me back.

"He protected his son's interests. That makes more sense."

"When Benjamin goes after something, he gets it. He doesn't have the word no in his vocabulary." I lifted my face so I could meet Sean's eyes. "If there are skeletons in your closet, you need to tell me now. If Benjamin wants to cause issues, he has his dad's power behind him to do it."

Sean lowered his face, rubbing our noses in an Eskimo kiss. "I have nothing to hide, Holly. I am the man you see in front of you."

I lowered my eyes. "I can't see all of you."

Sean's eyebrow jumped. "Well, I'm happy to bare myself to you, Holly, but you need to reciprocate."

A butterfly fluttered in my stomach. "How about you stand naked before me, and then I let you strip me bare?"

Sean's eyes lit up, his hand sliding along my thigh, lifting the nightdress to my hip, waist, stopping to stroke beneath my ribs. An uninhibited moan echoed through my chest.

"Let's turn that around. The female should always come first."

Trembling at the promise of his words, I lifted my body to help Sean remove the nightdress. Climbing to his knees, Sean dropped his mouth to my breasts and licked my nipple. My entire body tightened, muscles tensing from toes to head. Hot wetness encompassed my nipple, sucking and flicking the sensitive bud till I was squirming, gripping his biceps, and panting for breath.

"I love how you react to just my smallest attention, Holly."

"It's been a while. Be kind."

Closing my eyes as his mouth kissed my abdomen, knowing he had no intention of taking it easy on me. His fingers gripped my knickers peeling them down my thighs as his mouth found the pearl hidden below my mound. My hand gripped his hair as his tongue snaked between my folds and squiggled across the over sensitized bundle of nerves.

Lifting one leg, and then the other, I flicked the soft fabric of my panties off one ankle and let it pool around the other. Sean's hands pushed my thighs wide apart, moving his body square between. Strong hands gripped my hips and yanked me forward to meet his hungry mouth. Air rushed from my lungs in a gasp. The timber of the bedhead clutched in one hand, a mess of sandy blond hair in the other.

Wet heat worked my body into an inferno in a matter of licks, and breathing became difficult. Sean's tongue circled my entrance and then delved in. The tip of it flicked the front wall inside me repeatedly. My eyes folded back in my head, toes curled, and the world disappeared as I called his name to the ceiling and melted into a puddle.

Sean chuckled when I flopped beneath him. Rising from between my thighs, Sean peered at my sex. "Was that too much, too soon?"

"Don't be cheeky and get naked already."

Sean stood beside the bed. "Look at me, Holly. I'm baring

myself for you and only you."

My eyes traversed the tall, muscular man before me, his eyes glimmering jewels of honesty. I knew he meant those words sincerely. My tongue darted across my lips as his hands slid his boxers down, and Sean revealed himself to me entirely. Long, thick, hard, and already seeping in readiness.

Kneeling back on the bed, Sean spread my knees and moved between them. "I want you bare. Are we okay to do that?"

"Yes." I wasn't ready to start a family yet, so I was still on the pill. Sean lifted over me, his lips finding mine. Slow, breathy kisses as our bodies aligned with each other. My nails gripped his back as he niched himself, that first stretch catching my breath.

"Don't ever leave me again," Sean panted in my ear.

"I'm all yours."

Biting my lip as he surged forward, stretching me, owning me, my body opened to him, slick with desire, heated with lust, safe in love. My senses lit up across my body. Every touch, kiss, and stroke felt to the tips of my fingers and toes. Sean waited till my moans changed octave to pull away and turn me over. Pushing back into me, he made me feel him deeper, stroking me differently, making sure he touched every bit of me.

My fingers were twisting in the sheets as he pumped me hard and deep. Every moan, whimper, and curse urging him harder and faster. His hands slid along my skin, lubricated by the sweat of our physical exertion in the tropical humidity. With a loud grunt, Sean pulled away. Grabbing the base of his cock in a stranglehold, he focused on his breathing, closing his eyes and pulling himself back from the edge.

Mouth lifting as I watched the pulse in his cock throbbing in his hand. Sean's hand ran over my bum and gave it a swat. Flinching, I moaned as warmth rushed to his handprint. He rubbed the sting, and when I looked back, his eyes were glazed and dilated and focused entirely on my arse. I wiggled it. Sean lifted his face to the ceiling. "Fuck, Holly, I'm trying to last here."

My cheeks swelled with a broad grin. Turning, I lay back beneath Sean and started touching myself. "Does this help?"

Sean's chest vibrated with a throaty growl. "No, it certainly doesn't." He fell upon me, sucking my nipple into his mouth, making me whimper with the bite of pain, and release to pleasure. "I want to fuck you so hard, Holly, but I want to make love to you too."

"Love can be hard and passionate too."

Sean rose above me, teasing the seeping head of him across my clit, making me moan and bite my lip. "What do you want, Holly? I'll give you anything you want."

His kiss stole my answer, tongue thrusting, and curling as he explored my mouth. Pulling back, Sean lifted my thighs to his waist, holding my body to his as he knelt, folding back on his ankles, picking me up in his arms.

It didn't matter my answer; Sean needed to fuck me, to know I was his again, and I was onboard with that. Mouth to his ear, I gave him the green light. "Claim me. I'm yours."

Cursing in my ear, Sean thrust forward. With skin on skin and heat on heat, we burned away the last seven months till we were breathless and calling each other's names as our world's exploded into stardust.

Once we had our breaths back, Sean laid us gently on the bed, his eyes glancing at the clock. "I need to shower and go to work. I'm meant to be meeting contractors in thirty minutes."

"Unless you want me running around your resort in my nightdress, I think I'll stay here. I have two hours till I'm due in the spa. With any luck, my clothes will turn up by then."

"I'm highly tempted to make sure your clothes don't turn up."

I whacked his arm. "I'm here for work. I need to do my job."

"Work?"

"The Retreat Resort is up for sale. Roger is interested in turning it into the next Holmes resort."

Sean's brows bunched. "Holly, I purchased the Retreat three weeks ago. It was the meeting I was flying back for when I left you. I own the damn island."

I blinked. "Three weeks ago?" Sean nodded. "But it was only two weeks ago Roger told me to come here and gave me the tickets. He would have known by then."

Sean's brows lowered further. "Certainly, he would have. Do you think he was planning to make me an offer?"

My eyes widened. "No, Roger set me up."

"What?"

"He kept saying I had to come to the Hideaway and compare it to the Retreat, to make sure the management of both resorts were working together. The bastard set me up to see you again." I couldn't believe Roger did that to me.

When Sean laughed, I glared at him until his face softened. "Holly, they knew I purchased the Hideaway months ago.

Roger and I talked about it at the conference. He sent you here specifically to see me. I owe him a Christmas present."

"Yeah, well, I hope he's ready to accept my resignation," I scoffed.

Shaking his head, Sean kissed me into silence. Once I was struggling to breathe again, Sean stood up and picked up the landline. "Morning, Daniel. Have you been down to survey the damage in daylight yet?" Sean listened as he picked up his smartphone and checked his emails. "Did you retrieve Miss Claire's belongings? Just have them delivered to my villa." Sean smirked. "No, she didn't end up needing her villa. Send her bags over, and I'll come over before lunch with the contractors to organize repairs."

Hanging up, Sean reached out, snagging my hand. "Let's have a shower. Your clothes should be here by the time we finish."

"Are you planning to get me dirty before I get clean again?"

Sean smiled over his shoulder. "Very much so." I started laughing. "What?" Sean asked as he turned to face me.

"I need to get Roger and Sammy a better Christmas present too. A couple's massage isn't going to cut it now."

"You think Roger's wife was involved?"

"Oh, I'm damn sure it was her idea. Roger is a good man, but he wouldn't have crossed this line of professionalism. Sammy will without question."

Grinning, Sean pulled me under the water with him. "Then tell me, what should I get your boss' wife as a thank you present for sending me the woman I love for Christmas?"

"That's easy. Two turtle doves and ten lads a leaping."

CHAPTER TWENTY

"Wʜᴀᴛ's ʜᴀᴘᴘᴇɴᴇᴅ?" Rᴏɢᴇʀ ᴀsᴋᴇᴅ ᴀs sᴏᴏɴ ᴀs I ᴘɪᴄᴋᴇᴅ ᴜᴘ the phone that night. "The accommodation cost was refunded today."

"Yes, there was an incident last night?" I smirked as I sat down at the restaurant to wait for Sean to join me.

"Did she go yet?" Sammy whispered in the background.

"What kind of incident?"

"Well, after I hung up from you, the storm picked up a beach chair and threw it into my villa. Luckily, I wasn't in bed, or I would have been getting this call in the hospital."

"Shit, Holly, are you okay?"

"I am. I wasn't injured, but it destroyed the villa. The Retreat's booked out, so they refunded the cost of my accommodation and transferred me to the Hideaway for the rest of the week." Roger was quiet on the other end. "The owner of both the resorts came to get me personally once he heard my name."

"Oh, and how did that go?" Roger choked.

"I spent the day writing my resignation letter, that's how it went."

"Holly..."

"You played me. You were never buying the Retreat. This work trip was a setup."

Roger took a deep breath. "Holly, you were miserable. Sammy called Trisha and found out you'd been on a date with Sean, and when Trisha came home, you were more depressed than when you came back from Hawaii. It didn't take much to figure out the cause. Especially since Trisha found the note."

"Roger, shh, she doesn't need to know that," Sammy scolded.

Covering my face with one hand, I vowed to have a serious word with Trisha about why she was scrounging around in my underwear drawer.

"Look, we want you to be happy, Holly, but I don't want to lose you as an employee. Sammy and I have been tossing around ideas of how to make this work. Just enjoy the week. When you get back, we'll sit down and work it out."

"It needs to be something that doesn't require my regular presence, Roger. I've decided I'm going home with Sean."

"To Hawaii?"

"Yes. Though, I'll come back to Sydney when he comes over for his businesses here."

"So, there is no chance Sean could make Sydney his home?"

"Oh, I think we will both be happier in Hawaii."

Roger cursed on the other end of the line. "We'll work it out, Holly. The important thing is that you are happy again."

My mouth pulled up on one side as Sean walked into the restaurant, spotted me, and bestowed the sexiest grin on me. "I am, Roger. Thanks to both of you."

"All we did was put you both on the same island, Holly. The rest was up to the two of you."

"So, should I just hand all my research over to the new owner?"

"Hell, no. You did that on my dime. That research belongs to me. Cassidy is going to have to pay for that information," Roger answered with certainty.

Tilting my head in thought, I considered how Roger didn't even have to think about his answer. "You plan on fronting my business idea."

Roger cleared his throat. "Sammy and I want us all to go into business together. I'll run the business, Sammy will organize bookings, and you'll work your magic as an advisor. People like Benjamin, who once utilized your knowledge for free, will have to pay for it."

"I'll let Mr. Cassidy know. Do you know the costings yet?"

Sean lifted a brow at me before signaling the waiter.

"I'll work up something with Sammy which we can go over when you get back next week," Roger informed.

"Righty-o, boss."

"Don't give me sass, Holly. I get it enough at home."

"You love it. I'll see you on Thursday. My client is sitting waiting for me to order dinner."

"That just sounds wrong, Holly. Enjoy the rest of your time there." Roger hung up.

A wicked smirk covered Sean's face. "Client? Does that mean I get to request kinky stuff?"

"I meant it in the way that I'm here for work. It just so happens that you get to be the beneficiary of my hard work." Sean pressed his lips to prevent laughing. Blood rushed to my face. "That came out wrong."

"Not to me, it didn't. What did Roger have to say for himself?"

"That he was hoping, we would make Sydney our home. He and Sammy have a business proposition for me when I get back."

"They want you to do what you did here this week for other people, and they'll take a commission on the fee," Sean answered confidently.

My brows furrowed. "How did you know?"

"I was thinking about it all day today, and I realized that they'd beaten me to the idea. Roger is a perfect businessman. His hotel goods and services company is one of the best out there; it's why I'm a client of theirs. Rumor at the conference was Holmes was looking to branch out and offer more than bathroom and minibar products." Sean sipped from the glass of table water. "What we need to be sure of is that you get paid what you are worth, and you have flexibility in where you work or who you work for."

Narrowing my eyes, I tilted my head. "It sounds like you plan on negotiating my contract for me, Mr. Cassidy."

"I would hope you plan to include me in your decision making, Holly, and I don't want anyone else taking advantage of you."

My lips pressed together as I dropped my eyes to the menu. "You're a little domineering sometimes, Sean."

My heart stuttered at how gorgeous Sean looked when he blushed and smirked. "Sorry, it's the lawyer in me. I do have a lot more life experience than you, Holly, but if you ever feel I'm overstepping, just let me know, and I'll happily listen to what you want."

"Do you know what I want right now?" Batting my lashes, I leaned forward on the table.

Sean's eyes dropped to where my cowl-necked dress fell forward, giving him a good view of cleavage. He shook his head and licked his lips. "To order room service." Standing, Sean took my hand and was walking us toward the exit a heartbeat later.

"That's him, the American she was engaged to," the woman from the helicopter squawked to her partner as we passed. "I bet her father doesn't know she's here."

Sean stopped at the waiting area on the way out. "Carissa, the couple at table nine get a complimentary bottle of wine. Tell them it's from the owner."

"Yes, Mr. Cassidy. Are you not eating?"

"We've decided to get room service. Too many busybodies."

Carissa smiled and nodded. "Yes, Mr. Cassidy. A few people have commented on your guest since you sat together."

"Not my guest, Carissa. My fiancée." Sean winked at the surprised smile on the girl's face, then he hauled me back to his villa and ate me for appetizers.

————

"LOOK AT THAT SMILE," Roger greeted when he walked in the cafe on Thursday morning.

Blushing, I pushed my typed notes across the table to him. "Everything you need to know about a hotel that's not yours."

Sitting opposite me, Roger smirked. "You know, Sammy and I met when she came to review my father's hotel. We had some very passionate nights together. Before she could leave, I saw her notebook and realized she was a reviewer. I didn't tell her I knew, but when the review came out, I realized who she was. I tracked her down and asked to date her. Our relationship was very intense, and we fell in love, but Sammy wouldn't marry me because I was a hotelier's son, and was being groomed to take over."

"Is that why you chose a different path in the industry?"

"It was my compromise to be with the woman with whom I fell in love. Opening the city resort, that was something Sammy had to agree to, and we did it because she was planning on pulling back on the reviewing." Roger adjusted himself in his chair. "Now Nina is here, Sammy has decided to call it quits altogether. She doesn't want to be away from her family."

"That makes sense. Sammy's been complaining about the travel the last few times I've talked to her."

"Holly, Sammy and I sent you north because we know how miserable you've been since your date with Cassidy. We both experienced the same thing when neither one of us wanted to give up what we had, but someone has to give, Holly. Cassidy purchased a Resort here, just to be close to you. You need to be the one to sacrifice your dream now, and perhaps, like me, you'll find time for it again in the future."

My brows furrowed. "You're firing me?"

Roger exhaled. "I'm kickstarting your next career. Between Henderson hotels and Holmes resorts, I'm sure we can keep you busy throughout the year as a consultant."

"What about my role?"

"Sammy will take that over. She's more than capable, and the bonus is, we can talk about work at home."

"Wow." Sitting back, I looked down at the computer, elated, but disappointed.

"Sammy and I have been tossing around several different ideas since she decided to quit the review circuit. Since we realized we were going to lose you, this is the best we can come up with, but if you have a better idea, we'll be happy to hear it."

"I need to think about this, talk it over with Sean," I excused, still unsure about how quickly this all happened. "But, it does sound similar to what I thought before I met up with Sean again."

"What is your hesitation?"

I chewed my lip. "This was my dream job, and I love working with you and Sammy."

The side of Roger's mouth tilted upward. "Do you know the problem with achieving your dreams, Holly?" I shook my head. Roger reached across the table and patted my hand. "You have to find new dreams to chase." Standing up, he pushed the file back to me. "Type this up into a formal report. I'm going to make Cassidy pay for stealing you away." Roger turned to leave. "Oh, Sammy said we expect you both for dinner on Friday by seven."

"Both of us?" I blinked surprised.

Roger lifted a brow, a smile spreading across his face. "Cassidy didn't fly back with you?"

My cheeks were hot as a blush crept all the way to my neck. "How did you know?"

"That man isn't a fool. He's not going to let you fly home alone again. He wouldn't take the risk of you not wanting to leave. I'll see you tomorrow morning for a proper meeting. Have a good day."

"Roger?" I waited till he turned to face me. "Thank you, for the job, for the trip, and for understanding."

"It has been and still is my pleasure. Beautiful ring by the way." Roger winked and walked out the door. Admiring the diamond adorning my hand, I sighed. I'd told Sean it wasn't formal. I expected him to propose a second time and not cock it up this time. Until then, I was wearing the ring to get used to it.

———

"I'M HOME!"

The living room held the best sight I could find at the end of the day. Sean sat on the sofa, Mitchell sitting there talking with him.

"Hey, Mitchell dropped over to say hello." Standing, Sean pulled me against him, kissing me heatedly. "I missed you. How did it go today?"

"Surprisingly good." Smiling up at Sean, I knew Sammy and Roger had done me the biggest favor sending me to Sean's island. Happiness was bubbling in my chest, radiating down my arms. "Out of curiosity, how much did you pay Roger to fire me?"

Sean smirked, playing along instantly. He Eskimo kissed me. "I'd pay double again because you're worth it."

I swear I was glowing with the light and the heat that was filling me to the brim. Sean's mouth found mine, and I found my new home, in his arms.

"Okay, I'm just going to go. Tony and I will meet you down the restaurant in an hour." When Sean and I didn't move, Mitchell huffed to the door. "You two are too fucking cute. I'll show myself out."

When the door closed, Sean lifted me in his arms. "We have an hour."

"We have the rest of our lives."

Sean exhaled, touching his forehead to mine as he carried me into my room. "That's a lot of movies and popcorn."

"Are you scared?"

"Just eager to get started."

Falling to the bed, I closed my eyes and made a wish. I didn't believe in happy ever after, but, I hoped, like Sammy and Roger, Sean and I would always have our passion for one another. Everything else, I knew we could work our way through, as long as our love stayed.

EPILOGUE

THREE MONTHS LATER

Thunder was trying to break down my door. "What is that?" Trish grumbled from her bedroom.

"I've got it."

Yesterday, Sean and I flew back into Sydney from Hawaii. This morning, I was due to meet with Benjamin to start my week-long assessment of Hotel Henderson.

Opening the door, I found beefy bodyguards surrounding my father. Stepping out of the way while the security barged into my apartment to ensure it was safe. "Prime Minister," I gritted my clenched teeth.

Dad waited till they gave the all clear and the door closed with his security outside. Removing a piece of stationary from his jacket pocket, my father held it up for me to see. "What is this?"

"It's a wedding invitation."

"This is how you tell your family you're engaged? I haven't

even met the man, and you send me an invitation to a wedding?"

"Are you saying you don't want to come?"

"You couldn't pick up the phone and tell us personally?"

"I did that for the people who are in my life. The other must-invites got the invitation." I crossed my arms defensively. "It's not like you ever call me to see how I am."

"I guess I should count myself lucky I even got an invite." With a huff, he turned to consider me. "I want to meet him."

Looking over my father's shoulder, I spotted a half-dressed Sean watching from my bedroom door. The sight of him in his jeans with no shirt made all the delicious bits tighten in memory of how he woke me up this morning before our surf. "Okay. Dad, I'd like you to meet Sean Cassidy, my fiancé."

My father turned to find Sean stepping towards him. "Prime Minister Claire. Nice of you to stop by so early. Another half an hour, and you would have missed us."

"I know my daughter's schedule. Holly may think I don't care, but I keep tabs as best I can on my youngest."

"You spy on her?" Sean raised a brow.

"I learned a long time ago that a wild thing couldn't be tamed or chained. The best for both is to let it roam free and track it from a distance. Then, when it needs you, you can be there for it. I'll always give Holly her space, but I'm here for her if she needs me." Dad raised both brows. "She never does, mind you, but she's my daughter, and I love her despite our differences."

Sean nodded. "She is fiercely independent, but that's a trait I do adore about her."

"What's all this noise?" Trisha came out of her room. She spotted my father and groaned. "You again. I'd offer to make coffee, but I'm worried it will end up repainting the wall." Ignoring my father's glare, Trisha scuffed her way into the kitchen.

Sean glanced at me with raised brows and shoulders. "Not important." Scrunching my nose, I shook my head on the memory.

"My daughter has her father's temper," dad muttered to Sean. Taking a deep breath, the Prime Minister pulled out his phone and sent a message. "I won't keep you. We'll have dinner tonight. My assistant will send you the details. It's about time Holly came to Kirribilli House for a visit." Without any further comment, he left.

"Kirribilli House?" Sean stared at the closing apartment door.

"Second official residence of the Prime Minister. It's where he lives when he's in Sydney."

Sean hugged me. "I'll be right there by your side. Always will be."

"Ick, too much soppy for this early in the morning. I'm going back to bed. Try not to make people puke with these open displays of lovey-dovey cuteness."

Chuckling as Trisha walked out, I lifted my eyes to Sean's. "That went way better than I expected."

"Just wait till tonight. I've had years of being around American Senators. I'll have your dad eating out of my hand."

"Well, just don't let the media capture it and start a scandal."

"Speaking of scandals, how long till you are due to meet Henderson?" Sean started leading me back to my bedroom.

"An hour. Why?"

Sean raised a brow, the smirk of mischief lighting up his eyes. "Plenty of time.

~THE END~

CALYPSO

ELERI ROYALS SERIES

In my town, there are two kinds of people; those from the sophisticated Eleri, and those from the gang-run Riverside. The natural divide is the Eleri River, the human divide is money.

CALYPSO PREVIEW

CHAPTER 1

I was wet!

Actually, wet might have been an understatement. I'd walked five kilometres in torrential rain. Two kilometres of that in heels, which seemed like a feat in itself. I'd taken my heels off when my second blister busted, and the pain became unbearable.

Not that I was unhappy. I was damn near elated. The date my mother had set me up on was horrible. The asshole son of one of her colleagues was a self-entitled and conceited son of a bitch. When he tossed me out of his car forty minutes ago because I wouldn't put out, I'd smiled happily and waved goodbye.

Why? Because doing my mother the favour of dating her colleague's son had bought me a two week holiday in Hawaii. That's why I didn't care how sore my feet were, how wet I was, or that I probably looked pretty pathetic skipping towards the late night Pitstop Cafe resembling a drowned rat. The Pitstop was a heritage listed building converted into a cafe, adjoined with a seven-eleven service station.

Bouncing up to the doors with a smile on my face, I was daydreaming about the sort of bikini I should buy for my first vacation in two years. That was the only reason I went on this date from hell. Once I was under cover of the awning, I attempted to wring myself of excess water. The glass doors slid open, and the buzzer sounded to let the employee know he had a customer.

Joshua, a high school senior and night shift employee, stepped around the corner from the cafe, his blue eyes going wide as I stepped inside the doors. His pouty mouth moved, but no sound came out. Joshua was two years behind me at school, and under normal circumstances, I would have no idea who he was, but I tutored him for my two senior years. I was a quarter of the way into my second year at university now but continued to mentor Joshua, so we knew each other well.

"Band-aids?" I asked, pulling my dripping, sable-coloured hair back off my face. That was my one regret tonight, wearing my hair down. I probably looked like the psychotic dead girl from 'The Ring.' Instead of crawling out of the television, I was walking through the door.

"The second row from the back," Joshua answered then dashed around the corner back into the cafe.

Okay. Guess I've looked better, but I wasn't used to that reaction. Looking behind me as I squatted to get a packet of band-aids, I realised I'd left puddles in my wake. Joshua probably ran off to get a bucket. As if on cue, he appeared in the doorway, setting up a wet floor sign before quickly moving towards me as he mopped the floor.

"Sorry," I apologised. "I did try and squeeze all the water out before I came in."

"It's okay. I've been mopping all night." Joshua smiled holding out a dry towel. "Give me your coat. I'll hang it in front of the fire in the cafe."

Lowering my handbag and heels to the floor, I smiled unbuttoning my ivory duffel coat and swapping him for the towel. "Thanks, Josh." Joshua graced me a natural smile as he went back to the cafe. He'd changed a lot in the last four years. No longer the cute kid, Josh had filled out a little and was previewing the handsome man he'd become. At eighteen, Joshua wasn't there yet. There was still a boyishness about him that made me think of him as a kid.

Using the towel to dry my face, hair, and legs, I then grabbed the band-aids with my stuff and walked over to the counter. I retrieved my comb out of my bag and pulled my hair back into a ponytail. Joshua still hadn't come back, so I took out a make-up wipe and my compact and cleaned all the make-up off my face. The mascara smudged black around my eyes, but I cleaned it till it just looked like eyeliner.

"Now you look like yourself," Joshua teased coming to serve me on the other side of the counter. He picked up the band-aids and scanned them. "Need anything else?"

"A hot chocolate and something hot to eat," I chuckled, handing over some cash.

"Kitchen in the cafe is closed, but there are a few hot dogs left if you want that?" Joshua offered, pointing to the hot dog machine.

I eyed him. "Two hot dogs would be awesome, as long as there is cafe quality hot chocolate to go with it?"

Joshua smiled and rung up the hot dogs for me. "Grab your food and come into the cafe and get warm." He handed me my change, his eyes dropping to my cleavage before he moved around to the cafe.

I looked down and blushed at my nipples high beaming through the sapphire silk of my dress. As far as dresses go, it was conservative. It showed more leg than anything else. However, when you've walked barefoot, through torrential rain in Autumn, your body tends to tell you in any way possible that you are cold.

Wrapping the towel around my shoulders like a shawl, I grabbed my hot dogs. With my handbag over my shoulder, heels in one hand, hot dogs in the other, I moved round to the cafe. If I'd been paying attention, I would have noticed the voices coming from the cafe before I walked around. I didn't.

At first, all I noticed was a table with seven men sitting around it playing cards. An assortment of hoodies, leather jackets, and sport team jackets hanging from the back of their chairs. It didn't faze me. This cafe was a favourite hang out for a lot of the local seniors during the week, but usually, they'd all be at a party on a Friday night. It wasn't until one of them lifted his head to watch me walk to the counter, and a few others looked to see what caught his eye, that I became unsettled. Most appeared to be decent enough, but at least half of them could pass for members of a drug syndicate in a Hollywood movie.

At the far end of the table, were the last set of eyes I expected to see hanging in a service station cafe on a Friday night. Crystal blue, those eyes were almost a perfect match for my dress. Thick long lashes that most girls would kill to have naturally surrounded them, and as those eyes dropped to scan my appearance, they drew my gaze down to his perfect pout, enclosed in a couple of days worth of scruff.

Pulling my focus back a little, I took in the olive skin, mop of unruly black hair, and the long sleeve black heavy metal shirt with a hood that while generous, still managed to draw attention to the broad shoulders and hard physique it hid. Biting my lip, I turned my focus forward, and pointedly ignored Aaron Wish, the catalyst of my raging hormones. Suddenly, the only part of me that had managed to stay dry all night was just as drenched as the rest of me.

Aaron had been a year ahead of me at our high school. Like Joshua, he'd been a scholarship student - poor kid at a rich college - and rumoured to be a local drug lord, womaniser, and voted most likely to become an assassin. I had crushed on Aaron Wish something fierce from age fourteen. I want to say that when he left for university, my crush went with him, but it didn't.

As an Excelsior student - an advanced learning student - I had chosen to leap ahead with my university studies by taking two first year units each semester for my two senior years of high school. So instead of Aaron vanishing from my life when he finished high school, we'd ended up having two university units of study together each semester in his first year, all the same classes last year, and one class each semester this year. The saving grace I had, was that Aaron Wish didn't even know I existed. Sure, he remembered me from school, but I kept my head down and hid up the back of my classes at University, so no one even knew I was there.

Joshua slid a mug of hot chocolate across the counter to me as

I reached it. "There you go, Caly. Go sit by the fire and thaw yourself out."

Putting my money on the counter to pay for the drink, I gave Josh a warm smile. "Thanks, Josh." Taking a sip while I waited for the change, then I dropped it all in the tips jar.

"You're too generous, Caly," Joshua sighed. Joshua was a scholarship kid too, and when our math teacher suggested he get tutoring and introduced me, he'd had to admit that he couldn't afford it. I'd volunteered to tutor him for free at lunch in the libraries in exchange for Mr Downs writing me a glowing recommendation for early entry to Eleri University. Despite no longer being bound by that deal, I'd grown to like Joshua and wanted to see him get into medicine as he hoped.

Moving to a table by the fire that was still far enough away from Aaron Wish and friends that they'd hopefully forget I was there, I put my back to the group, took a large mouthful of my hot chocolate before retrieving my mobile from what I was grateful was a waterproof handbag. "How'd the date go?" Penny, my best friend and roommate, answered on the second ring.

"It was a total bust. Bastard ditched me halfway between Charlie's and the Pitstop Cafe because I wouldn't blow him," I informed her before taking a big bite of my hot dog.

"That asshat!" Penny exclaimed venomously. "It's pouring rain, and he left you in the middle of nowhere at night?"

"Yep," I answered around my food. Unladylike, I know, but I was cold and starving. Charlie's was a five-star restaurant that barely served enough to satisfy a gold fish's appetite.

"Shit! Where are you now."

"Pitstop," I answered, then swallowed the last bite. "I've busted my favourite pair of heels, I've got blisters the size of Mount Olympus, and I'm drenched to the bone. But, I have a holiday to Hawaii secured in the bag."

Penny chuckled. "No wonder your mum had to bribe you to go out with such a prick."

"Agreed. Can you pick me up?" I pleaded.

Penny groaned. "God, Caly. If you'd phoned an hour ago I'd be in the car in a heartbeat, but I went over to see Simon, there is a party on at his place and I'm about three drinks over the limit already."

My head dropped in disappointment. "Well, shit."

"I'm sorry, hon," Penny said sincerely. "Can you afford a cab?"

Not really. "Yeah. I'm guessing you're staying with Simon tonight, so I'll see you in the morning."

"Okay, hon. Let me know when you're home safe," Penny insisted. She was the motherly one out of the two of us. Wild, but motherly.

Hanging up, I took another bite of the hot dog as I contemplated how I was going to get back to campus tonight. It was over a thirty-minute drive from the Pitstop. Slumping down in my chair, I pulled out my iPad and searched the bus timetable using the cafe's free WiFi. The only bus that came by here towards the campus for the rest of the night was still another hour away.

With some free time up my sleeve, I logged onto my blog site and wrote a new post while I devoured my food. I hit the publish button, finished my hot chocolate, and called my mother. "Caly, I didn't expect to hear from you until tomorrow," My mother's voice came over the line rushed.

"I expected to get your voicemail. Aren't you at a conference in Singapore?" My mind raced over the schedule I'd memorised for my mum's whereabouts this week and the calculation of time difference between countries.

"I'm just walking into the dinner. How did the date go?"

"He wined me, dined me, then dumped me by the side of the road when I wouldn't let him sixty-nine me," I answered honestly. "I've already blogged it, so you can read it when you get a minute."

My mother's heels stopped clacking across the marble floor. "Are you safe?" She asked with genuine concern. My mother was a high powered businesswoman in the world of biochemical engineering. She'd given birth to me between replying to work emails and directing her team via phone calls, worked from home for two weeks, and then I went to work with her.

"I am," I assured her. "I broke those Jimmy Choo's you got me for my birthday last year, but I'm safe. The blisters are worth a holiday to Hawaii."

My mother released a small laugh and the echo of her high heels striking marble started up again. "A deal is a deal. Tell me the dates in summer you want the flights booked and where you want to stay, and I'll get it organised."

"I'm doing summer school this year, so I think that cancels out summer as an option," I informed her. "How about during winter break?"

"I'm heading into the dinner. We'll have dinner next week and discuss it then. Love you."

"Love you too, mum," I replied as the call disconnected. With a sigh, I looked at the time and then checked my cash flow. Despite my family being well off, my mother insisted on me earning my way, so I was very strict with my budget with what I received from work. Don't get me wrong; I wasn't doing it tough. My mother paid my student fees and dorm costs. However, all the day to day expenses were mine.

For that reason, I withdrew cash each week which allowed for coffee's and transport to work or to go to the bar with my friends. Seeing there was enough cash for the bus ticket home and a least one more hot chocolate, I made my way back to the counter, which, unfortunately, took me close to the table of men.

Keeping my eyes on the counter where Joshua was leaning reading, I didn't allow the laughter and shenanigans at the other table catch my attention. Joshua looked up with a smile when I stopped in front of him. "Hot chocolate or something stronger?"

"Unless you sell Bourbon, it's hot chocolate," I smirked putting my money on the counter and picking up his book. "Mary Shelly's Frankenstein?"

"Set reading," Joshua informed me.

With a nod, I placed it back down so he wouldn't lose his page. A masculine laugh burst out behind me. The way it heated my body better than the fire had made me cringe. "What's so funny, Ayah?" One of the guys asked.

"There's a blog I started following in high school. It's by a girl who calls herself Nymph," Aaron chuckled. "It's effectively her dating life. She called it Blue Balls because it started off as a blog about all the ways her boyfriend used to try and get her to have sex with him. They broke up a few years back and now it's about her dates."

It was like instant freeze, holding my breath, realising he was reading my blog. My mum and Penny knew it was my blog, but I'd never told anyone else. The desire to get my stuff and wait at the bus stop was overwhelming, but at the same time, I was impressed that he liked it. "Is it dirty?" One of the guys asked.

"Sometimes, but it's not graphic sex or anything," Aaron answered. "It's still all about what guys say or do to get girls to have sex with them. Like tonight," Aaron chuckled. Now, I wanted to melt in a puddle of embarrassment as he started reading.

"I went on a blind date. Normally, I would never do a blind date. Let's just say someone coerced me into it, and no matter how bad it went, I was still going to be the winner. So, I went on this blind date with a guy in his mid-twenties. He's the son of a successful businessman and now works for his father's company. He's good-looking, well-educated, and wealthy. I couldn't understand why this guy needed to be set up on a blind date. Accepting he may be too busy to meet women, I went along thinking I might at least enjoy a nice evening."

Aaron chuckled again, taking a sip of his hot beverage as he scrolled the screen on his phone. "He arrived on time, was dressed well and even opened the car door for me. So far, so good. He took me to a posh restaurant. Not my scene, but, obviously, he was trying to impress. He insisted on ordering for me, instant turn off, and then proceeded to talk about himself and how good he is at everything. I was bored before the entree arrived."

Joshua pushed my mug of hot chocolate across the counter along with my change. He was also listening to Aaron and captivated. "After two hours of listening to this guy talk himself up, and replays of American Psycho happening behind my eyes, the waiter arrived with the dessert menu. Finally, the night was looking up. The desserts at this restaurant were orgasmic. So, considering it was the only orgasm I was getting tonight, I was all for dessert. You know what Ego did? He told the waiter we wouldn't need dessert. He followed this up by leering at me over the table and saying, and I quote, 'you're hot, you don't want to ruin it by eating desserts.'" Aaron burst out laughing.

His friends made combined hissing and sounds of imminent danger. "Ouch!" One guy laughed. "I'm surprised he's still walking."

Aaron started again. "So we leave the restaurant. I plan to say goodnight; I understand why no one will date you, good riddance when he pulls the car off onto a side road. Ego then proceeds to remove his seatbelt, unplug mine, push his seat back as far as it will go, unzip his pants, pull out his Johnston, and tells me to climb aboard."

"This guy is an idiot!" someone exclaims. The others murmur agreement. I nodded ascension. Chuckling at me, Joshua leaned over the counter to hear better.

"Needless to say, I refused his offer, both for moral reasons, and the fact that he was either flying at half mast or, in my experience, was not god's gift to women - if you get my meaning," Aaron started laughing again. "Ego then informed me that if he shells out, I need to put out. When that didn't work, he tried to negotiate for a blowjob, and on my refusal, acknowledged he'd settle for a happy ending."

"Jesus! This guy obviously should stick to paying for it," Aaron's friend laughed.

"When none of his demands for me to 'take care of his needs' was met, Ego, ever so politely climbed out of the car, came around to my door, took my upper arm, and forcibly removed me from his car."

The crowd grew quiet. "I don't like where this is heading, Ayah." One of the more dangerous looking guys warned.

Aaron put up a placating hand. "Don't worry; I've already read it through. She's safe, or she wouldn't be blogging about it already," Aaron assures. The big guy sits back, crossing his arms in suspicious patience. "Where was I? From his car. He grips me rather tightly and tells me to get on my knees or walk home. Now, I must tell you, Ego hadn't bothered putting his little fellow away, and it was still poking out like a hitchhikers thumb. Yes, it's cold, and we were getting rained on, so I'll give him some shrinkage allowance, but it had been warm inside the car, so not that much."

By now all the guys are holding up their thumbs and snickering. "Give the girl my number. Shrinkage need not apply," the big guy leans in with a grin. His eyes lift to me, and he winks. With a chuckle, I pick up my hot chocolate and take a drink while the big guy lets his eyes check me out.

"So," Aaron shakes his head with a laugh, "on my knees or walk. All ladylike, I lift my knee rather forcefully, and as he falls to the ground cursing while I politely decline. The queen of England would be impressed with the grace in which I handled the matter. Collecting my bag, I enjoyed the walk home. Of course, who do I trip over on the way? Lancelot. The one place I wasn't wet from the rain, I am now," Aaron chuckles putting his phone away.

"Is Lancelot her fuck buddy or something?" Joshua asks. The question nearly made me spit up my mouthful of hot chocolate, but I quickly covered it as all eyes turned in our direction.

Aaron frowned in consideration. Leaning back in his chair, he shook his head. "No. He's the one guy she's never talked about more than a mention here and there."

"So why call him Lancelot?" Joshua considered. "Lancelot was Guenevere's affair. I would think they must be sleeping together, especially with her saying she tripped over him."

Aaron smiled shaking his head. "He's been on the scene since she was with her ex-boyfriend. She called him Lancelot for being her temptation, not because they hooked up. He's always just mentioned in passing," Aaron clarified.

The big guy was watching me again. "Speaking of lady's out walking by themselves at night... what's a pretty thing like you wandering around in this weather for?"

All eyes turned to me. I pasted on a false smile. "My roommate had a few too many drinks at her boyfriend's party tonight and decided to crash there the night. I'm just going to wait for the bus and get back to campus so I can sleep in in the morning," I bent the truth.

"Except you work the weekends," Joshua corrected me. If there weren't a counter between us, I would have kicked him in the shins.

"Yeah, but I'm closer to work if I stay on campus, so I get to sleep a bit later. Plus, I get my bed to myself instead of sharing with some jock who thinks he's entitled," I clarified. Joshua smiled.

"Hey, I am entitled," one of the guys at the table pouted in humour.

"Not to me, you're not." I winked. All the guys laughed.

"What about me?" The big guy asked.

"What about you?" I asked.

"Am I entitled?"

Opening my mouth to answer, Joshua beat me to it. "Dude, no. Caly is spoken for." I looked at Joshua surprised, but didn't refute it. Picking up my mug, I started walking back to my seat.

"Of course she is. She's too fit not to be," the big guy complimented. "I can still give you a ride home."

Chuckling, I saluted him with my mug as I walked. "Thanks, but the bus doesn't require me to get on my knees and worship, so I'll take that option, thanks."

All the guys chuckled and returned to their card game. Taking my seat, I opened an ebook to read while I waited for the bus. About ten minutes later, chairs scraping across the floor caught my attention. Aaron and his friends were leaving. All of them making their way outside except for Aaron and the big guy. The big guy instead, came to stand beside me. "My offer for a lift is still there. No expectations. I don't like women being out and susceptible at night. Bad things happen, even on busses."

"Thank you, but I was taught never to hop in a car with a stranger." I gave him a friendly smile.

He returned my smile. "You're friends with Josh?" Tilting my head, wondering where this question was leading, I nodded. "And you live on campus?" His smile grew when I nodded again. He looked over to where Aaron was straightening up the tables. "Ayah?"

"Yeah, man?" Aaron stood up looking our way.

"Give Caly a lift back to campus. I'll sleep better knowing she made it safely."

"No, really-" I tried to object.

Big guy put his hand on my shoulder. "Josh will be in the car for most of the ride, and Ayah lives on campus, so he's going there anyway. Aren't you Ayah?"

Aaron folded his arms across his chest, face stern. "Yeah. I'll get her home safe."

Big guy smiled. "Thanks, dude." He patted my shoulder. "Names Dwayne by the way. Josh can give you my number if you ever stop being spoken for." Dwayne winked and walked out.

Aaron's soul-eating eyes were still focused on me. "Pack up. Josh is just closing up. We'll wait in the car." The lights in the shop area went out a second later. Turning my attention to my gear, I shoved my iPad back in my handbag, along with the bandaids I was going to need for work tomorrow morning. Grabbing my coat off the chair, I pulled it on. Collecting his leather jacket, Aaron yanked it on, his eyes still on me.

Swallowing the massive glob of saliva suddenly filling my mouth, I picked up my empty mug and took it to the counter. "Leave it. The morning shift will deal with it," Aaron told me. When I turned around, he was holding my bag and heels in his hand, analysing the broken heel. "You were dressed up for a house party. Don't know many girls who would kill a pair of fancy heels and walk in the rain to the bus stop, rather than take the couch."

Taking my bag and heels from him, I shrugged off his interest. "I'm not the average girl."

Aaron squared himself to face me. "Caly Zilla, popular, but always reserved at school. You dated one of the most popular boys in my year, were top of your class, rich, but rarely showed it, right down to you even working as a tutor to give yourself spending money. And, you were an Excelsior student," Aaron listed off. "You were a year behind me at school, and yet, you've been at uni since I started."

"There a year before, actually," I corrected.

Aaron smirked. "I'm in my third year, and you are in half my classes."

"I know," I blushed. I wasn't sure if I was blushing because Aaron noticed me, or because I'd acknowledged seeing him.

Aaron's eyes lit up. "Let's go wait in the car."

"Does this lift carry the expectation of a blowjob?" I asked pointedly.

Aaron snickered. "No expectation, but I wouldn't turn one down if you feel the need to say thank you," Aaron teased. Rolling my eyes, I followed him out to the car park. Opening the door to a two-door sports car, Aaron pressed the lever for the front seat to slide forward. "Josh needs to get out first, so you'll have to take the back seat."

"There is an irony in that comment, I'm sure," I scoffed, stepping forward.

With a smile, Aaron slid the seat back into place, effectively locking me in the back of his car. Closing the door, he walked around dropping into the front seat. "You look good in the back seat," he winked.

"You probably say that to all the girls you get in your back seat," I teased back.

Aaron grinned. "Do I look like I fit in that back seat?"

No, no you don't. At well over six foot, Aaron Wish stood a head taller than me, and his shoulders were nearly twice my breadth. I wasn't short, but Aaron certainly made me feel it in his presence. Taking a deep breath, I decided to divert the conversation. "So, did you become an assassin like your classmates predicted?"

Aaron smiled as he pressed the button for the engine to start. "Can't fit many weapons or bodies in the trunk of this car."

"How does a guy on scholarship afford a car like this?" I asked straight out.

Aaron's smile faded. "It was a payout from the job I did through school."

"God, I wish I could afford a car."

"I'm pretty sure the rich girl complaining about money to the scholarship kid is ironic," Aaron huffed.

"I'm pretty sure the scholarship kid owning a car worth more than my annual income, is questionable."

Aaron met my eyes in the review mirror. "Life giveth, and life taketh away."

My smile faded too. My hand automatically went to the necklace at my throat. I couldn't remember a time I hadn't worn the locket. Even at school, where jewellery was banned, my mother had gotten special permission for me to wear it. It was a gift from my father to my mother. I'd never met him, had no idea who he was. As far as I knew, he was gone from her life before I was born. The locket was all I had of him.

The passenger door opened and Joshua slid in. He did up his seat belt and smiled at me. "Catching a lift to campus?" He asked. I nodded. Joshua's eyes flicked to Aaron. "She's the reason my grades are good enough to get into medicine next year, keep her safe."

Aaron looked at Joshua. "I know. I will."

There in the dark, illuminated only by the dashboard light, I saw the resemblance in their facial structure I'd never noticed in daylight. Aaron was all dark and brooding compared to Joshua who was light and upbeat. Joshua was more auburn in his hair, and his skin a little paler, but their silhouettes and eyes were a perfect match.

"Are you two related?" I asked as the meaning of that clicked in my head.

Aaron smiled. "Josh is my baby brother." Putting his arm across the back of the passenger seat, Aaron looked at me as he started reversing. "He's been telling me all about you for years."

JOIN THE BEAUTIFUL AND DEADLY

Join Ebony's Mischief List

Sign up to Ebony's mailing list for the following perks:

- latest news on new releases
- heads up on upcoming promotions
- exclusive freebies like coupons to read Ebony's stories on Radish for free
- first chance at Giveaways
- get a free book

Go to https://ebonyolson.com for more information

ABOUT THE AUTHOR

Ebony lives in Sydney, Australia, with her husband, daughter, and six cats. She loves to read fantasy, thrillers, and paranormal romance, spending most of her free time with her nose in a book or writing.

Having always possessed an over-active imagination she spent her younger years regaling friends with fantastic stories, holding her audience captive with the passion and suspense of her characters plights.

Now in adulthood she has numerous published works and shows no signs of stopping her imagination from spreading across as many pages as it can find.

If you'd like to follow Ebony or simply say hi you can find her here:

Website: http://ebonyolson.com/

www.ingramcontent.com/pod-product-compliance
Lightning Source LLC
Chambersburg PA
CBHW070152120726
47909CB00001B/84